peacetime's children

A catalogue record of this book is available from the British Library

First Edition: October 2003

ISBN: 1-84375-029-5

This is a work of fiction. Names, characters, places and incidents are the product of the author's imagination or are used fictitiously, and any resemblance to any actual persons, living or dead, events, or locales is entirely coincidental.

To order additional copies of this book please visit:
http://www.upso.co.uk/davidknowles.htm

Published by: UPSO Ltd
5 Stirling Road, Castleham Business Park,
St Leonards-on-Sea, East Sussex TN38 9NW United Kingdom
Tel: 01424 853349 Fax: 0870 191 3991
Email: info@upso.co.uk Web: http://www.upso.co.uk

peacetime's children

by

david knowles

UPSO

To Carol

The finest of peacetime's children

I've done some bad
I've done some good
I did a whole lot better than
they thought I would

Everybody Loves Me Baby
Don McLean

THE FAMILIES OF peacetime's children

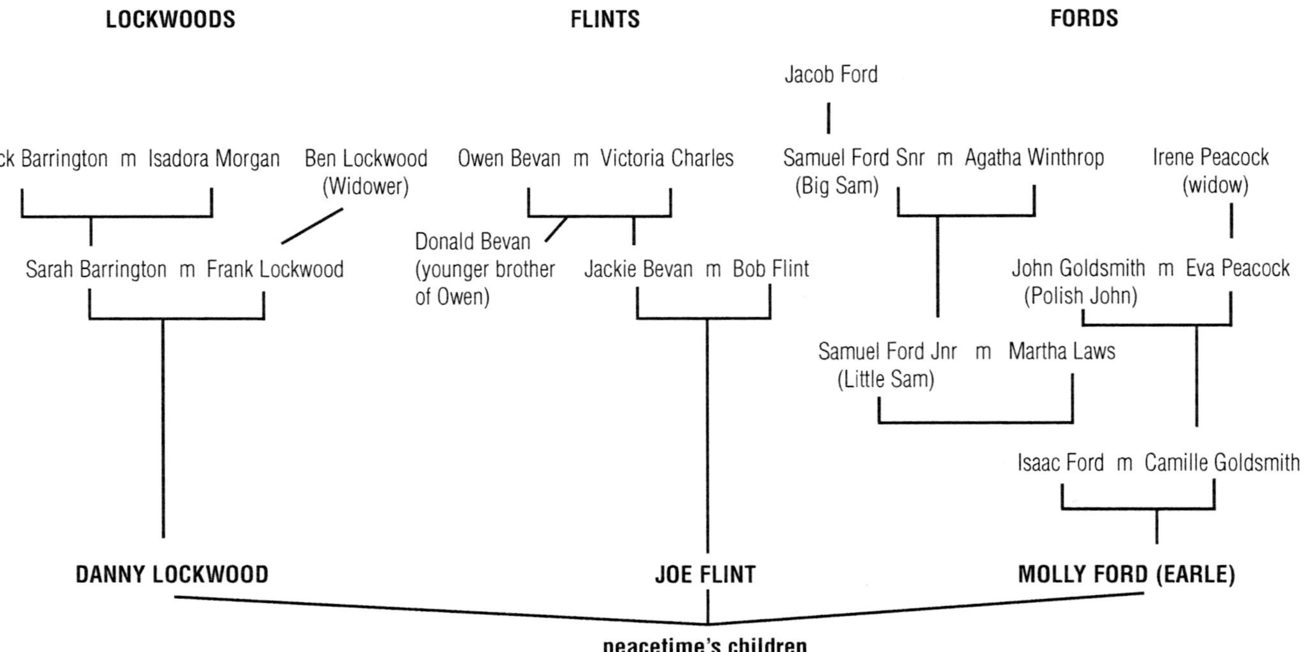

CONTENTS

Preface

The best year was 1953.

The faded sepia photograph on top of the bookcase showed it to be the case. Children's faces at the start of the new millennium don't look like that any more. Fresh. Optimistic. Resplendent in their innocence.

The standard bearers of the new age of peace and hope, and the embodiment of their family's wishes and dreams. And, being so, also of a nation's, in its search for a pathway out of the darkness of war.

The year marked the beginning of a new Elizabethan age, and the ending of the old Victorian order.

It was Coronation year. The streets of every British city, town and village were decked out in red, white and blue.

It was the year when heroes came forward to bring the nation alive with a spirit of patriotism and adventure at a time when it was still emerging from the shadows of a spartan post-war world.

The day of the Coronation began with the news that a British-led team had reached the summit of Everest.

The frontiers of science had already been crossed earlier in the year when scientists Crick and Watson announced that they had 'Found the secret of life'. They had just achieved the greatest scientific breakthrough since Einstein's Theory of Relativity – the discovery of the structure of DNA.

In sport, Matthews got his Cup Winner's Medal at last, Richards his Derby win, and Compton the winning run that brought back the Ashes.

After 1953, the country was ready at last to cast aside all the miseries of the years of blackouts, food shortages, sandbags, gas masks and clothes rationing and was primed to embark on a glorious renaissance.

It was a momentous year encapsulated by the words of Lord Hunt of Everest, 'There is no height, no depth, that the spirit of man guided by a higher spirit, cannot attain.'

The Alley

The bookcase was in the corner of the lounge of Joe Flint's house and along the top were rows of haphazardly positioned photographs, which spanned the lifetimes of members of the Flint family.

Joe was deep in thought, looking at the frayed and faded black and white one in the tarnished gilt frame at the corner of the front row.

He found it hard to believe that the fresh-faced, beaming boy with the short-cropped, slicked-down black hair had once been him.

Just half an hour before, his reflection in the bathroom mirror had told him a different story. The face that looked back at him while he spread the shaving foam over his cheeks and chin was of someone middle-aged, with furrows etched into his brow and at the corners of his eyes. Joe had smoothed down the greying hair on the sides of his shaven head, a style that had recently become fashionable amongst the young men of the day. But even this consolation and self-deception was short-lived for Joe, who was forced to concede to himself that the hairstyle had been borne of necessity – to disguise a rapidly-balding pate – rather than a personal choice to become avant-garde.

The reason Joe Flint was looking at his picture gallery was the arrival in his life of a new millennium and his feeling that this historic milestone needed to be marked in his mind.

Joe's reverie moved on. The old photograph on the front row

intrigued him. He was the middle one of three youngsters and remembered his mother had told him about the picture. That it had been taken on a post-war summer afternoon in Blackpool, on Coronation day.

The three youthful faces seemed to epitomise a fresh start from the ravages of war for three families who had endured the years of deprivation. Years that now had been consigned to history. The times of infinite promise lay ahead. It was there for all to see. In the faces of three children. In the photograph.

The girl on the left was Molly, Isaac Ford's daughter and granddaughter of Polish John and Eva, her mother's parents.

Molly was wearing a floral dress and her russet-coloured hair was tied in a bow. Her blue eyes sparkled and danced and seemed to be beseeching the camera to single her out from the three of them. Even then she knew she was a star.

'I was looking serious and shy', ruminated Joe, peering closer at the picture, as though by so doing he could peel away the intervening years and, just for a fleeting instant, re-live the moment and remember what he had been thinking as the camera clicked and made the three of them timeless.

The last of the three was Danny Lockwood, who appeared indifferent to both the situation and his two young contemporaries. He was immaculate in his dark suit and Windsor-knotted plaid tie, which he was wearing even on that hot summer afternoon. Meticulously prepared for the occasion. The public schoolboy. Always a cut above.

Danny. Slight and mild-mannered, with a knowing grin about to spread across his well-scrubbed features. Black wavy hair and dark intense eyes. 'A mystery man,' thought Joe.

Joe recalled the reason for the photograph and in his mind heard his mother's voice on the day ten years earlier, when she had given it to him.

'That was a marvellous summer, Joe. We always seemed to be celebrating that year. Not just us in Blackpool, but the entire country as well. This one you're looking at was taken on the day of the Queen's Coronation, 2nd June 1953.

All of us were full with bookings that year and the streets every day were crammed with visitors. At every house, as far down the road as you could see, people were thronging; standing outside and sitting on doorsteps.

They all seemed to be either mining families or mill workers; they were always discussing their jobs. You'd have thought that for one week a year that's the last thing they'd want to talk about.

I know where we were the day this picture was taken. We were all round at Eva's New Sands on Kensington Drive. Her son-in-law, Isaac, a wealthy businessman from Manchester, had bought them a TV set to watch the Cup Final a month before. I remember Eva telling me about the day they got the set. How Isaac hadn't said anything; just pulled up in his silver Mercedes and asked Eva and Molly to look in the boot, and there it was, a 12 inch Ferguson black and white.

We all saw the Queen being crowned. The whole street crowded into the lounge of the New Sands – well, it seemed like that, but, then again, it was a long time ago. It was magical. Unbelievable. Just like being there inside Westminster Abbey.

After that day, everyone round here soon seemed to get a television, but all rented, not owned like Eva's. We still listened to the radio, but only if here wasn't anything worth watching on TV.

And that picture of the three of you was taken before the Coronation, outside the New Sands by John. Polish John everyone called him. Eva's husband. We had all gone round there in the morning and had lunch with Eva and the visitors.

Made a real day of it. Look how you're all dressed up especially for the day, all three of you. Don't you all look smart?'

While his mother, Jackie, was telling him that day about the Coronation, a misty, distant recollection had crossed Joe Flint's mind, of something which must have happened the month before and would have been the day he had seen television for the first time. He was running up to anyone passing by in the street and joyously telling them 'We've won – Matthews won the Cup', even though, as a seven-year old boy, he had no idea at the time of the significance of the words, only the excitement he was feeling and that he was somehow a part of it all.

His Welsh grandfather, Owen, all his life kept a picture on his mantelpiece to remind him of that same day, Cup Final Day 1953, when he had been at Wembley Stadium to see the footballer he idolised, Stanley Matthews, being held on the shoulders of Mortensen and Mudie, proudly holding up his Cup-winner's medal.

The ecstasies of the Coronation, the Matthews Cup Final and the other epic events of 1953 had faded into the distant memories of Molly, Joe and Danny and only the launch of black and white television remained amongst them as a topic of conversation.

The dog days of high summer had returned to Blackpool boarding house land and the three children were to be found in the Alley; the long, narrow, cobbled back street that linked the garages of the exclusive Kensington Drive hotel properties, of which the Sands was the largest and most prestigious, with the back yards of the boarding houses which lined Park Avenue. The Alley may have been only several yards in width, but in terms of social significance in the hotel and boarding house community of the seaside town, it represented a chasm of immeasurable proportions, and unbridgeable dimensions.

Molly, as was invariably the case, felt the need to be provocative and to spark controversy.

It was her habit to make only rare appearances to play with the two boys and even then she chose to ration these visits to those occasions when she was feeling particularly bored and in need of amusement.

The times when she deigned to grace the Alley with her presence were usually marked by lively juvenile debate, following which the boys felt intellectually exhausted, and immediately returned to their less taxing physical pursuits of football and cricket.

Molly always returned to her home at the New Sands Hotel with her pristine appearance still unsullied after her brief incursions "slumming it" as the mothers of the two boys would say during their dialogues across their shared back wall.

If poise and composure can be qualities attributable to a girl of only ten, then it could be said that Molly possessed both. In abundance.

Molly's visit to the Alley that day was to make an announcement, 'My Nan's been taking me to tap lessons in town. I'm going to sing and dance at the London Palladium. I'll be the next Ginger Rogers. Her hair is the same colour as mine. Nan says she was my Mum's favourite.'

Joe and Danny both looked perplexed. The boys' shared glance indicated that they were picturing themselves inside the King George Cinema on Kingston Road, known as the 'flea pit', among the throng at the previous Saturday's morning matinee. Up on the screen had been Fred Astaire in top hat and tails, miraculously skimming across the dance floor; but the boys' thoughts at that moment transposed his partner into Molly Ford and it was a mental image that sat uneasily with both of them and resulted in an awkward silence descending on the group.

'My Dad took me to the King George to see Gary Cooper,' Joe Flint chimed in, wearing a self-satisfied beam, 'in High Noon.' He incongruously burst into tuneless song, to the astonishment of Danny and Molly, while, at the same time, making the motion of drawing a six-gun from a holster hanging low from his hip and firing an imaginary shot at Danny. 'Do not forsake me oh my darlin', on this our wedding day ...... Tex Ritter,' Joe announced, convinced that his awareness of such esoteric movie trivia would confound the star-struck Molly, let alone Danny.

Danny, however, was not to be outdone. 'My Dad's favourite's Bradman.' He proceeded to execute a pretend forward defensive stroke.

All of them now considered honour had been satisfied and the Alley fell quiet again.

Following exchanges such as these, the stars' names they had mentioned would be mentally locked away, to be re-introduced at a future date, for the next bout of one-upmanship.

The boys resumed kicking a football listlessly against a battered, discoloured garage door.

'Show us your birthmark, then,' Danny abruptly said to Molly, as though this was a prerequisite Molly needed in order to prove her claim to be a future Ginger Rogers.

The renowned birthmark, in effect a miniscule pale red blotch of no significance even to Molly herself, had attained mythical status among the Alley gang ever since the day Molly had unwittingly happened to brag about it in a misguided attempt to demonstrate her superiority among the three of them.

Molly, being Molly, responded ingeniously, 'Let me bat next time you play cricket and I will.' Danny and Joe were, as usual, wrong-footed by her quick-wittedness and the realisation that a girl could have such chutzpah.

Joe and Danny decided against pursuing their need to see the famed birthmark, which thereby retained its mystery. And Molly remained a goddess beyond compare to the boys of Park Avenue Alley.

The conversational template of the Alley was invariably Danny throwing down the gauntlet to Molly, only for her to promptly pick it up and witheringly throw it back, leaving both the boys dumbfounded.

Joe usually said little or nothing during their bouts of one-upmanship. He felt dull in their afterglow and would resort to trying to gain the kudos of reflected glory by constantly referring to his father, an electrician who worked on the Illuminations. Joe looked on him as an artist who produced magic each day of his working life; a 'sparks' who alone was responsible for the glory of the dazzlingly coloured trams that rocked and rattled along the promenade during the annual festival of lights that began at the summer season's close and continued until the chills and gloom of winter ushered in the beginning of the town's hibernation for another year.

Other characters drifted onto the periphery of the group in the Alley during the summer months: locals from neighbouring streets and visitors' children, who brought with them exotic, apocryphal tales of their exploits in far-flung inland towns with peculiar sounding names, such as Barnoldswick, and which invariably resulted in an undignified scrap in the midst of cheering, transfixed onlookers encircling the protagonists while they kicked, punched and scrambled; locked together on the dust-encrusted cobblestones.

The end would come with an irate parent hauling one of the fighters to his feet by the scruff of an unwashed neck and dragging him off down the Alley, and bringing a summary conclusion to the afternoon's entertainment and a signal to the rest of the children to straggle away to their respective boarding houses for tea.

And so, the scene has now been set, and the introductions have been made to Molly, Joe and Danny. Peacetime's children.

The heralds of the post-war era for a famous seaside town.

Wish them well on the odyssey of their lives.

May Fate be kind.

From the Village

Sarah's mother, Isadora, a lady of impeccable grooming and striking appearance, had always felt that her only child had married beneath her and while her father, the village shopkeeper, doted on Sarah without reservation, Isadora always wanted more for her than the undemanding tranquillity of married life in a small rural backwater of Nottinghamshire.

Isadora, in harbouring such ambitions for the teenage Sarah, had introduced her to Miss Bottesford for piano tuition; and the following year to Miss Cook for elocution lessons.

The two unmarried ladies were looked on as the charming eccentrics of the timeless community of Brackley, each with a large rambling house at opposite ends of a muddy and isolated country lane. The ladies immersed themselves in their respective occupations to the virtual exclusion of any social activity; the exception being a stroll together each afternoon to Jack and Isadora's store by the village green, to pick up just sufficient groceries to last until the next afternoon, plus two copies of The Times.

None of the other residents of Brackley could remember a time when Miss Bottesford and Miss Cook had not lived at their respective ends of Hawthorn Lane.

As Sarah grew older, she thought it remarkable that such a little village should have so large a proportion of people who were able to play the piano and who also seemed to speak exaggeratedly correct English. She later learned that Miss

Bottesford and Miss Cook gave substantial discounts to locals while charging full rate to outsiders.

So reclusive were the two old ladies of Hawthorn Lane that they did not attend even one of Isadora Barrington's renowned monthly soirées. This was a source of continual regret to Isadora, who longed for the social cachet that the attendance of just one of the two erudite ladies would have brought her amongst the Brackley villagers.

While her husband, Jack Barrington, was managing their Brackley store, Isadora would be indulging in her passion. Cookery. Not common-or-garden home cookery, but strictly haute cuisine.

To Isadora, owning a village store, notwithstanding its location in a spot as idyllic as Brackley, still made her a glorified shopkeeper, and was a poor substitute of a life for someone like herself, who burned with an unquenchable fire to cater for those who possessed a sophisticated and discriminating palate.

Isadora had been helped in coming to terms with what she regarded as her diminished status in life by the compensation of her monthly soirées for regular shop clientele from among the Brackley villagers, with the perennial exception of Miss Bottesford and Miss Cook.

Isadora's dream, however, remained: to be a co-owner, with her husband, of an exclusive city centre restaurant, in which she could combine a role of preparing exotic dishes to an elite clientele, with parading herself in the diningroom in all her finery, and engage in refined conversation.

Isadora's one fervent hope during Sarah's formative years was that she would go on to achieve this dream on her behalf, and it was with that in view that she sought to inculcate in her daughter her own culinary infatuation.

Sarah in adulthood recollected overhearing a conversation between her mother and father prompted by the son of one of their customers having passed his final examination to become an articled accountant. The phrase from her mother, 'Sarah one day will make an excellent wife for a professional man' had stuck in her mind. Although at the time she had heard it, Sarah could not quite understand the import of the statement, nonetheless she had taken it to have been complimentary, mainly from the enthusiastic tone in which her mother had spoken. It never occurred to her to bring up the matter with her mother, and it just stayed tucked away, disregarded, at the back of her mind, amongst the rest of her childhood detritus.

While Sarah remembered her mother's involvement in her life as being a constant one, even to the extent of ensuring that her appearance was always just so before she was allowed to venture from the store into the village, she recalled that her father in contrast always seemed to be in the background during her childhood, totally absorbed in the store during the day and each night discussing the domestic lives of the customers with her mother.

It seemed to Sarah that the customers entered the store primarily for the purpose of gossiping about the activities of their fellow villagers.

Her father, Jack, enjoyed this immensely and always made a point of passing on the latest titbit to Isadora at the earliest opportunity, with added relish and appropriate embellishment of his own inimitably ribald sort.

The other centre of intrigue and gossip in the tiny village was the local church, St Cuthbert's, and this could have been a significant reason why her father had insisted on his family's regular attendance there from the time that Sarah had been able to walk from the store across the village green.

Jack would make an excuse to linger after the service and could be seen hovering around the church doors, to see which of the villagers was the latest one to be stepping into the confessional.

The social life of Brackley was restricted to weekly church fellowships, a fortnightly barn dance in the village hall, and a yearly coach outing to Mansfield.

The first year that Sarah expressed an interest in going on the coach trip, Isadora ensured that she was not able to go by telling her that they had decided to close the store for the day, so as to pay their yearly family visit to Sarah's aunt in Chesterfield.

The change in Sarah's life in Brackley began on the day she chanced upon Frank Lockwood.

Frank's father, Ben, a widower, had been a miner who had retired from the pit due to a lung condition and, with his pension from the Coal Board and a sizeable family inheritance, had decided he was now at the stage of his life when he had earned the right to sample the peaceful delights of rural life, after a working lifetime spent in the dust and grime of a mining village.

So Ben and his son Frank moved to Brackley.

Frank continued his job at the pit and cycled the nine miles every day from Brackley to work.

Ben and Frank were sauntering alongside the village green, on a spring Sunday morning, when they came across Sarah and her parents, on their way home from church, standing at the edge of the duck pond, tossing small pieces of bread into the water.

Sarah looked at Frank and something magical happened between them.

Over the following months, romance blossomed, despite discouragement from Isadora, who even suggested to Sarah that perhaps Frank may be interested in elocution lessons, but demurred at also proposing piano tuition after her first sight of his enormous miner's hands had caused her to inwardly wince, which she did at the same time as politely smiling and passing him a cup of tea served in her best china cup.

Also, being sartorially obsessed, to Isadora the sight of Frank entering the store in shirt sleeves, rolled up tightly above his elbows, was enough to cause her to retire to the lounge at the rear of the store and pour herself a reviving glass of brandy.

But Isadora had Sarah's happiness continually at heart, even above her own sensitivities, and had the good sense to resist from openly displaying even the slightest hint of opposition to her beloved daughter's chosen male companion.

The adoption of such a prudent approach was put to the test six months after the day Sarah had met Frank by the duck pond when Sarah announced to her mother and father that Frank would be visiting them both to discuss a matter of particular importance.

Over tea that night, Sarah refused to pre-empt Frank's visit by answering any speculative parental questions. However, the visit by Frank both confirmed Isadora's fears and answered Sarah's dreams; Frank and Sarah announced they were to marry.

On the eve of the wedding, a resigned Isadora sought consolation from her husband Jack with such remarks as 'He's always been respectful enough to us, and there's a lot to be said for that' and 'After all, her friends have now all married and the last one had a child just a few months afterwards; at least our Sarah will be doing things properly, won't she Jack? ... won't she Jack?'

Jack, at this point, would glance at his wife over the top of his newspaper and attempt to assuage her anxieties by his routine closing riposte, 'As long as Sarah's happy, that's all that really counts.'

The year after Sarah and Frank's wedding at St Cuthbert's was a tragic one for the newly-married couple.

Early in the year Isadora and Jack died within two months of each other.

The sadness of Christmas that year was alleviated when Sarah, now running the store single-handed, was told by Frank in his stern, self-effacing manner, that he had been offered a supervisor's vacancy at the pit.

Sarah was successful in overturning her husband's initial reluctance to accept the promotion and the thought flashed across her mind of the gratification her mother Isadora would have gained from slipping into casual conversations with shop customers the news that her son-in-law had attained a managerial position.

The years that followed were prosperous ones for Sarah and Frank.

Under Sarah's diligent management, the village store expanded and this, allied to Frank's higher wages since his promotion, meant that, when Sarah announced to Frank that she was pregnant, they were able to afford to employ an assistant to help them run the business.

When their son Danny was born Sarah and Frank resolved that he would be the first in several generations of the Lockwood family not to go down the pit. The announcement was greeted by sullen silence from Frank's father.

One evening in the Lockwood house, after Danny had gone to bed, Frank began reminiscing about the family holidays he had spent in Blackpool when he had been a child and, in his wistful mood, he painted an idyllic picture to Sarah of weeks of unbroken sunshine, with days spent at the funfair and nights strolling along miles of golden sands.

At that moment Frank sowed the seed in Sarah's mind of a glittering new future for the Lockwoods in an ideal location for an ambitious young family ready to take on a new challenge.

Before the end of the year, Frank and Sarah Lockwood had become the new owners of a ten-bedroomed boarding house at number 3 Park Avenue, Blackpool.

From the Valleys

On the first day of the new millennium Joe Flint's gaze moved away from the black and white photograph of Molly, Joe and Danny to one alongside that he had taken himself of his grandparents and uncle in the shade of a giant oak tree on a midsummer day in a country park. This picture of his family frozen in a moment in time evoked in Joe a need to explore the role each of them had played in his own life story.

Joe looked closely at the faces of the two men in the picture. His grandfather Owen and his uncle Donald. He wondered how different they were, these men forged in an era of war and depression, to himself, who had grown up during the age of the welfare state.

The answer that came to him was 'No different'. The difference had been luck.

Joe's maternal grandmother, Victoria, was to the left of the photograph. Tall, grey-haired, and with a regal no-nonsense manner, leaning on her ornately carved walking stick that she took everywhere with her.

She married Owen Bevan, Joe's grandfather, when he returned home to Wales at the end of the First World War.

The hardship Owen and Victoria had gone through was never spoken of to the growing Joe by his grandparents. They looked upon their marriage as but one tiny thread in life's giant patchwork tapestry, with the bad and the good interwoven indistinguishably; not designed to be studied closely, merely to be glanced at for a second before moving on.

Standing next to Victoria were Joe's grandfather and his uncle.

Owen was standing with arms folded; stocky and square-shouldered with bushy white hair and cheery round face; and alongside him, Donald, a thinner, younger version of his brother Owen, ramrod straight, blue eyes twinkling with impish mischief.

Joe's thoughts took him back to a Christmas Day when they had visited.

He recalled how Donald, as eager to relive his youth as Owen was reluctant, had glanced at his brother. Their glasses of beer had just been re-filled, and Donald's lively mood been ignited by the effects of Christmas lunch.

A knowing smile had appeared on his grandfather's face followed by a wink at Joe when Donald began to speak. It was a wink that seemed to say to everyone in the room, 'Take all what Donald's about to say with a pinch of salt, you know what he's like.'

Donald began his tale of a bygone spring day in the Welsh valleys.

'Do you remember that day you carried me, Owen, like you always did - on your back - down that cobbled street that ran all the way from the gates of the steelworks at the top of the hill into the town centre? I had come to meet you at the end of your shift, to surprise you. You used to tell Ma and Pa how you liked to carry me because it made your back strong. I always liked to hear your stories of what had gone on during your shift and any new jokes that were doing the rounds.

That day, though, was different. You said you had something important to tell me.' Donald nudged Owen, who had started to doze off, the heat from the fire had begun to redden his cheeks, but Donald was now in full flow, his eyes evidence that he was re-living that day, now long gone, when the two brothers had been young men.

Owen lifted young Donald down off his back, and they leant against a garden wall.

'I've done it,' Owen said to Donald, 'I've joined up.'

Owen's words drifted silently away down into the valleys, in the warmth of a Welsh April afternoon; they were spoken softly and modestly, Owen casually flicking a stone away with his big heavy work boot as he spoke, not looking up at his younger brother, his eyes downcast towards the cobblestones.

Owen assumed Donald had heard him, and continued 'Let me tell Ma. I need her to understand.'

Donald realised then the significance of his brother's initial words. The talk between the young men in the valleys that year, 1914, had been of little else. Donald knew he should have anticipated it and not have been surprised but, in fact, he was dumbfounded. He began to absorb the personal implications of Owen's portentous words. His older brother going to war. Losing his best friend. Not seeing him again for years.

To Donald, Owen was peerless. 'What will happen to me? How will I manage? Let me come with you.' Donald breathlessly let the questions tumble out.

Owen tilted his cap to the back of his head, sunk his hands deeper into the pockets of his heavy black work trousers, and carried on studying the cobblestones. Donald felt his eyes begin to moisten, and a lump form in his throat. He was trying to stem a rising tide of panic, a feeling that his secure, cosy world of just a moment before had now been irredeemably shattered into a mass of tiny fragments that even the most consummate craftsman would never be able to repair.

But, from that afternoon, there was to be no turning back for either Owen or Donald. The brothers had crossed the Rubicon, that divided a past as boys from a future as men.

On that Christmas Day afternoon at Joe Flint's house, Donald noticed that his disclosure had embarrassed his brother, so he moved on to another story from his well-stocked mental library of tales from his youth ... 'When we were little Ma would bath us together in the giant tin tub, in front of the fire, and scrub the coal dust off us and, during the depression, we used to go searching in the slag heaps for lumps of coal to put on the fire at home. Youngsters these days don't know they're born.'

Joe's reminiscences about his grandfather moved away from the picture of him amongst the family group in the park, to the oil portrait he had in his attic. It was of Owen in war uniform. His serious expression. Slicked-back hair parted down the middle. His determined, firm-set jaw. The look of defiance on his young, fresh face.

Joe had been given the portrait amongst other wartime belongings after his grandfather died and he treasured both the portrait and a box of medals. The bronze star with crossed swords and 1914-18 inscribed on the front, attached to a red, white and blue ribbon held together by a safety pin. The large, silver George V First World War medal with its orange, blue and black ribbon. Owen's Royal Welsh Fusilliers capbadge. And, for Joe, the medal nonpareil: gold with a ribbon of purple, green, yellow and red, and inscribed, 'The Great War For Civilisation, 1914-1919.'

Owen Bevan returned home from war ostensibly the same unassuming man he had been on the day he left, but whose quiet, courteous manner now disguised an inner core of steel. And the only job open to him in his Welsh village was to work down the pit.

Owen's character was formed during times of deprivation and unremitting struggle that had taken him on an epic journey from the white heat of the steelworks, through the battlefields of war and the harshness of the coalmine, to the desolation of the depression and then again to war, in 1939.

The stamping ground of Owen and Donald had been the hills and valleys of Wales in a time when wealthy patrician mine owners held dominance over workers who earned their living crouched in cold dark tunnels running with water, swinging pick-axes at a coal face, while listening constantly for signs that the earth overhead might at any moment cave in and bury them.

And yet, in Joe Flint's eyes, his grandfather had always remained the least cynical person he had ever known. He appeared to have been ennobled rather than crushed by his life of formidable challenges.

A particular day that had stayed in Joe's memory, as a man of the television age, had been the day of the funeral of Winston Churchill.

On that Saturday morning, all his family had been gathered round the black and white television set, an unusual occurrence that had marked the day in Joe's mind as being a momentous one. The room was quiet and respectful.

Joe had been aware at the time that his grandfather's hero was Lloyd George and was unsure as to the extent of his esteem for Churchill, although he had heard him refer to the Dardanelles as being Churchill's nemesis in the early part of a long and distinguished political career; a view which had seemed to hold sway over his reticence concerning Churchill's later re-emergence from the political wilderness to become a Prime Minister who embodied the spirit of a nation in wartime and led it on to victory.

Joe had attributed this attitude to his grandfather's lifelong political allegiance to the Labour party, an attachment he maintained unswervingly while also viewing politicians as a species through a jaundiced eye.

Also, Owen's Welsh roots ran into very deep soil, and this was permanently to the fore in his expressions of opinion, his proud boast being that the brotherhood of the Welsh and the Scots were the pure stock of the Sceptred Isle, and the English mere usurping hybrids.

Of course, on the rare occasions Owen made such views known, his chosen phrases were always a rich blend of irony and mischief, with an underlying desire to provoke heated family debate added for extra flavour.

Within Owen, as with his wife Victoria, was an inherent sense of the absurdities of life, and this had been an enduringly strong link in their marital chain, along with an ingrained obligation, which they both felt, to prick pomposity in whatever guise they happened to discover it and then to relish the outcome.

Respect had to be earned from Owen Bevan in much the

same way as the miner who had worked alongside him, hacking at the coal face, or the soldier at his side as they went into battle together, had earned his respect, except in their cases, respect grew to become akin to devotion.

On the evening of Churchill's funeral, Victoria had been out, and returned home quietly. She felt there was an eerie silence throughout the house, which was in darkness, with the exception of a sliver of light from underneath the door of the back room. She turned the doorknob quietly. And saw Owen. The National Anthem was playing from the radio, to mark the end of a day's broadcasting that had commemorated Churchill's passing. Owen was standing. Motionless. Erect back and shoulders. Eyes moist with tears. Beribboned medals laid in a straight line on the table.

'Come to bed, Owen,' Victoria whispered as she gently took her husband's hand and led the way out of the back room.

Churchill's day was over. Respect had been paid by a Royal Welsh Fusillier.

Donald Bevan grew up to be a smaller, thinner, spry version of his staunch Welsh brother, Owen. If Owen could be said to be Edward G. Robinson, then Donald was James Cagney. The Hollywood comparisons were appropriate not only in terms of physicality, but also in regard to mannerisms and personality.

Owen and Victoria moved to the boarding house at number 5 Park Avenue, Blackpool, after Owen's demob at the end of the Second World War with their daughter Jackie, her husband Bob and baby Joe, and it had not been long before Donald and his wife had joined them and bought a boarding house of their own a few streets away and a whole family enclave from the Welsh valleys had re-formed to build new futures for themselves at the seaside town.

The brothers would meet up for Saturday nights out at the King George Cinema. These weekly meetings were opportunities for Owen and Donald to catch up on family news.

One occasion in particular was memorable to Joe Flint as he had been invited to go with them.

In the tradition of the day, the National Anthem was played after the film finished, before the audience left the cinema.

Donald caught sight of a man in a white raincoat stepping into the aisle in an attempt to be the first to leave the cinema by avoiding the rush that always began on the appearance on the screen of a giant image of a uniformed Queen Elizabeth on horseback to the resounding strains of the Anthem. He noticed Owen from the corner of his eye jumping to his feet, and immediately feared the worst. Donald put out a restraining arm to block Owen's path. 'Disrespectful lout' Owen was muttering under his breath. 'Leave it, Owen,' Donald said to his brother, but it was too late, Owen had gone and an unseemly scuffle was in progress in the aisle.

The projectionist, having had a long and tedious evening, and in desperate need of excitement, fixed the scrapping pair in the full glare of his spotlight. Other members of the audience edged their way past the brawlers, leaving the two of them dishevelled and still grappling.

Joe recalled that Donald ushered him outside, where an unkempt Owen eventually appeared and proceeded to comb his hair, straighten his best jacket and put his trilby back squarely on his head. Not a word was spoken between the three of them on their way home and no-one ever got to hear of the lot of the man in the white raincoat.

Owen was certainly not the type of man to brag, nor to disabuse all those people who, as a result of Donald's propensity to gossip, were compelled to listen to his brother's amplified recountings of the unfortunate episode, which led them to believe that Owen had emerged completely unscathed and without a hair out of place, whereas the man in the white raincoat was carried off feet first.

The consequence was that Owen, from that day onwards, acquired the reputation in the neighbourhood of being a dyed-in-the-wool Royalist – to his continuing dismay, since he felt he was simply a believer in correct behaviour.

However, the die had been cast for him by Donald and Owen was much too considerate a man to set the record straight and thereby cast a shadow over his younger brother's veracity, or the reflected glory he had gained from the eventful night out at the King George.

From the Old West

Old Glory had fluttered proudly in the breeze from its position on the immaculate lawns outside the majestic white pillars of Red Pines since the day when 'Big Sam' Ford had personally placed, at the foot of the imposing gleaming white flagpole, the last symbolic spade of soil.

This indicated to everyone watching that day, from behind the windows, and from upon the lawns of the magnificent colonial-style New York mansion, that they had all just witnessed a momentous occasion in the auspicious history of the Ford dynasty.

That day later became crystallised in the memory of each person present into one moment.

As he placed his spade down onto the lawn beside him, Big Sam had bowed from the waist, with an exaggerated extended flourish of both arms, and a circular twirling of his hands, to acknowledge the rapturous applause of his wife, Agatha and his son 'Little Sam' who were standing proudly in the entrance of Red Pines.

A distinguished actor of the London theatre, in taking his curtain call, and acknowledging the applause of the audience at the close of a successful performance could not have accomplished the movement of Big Sam with such élan and flourish.

Samuel Arthur Ford Senior, was known as Big Sam by

everyone who knew him, in order to distinguish him from his son, Little Sam, Samuel Arthur Ford Junior.

Big Sam was a swashbuckling, ruddy-complexioned, Buffalo Bill character of the Old American West, with hooded blue eyes, piercing out onto the world from beneath bushy eyebrows, and a big moustache that curled downwards, before disappearing into a resplendent auburn beard, that appeared to swallow up the entire lower half of his face.

Big Sam's earliest memory was of a much grander celebration on the lawns of Red Pines, when he stood alongside his mother and tried to hold on to the edge of her voluminous floral skirt, as she danced round in a circle, in celebration of news of the surrender of General Robert E. Lee to Ulysses S. Grant at Appomattox, an event which had marked the end of the American Civil War.

Big Sam was too young to appreciate that his mother's euphoria at that moment was just as much in celebration of the fact that she could now anticipate the return from the war of his father.

Big Sam, in later life, always recalled the first sight he had of his father was the day he saw him in his dark blue uniform of the Union, with his shining sword swinging from his hip, and dazzling rays from the sun flashing from its glorious gleaming blade.

He remembered his father sweeping him up into his arms, and the magical moment when he had let him run his tiny finger down the edge of the blade, and had said to him, 'One day, my boy, this sword will be yours.'

Even as a venerable old man, when he was reminiscing over his long and distinguished life, Big Sam still told people that the moment in his father's arms was the happiest.

Big Sam also recalled the joyous months at Red Pines that had followed his father's return from the war.

Samuel Arthur Ford Senior, Big Sam, was a chip off the old block. His soldier father, Jacob Ford, had been a fighting man of principle, an abolitionist who went to fight in the Civil War because of his heartfelt detestation of slavery, and returned home at a time when a vast tidal wave of immigrant humanity was beginning to flood into the promised land of New York, to establish a financial empire with the inspired use of the Ford family wealth.

Jacob Ford was one of the first venture capitalists.

His imaginative vision was to loan money to the impoverished new immigrants, at low rates of interest, to give them a start in their new lives, so they could rent apartments in the teeming tenement blocks of New York, and feed and clothe their children, the next generation of Americans.

Jacob Ford's empire was already firmly established when his health began to decline and his plethora of loan companies, spread over the length and breadth of New York, was brought under a single enormous umbrella and given the title S.A.F.F., the Samuel Arthur Ford Financial Corporation, succession having been passed to his son and heir, Big Sam, who officially became president of S.A.F.F. upon the death of his father five years later.

Big Sam's only pastime, when he found time to get away from the incessant demands of the fledgling corporation, and indulge himself, was to ride the roller coasters at New York's Coney Island.

Big Sam, a hulking, grizzly of a man, had no hesitation in using his imposing bulk as an intimidatory weapon in order to ensure his place at the front of the queue for the roller coaster rides. By doing this, he guaranteed himself a seat in the front car of the coaster.

Big Sam set an incongruous figure, at the head of a queue of small, fresh-faced New York boys and girls.

'The coaster creaks and rattles, and then bursts into life, and begins to slowly rise up the wooden track, and climb towards the blue New York heavens. It then pauses for a moment, before plunging downwards, at the speed of light, to the depths of the oceans,' was how Big Sam imaginatively described the coaster experience to Little Sam, on the day he and Agatha took their son to Coney Island for the first time.

Little Sam's stomach churned at the imagery his father had created in his impressionable mind.

Once at Coney Island, Little Sam stood, hand-in-hand

alongside his mother, and looked up in awe at his father, who seemed to lead the soaring, shaking, giant caterpillar as it wound its sinuous path slowly up to the peaks, and then came hurtling, at breakneck speed, down to the ground. And then do the same again, over and over.

To the little boy, the accompanying sounds were mesmerising; the silence he could almost touch as the coaster climbed, followed by the high-pitched screams and shouts as it swooped, with its attendant sea of arms flailing in the air.

To Little Sam, who had never before even seen a roller coaster, his father was a supreme illusionist as, at the highest point on the track, he would disappear from view, as the coaster slowly turned a corner, and then, as if by magic, appear again, seemingly from out of the clouds.

But, following many future visits to the pleasure park after that day, what convinced Little Sam, above all else, that his father was made by God to be above all other mortal beings, was that he was always the only one on the ride who refused to grip the metal safety bar that the attendant dropped in place across the tops of his legs at the start of the ride, and, as the coaster made its hair-raising final swoop, could be seen, standing magisterially upright in the front car, arms extended aloft towards the heavens, looking for all the world like Moses preparing to descend from Mount Sinai to the seething multitude of the Israelites waiting below to receive the Ten Commandments.

After leaving the coaster, and walking out through the exit gates, to rejoin his wife and son, Big Sam would invariably be reprimanded by the brown-jacketed coaster attendant for having lifted the safety bar, and for his blatant exhibitionism on the ride, which, by flagrantly ignoring safety regulations, had, in the attendant's words, 'set a dangerous example and precedent to the young people who visit Coney Island.'

On such occasions, Big Sam would merely brush past the attendant, paying him no more heed than he would have to a gnat, idly buzzing around his head on a drowsy summer afternoon, and would proceed through the gates to Agatha and Little Sam as though no-one had spoken to him, and then, at the last moment, turn to face him, and boom out, in his bass stentorian voice, that seemed to rise up slowly from his boots, 'I assume you know to whom you are speaking, Sir?' said with such imposing authority as to render his hapless accuser mute. And Big Sam always ensured that his riposte was said within earshot of Little Sam, waiting with his mother, beyond the exit gates.

It is scarce wonder, then, that Samuel Arthur Ford Junior, Little Sam, developed into a reticent, introverted man by growing up in the shadow of such a colossus as his father.

Big Sam would scathingly remark to his wife Agatha that 'the Ford genetic thread must have snapped the day you presented me with Little Sam.'

In passing such a harsh judgement on his offspring, however, Big Sam would come to be proved only partly accurate, for, although Little Sam did grow into adulthood without the slightest intention of ever riding a roller coaster, let alone doing it with such bravado as his father, he did, in fact, inherit Big Sam's intuitive feel for what made the American working man tick, his pulse beat faster, and how to excite him.

It could have been simply that he had failed to inherit his father's childlike innocence, because Little Sam became a quiet, solemn man, lacking even the slightest smidgeon of his father's exuberant joie de vivre.

Big Sam looked upon life as a plaything, in much the same way as a young boy would regard his puppy dog, romping with it, teasing it and tugging its ears, on a bright summer morning, and waiting to see if any reaction was forthcoming and, if there was, proceed to tease the dog even more.

Little Sam, however, in contrast, saw life as a shadow, following him on a walk at the onset of evening which caused him to keep stopping to glance behind, with suspicion, to see if it might have substance that could threaten him, and only when the shadow had moved on its way, could he then resume his walk, free from anxiety.

Upon meeting a stranger, Big Sam would always be the first to thrust forward his strong right arm to shake hands; Little Sam never did; he would wait to see the other person's open palm first, and then proffer his in return.

But, notwithstanding such idiosyncratic distinctions between them, Little Sam grew up to resemble his father in the manner in which he approached the cut-throat arena of business, where he displayed an indistinguishable dynamism, and originality of thought, which proved to be the Ford genetic thread that had not snapped, but was made of unalloyed steel, not only in the person of Little Sam, but also later in his son, Isaac Ford.

Big Sam, and his son, Little Sam, embarked on a world tour in the early years of the new century. Agatha was unable to join them, as, at the last moment, she fell ill, with a minor chest ailment, but she insisted that they went on without her.

As a part of the tour, they stopped off in the British Isles, and included, during their stay, a walking tour of the Cumberland Lake District, followed by a short stay in the North-West English seaside town of Blackpool. The result was to be momentous in the histories of both Blackpool, and the American S.A.F.F. corporate giant.

The Blackpool of the early 1900s was a revelation to the Fords – a father and son who were the prototype metropolitan Americans.

Blackpool
Lancashire
England
2nd July 1902

My dearest Aggie,

Well, here we both are at the English seaside.
I do hope you are now fully recovered. We are looking forward to hearing from you soon. Try to write when you can.
Blackpool is amazing!
We have been here only a week, and feel that we have seen more than most people see in a lifetime.
First of all, the sea air is so bracing! So different to the Manhattan smog! We only wish that you could be here to share it with us.

It is impossible to convey in words how unique a place this is, but I hope this letter will help give you a flavour.
I had always been under the impression, before I came here, that the British were a reserved race, but Blackpool has shown that such a preconception was misplaced.
It is a town built for the working man and his family, a place where, for one week each year, they can forget about the work clock, and the pressures imposed upon them by harsh working lives in the mills, the factories and the shops.
And how they relish their freedom!
Earlier this week, Samuel and I visited the Winter Gardens, a giant palace of entertainment, with everything under one enormous roof, A wonderful idea – indoor promenades, concert hall, etc, etc...
Blackpool is all crowds – and noise – and life! In a word – RAZZAMATAZZ!
But, perhaps, the easiest way to give you a taste of this special place is to tell you what Samuel and I did here today. It will help give you an idea what every day is like here.
We woke early, and made our way through the streets to the seafront.
There are stalls on either side of the street, selling everything you could possibly imagine – oysters, crockery, ice cream and such a variety of sights that even New Yorkers like us have never cast eyes on before – German bands, organ-grinders, musicians of all kinds.
And pubs on every street corner.
At times we had to force our way through the crowds but, eventually, we reached the heart of Blackpool – the famous giant Tower and the piers, stretching out to sea. Here the crowds were even greater than before. An ocean of people!
And, between the piers, the fairground – even in New

York I have never seen so much enterprise – fortune tellers everywhere, folk reading the bumps on top of others' heads – they call it phrenology; folk cutting the corns on others' feet. And many entertainers, from ventriloquists to conjurers.
Samuel and I had our photograph taken, in the middle of the crowds, on the beach – just in case you wouldn't believe our story when we got home! – In the photograph we are both eating Blackpool rock.
Then we both rolled up our trousers, and paddled in the sea.
We rode on the public electric tramcar – the first anywhere in the world.
Everywhere is like one giant carnival of working people, in fact, here they call it 'the Carnival of the Sands'. Even on the beach, especially on the beach. All playing as hard as they can.
And everyone you meet here is so good-humoured. There is an excitement – an energy – in the air here, perhaps being near the sea causes it, and that is why they all come here in such vast numbers.
They cater for the working man here in every respect that he could wish for, more than anywhere else I have been to, even including the US, and that is the lesson I will bring back home with me, and hope to make use of. We are over here to learn, as well as to enjoy ourselves.
The folk here take to the sun on the warm days, by lounging in deck chairs, and the men keep on their thick jackets, even on the hottest days.
We passed doctors selling cures for every ailment known to man, and auctioneers, selling heaven knows what.
I have learned that ordinary folk are looking for ways to spend their hard-earned money, in having fun that is no more than their due, and that it is up to me to help them find new ways that will excite them. We must

continually try to innovate, and help find them the thrills they are seeking.
There was one particular sight that especially intrigued us, and we stayed half an hour in the crowd that had gathered round to listen to him. He was an orator, standing on a soapbox, so the crowds could hear everything he was saying. He was a rabble-rouser, stirring up excitement in the crowd, who began to cheer and applaud his every word. He spoke all about the rights of the working man, about rising up to throw off the oppressor; that we should all fight for our freedom, and unite. I spoke to many of the folk listening to him. Their work was cotton-spinning and weaving in the inland mills, and they came to Blackpool every year. They all seemed happy with their lot in life to me, but who can tell, as they were on holiday. They were all exuberant folk, full of life, especially the women – some of them were linking arms and kicking their legs in the air; they seemed without a care in the world.
The orator was still going strong when a police officer – someone in the crowd shouted out 'Here's a bobby, coming to get him' - grabbed him by the collar, and took him away. All the crowd cheered their hero, and yelled 'Shame! Shame! Leave him alone.'
Late in the afternoon, we rode on the Gigantic Wheel, that took us high up into the sky, and we could look down on the crowds, who seemed from up there to be like an army of ants on the move.
Before I sign off, Aggie my dear, let me tell you about tonight. Samuel and I came down again to the promenade, and watched the sun going down behind the sea, on the horizon. For as far as the eye could see was a continuous stretch of golden sands. The fairground folk had made their way home for the day. The sun was a giant, vivid orange ball, slowly fading away behind a sea as still as a millpond. Seagulls were wheeling patterns in the distance, silhouetted against a

darkening sky of the deepest blue, with gossamer wisps of white cloud drifting back and forth in the cool breeze of the evening.
Even the most inspired landscape painter would have struggled to do justice to such an exquisite scene.
If only you could have been here with us, but, God willing, we will have the chance to return here together.
I will write again soon,
With my deepest love,

Yours ever
Samuel

P.S. Junior sends his love

Big Sam returned to New York invigorated by the time he had spent in Blackpool and eager to put into effect the lessons he had learned.

He had seen, with his own eyes, the insatiable demand there was for leisure. Exciting leisure.

Already, by this time, the S.A.F.F. Corporation was a giant conglomerate, but specialising only in loan finance.

Big Sam's plan, on his return, was to complete a circle.

He knew from his days spent at Coney Island, the overpowering feelings of exhilaration and freedom he would get when standing up in the front car of the roller coaster, and had never understood anyone who didn't feel the same way.

He had also seen Blackpool, a town where working people were seeking a multiplicity of thrills that he knew a pleasure park could satisfy.

So he drew the inevitable conclusion: his loan corporation was already providing the money to people to establish them in their daily working lives and earning a living, so he would now provide the outlet for them to spend their dollars in enjoying their leisure, in ways that excited them.

Big Sam was going to take his corporation into the pleasure

business in a big, modern way and, by so doing, cater for the full spectrum of an American life.

In his imagination, Sam envisaged taller and faster roller coasters, crazier helter-skelters, more nerve-wracking switchback rides, all to be built to induce heart-stopping exhilaration and dizzying rapture, on a scale never before conceived.

S.A.F.F. Leisure would be formed as an offshoot corporation, specialising in all aspects of the pleasure park industry, from research and development to design and production; not only in the USA, but also overseas.

Both Coney Island and Blackpool had shown Big Sam that leisure was as vital an ingredient in the life of a blue collar American immigrant, building a new life in New York, as it was to an English woman toiling in a Lancashire cotton mill. As essential to their well-being as the life-blood that coursed through their veins and, to Big Sam, this was the reason why only the very best was going to be good enough for them.

In Big Sam's vision he saw himself as the missionary who was going to re-ignite, if only for a glorious, sparkling instant, the fires of joy inside human personalities that every day were being harshly extinguished by the austere, mundane tedium of bitter and harrowing working lives.

In the working people he had witnessed he instinctively felt that the innocent, fun-loving child within the grown-up had been lost somewhere deep in the mists of life's disillusionment and despair, and needed to be re-discovered, and led out again to play in the sunlight of a new day, and, at night, to dream and re-live that day.

And Samuel Arthur Ford Senior, intended to make S.A.F.F. Leisure a dream factory.

Since his return from the first visit to Blackpool, he had in the forefront of his mind the building of an English equivalent to his beloved Coney Island; he knew the demand was already there, as he had seen the vast numbers of holidaymakers and, in fact, felt that Blackpool offered even more potential, as Coney Island was a magnet for day-trippers only, whereas Blackpool had a captive audience of week-long visitors, many of whom returned year after year.

But Big Sam's experience in Blackpool, as intoxicating as it had been, had also been a salutary one for him. It had shown him the scale of the task ahead, if his dreams were to be realised. There was no time to waste.

In the first decade of the twentieth century, in his capacity as overlord of S.A.F.F. Leisure (UK), the newly-formed British arm of his corporate empire, Big Sam paid regular visits to Blackpool, before moving into new corporate offices in Manchester, from where he could personally put into operation the designing and development of a giant pleasure park in the town he had so warmed to on his visit there with his son.

He found the land he wanted in a vast tract of sand dunes at the southern end of the town, which was being occupied by gypsies as an encampment. When Sam had paid his original visit, as well as the gypsies there had also been exhibitions, displays, shooting galleries and the ubiquitous fortune tellers. But there had also been several mechanical rides.

In essence, Big Sam had witnessed a pleasure park in embryo.

Big Sam formed a syndicate of American and British financiers and lawyers to buy the land and negotiate with the Blackpool town corporation to build a pleasure park on it.

Once the financial and legal arms of S.A.F.F. (U.K.) had completed their tasks, the planners and developers took over and finished the work.

Samuel Ford's Coaster World had been born, and the American invasion of Blackpool was under way.

The years between the two world wars were a boom time for Coaster World, as the people of Britain luxuriated in their release from a war that had taken away four years of their lives.

At the start of the Second World War, the octogenarian Big Sam returned to live in New York, and his son was appointed chairman of S.A.F.F. (U.K) and took up residence in the Ford family home at Woodlands, the mansion in the Cheshire village of Westhall, vacated by his father.

In 1923, Samuel Ford Junior's son was born, to take his place as next in the eminent line of the American Fords, the moguls of finance and leisure. The boy's name was Isaac.

Isaac learned his trade, as expected of a Ford, in the manner of his father and grandfather.

Samuel Ford Junior had become a big and imposing man, but had retained the reserve he had shown as a young boy in the days he had watched his father, Big Sam, riding the Coney Island coasters.

Sam Junior was now also different in other respects from his father.

He was a man of the new century, close to his son in his formative years, not remote like Big Sam had been with him.

In his business dealings, he achieved by suave diplomacy and quiet persuasion what Big Sam had done by bluster and power.

Sam Junior was loved by his people at S.A.F.F. (UK) whereas Big Sam was respected, and even revered, by his employees, but few ever claimed to have loved him. He had never been that type of man, although, sadly, he had always wanted to be, until he became resigned to the fact that perhaps only Agatha, and not even Sam Junior regarded him in that way, as his son had always seemed intimidated, and at times, even fearful, in his presence.

Samuel Arthur Ford Junior, Little Sam, when in conversation at his Woodlands home in Westhall, with his wife, Martha, and son, Isaac, always referred to the workers at S.A.F.F.(U.K.) as 'our people', even though they were British, and he was an American. This became a particular source of puzzlement to young Isaac, who had been born in Cheshire, England, and whose early years had imbued in him a reverence for American history, as taught to him at home by his father, who made only superficial reference to the history of England, the land of Isaac's birth.

Such scant knowledge as Isaac had gained about English history had been acquired by paying a passing interest to the subject during history lessons at his exclusive Cheshire public school, where his enthusiasm had centred around mathematics and the sciences.

The Ford Woodlands home contained a vast library of

American literature, most of which had been imported from New York, upon the family's removal before the Second World War.

Isaac's happiest moments as a small boy at Woodlands were spent huddled in the corner of the cavernous walnut-panelled sitting room, by the side of a roaring log fire, on cold winter nights, his father by his side, reading to him from the enormous, leather-bound volume spread across his knees.

The pages Isaac came to love the most, and the ones which fired his youthful imagination, were the ornate, glowingly-coloured plates which depicted the Old West of the pioneers and the prairies, the men of the wagon trains and the cattle trails.

Later, when he was older, his father had introduced him to stories of the birth of the United States of America.

Isaac's father, Sam Junior, although a big man in size, in facial appearance had become a man who bore little resemblance to his father, Big Sam.

Sam Junior was sallow-cheeked and clean-shaven, with short, black hair and deep-set, hazel eyes that reflected his cautious, taciturn disposition.

Sam Junior, in his readings to Isaac, would emphasise the likeness in facial appearance between his father, Big Sam, and Abraham Lincoln, and, although this was a considerable distance from actuality, it served a dual purpose, in that it simultaneously brought to life, and also linked, in the boy's imagination, the gods in the pantheon of American legend and, by association, the giants of the Ford dynasty.

Also, by adopting such an approach, not only did the historical figures become alive again, but so also did the values which they had incorporated into the American constitution, and the Ford family line.

Samuel secretly hoped that by doing this, Isaac would absorb these same values, and come to an awareness as to what being a Ford, and an American, had always meant, and should continue to mean through the generations to come. In particular, the Ford belief that the pursuit of happiness, as enshrined in the American constitution was an inalienable right, alongside life and liberty, and should be a constant endeavour of every individual.

And so, through Isaac's history lessons with his father, the boy learned the significance of such landmarks as the abolition of slavery in the American and Ford family past.

Samuel would begin by telling his boy of Thomas Jefferson, who he described as 'a slave owner, who was, in principle, opposed to slavery, who became the third U.S. President, and the primary author of the Declaration of Independence', and conclude with Abraham Lincoln, 'the man responsible for the ending of slavery in America, who ensured the secession of the Southern slave-owning states by becoming President in 1860, and the man who issued the Emancipation Proclamation of 1862, and finally ended the war for slavery in 1865.'

Samuel would end his narration on his hero, Lincoln, with a reference to Isaac's great grandfather, Jacob Ford, 'a man who hated slavery with all his heart, and believed in freedom and independence above all things. Enough to go to war and fight for it.' He would recall the day his father, Big Sam, had told him about Jacob's return from the Civil War, and touching the gleaming sword on his dark blue uniform and how all this had been held in celebration of the surrender of Lee to Grant, to end the Civil War.

Samuel would end Isaac's American history lesson in dramatic fashion. 'Five days after the surrender of Robert E. Lee, Lincoln was shot by John Wilkes Booth, a southern sympathizer, and died the following day.'

With this, Samuel would close the massive volume and tell Isaac it was time for him to go to bed.

One saying of his father's that was to make a lasting impression, and may well have been the spark in his subconscious that ignited Isaac's remorseless energy and immutable resolve was a Ford family dictum that, although human beings were believed to have a congenital fault, in that they were never satisfied, this, in fact, was one of their greatest strengths, as it set the species apart, and above the animals, who are satisfied with what they have.

Isaac's mother, Martha, had minimal involvement in her son's intellectual development. Isaac remembered her as a peripheral figure in his young life, remaining mainly in the background as a support to his father. She was the polar opposite to her husband, for, whereas he was tall and imposing in appearance, yet reserved and chivalrous in temperament, Martha was frail and unprepossessing, but endowed with such force of character that, merely an arched eyebrow, or a furrowed forehead, from the elfin-like face of this tiny woman, who would have struggled to remain upright in any but the gentlest zephyr of a sea breeze, was sufficient to render anyone with the gall to oppose her into meek obeisance.

At the start of the Second World War the S.A.F.F. (UK) premises were taken over by the government, and converted into a munitions factory for the duration of the war. The male employees went into the armed forces, replaced by a wartime workforce comprised almost exclusively of women, many of whom were in employment for the first time.

When the end of the war became imminent, and the sixty-year old Samuel Ford was drawing up plans to resume peacetime production at the corporation, he received an unexpected visit at Woodlands from his old S.A.F.F. (U.K.) trade union leader.

Before the wartime closure of the corporation, Samuel and Jimmy Murray, although far from being friends, had enjoyed an amicable and respectful relationship for two figureheads who stood on the summits of opposing peaks across the working divide.

Jimmy Murray was a diminutive, bluff, ferret-like Glaswegian of unkempt appearance, who discerned in his counterpart, Samuel, not least from the steely glint in his eye, a similarly tough and uncompromising man as himself, although one who exuded in abundance, unlike himself, a cultural veneer. This, in Jimmy's view, could only have been acquired by someone who had lived his long life ensconced in opulent settings such as the one in which Jimmy now found himself, as he sank back into the red Chesterfield armchair, opposite Samuel, in the sitting room of Woodlands.

As Jimmy had been ushered in by the Ford butler, to meet his erstwhile employer, he had noted that Samuel, in the manner of their previous few meetings at the corporation, had seemed reluctant to take his outstretched hand in greeting; Jimmy, mistakenly on his part, attributed this to what he perceived as an inherent feeling of superiority that he believed Samuel, the wealthy American, must believe he possessed over him, whereas it was, in fact, simply an aspect of Samuel's diffident disposition.

In fact, no such thought would ever have occurred to Samuel, in his dealings with anyone, as he regarded each person with whom he came into contact as an equal, and expected the same from them in return.

Jimmy Murray opened the conversation, 'Thank you for seeing me, Mr Ford, I appreciate that you must be a very busy man.'

Samuel sat upright, crossed his legs, and folded his hands across his lap, 'Not at all, Jimmy, not at all. I trust you and your family are all well.'

'They are, Mr Ford, and yours?'

'All fine, Jimmy, thank you.'

'Been difficult times, Mr Ford, difficult times.'

'Indeed, Jimmy, indeed.'

Both men had always been uncomfortable with preliminary small-talk; they liked to establish the ground on which they were to engage battle from the outset of a meeting.

To a disinterested observer of the proceedings at Woodlands that morning, noticing the reluctance of both parties to observe the protocol that customarily preceded formal discourse, it would have appeared that the war had never taken place in their respective lives, and that he was merely witness to nothing more significant than a continuation of a routine daily business meeting of six years earlier.

The observer would also have been disconcerted by the incongruous disparity in articulation, between Samuel's mellifluous American, on the one hand, and Jimmy's gruff Glaswegian on the other.

So Samuel and Jimmy, having exhausted their small-talk got right into the big-talk.

Jimmy began, 'I came to see you, Mr Ford, to discuss the agreement ... the meeting we had at the start of the war, about the men at S.A.F.F. who had volunteered for the forces, and how they would be able to have their jobs back when the war ended.'

Samuel studied Jimmy closely, and raised his right hand to his chin, before he replied, 'I remember, Jimmy. But you must appreciate that was then, and now is now, and there's been a war inbetween. I never promised anything, I said I'd see what I could do for them, depending on the circumstances at the time, and not long after we had spoken, the factories were closed down – for the duration – and the government took them over, for war production purposes. I wasn't given a choice.

I've always prided myself on being a man of my word, Jimmy, but no-one can legislate for circumstances following the outbreak of war.'

Jimmy began shifting uneasily in his chair. He was waiting to come in and break the flow of what might, if he wasn't careful, develop into a lecture.

'With all due respect, Mr Ford, we all knew the government wouldn't allow the S.A.F.F. plants and offices to lie idle for who knows how long, so what they did wasn't exactly a surprise, and should not have played a part in our agreement. And we shook hands on it, and, on the basis of that handshake, I went back to my men and promised them that their jobs would remain secure, and would still be there for them when the war ended. I put my reputation at stake. Also my honesty and integrity.'

A look of irritation crossed Samuel's face. 'Please don't make this any more difficult for me than it is already, Jimmy, but if you'll please allow me to finish. I accept everything you've just said, and, I, too, value my reputation, my honesty, my integrity, and would never compromise them under any circumstances. I was about to add, before your interruption, that S.A.F.F. has had a new workforce during the war – almost entirely of women – and they, too, have a representative whose views I am obliged to take into account.

In fact, Jimmy, when it was announced that the war was to end, the lady in question – Sylvia - Sylvia Jones – came to see me. She'd had a meeting with her workforce. I know I'm not speaking out of order in telling you this, because of your interest on the lines you've just explained to me – you're entitled to know – in fact we are still awaiting a resolution following my meeting with Sylvia, after which I was going to get in touch with you, but you pre-empted me, by coming to see me today.'

Jimmy remained silent, and consumed with trepidation, at what he was about to hear.

'I'll cut to the chase, Jimmy.'

Jimmy nodded his head, and Samuel continued, 'Sylvia Jones told me that a substantial majority of her members have requested that all jobs are kept in force until the women's menfolk have returned home, and each individual has been given the opportunity to assess her position, at which time a further ballot will be taken, about the agreed future of the workforce.

It seems that it is no longer certain that the women will want to return to the status quo that existed before the war, when most of them were housewives. But we'll have to wait and see the outcome of the ballot, before we know for certain about that. And, Jimmy – this is cards on the table time – from my personal standpoint, the women have been working on wartime rates of pay, which is considerably less than the men received during peacetime, and, following the end of the war, they may well want to keep their jobs, which would mean considerable cost economies for S.A.F.F.

Also, Jimmy, post-war will be a new world. We won't know how S.A.F.F. is going to be affected. What the demand for leisure entertainment will be. It may be greater than before the war – or less – it will take time before we're going to find out for sure.

But, on the other hand, Jimmy, cost isn't everything. S.A.F.F. also needs the expertise, the experience, of the men who worked for us pre-war. But we also need to pay as economical pay rates as possible, especially in the immediate post-war period, until the wheels of the country start turning again.

So, Jimmy, you see the bind we're in at S.A.F.F. And now you know as much as I do.'

Jimmy Murray felt that the wind had been taken out of his sails, and he had no alternative but to withdraw, and hope to fight again another day.

The men of S.A.F.F. returned home from war to a changed world. Not least in their relationships with their wives.

The wartime women of S.A.F.F., in common with a multitude of other British women who had also worked for the war effort, had gained, through their work, a new-found and liberating independence, and were not content to return to their pre-war lives, when they were purely homebodies. They wanted a full share in the new post-war British order, in which they expected this new dimension in their lives to continue.

The results of the ballots held by both S.A.F.F. union leaders, Jimmy Murray, and Sylvia Jones, were both unanimous; the men wanted their jobs back, and the women wanted to hold on to theirs.

The situation was a classic impasse, and one in which Samuel Ford found himself caught in the middle. And which brought him to the verge of destroying himself.

Samuel had no alternative but to allow the wartime staff situation of a female workforce to remain in place, while a resolution was sought between himself, and the two warring parties.

Battle lines had been drawn, and all three parties in the dispute, Samuel Ford, the unemployed S.A.F.F. men and the employed S.A.F.F. women, became deeply entrenched in their intractable positions.

Samuel's suggestion that a compromise solution should be sought as the way out of the morass was instantly rejected by both unions. They dismissed out of hand any possibility of a mixed workforce comprising equal numbers of men and women. The pre-war men with the expertise would not work alongside the unskilled wartime women. With both parties, it had to be all or nothing.

The months dragged by, and there appeared to be little prospect of a break in a stand-off that became increasingly acrimonious with each passing day.

The union coffers of the unemployed men's union became almost exhausted, and the men were finding the struggle to put food on the family table almost overwhelming.

And, through it all, the gates of Coaster World remained

firmly locked, waiting for the day when the situation was resolved.

And, with Jimmy Murray's workers' hardship fund almost run dry, Samuel Ford himself began to become fearful for the future of S.A.F.F. (UK), including his own position as head of the corporation.

He was still accountable to his father who, despite his age, had remained President of the parent US corporation, and Big Sam was beginning to demand answers from his son, and a solution, and quickly.

Big Sam, as much as he loved his son, would not tolerate failure, even by a Ford, especially by a Ford, and, for the first time in his life, Sam Junior felt powerless, squeezed from all sides, and especially from above.

So Sam Junior, a lifelong teetotaller, at sixty years of age, took to the bottle, to ease the depression that had taken root within his mind, mildly at first, and then, all-consuming and paralysing in its force.

Samuel established secret hiding places, spread out at all points of Woodlands, for his supplies of Jack Daniels, and even a permanent bottle, for personal and surreptitious use only, in his S.A.F.F. office, to help him get through his working day.

He was desperately seeking a solution to the corporation problems by plunging himself into the blessed oblivion that could be found at the bottom of an empty whisky bottle. But his drinking only served to feed his depression, and propel its destructive force into an extra dimension.

As the severity of the depression worsened and with his alcoholism tightening its grip, he began to take increasing absences from his duties at S.A.F.F., and would lock himself in his study at Woodlands, with only Jack Daniels as a consoling companion.

Samuel's wife, Martha, failed to recognise any more the man she had known for over forty years, but was at a loss to help him.

Martha's approach to most problems in life had always been to charge at them head on, and so remove them by dynamic force of will alone, but she was impotent when confronted by the insidious psychological forces that were enslaving and overwhelming her wretched husband.

The result between Samuel and Martha was a nightly battleground of ferocious accusation and recrimination, much of it overheard, in its varying degrees of intensity, by twenty-two year old Isaac.

Isaac would view the broken look on his father's face, at the moments during the arguments when his mother was unleashing on her husband the full venom of a lifetime's disillusionment, and feel inside himself a war being waged for the supremacy of his emotions, between sorrow for his embattled father, and anger at the circumstances that had brought such affliction down upon the once-proud, unassailable Ford family.

Isaac went away and weighed the import of the savage words he had heard between his father and mother, and looked for a solution that could rescue his pitiable father; a key that could unlock the door of the deadlock, a secret passageway to lead the way out of the cul-de-sac.

The day arrived when Isaac decided to act.

He had overheard Samuel discussing a meeting that was to take place in his office at S.A.F.F. headquarters in Manchester, between the two union representatives, and himself as mediator. He had heard his father say that he would be unlikely to attend, due to illness, and would, in his absence, be arranging for his deputy chairman to stand in for him.

On the night of the meeting, the weather was stormy, with rain driving down relentlessly from leaden skies, and a stygian gloom hanging over the city.

Isaac strode purposefully along the winding corridors of S.A.F.F. headquarters, and walked unannounced into his father's capacious office.

Only Bill Johnson, the deputy chairman, recognised Samuel's son, as Isaac stood in the doorway, and his first thought was that Isaac must be there to deliver a message from Samuel, so he smiled and waited for him to speak first. Instead, Jimmy Murray spoke, 'This is a private meeting, son.'

Isaac assumed, by his dishevelled appearance, that the man

addressing him was the one-time S.A.F.F. union leader, whose unflattering description he had overheard during the heated exchanges at home between his mother and father.

Isaac was undaunted at finding himself in the citadel of Ford power and now actually facing up to the eminent figures who surrounded his father, and played their roles alongside him in the daily functioning of his corporate empire.

Isaac squared his shoulders, and fixed his gaze at a point equidistant between Jimmy Murray and Sylvia Jones, the two union heads, and, as he spoke, switched his look between them, as, by so doing, he was indicating to them that they were of equal importance.

Isaac kept his head held high, and did not allow his gaze to waver, or to drop, even for a split second.

'I know I shouldn't be here tonight, but I'd like just a few minutes of your time.'

'Why should we listen to you, and not to your father?' The gruff, white-haired Bill Johnson's welcoming smile now vanished from his face as he spoke, and Isaac felt irritated that he had not even addressed him by his name, nor introduced him to the two union bosses, but had merely looked at him as though he was a complete stranger he was passing on the street.

Isaac walked over to the big bay window. The concealed pale orange light above the centre of the polished oak table cast a shadow across his face. He sensed intuitively that this tactic could make a difference to his plea for consideration by the group of three in the room.

Isaac spoke directly to the deputy chairman, 'My father does not know I'm here this evening, and I'm not here as his spokesman, but, nevertheless, I think you'll find what I have to say is of significance. Also, my father is unaware that I know any details about the current labour dispute, but I have recently acquainted myself with the full facts.'

The faces of each of the three listeners registered a shared look of bemusement as Isaac spoke.

'Take a seat. We'll give you fifteen minutes. Not a second longer. Then please leave.' Bill Johnson spoke in a manner even more abrupt than usual. He was concerned about what Samuel's likely view was going to be when he eventually got to hear of his son's bravado. He decided the prudent approach, as Samuel's understudy, was to adopt a middle course, between admonition of Samuel's boy, and cautious respect towards him for what he was about to say, until the outcome of his address had become apparent.

Bill Johnson felt the moment was right to at least introduce him, 'Oh, by the way, this is Samuel's son, Isaac.' Jimmy and Sylvia looked at each other incredulously, and then back at Isaac, who nodded and smiled at both of them, and then at Bill Johnson.

It was Jimmy who spoke first, as was his wont, 'I've known your father for a long time. A fine man. Always found him tough, but also fair, in any dealings we've had together.'

Jimmy had provided Isaac with exactly the introduction he needed, 'And now been abandoned, by the very people he trusted,' Isaac said sharply, making a conscious effort to keep his gaze from drifting back towards the face of Bill Johnson, and continuing to switch between Jimmy and Sylvia, 'simply because they are not prepared to get together and compromise. To find a way out that would benefit everyone, especially the corporation that has provided your comfortable lifestyles – and mine.'

Isaac had decided that a forthright approach was the most likely to pay dividends, and he was driven on by the alternating pictures in his mind of his father's distressed face when he had last seen him, and the childhood image of his father reading to him about the heroic figures of the American past, not least his hero Lincoln delivering his immortal Gettysburg Address.

He knew he had nothing to lose, and, at that moment, he envisioned himself as the standard bearer of the Ford heritage, the latest in a long and distinguished line that stretched back to his great-grandfather Jacob, then his grandfather Big Samuel, then his father, and now himself. A whole American history, now being distilled into a fleeting fifteen minutes of time, during which both his father's sanity and the corporation's future would be balancing precariously on the high wire of his youthful oratory.

Isaac's neatly combed, short, dark hair, was beginning to feel matted to his scalp due to the perspiration that was now also starting to trickle down the back of his neck, making the tightly-fitting collar of his pristine, white shirt contract into his neck, and begin to bite into the skin with the intensity of cheese wire slicing through a block of stilton.

Isaac ran his right index finger around the inside of the shirt collar, to relieve the pressure, and gently loosened the knot of his dark blue tie; he then tugged at the sleeves of his ill-fitting navy blue suit, an article of clothing he had always avoided wearing, but had chosen that night to initiate with the intention of making a visual impact to support the eloquent persuasion he was hoping to summon up.

Every person in the room, at that moment, sensed an inherently steely quality about Isaac. Something indefinable that demanded their attention, and that would brook no unwarranted questioning or criticism. So they remained silent and allowed him to continue.

If the three people in the room listening to Isaac had been asked at that moment to define in one word the quality in him they recognised and respected, they would unanimously have chosen 'ruthlessness.'

They all instinctively knew that Isaac was a lion pack member, like themselves, whose natural habitat was the corporate jungle, the environment in which they all hunted for prey.

Bill Johnson looked at the two union leaders, and then addressed Isaac, 'Carry on.'

All three onlookers, Bill Johnson, Jimmy Murray, and Sylvia Jones, were thinking the one thought, 'What have we got to lose, let's hear what he's got to say.'

Isaac now had their undivided attention. His first objective had been achieved.

He had prepared well for this moment, by rehearsing at home, so as to anticipate every possible contingency in the cross-examination that he knew was bound to follow his proposals.

'I have a plan that would resolve the dispute. I have approached it from the opposite direction, that is, not to wait until the dispute is settled before opening Coaster World, but to open it up without delay first, and this would lead to the solution of the disagreement.'

'How?' asked Sylvia Jones.

'Because, by doing this, the way would be open to offer more work to more people, instead of all the people in both unions, men and women, wanting jobs only at S.A.F.F.

But, for this to succeed, a prerequisite would be good faith on the part of the members of both unions.'

Isaac glanced at Sylvia, and then at Jimmy.

'How I see it working is as follows: continue to pay the present women's wartime pay rate, after the war ...' Jimmy was about to interrupt, a look of annoyance on his pinched and flushed features, but Isaac held up his right hand, and went on. 'Please let me explain ... But link it with a percentage increment, a bonus, month on month, linked to increased turnover at S.A.F.F., as business picks up after the war, which we all hope, and expect, that it will.

But, in addition ...' at this point Isaac removed his hands from his trouser pockets and leaned forward onto the ornate table; he adopted a tone less conversational and more intense, ' ... link this with an offer of jobs at Coaster World to the members of both unions, men and women. The full range of jobs: supervisory, clerical and manual. And make them permanent, secure jobs, not casual and temporary like they were pre-war. Also, put anyone who accepts these new jobs on the same rate of pay as the S.A.F.F. rate, but with the added inducement of a productivity bonus, on the same lines as the one I've just outlined for S.A.F.F. And, as an extra sweetener, a second bonus, free use of Coaster World for workers and families for the duration of employment there.

By adopting this plan, everyone in both unions will be able to be given the offer of a job immediately, post-war, and the deadlock would be broken.'

A silence fell over the room, while Bill, Jimmy and Sylvia absorbed the likely implications of Isaac's proposals for each of their respective interests.

They each racked their brains and the depths of their

experience to find a loophole, a flaw that would bring Isaac's proposals crashing to earth. And they were all thinking of where Samuel came into all this.

The deputy chairman was the first to speak. 'We'll need to know Samuel's views on this.'

Isaac replied, without hesitation, 'I'm sure you will find the proposals will meet with my father's complete approval. Thank you for your time.'

With this, Isaac walked away from the table and strode purposefully towards the big wooden doors. He turned the gleaming brass knobs, and stepped out into the corridor.

The building already felt like his natural home.

Within weeks, Samuel Ford had become a teetotaller once more. Not a single bottle of Jack Daniels was ever seen again at his home or in his office.

He was a man reborn. And with a full grasp again of the reins of power at S.A.F.F. (U.K.). Only with a new deputy chairman, to replace Bill Johnson, who was offered, and reluctantly accepted, early retirement.

Samuel Ford's new right-hand man, to help him begin his renaissance, was his son, Isaac, who had received a substantial reward for his bravura fifteen-minute performance. He had won his spurs in the eyes of his grandfather Big Sam in New York, who agreed to his appointment on a recommendation from his son.

Isaac's first task in his new role was to oversee the resolution of the S.A.F.F. union dispute.

The impasse was broken, and the man to lead the Ford dynasty into the new peacetime era had been found.

Isaac Ford and his new bride Camille were among the wealthy new socialites of the post-war North West England scene and their names were continually in evidence at the head of invitation lists for social and business gatherings of the great and the good of the region.

Camille's photograph had been displayed on the front cover of North West Society, a publication with a select readership that sought out for the monthly honour only the glamorous people from amongst the ranks of the seriously moneyed of the region.

And Camille Ford fulfilled this requirement in abundance. She was taller than Isaac, willowy and graceful, with auburn hair and dazzling dark brown eyes. And a vivacity inherited, as said by people who knew her family, from her effervescent mother Eva, whom she was also said to favour in looks.

Few of her father John's manifold idiosyncrasies were apparent in his daughter, who displayed none of his inscrutability and introspection.

Camille was indisputably Eva's girl with her equable, gregarious and high-spirited disposition.

At the functions Camille attended with Isaac, during those times when he was obliged to leave her on her own while he fulfilled his back-slapping and glad-handing obligations, the eligible men in the room would noticeably converge on Camille. This became such a routine occurrence as to cause irritation to her husband, which was usually outweighed by his understanding of such unrestrained zeal as being due to envy of him for being so fortunate as to be the husband of a creature of such attractiveness.

One day, towards the end of their first year of marriage, Camille crept up on Isaac on a quiet, bright Sunday morning while he was reading the newspaper. She placed her hands on his shoulders and gently kissed him on the cheek, as delicately as a butterfly landing on a flower stem, and spoke in her soft, lilting voice, 'Isaac, I've something to tell you.'

Isaac folded his newspaper and placed it on the table at his side. He swung Camille around onto his lap, resting his arms around her waist.

'Isaac, we're going to have a baby.'

For the first time in his life, Isaac Ford was lost for words.

And so, Molly came into the world of Isaac and Camille.

Tragically, later on that same day, Camille left the world.

Camille had a difficult pregnancy, but hid her concerns from her husband.

As the months progressed, the movement of the child within

her did not seem to be happening in the way her friends with children had led her to expect.

On the mornings they met for coffee Camille deftly deflected their probing questions by switching the conversation to other topics. But the more discerning of her coffee morning coterie had gathered that all was not as it should be with Camille.

Molly arrived a month early, and Isaac was summoned from a meeting in the Lake District, to Blackpool Central hospital, to find Camille in the agonising throes of childbirth.

Immediately after seeing his wife, briefly clasping her hand and wiping her brow, he was summoned away by a doctor into a side ward.

The look of concern on the young doctor's face transmitted to Isaac a bolt of numbing anxiety.

'This is difficult for me to have to tell you, Mr Ford,' said the doctor solicitously, as he gestured to the only chair in the room, 'Please take a seat.'

'I think I'd rather stand, thanks all the same.'

'Your wife has been suffering complications since her admission. We're doing our best for her.'

'I'm sure you are.'

'It's the baby's position in the womb. It happens, but not very often.'

The doctor's small consolatory offering was lost on Isaac at that moment.

'If she proceeds there is a risk. How great, we're not absolutely sure. But definitely a risk.'

'A risk to who – my wife – or the baby?'

'Both, I'm afraid. I'm sorry. Unfortunately we haven't got much time. Soon we'll have to continue – or not – according to your wishes. We need an answer as to what you would like us to do.'

'What's your advice, doctor?'

'There is an equal danger for mother and baby, as the labour has been in progress for a considerable time. Perhaps you would like to speak to your wife. We've had to give her a sedative for the time being. She was in pain and struggling.'

'Poor Camille. Poor Camille,' thought Isaac. 'Why wasn't I with you?'

Isaac walked back into the ward. Camille was breathing deeply and rhythmically. She opened her eyes and smiled. 'Isaac, I'm glad you came.'

Isaac was about to ask her, but Camille put her hand over his and spoke to him first. 'I know what we need to decide. What do you want to do?'

Isaac did not need to think any longer as he looked lovingly into Camille's weary eyes. 'We can have another child.'

Camille was silent, but Isaac knew from her face there was something both she and the doctor had kept from him. Then Camille took hold of his hand and told him. 'Isaac, I can't. If I don't go through with it, too much internal damage will have been done. I want to go ahead. It means it's the only chance we'll have – ever – to have a child. You know how much having a child means to me - means to both of us.'

Isaac experienced a fearsome shudder, his throat tightened and he heard himself saying the most difficult words he had ever had to speak,

'If you're sure that's what you want, then I want it too.' The knuckles on his right hand were white from the ferocity of Camille's grasp. She gave her husband a gentle smile and closed her eyes. At that very moment the doctor appeared around the corner of the room.

'I'm sorry, Mr Ford, we'll now have to proceed.

Have you decided? I hate to have to hurry you. I appreciate how difficult it is, what you're both going through.'

Isaac answered him firmly, 'We've both decided we want to have the child. Please do everything you can.'

'You can be sure that your wife is in the best of hands.'

The joyous cry of life when the beautiful red-haired baby girl entered the world rang throughout the maternity ward.

Camille cradled the tiny baby in her arms, and her world at that moment was complete, with Isaac sitting on the bed, by her side.

She passed the baby into Isaac's arms, and closed her eyes,

letting the exhaustion from her ordeal seep out of her body, floating out through each of her fingers, and each of her toes.

Camille slipped into unconsciousness with her last waking image on earth being her husband's smiling face as he cradled in his arms their creation of such fragile beauty, with her tiny eyes tightly drawn together in blissful newborn sleep.

When Isaac noticed the change in Camille's breathing, his face at that moment was alongside her mouth, trying to catch the words she was struggling to tell him, 'Molly, our little Molly.'

Three hours later Isaac had to break the hardest news of his life, when he telephoned Eva. He was tormented as to the means of conveying what Eva and John needed to know, even beyond the moment when he dialled the number of the Sands hotel, heard the answering tone, and the voice on the other end. He began to speak, 'Hello, Eva, it's Isaac.'

Eva instinctively knew, but remained silent.

'Eva, you're a grandmother; the most beautiful little girl. We've called her Molly.'

Eva still stayed silent. She didn't even ask about her daughter. She knew.

'We've lost her, Eva, we've lost her.'

The telephone dropped from Isaac's hand - the black spiral cord swung back and forth in space, as Isaac slumped against the wall.

A distant voice could be heard through the receiver, a voice with a foreign accent.

'Isaac? Are you there, Isaac?'

John had come to the phone. Eva lay at his feet.

The Ringmaster and the Fortune Teller

Even if entertaining was not in Molly's blood from birth, then eccentricity most certainly was.

The patriarch of the Goldsmith family was John, known as Polish John by everyone outside his immediate family. This was a sobriquet John had acquired during an afternoon of drunken revelry and bonhomie at the 'Polish Palace', a gaming establishment which catered for the expatriate Polish community of Blackpool, only a stone's throw away from the family hotel on Kensington Drive.

Polish John had always endeavoured to shroud knowledge of his precise national origin in mystery, to everyone except his wife, Eva.

Some said that John must have been a refugee from Poland, solely because he attended the 'Polish Palace' on such a regular basis. Far too regular, in the opinion of Eva.

In point of fact, John's origins were Russian.

One indication of this was the bottle of vodka perpetually in evidence on the table next to his armchair, from which he took periodic swigs, without any discernible effect on his disposition.

This time-honoured practice had never been known to lighten John's mood, which was continually sombre; an impression magnified by his occupational attire of black tail-coat and top hat. Polish John was an undertaker.

John was a taciturn, aloof man, with exuberantly long, dark wavy hair, on top of which the top hat perched at a precariously jaunty angle, to add an extra element of incongruity to the melancholic demeanour he displayed to the bright and breezy, candy floss, kiss-me-quick habitat that was his adopted seaside home.

In addition, his alabaster pale complexion and overhanging dark beetle brows added a forbidding dimension that John felt was appropriate in his occupation, for the attendant relatives, in order that due respect would be accorded to clients who were about to embark upon a journey for which none of them required a return ticket.

In the Old Country, as Polish John referred to his Russian homeland, he had been a ringmaster with the Moscow travelling circus and Eva had always felt that her husband's bearing and demeanour emanated from these early years.

John always relished the opportunity to recount a Moscow Circus performance to Eva.

He liked to describe it in the fashion of an orchestra playing a symphony: using a soft, soothing voice to start, then slowly gathering speed and volume as other instruments joined in, and finishing in a percussion crescendo of drums and crashing cymbals, when his arms would be waving patterns in the air to accompany his high-pitched shrieks and deep rumbling roars.

The performance having been described in this manner, he would then immediately revert to brooding silence with accompanying swigs of vodka.

He would always begin by describing the children in the audience. 'They are always open-mouthed in wonder, Eva. Throughout the entire performance ... from the first minute when they see young Nadia up in the roof of the Big Top on the high trapeze in her sparkling white costume ... waiting for her moment, and then diving without warning off the platform, like a swallow, hanging onto the bar as it flies through space ... to meet Ivanov who is in mid-air, upside down, gripping his swinging bar behind his knees ... they time it to meet perfectly ... and Ivanov reaches out to catch Nadia's outstretched arms, and they swing together onto the safety of the platform ... and you can feel the breath of the crowd as they gasp in astonishment.

Then the mood of the children will switch to laughter. They clap and jump in delight as the bucket of whitewash is thrown over the immaculate costume of the sad-faced clown.

I would watch from the wings, observing the stern icy faces of the parents when they arrived being thawed by the warmth of laughter during the show. And they would leave with expressions filled with joy, walking from the tent hand-in-hand with their excited children. This is the power of the Big Top, Eva.'

John's favourite moment of his performance as ringmaster had always remained his nightly announcement of the spectacular grand finale.

'I could build the tension to achieve maximum impact, with my flamboyant introduction and then melodramatically stand to one side to let the floor of the circus ring open up to reveal the dazzling sight of a host of fountains shooting jets of brilliantly coloured water up to the roof. And each of the performers, in order of star status, would leap from behind the stage curtain onto a concealed platform and jump, bounce and cartwheel with acrobatic panache, the illusion making it appear to the spellbound audience as though they were performing on water, amid cascading fountains.'

It was, in fact, a finale to match John's concluding words, histrionically announced to Eva in his fractured English. 'The Circus both amuses and astounds in equal measure. It is an arena where magic is commonplace. Circus is extravanganza supreme.'

John Goldsmith had taken employment as an undertaker after his arrival in Blackpool as an émigré from Russia. He attributed his decision as being an eccentric expression of his ringmaster's love of presentation that was still inherent in him from his Moscow circus days, and he continued to nurse a desire to one day return to the circus, but only at his previously elevated level.

Eva Peacock was a Blackpool girl who worked backstage with the elephants at the Tower Circus.

John came to regard Eva as his talisman for success and happiness in his new land as, from the day he first set eyes on her, his life was transformed.

Eva Peacock was small, blonde and vivacious.

John's first encounter with Eva took place when she was on central beach in the early morning, walking alongside a line of circus elephants out for their morning exercise.

John walked over to stroke the side of the lead elephant, but was at a loss to think of anything more to say to Eva than asking the elephant's name.

In contrast to the laconic John, the garrulous Eva found no discomfort in prolonging their conversation beyond discussing her elephants, and John discovered that she lived with her mother at a run-down boarding house in the centre of town.

To a lonely immigrant with too much time to dwell on his miserable situation, Eva was a heaven-sent angel of mercy. Their meeting was a classic case of an attraction of opposites.

Eva's mother, Irene, was dismissive with John from the day they were introduced. She thought him withdrawn and monosyllabic and was at a loss to see what her vivacious daughter could possibly find attractive about him but, fortuitously for the couple, most of the time she was too busy running her boarding house to dwell on her daughter's comings and goings.

The day that Eva and John announced plans for their marriage, Irene Peacock shrugged her shoulders resignedly, and agreed to John moving in to live at The Sands when he became Eva's husband.

'After all, one extra mouth to feed won't make a blind bit of difference' and 'You both seem happy enough together' were two of her typical responses to the glad tidings.

Eva and John remained sanguine in the face of Irene's lukewarm response to their relationship and the idiosyncrasies of the couple increased rather than diminished following their marriage.

Irene felt that John the undertaker was in a singularly appropriate occupation for his sepulchral nature and that Eva's desire to be a fortune-teller was bizarre for a girl who never planned her own life beyond the next minute. And, most puzzling of all to Irene was the birth of such an exquisite child as her granddaughter Camille to a pair Irene perceived as being as different from each other as chalk and cheese.

Eva and John, however, had one thing in common.

Both of their personalities fitted in with the town in which they were living. They both had an intrinsic need to exhibit themselves. To show off. John's was hidden below the surface of his gloomy nature, but was there nonetheless, as made apparent in his choice of occupation. Eva's was on daily display, usually to the amusement of the boarding house guests, to whom she frothed and bubbled while her mother slaved away doggedly in a steaming kitchen at the back of the house.

John's decision to continue as an undertaker and not return to the circus ring may well have been made on the evening he was walking through the cavernous interior of Blackpool Tower. This was in the days when the Tower incongruously contained within the same building as the ballroom, an aquarium and a menagerie with lions, monkeys and other animals. John was walking down a passageway alongside the ballroom, when he caught sight of a group of drunken youthful revellers pacing back and forth in mockery of a majestic lion lying inside a cage that had been placed near the ballroom.

A mixture of sadness and fury had seethed within him to see a beast of such grandeur being ridiculed, and reduced to mournful impotence.

John thought what a curious world his new homeland was, and not like his old world where such a noble beast would have been revered, not humiliated.

A debate was triggered off in his mind by what he had witnessed. He had never questioned animals in a circus being used as an entertainment as this had been his life and he had just accepted it as part of the natural order of things. As performers, the animals were as indispensable as the humans; both provided happiness to people who paid to watch them.

Also, in Russia, he had lovingly washed, fed and exercised the animals. He had loved them all.

Now, here, in a country he had been led to believe was the acme of civilisation, an animal was being displayed as no more than an object of scorn. This confused and angered him in equal measure.

'I want no part of this,' he told Eva that night when he arrived home.

But, despite his experience that night and this remark to Eva, John's love for this exuberant town by the sea, with its spectacular circus built inside a tower, remained undimmed, and he associated the Tower with circus people, and was to be seen in the town speaking to the animal trainers, and patting the elephants as they trooped in a linked line along the sands for morning exercise.

John even opened a donkey concession on the beach for the children of the holidaymakers during the summer season.

But John knew that his previous employment as a ringmaster was finished forever. After seeing the lion, he never again set foot inside a circus.

He realised that his love for circus animals ran deeper than he had expected. It had been challenged, and contradictions upon the inter-relationship between people and animals never became resolved in his mind after the night he had seen the lion.

The annual family Christmas gatherings at the Sands began in the early years of John and Eva's marriage when they lived with Eva's mother, Irene.

The get-togethers were invariably replete with tales of the past, many of which concerned John and his circus experiences. He was the only one who really knew the distinction between those stories which were grounded in reality and those which were merely apocryphal.

That was how John liked it, as by maintaining a cloak of mystery, over time he hoped the myths about him would amplify. This did happen, and his legend flourished throughout his lifetime, and beyond, to such an extent that, given even the slightest encouragement, Eva would describe in detail her husband's funeral day, as she regarded this one day as having encapsulated an extraordinary lifetime, which, by her recounting, would thereafter be treasured by other people as John would have wished.

Eva always began in the same way: 'Would you believe there was a jazz band leading the cortege, all wearing candy-striped blazers and straw boaters. Then behind them came a llama; no-one watching knew what it was doing there. Next was a clown in full costume, followed by a juggler and the stilt man. Then came the lion tamer cracking his whip. All of them were from the Tower Circus.'

Eva, at this point, would hesitate for a moment and look at the listener's expression to see if she was re-creating the spirit of that day, and to gauge the reaction of her audience to her narrative.

'All along the promenade they went. In the middle of summer. You should have seen the crowds. Open-mouthed in amazement. Some even forgot to eat their ice creams and candy floss and were holding them in their hands, just staring in wonder, as though this was the kind of procession that happened in Blackpool every day. That it was all part and parcel of the week's entertainment. We did him proud. I know John would have loved every second of it.'

Eva would then take a sip from her tea and sit back in exultation, her hands clasped in her lap and would begin to twiddle her thumbs, always a sure sign she regarded her tale as having been well told.

After a suitable interlude, she would continue. 'Out of respect to John the jazz band were playing 'I've got a lovely bunch of coconuts', his favourite. It never sounded better than on that day. I heard the holidaymakers clapping and singing along to it as we passed, even though it was a funeral.'

The Polish John legend would be re-enacted to any new listeners at Christmas when family, friends and neighbours would huddle round the glowing embers in the coal-burning stove in the front lounge at the New Sands, listening to the sound of the bitter wind as it roared through the town from the Irish Sea.

Eva would conclude her story. 'We came out of the church to the sound of the jazz band playing 'I do like to be beside the seaside'. Relatives who saw John at rest that day, in his ringmaster's costume, say a smile had appeared on his face, the first time they had seen him smile, and this was how he passed on.

And the next week I scattered his ashes across the circus ring – before the audience came in for the show.'

Eva would sigh at this point, her final memory of her husband a sweet one, inviolably locked away in her mind, waiting to be re-introduced into the light of day only at the next appropriate moment.

In her old age, when Eva told the tales of Polish John she had become a pale shadow of her former ebullient self, as she had succumbed to the ravages of Parkinson's disease, and would fight to steady her trembling hands, which in her younger years she had loved to wave around ecstatically in order to add dramatics to her story.

She would often have to struggle to complete the tale and would be exhausted and breathless at the end, but with a look of transcendent serenity in her moisture-filled twinkling blue eyes.

Eva and John inherited the Sands on Irene Peacock's death and ran the boarding house while bringing up their daughter Camille, who then left home after her marriage to the wealthy industrialist, Isaac Ford.

Following Camille's death, after giving birth to Molly, Isaac had been considering the Sands as a future home for his daughter and, with this in mind, he began discussions with Eva and John on the advisability of modernisation, under his auspices, and the ownership of S.A.F.F., re-naming it New Sands and bringing in a professional manager and staff, with Eva and John adopting supervisory roles and being less involved on a day-to-day basis.

Isaac began extending and refurbishing the Sands beyond recognition, with the same urgency evident in his drive to reconstruct a large tract of the Blackpool seafront into his planned hotel and casino complex, with an Egyptian theme, Cleopatra's.

Isaac foresaw his plan for the New Sands, once completed, as freeing him to devote all his time to business, without the encumbrance of having to rear his child.

Eva and John agreed to Isaac's proposals for the future of their business and their new, less demanding roles, and began to see the changes as an opportunity to indulge themselves in areas of life that had been closed off to them over the years because of the boarding house's incessant demands on their time.

Eva had sought assurances, in the hand-over of ownership of her hotel to Isaac's corporation that the futures of John and herself would be protected and Isaac had done his best to allay her concerns as they sat together in his solicitor's office by telling her that 'You and John will both be secure for as long as you live. You need never concern yourselves about that.'

From the day her daughter Camille had introduced Isaac to them, Eva had been uneasy about him despite his background. However, from the day he became her son-in-law she accepted him gracefully for her daughter's sake, in much the same way as her mother, Irene, had done with John.

The increasing prosperity of all the family as a result of Isaac's business acumen with the New Sands had forced upon Eva the adoption by her of a more considered and less condemnatory approach to her son-in-law; but this remained at little more than surface deep, even after Isaac agreed to bank-roll the construction of Eva's longed-for theatrical agency and fortune-telling booth, two businesses he had agreed to fund at Eva's request, as intended sidelines after she and John had gone into semi-retirement at the New Sands.

Of course, Isaac's agreement to fund Eva's plans was based less on family sentiment as hard-headed considerations of the money-spinning possibilities of the new enterprises. And besides, Isaac felt his involvement in helping to realise Eva's dreams in concrete form, would curtail his mother-in-law's increasing propensity to gossip adversely about him.

There remained within Isaac Ford a deeply hidden resentment at the death of his wife at a time when his meteoric rise at S.A.F.F. had fired him with a passion to drive forward his plans for a new stage in the transformation of the Blackpool holiday scene, following on the heels of the revived Coaster World.

It could have been said that his baby Molly was the embodiment of this resentment but Isaac would have vehemently refused to openly recognise his daughter in this way. In fact, he spoiled the little girl, but only materially. He gave her everything she wanted, but his time.

The loss of Camille had served to add fuel to the flames of his burgeoning ambition, and given fresh impetus to his expansionist ideas.

In Isaac's mind, now that his wife had died, he had only his own burning desire for success to satisfy, and it had become all-consuming. An end in itself.

He salved the emotional demands of his conscience by attempting to ensure the happiness of Molly, and the comfort of Eva and John, by materialistic means, as, by doing this, he felt he was carrying out his continuing obligation to his dead wife's wishes.

It was as though the love and tenderness in his being had ceased to exist, and, in its place a hard scab of familial duty had formed.

Isaac wanted to extend his father's vision. He saw the British working man in a post-war world as wanting more than the transitory thrill of a coaster ride to give him fulfilment in his precious, hard-earned leisure time. He also had an inherent need, a built-in urge, for risk. Financial risk. To stake everything on the spin of a coin, the turn of a wheel, and the throw of a dice.

Isaac was planning to incorporate this need for individual risk-taking into a post-war Britain where he found a set of auspicious circumstances had arisen which had provided him with an ideal opportunity: the imposition of exchange controls, and transport difficulties, were restricting competition from abroad; paid holidays were becoming more widespread, and the entertainment and service industries were exempt from rationing.

This combination of disparate elements had produced a climate in which the S.A.F.F. Corporation could launch an assault on the dilapidated stretch of central Blackpool seafront; demolish the crumbling arcades and replace them with Cleopatra's, Isaac Ford's inspired conception of a hotel and gambling complex contained within a gargantuan Sphinx, where all the gambling diversion any visitor to Blackpool could possibly desire could be satisfied under one roof.

The flow of the River Nile was being re-directed into the Irish Sea.

Within Cleopatra's, entire floors were occupied by hordes of holidaymakers, young and old, playing only on slot machines.

The sound of a human voice was never heard. Only a continual discordant cacophony of squeaking, buzzing, jingling and clanging, that reverberated day and night from inside this gleaming new temple of mammon at which visitors to the town had come to worship.

Isaac was the orchestrator of the entire project from conception stage all the way through to over-seeing the final construction of the Sphinx itself and the installation of the multitude of gaming machines.

Cleopatra's was so all-encompassing that, if he so desired, a holidaymaker need not leave the sanctity of the air-conditioned ersatz Egyptian monolith for the entire stay of his holiday, despite the fact that, a few yards away, on the other side of the promenade, other tourists would be lazing in deckchairs wearing swimming costumes and developing sun tans in a heat of such intensity that they would still be unable to cover their blistered bodies on the day they returned home.

The spectacular success of Cleopatra's prompted Isaac to spread his wings in his personal life, and he moved to the majestic Camford Castle at the edge of the Lake District.

On the day Isaac moved in to take possession as the new owner, he climbed up to the battlements with John, Eva and Molly, and hoisted Molly up onto his shoulders so she could survey her father's new kingdom spread out in glorious living technicolour beneath her awestruck gaze.

That same evening, he took John and Eva to one side and asked them if Molly would be able to live with them at the New Sands, citing 'the demands of business' as the reason why it would not be possible for his daughter to live with him at Camford Castle, although he was at pains to point out to them that 'he would endeavour to get over to Blackpool to see his daughter at every possible opportunity.'

Eva had known, while he was offering to fund her theatrical agency, that her son-in-law would exert a price for such generosity, but fortunately for Isaac, bringing up Molly was a price they were only too willing to pay. Eva at that moment resolved that their plans would continue unaltered and Molly would be a part of them, all the way.

Later that evening, back at the New Sands after her grandparents had told her the news, Molly tried to make sense in her whizzing mind of the heady events of the day. Of course, she loved John and Eva deeply, but her father, after that morning on the battlements had become King Arthur come to life from the pages of her storybook, showing her their Camelot, and she was now puzzled as to why she was no longer to be a part of the magic realm.

Molly took out the photograph of her mother that she kept underneath her pillow and smiled at her face and longed for the photograph to come to life in the way Camelot had earlier that day.

Despite her efforts, no miracle took place and she began to think, 'I might need to do things on my own from now on,' and cried herself to sleep.

The New Sands established a reputation as a theatrical hotel. Performers from the shows on the piers and in the theatres of the town were regular guests at the hotel.

Show business rumour and gossip became common currency in the Goldsmith household.

Eva would take Molly backstage at the town's season shows to meet the artists and have her photograph taken with them, and these were then displayed around the walls of the hotel to be proudly shown to visitors.

The end of season parties at the New Sands became famous among the show business fraternity and the hotel's visitors' book was a veritable 'Who's Who' of British entertainment.

Growing up in such a environment, it was inevitable from an early age that Molly would be stage-struck and show business connections were fostered by Eva from among her New Sands clientele as being of possible future benefit to a granddaughter who, from within only a few years of her first tottering steps around the lounge of the New Sands, she groomed for a future on the stage by taking her to singing and tap-dancing classes, at which Molly was always the youngest pupil by several years.

Roderick Sterne was a young, ambitious show business impresario who stayed regularly at the New Sands and was made aware by Eva of her granddaughter's stage ambitions.

The impresario spoke to Eva about a new television talent show called 'Select A Star' that was beginning soon, and that the producers were planning a nationwide search the following summer for performers to appear on the show.

He also told her that he would be hosting the programme and running one of the auditions at Blackpool's North Pier theatre.

When Roderick Sterne said, 'Bring your Molly along. Let's see what she can do,' Eva did not need a second invitation.

The day she had been waiting for had arrived.

Even from being a young girl Eva had been enchanted with the glitz and pazazz of her hometown of Blackpool.

It had been a love affair as deep and enduring as her husband, John's, had been with the Moscow Circus.

The modernisation of their hotel to the New Sands by their son-in-law Isaac, and his appointment of a manager had released Eva to achieve her dream of running a theatrical academy.

She had always wanted to help people with talent realise their potential. And to display themselves to full advantage.

'And what better place for an academy than Blackpool?' Eva had reasoned to herself, 'I could build up a clientele of every type of performer – from chorus girl to top-of-the-bill singer or comedian.'

And, most important of all to Eva, was the consideration that, if her teenage granddaughter Molly began to achieve success with her singing ambitions, she would have someone to promote her career.

'With the contacts I can establish, I could then be Molly's agent. Also someone she could trust, always with her best interests at heart, not an agent who would be managing her just for financial reasons,' Eva told herself.

Eva had asked John to help her find a suitable site for the

building of her academy. They strolled together on the promenade and the streets of the town, in a way they had not done since they were newly-weds.

Freed from all her years catering for other peoples' pleasure before her own, Eva felt liberated. Sauntering along, drinking in the salty sea air, she suddenly felt the urge to be a little girl again, and wanted to skip. John, however, maintained his steady, measured stride, so Eva restrained herself, in order to stay alongside him, linking his arm.

Eva tried to absorb everything about Blackpool that bright, hot summer afternoon and look at her hometown as through the eyes of a holiday-maker.

'John, let's pretend that we've come on holiday – to Blackpool – for the day – and it's the first time we've been here,' Eva had said enthusiastically over their cooked breakfast of eggs, bacon, sausage and tomato. She looked down at her plate and laughed, 'Look, we've already started. A 'New Sands Special' breakfast.'

'Eva, I know your heart's set on running a charm school,' John said in reply.

Eva was vexed by John's use of the alternative name for her prospective enterprise, which she considered disdainful, but let his gibe pass.

'So let's make it a success', he continued. 'In fact, the best. We did it with the Sands,' John swivelled in his chair, pointing from wall to wall of the gleaming, revamped dining room, 'so we can do it again.'

John and Eva's first port of call after breakfast was the railway station. They stood and watched the crowds, laden with luggage, leaving the trains and getting into taxis.

There were visitors of every complexion ... Honeymooners hand-in-hand, floating along on an intoxicating cloud of romance, oblivious to all around them ... Packs of boisterous young men wolf-whistling and shouting to passing groups of disregarding young girls ... Exhausted families with father, suitcase in hand, staggering along the platform, being chased by his harassed wife endeavouring desperately to stop their excited children from running out of the station into the crowded street.

Then came a group of older married couples, perennial visitors to the town, strolling arm-in-arm out from the gloom of the station into the sunshine, each one's thoughts straying back to the day when Blackpool had become a place ordained to be treasured in shared memory; where a lifelong romance had begun, and, for them both, since that day, a town that would remain incomparable and changeless.

Eva and John wandered from the railway station to the promenade.

They watched people thronging the sands, and bathing in the grey waters of the Irish sea.

On the beach children were riding donkeys, and building sandcastles. A father struggled to stand up his deckchair in the gusting breeze, while his wife decorously removed her clothing behind a beach towel, held aloft by her mother, and changed into her bathing costume. Meanwhile grandfather was lifting up the top slice from his cheese and pickle sandwich and attempted, forlornly, to remove some fine grains of sand, before starting to eat it.

Eva and John walked to Coaster World at the south end of the promenade.

John contemplated the 'Laughing Policeman' in his glass case, outside the 'Fun House'. Screams resounded from panic-stricken girls on the 'Giant Rocket' as it swooped, shook and then rose to the sky at terrifying speed. Before starting all over again.

Eva and John were unaware, at that moment, that this ride was the brainchild, the pièce de resistance, of Isaac's father, Samuel Ford Junior, and had been the first ride he had designed and built in Britain.

It was now early evening. Eva and John were by the entrance to the South Pier, standing reflectively at the end of a day that had sizzled with the heat of high summer. The sun was only now beginning to slip below the horizon, suffusing the scene with a spectacular orange glow.

The bathers had long ago left the sea and the sands were deserted.

Attendants were stacking away the deckchairs for the day.

Blackpool at night was about to begin.

A palpable stirring of anticipation pervaded the air as visitors descended from trams and bustled their way along the wooden pier to the theatre at the end, passing fishermen carrying their clutch of rods, returning home for tea after a day's fishing from the jetty beyond the theatre.

Girls were fighting to hold down their billowing floral skirts against the blustery evening breeze, and precariously balancing on the high-heels of their stilettos as they struggled to make headway along the narrow gaps between the pier's wooden planks, above a sea now awakening from its daytime repose and beginning to ripple and swirl.

From the far distance of the pier Eva and John made out the discordant sound of a band tuning up for the start of the second house of the show. The crowds from the first house began to leave the theatre and were chattering excitedly as they crossed paths with the people arriving for the evening show.

The reverberation of laughter floated along with the hurrying crowds, everyone being sprinkled with flurries of brackish sea spray off the incoming tide. And, emanating from the multi-coloured stalls lining the seafront, a growing ambience redolent with the intoxicating aroma of fish and chips and cockles.

At that instant, Eva intuitively felt they were close to the heartbeat of the essential Blackpool. Her home. Her birthplace. At the edge of the sea. Showland, the funfairs, the hustle and bustle, the laughter, the heady sea aromas. People savouring the joy of life.

'Here's where we'll build the Astra,' Eva smiled to John. She was convinced.

And so Eva's theatrical academy was born, and became the talk of the showbusiness fraternity of Blackpool and beyond.

Eva's office as proprietor of the Astra Academy was at the front of the low, shining new building which was lavishly furnished, and decorated in warm, welcoming pastel colours. Secluded rooms led off from a long, narrow corridor, lined with a deep white carpet.

Eva began to recruit specialists in various diverse fields of artistic performance and self-improvement, each being responsible for teaching their own forte.

Eva's instructors included a large proportion of retired ladies of impeccable pedigree in their field of expertise who were delighted to be given the opportunity to resume successful careers at an age when they had become resigned to a life of pruning the roses and baby-sitting the grandchildren, and the more energetic ones to accompanying husbands around the golf course.

The Astra Academy was open to all. Rich and poor. Anonymous and famous.

Any visitor with either an ambition to be famous, or simply seeking self-improvement, could enrol at the academy, for initial assessment by Eva, before being allocated to whichever departments were appropriate, where the requisite gloss could be applied.

A few doors down the promenade from the academy was a tiny fortune teller's booth, built at Eva's request, with Isaac's money, as a sideline to the academy, allowing Eva to don a costume and pander to the performing side of her character which she always felt had lain dormant during her years of running a hotel. It also appealed to another facet of her personality. Her nosiness about people.

Eva intended to lead a double life.

To be the immaculately groomed and dynamic businesswoman of the academy for part of the week, and the rest of the time a mysterious gypsy fortune teller. The latter incarnation to supply the fun and frivolity essential to appease the child in her who was permanently hiding, just out of sight below the surface, waiting for the opportunity to burst forth into the daylight and create mischief.

Eva would leave the academy office twice a day, for an hour and a half on each occasion, being replaced by Daisy, one of her close friends.

She would then assume the mantle of Gypsy Pandora.

After her one and a half hours in the booth, she would return to the academy and Daisy, as Gypsy Sibylla, would replace her in the booth.

Eva and Daisy had chosen their gypsy names after a long and

heated discussion in a back room of the academy over several large glasses of sweet sherry.

A small pile of reference books was stacked between them as they sat face to face across a round table, the large sherry bottle in the middle and the pile of books next to it.

Eva, after considering and rejecting several options for her gypsy name, opted for 'Pandora,' as one of the books stated that the word was derived from the Greek meaning 'gifted'. When she read the following paragraph that 'Pandora's box' was a part of Greek mythology, and was said to have contained all the troubles of the world, which escaped when the box was opened, except one – hope – that sealed it for Eva.

The reference book was speaking her language. The name was meant just for her.

Daisy, not wishing to be outdone by her friend, sought out a name for herself also with a Greek root, eventually opting for 'Sibyl,' which her reference book told her was from the Greek, meaning 'able to prophesy.'

Daisy scanned further down the book, as, although she appreciated the direct relevance of the definition to her new employment, she felt the name too prosaic, so settled on the more exotic-sounding Dutch 'Sibylla'.

The fact that Eva preferred Daisy's choice of name, but was unable to do anything about it, became a continuing source of irritation to her, especially on the occasions when she stumbled across one of Gypsy Sibylla's name cards in the booth, which were handed out to visitors strolling along the promenade.

To Eva fortune telling was an engrossing sideline to her main work at the academy, and her double life resulted in several occasions when she had addressed the same person in both of her contrasting guises.

But after all, she told herself on such occasions, versatility was one of the qualities the Astra Academy stressed to its applicants, so Eva felt she was probably setting a good example by her schizophrenic behaviour.

Eva began to groom Molly at the academy in readiness for her audition to appear in Roderick Sterne's Select A Star. She intended to make Molly into her most successful protégé.

Molly spent time in every one of the departments, from the day the Astra Academy opened its doors for business.

As well as singing and tap dancing lessons which were always the most fully attended classes, Molly was also required to take on instruction at the more esoteric departments of the academy. Mrs Pilkington taught her elocution in a style of which Henry Higgins of Shaw's Pygmalion would have been proud, and all traces of her Lancashire accent disappeared.

Elocution was a class that had been in great demand from aspiring actors in local repertory companies, who booked an additional week of annual leave from work when they noticed the advertisement for the academy in the town's tourism brochures.

From elocution, Molly moved on to Miss Walker's deportment class, much to her pleasure as she had become bored with the speech routines required by the demanding Mrs Pilkington. She particularly enjoyed the sessions of deportment when she was asked to carry out laps of walking around the room while balancing a book on her head, and she attempted to become the pupil who could balance the most books. She accepted defeat only with the collapse of three thick books on the completion of a fourth lap of the room.

With the reputation of the academy spreading rapidly, Eva's enterprise began to burgeon beyond the theatrical and artistic world, and the wives of the town's successful businessmen started to enrol in droves for Miss Snooks' etiquette class, in order not to compare unfavourably with one another when meeting at prestigious functions in the North West.

Miss Snooks was a tall, blonde, middle-aged woman of exceptional elegance who taught all the skills necessary for the aspiring hostess, including how to dress immaculately for different occasions, and appropriate manners, both at and away from the dining table.

Molly was asked by Eva to sit and observe Miss Snooks' sessions in the hope that it would provide the perfect finishing touches to round off her education at the academy.

Eva began to find the administrative side of her business becoming tedious, so, at every opportunity, she would wait outside the theatres of the town, distributing her brochures about the academy to entertainers from the shows, and, in time, extended this into a new branch of the business: the representation of artists as a negotiator who could secure work for them, both in and out of season.

Eva's network of contacts in show business was only at an embryonic stage, and was based primarily on those entertainers who had stayed at the New Sands, but she had every confidence that this area of her venture would blossom to become the jewel in the crown of the Astra Academy.

In addition, the contacts she was establishing as the academy grew would be invaluable to Molly when she made the breakthrough in show business and put her foot on the first rung of the ladder to stardom.

Eva hit on a ruse that was to prove spectacularly successful in boosting the enrolment numbers of the Astra Academy.

It happened on a day of torrential rain on a desolate seafront, when Eva was sitting, dressed in her costume, behind the thick red velvet curtain of Gypsy Pandora's fortune telling booth and allowing her fertile imagination to idly wander.

A drenched and bedraggled man of about forty years of age stepped inside the doorway of the booth, to shelter from the deluge, and with not the slightest interest in knowing his future, only in trying to dry out before the start of the Tuesday music hall variety show at the South Pier theatre. His curiosity got the better of him and he could not resist pulling back the curtain of the booth. He peered into the blackness.

'You look wet, dearie. Have a sit down.' Gypsy Pandora gestured across the small table that separated them and on which stood a crystal ball.

The dishevelled man wore a melancholic look and a solitary dewdrop hung pathetically from the end of his glowing, runny nose.

He appeared not to have the energy even to reach into the pocket of his sodden grey mackintosh in order to unearth his handkerchief so he could wipe it away.

'Never mind, luvvie, the forecast's good for later on,' Pandora realised what she had said and burst into a cackle of crazy laughter, rocking back and forth in her chair ... 'and I should know ... if anyone does.'

At that moment fate smiled on Eva.

The dewdrop was beginning to tickle the end of the man's nose and he had no alternative but to stand up to search for his handkerchief.

'Take your time, dear, there's no one else waiting – not on an afternoon like this.'

And then Gypsy Pandora noticed that a dog-eared photograph had fluttered out of the man's pocket and landed on the desk.

The man was too preoccupied wiping the rain off his face and attending to the offending drop to have noticed the missing photograph.

Pandora sprang into covert action and moved the crystal ball on top of the photograph, then slid it back slowly towards her as though she was about to start the prediction.

Pandora engaged the man in small-talk, to distract him while she lifted the photograph from under the crystal ball and on to her lap.

She took quick glances at it while continuing to talk to the man.

The photograph was of a woman, smiling and standing on a lawn, alongside her two daughters and a black Labrador dog.

Pandora turned the photograph over. On the reverse was a message, written in a neat, precise hand.

'To James. With all our love. On your 39th.

From Christine, the girls, and Prince.

Counting the days 'til you come home.'

'Look, I really will have to be going.' The man was growing impatient.

'Alright, love, it won't take long, let's make a start.' Pandora smiled reassuringly, and laid her hands back on the table.

'What would you like, tarot cards or crystal ball?' Pandora produced the cards from a drawer in the desk, and laid them face down next to the crystal ball.

'Neither, really. I only came in to shelter from the rain. I don't really believe in all this nonsense. This witchcraft,' the man said, pointing at the crystal ball. 'O.K. then ... why not ... crystal ball.'

Pandora centred the crystal ball directly below her gaze as she leaned forward, and began to make slow circular movements across the top of it with both her palms.

'Of course my wife, she swears by this sort of thing. Reads her horoscope in the paper every morning.'

'That's quite common for ladies whose name begins with a 'C',' Pandora said nonchalantly.

'What? What was that?'

The man thought that his ears had deceived him, so let it pass.

Pandora looked up and studied his face. She detected that he had been slightly unnerved. She would now begin to entangle him in her web.

'Go on, tell me what you know about me, what's in store for me,' the man said impatiently, feeling the water dripping from the cuffs of his mackintosh on to his trouser legs.

'The crystal ball will tell all – when it's ready,' Pandora said, with tongue firmly in cheek ... 'the crystal ball is all-knowing and all-revealing.'

'Is that right? How clever of it,' said the man, a sneer forming at the corners of his mouth.

'Wait ... wait ... yes ... yes ... I can see something now ... it's getting clearer ... it's telling me something important ... it's about you ... it's telling me that important things will happen for you when you reach the age of forty. Next year.'

The man looked surprised but attributed Pandora's news to a lucky guess. A long way short of inspirational ability. But he stayed silent, just in case she might be on to something. Intrigue had swooped down and come to rest on his shoulder.

'You have a dog with royal connections ... Queenie ... King ... no ... Prince ... that's it ... Prince ... he's the black Prince ...'

The man remained quiet.

Eva now looked more intently at the crystal ball, as though her staring eyes were boring into its soul. 'The crystal ball wants to tell me more ... we will have to listen ...'

That instant the thought clicked into Pandora's mind that the man could only have been on his way to the music hall matinee on such a a wet afternoon ... perhaps he was a frustrated comedian ... or singer ... the idea fascinated Pandora ... she would take a gamble ...

'I can see you on a stage ... watched by Christine and your children ... I can just make them out ... in the front row of the audience ... applauding.'

Now the man was amazed. Dumbstruck in fact.

'I'm counting ... yes, that's it ... appearing in clearer focus now ... a girl ... another girl ... two children ...'

'You're incredible ... a genius,' the man spluttered. Thoughts had now passed of his miserable predicament.

'All in a day's work, luvvie ...' Gypsy Pandora looked up from her crystal ball and smiled at the man, his rapt face open-mouthed in astonishment and admiration.

'Tell me more.'

'It's now gone cloudy ... we'll have to wait ...'

The silence hung in the air between them.

The man dared not speak for fear of breaking the spell. Of forcing the magic to evaporate. After a few minutes that seemed like an eternity, Pandora said. 'It's coming back ...'

'What is it?'

'You're singing ... on the stage ... sounds like Bing Crosby... You know you've got talent, don't you? Have you ever thought of doing something about it?' Pandora's eyes twinkled at him ...

'Well, when I sing in the bath, Christine always says I've got a nice voice. And I can always remember the words to the hit songs. I bore the children with them all the time. In fact, come to think about it, once I start singing, I can't stop.'

'There you are, then.'

Pandora was now massaging his ego so rapidly it was likely to ignite and burst into flames before her eyes.

'If you want to know more ...'

'Yes ... Yes ...'

'I might be able to do something to help you.'

The man fell silent again. Desperate for Pandora to continue.

'Someone singing in the crystal ball is very rare ... very rare indeed ... a portent ... of a successful future ... even perhaps ...'

'Yes ... Yes ...'

'Stardom'.

The spider was now trapped in the web.

Pandora sat back in her chair ... 'The crystal ball is cloudy again. It has told us everything.'

The man felt drained ... But still wanting to know more ...

'You mentioned ... you know ... being able to help ...'

'Well ... there is a place ... luckily for you ... here ... in Blackpool. It's just a short walk down the prom in fact ... The Astra Academy ... Might be worth your while calling in while you're in town. I know they're very good at producing all different kinds of stars ... now, if you'll excuse me ... ' Gypsy Pandora slowly rose from her chair to accept payment from the man, and then moved towards the door, stopping just as he had risen to his feet. She leaned forward, and with her outstretched right hand pulled back the velvet curtain, and pushed open the door.

'Look. The rain's stopped. Lovely afternoon now,' Pandora said to the man, putting her arm round his waist, as though to usher him from the booth and out into the street, and then, while he was peering through the open door to look outside, Pandora deftly slipped the photograph into his mackintosh pocket.

It was sleight-of-hand of such dexterity that even her husband John, with all his years in the circus, in the company of conjurers, wizards, and sorcerers would have been open-mouthed in admiration.

The man stepped out from the booth onto a promenade now bathed in a watery sunlight.

Pandora took off her headscarf, and cleared her throat. 'When he calls at the academy, if I'm on reception, I hope he doesn't recognise me,' she mused to herself, 'but it's dark in here and my appearance and voice were well disguised.' The headscarf removed, she was now Eva again. She jumped in the air, and clicked her heels together in delight.

Eva knew that Gypsy Pandora had given a consummate acting performance.

On that wet afternoon in Blackpool, serendipity had smiled on Eva.

Her brainwave had made her feel like a gold prospector who had just struck the mother lode.

It had opened up the way for a link between the two arms of her entrepreneurship – the Astra Academy and Gypsy Pandora's fortune telling booth.

After that afternoon, Eva spent an increasing amount of time as Gypsy Pandora, and Daisy less as Gypsy Sybilla and more in the academy, deputising in Eva's absence.

Eva not only relished the change in her routine, but it provided the additional advantage of avoiding the possibility of her double life being unmasked.

Enrolment numbers at the Astra Academy skyrocketed overnight.

Seaside Lives

The first encounter between Jackie Flint and Sarah Lockwood was shortly after the arrival of the Lockwoods as the new occupants of number 3 Park Avenue.

Sarah, while hanging out her washing in the yard at the back of the house, had noticed Jackie and walked over to the small brick wall that divided the two houses.

She wiped her hands on her floral apron and extended her right arm across the wall, 'I'm Sarah. We moved in last week. Sarah Lockwood.'

Jackie smiled at her new neighbour and shook her hand. 'Nice to have someone new round here. My name's Jackie Flint. Pleased to meet you.'

'How's business?' Sarah asked, the first thing that had come into her head as an appropriate means to break the ice.

'Musn't grumble. Are you local?' Jackie asked, propping up the brush she had been using the sweep the yard when Sarah had walked over.

'No, we're from Mansfield. Shopkeepers. A little village called Brackley.

We decided it was time for a change of scene and Frank has always liked the seaside, from when he was little and came here on holiday,' Sarah replied, and, with this, they both peered through the open wooden gate that led to the Alley, 'Our two boys look as though they get on well together,' Jackie said as they watched Joe and Danny dribble a heavy leather football between them.

The two mothers had chosen a fortuitous moment to watch their sons, as ten minutes earlier, Joe had pinned Danny round his neck against the wooden garage door, for presuming to suggest that Trueman was a better fast bowler than Statham, one of the many daily skirmishes that broke out between the two boys following Danny's arrival in Park Avenue.

The washing having been hung on the line to dry, the two mothers felt there were no other appropriate topics of conversation for an introductory meeting, so Sarah decided to invite Jackie and her husband round to number 3 in order that the neighbouring families could become better acquainted.

The meeting that morning became the forerunner of a daily routine whereby snippets of family news were exchanged over the wall between Jackie and Sarah.

The next week, Bob Flint reluctantly went round to number 3 with Jackie. Frank opened the door.

'Hello, I'm Jackie, from number 5. This is Bob, my husband.'

Bob reached round the back of Jackie and offered his hand to Frank.

Frank led the way to the back room of the house. They overheard the chatter of visitors from the dining room at the front of the house. Jackie was mentally counting the number of voices she was hearing, trying to establish if Sarah's current bookings were in excess of her own.

After Bob had been introduced to Sarah, the four of them settled down with drinks in the lounge.

Jackie opened up the conversation, 'We live with my parents. Mum and I run the boarding house. What about you?'

'Just the three of us,' Sarah replied. 'Frank's father is back at Brackley. We ran a village store there. Sold up and came to Blackpool. Wanted a new challenge. A fresh start.'

The two women walked into the kitchen, leaving Frank and Bob alone together in the lounge, with the necessity of having to make small talk.

Frank was the first to break the awkward silence. 'We've found now where we're going to stay for good. The seaside.

Can't beat it. Worlds away from Brackley,' Frank barked in a stentorian manner. Bob blanched visibly at the prospect.

Meanwhile, Sarah was showing Jackie her refurbished kitchen, waving her right arm in a proprietorial way as she proudly showed off her sparkling, freshly polished domain.

After this first meeting between the neighbours, the two women spoke again the following Monday, washing day at Park Avenue.

Jackie was pounding the clothes in the sudsy water of the dolly tub, and then placing them between the rollers of the mangle while Joe turned the wooden handle to rinse off the water; she spotted Sarah coming out into the yard, put down the washing basket and walked over to the wall, 'Bob didn't get chance to mention something to Frank the other day when we called round.

Bob and Owen, my Dad, are both in the local Bisons Lodge. If he was interested, Frank would enjoy it. It's a good way to meet people, particularly with you being new to the area.'

Sarah's relaying of the message to her husband that night met with a frosty reception.

Frank invariably baulked at the prospect of any form of social interaction, but this time his resistance eventually withered under Sarah's continued insistence that it 'might help the business,' followed up with, 'Jackie has told me that I'll be looked after by the Bisons if anything happens to you.'

Sarah disregarded Frank's look of irritation brought about not least by the unwelcome thought of his demise, and continued on her Bisons theme, 'Jackie says that if you want to join you'll need to ask Bob, as the rules of the Bisons don't allow the first approach to come from a Bison to an initiate, but that once you've made an enquiry Bob can then set the wheels in motion.'

Frank remained silent, but was feeling increasingly powerless to resist Sarah's persuasive powers as she continued, 'Bob goes to the monthly meetings with Owen and his brother Donald. If you don't join you'll be the odd man out and we'll be missing out on things.'

'Precisely what?' was Frank's immediate question to himself, which he prudently resisted vocalising, and, despite his reservations, by the end of the week Frank had made a point of crossing Bob's path, to make the requisite formal approach to join the Blackpool Lodge of the Esteemed Ancient Order of Bisons.

The newcomers to Park Avenue continued to be a source of interest and curiosity to their neighbours for a considerable time after their arrival, but the only means by which gossip could be gathered and passed on was during the daily meetings across the back wall between Jackie and Sarah.

House visits between the Lockwoods and the Flints became rare events and when they occurred were invaluable opportunities for the information stream to surge forward, before resuming its habitual daily trickle between the two women of the adjoining households.

Between Joe and Danny, visits to one another's houses were usually errands which did not go beyond the front doorsteps.

Joe's life at number 5, as the only child of Jackie and Bob, and also living in the same house as his grandparents, Owen and Victoria, had shaped his psyche and his personality entirely differently to Danny's, who lived only with his parents.

The boys regarded each other only in adversarial terms; on the basis of football and cricket abilities while playing in the Alley, and otherwise on who had the superior collection of sporting magazines, which they would rifle through at night in the gloom of the Lockwood's garage.

There had been little beyond this limited world between them, until the day of Joe's momentous visit with a message from number 5 to number 3, when he was invited inside the Lockwood house for the first time.

Sarah answered the door. 'Joe. Come on through.' She led him through the hallway and into the back room.

Joe's first thought was how quiet the house was. At number 5, there was always the rattle of pots and pans from the kitchen, and the constant chattering and eruptions of laughter from the visitors' lounge. Always people coming and going through the permanently open front door.

'I'll tell Danny you're here. Have a sit down. He's just having a wash. Shouldn't be long,' Sarah said as she walked out leaving Joe on his own.

Joe's gaze panned the room. Everything was neatly stored away. No clutter. He could hear music from upstairs. He was transfixed by the sound. A throbbing, insistent, muffled drumbeat, accompanying a deep, rich, powerful singer's voice ...'Don't be cruel...'

Danny's fifteen-year old cousin, Sadie, over on a family visit, walked into the room. A waft of strong scent hovered around his nostrils, and then disappeared. 'The latest Elvis,' she announced, as though it was common knowledge. 'I got a record player for Christmas. Automatic. Plays eight records. Automatically.'

Joe nodded knowingly and tried to visualise this exotic present, but his imagination was only able to form an image of the wind-up gramophone at home, a square wooden box with a handle at the side that was turned to play each of his father's Glen Miller or Mario Lanza 78 rpm records placed on the turntable at the top.

Danny then walked into the room, looked over at Joe, and asked, 'How many 45s have you got in your collection at home?'

Joe's mind raced in its panic to interpret the devilish question and come up with a coherent answer.

'A few. Mum and Dad have got a lot in theirs: Glen Miller, Mario Lanza, Big Band music, and Opera.'

Danny and Sadie doubted it, but were unable to issue a challenge to his veracity as Joe deftly switched the conversation onto a new topic. 'Going to the match on Saturday?' in an attempt to change the direction of the whirlpool of musical naivety into which the pair had pushed him.

The boys were continually seeking to exhibit a superiority of wisdom over one another, but the added ingredient of a pony-tailed cousin, standing in the corner with hands on hips and chewing gum, had, on this occasion, significantly tilted the balance of power towards Danny.

'What's wrong with your hair?' Danny asked Joe, not prepared to surrender the verbal initiative to him. Sadie put on her bright pink, horn-rimmed spectacles and peered at Joe.

'Bill Haley's kiss curl. You know, 'Rock Around the Clock',,'

Joe answered, proudly fingering the black curl of hair in the middle of his forehead, that his Mum had painstakingly plastered down, firstly with water and then Brylcream to hold it firmly in place.

While giving this explanation to Danny and his cousin, Joe could still hear in his head the pulsating beat and rhythm – the sheer exciting buzz – of the Elvis song he had heard when he had sat down in the lounge. His thought at that moment was that this was something deep and powerful, magical even. Beyond Bill Haley. And that Danny had discovered it first. He was a pirate who had reached the treasure chest before him and was now kneeling before the opened box, dangling the sparkling baubles through his fingers, in front of Joe's eyes.

'Mum says that next week I can have a Tony Curtis,' Danny had now decided to joust with Joe over hairstyles instead of music.

Joe didn't even reply. In this conversation the trends were being set and then shifted with greater rapidity than the speed of Sadie chewing her bubble gum.

'If that's how it is,' Joe thought to himself, 'I won't even bother to ask him about Elvis, like I wanted to.'

Sarah entered the room at the moment the juvenile verbal grappling had drifted into a morose silence that was hanging threateningly between the three of them.

Both boys had fired off their heavy artillery and a dignified retreat to barracks was now taking place, in order to re-arm for the next duel.

Sarah sensed the unease between Danny, Sadie and Joe and felt a twinge of concern that Jackie might get to hear of it, and begin to question the Lockwood family hospitality. So she attempted to lighten the proceedings and turned towards Danny to ask him, 'Has Joe seen your new Don Bradman bat?'

The final straw. Joe rose from his chair, 'Thanks for the orange juice, Mrs Lockwood.' He turned on his heel and headed straight for the door, on his way side-stepping Sadie but resolutely not meeting her gaze.

When Joe arrived home and his mother asked him if the

Lockwoods had given him a reply to her message, Danny could only return her question with a bemused look.

'That one's in his own little world,' Jackie said to Bob over tea that night, 'Like I've always said – if you want something doing properly – do it yourself.'

After that seminal afternoon at the Lockwoods, Joe would visualize Danny at night in his room at number 3, styling his Tony Curtis into place and listening to Elvis' 'Don't be Cruel'. And doing this after a day in the Alley with his new cricket bat trying to perfect a Don Bradman late cut.

But, this image notwithstanding, Joe envied Danny not one jot.

Because Joe's thoughts would then invariably return to the delights that the coming Saturday afternoon would bring

From when he was aged eight, Saturday was Joe Flint's day.

Joe remembered the family discussion that brought this about.

It was the day he became a person in his own right, within the family at number 5 Park Avenue.

They were all gathered in the kitchen and were discussing him.

Joe knew his life was about to change.

He had crept unheard into the doorway and overheard his mother speaking, 'But will he be safe in the crowds? He's still only small.'

His father had answered, 'We'll look after him. Don't worry. A lot of young lads go to the match.'

Joe knew that his father, grandfather, and his uncle Donald had all been to Wembley for the 'Matthews Final' and he had made repeated requests ever since to each family member in turn to be allowed to go to watch Blackpool play their home football matches. Before that day, his pleas had been in vain.

Joe's heart was beginning to pound with the thought that his luck may be about to change. He crossed his fingers, as he stood his ground in the kitchen doorway.

Stanley Matthews had filled his grandfather Owen's mind with glittering memories.

Joe had listened to him reading from the newspaper of

Matthews as 'a tormentor of hapless, floundering, chisel-jawed fullbacks,' of his 'mesmerising trickery,' and how he 'strolled up to the full-back, ball at his feet, and then away down the wing with an electrifying burst of speed.'

Joe's personal experience of football had been as a goalkeeper at school. He remembered one particular afternoon on the recreation ground, when he had dived to catch a penalty kick, and then, later in the same match, another penalty save when he had scrambled, full stretch, along the goal-line to push the ball round the goal-post.

The teacher, who was refereeing the match, had called him over at the end of the game, and put a sixpence in his mud-splattered hand.

That day he had run home from school to tell them all. Still in his football kit.

But, as exciting and memorable as that afternoon had been, this particular Saturday morning when he stood in the kitchen, remained a day without equal in his life.

The anticipation after they had agreed he could go to see his first match had knotted Joe's stomach.

At two o'clock, Joe, his Dad Bob, his grandad Owen, and his uncle Donald, headed off down Park Avenue making for West Drive, the main road that led to the Bloomfield Road football ground.

As they turned left at the bottom of Park Avenue, they met the oncoming crowds on West Drive. A mass of people that gathered in number until the ground came into view. It was a maelstrom of colour, movement and noise to young Joe.

They reached the ground, and Joe stood in line to go through the turnstile that led on to Spion Kop, the massed standing area behind one of the goals.

Joe was wedged between his father and grandfather, not able to see the sky when he looked upwards, his arms at his sides, and his right hand grasping his wooden rattle. His neck and lower chin had vanished underneath his thick woollen tangerine and white scarf.

An interminable half-hour wait later, Joe was in the ground and on the steep climb, step-by-step up to the top of Spion Kop and, at the top, laid out below, beneath his awestruck gaze, his Christmas present 'Subbuteo' table football field brought to magnificent real life.

'Well, what do you think, Joe?' one of the three men asked him. At that moment he couldn't discern who, as his mind was far away, his gaze transfixed ahead. The first archaeologist to look upon the treasures of Tutankhamun's tomb would have felt no differently to Joe Flint at that moment in his eight-year old life, and would similarly have struggled for a coherent response.

After that, the afternoon for Joe dissolved into a blur of activity.

Just before kick-off a mass of young boys were lifted up in the air by their fathers standing in the massed crowd on the Kop, and passed in unison over the heads of the spectators below, and on to the cinder track behind the goal.

At the end of the match, Owen and Bob came to collect Joe, and lift him back over the wall and among the departing spectators.

They all walked home along West Drive, and into the warmth of the lounge of 5 Park Avenue, for tea, 'the Groves,' and 'Dixon of Dock Green' on television.

That night when Joe closed his eyes to drift off into sleep, his life could not have been more fulfilled.

Sitting on the cinder track, right by the corner flag, he had been close enough to the wondrous Matthews to touch him as he crossed a corner kick – the ball had drifted through the air and arrived at the precise moment Stan Mortensen reached the crowded penalty area and powered the ball with his forehead into a bulging net, out of reach of a flying, desperate goalkeeper. Blackpool had won the match, and gone to the top of Division One.

When his Mum came to his bedroom door and called out, 'Goodnight, Joe,' he didn't answer. He had already drifted into sleep, his last waking thought, 'Life will never get better than today.' His wooden rattle was folded inside his scarf on the bed next to him.

Jackie Flint and her mother Victoria, being denied the

ecstasies of a fortnightly football ritual, adopted one all of their own while the match was taking place.

The visitors having been catered for, and the men at the match, they made up a packed lunch for two and a flask of tea, and set off in the family's new Austin Cambridge to the south end of Blackpool promenade, where they parked for the afternoon.

Their hobby was 'visitor watching.'

The location was one of Blackpool's busiest spots for arriving visitors, on their way towards the glories of the 'Golden Mile.'

The highlight of Jackie and Victoria's year was Wakes Week, when the factories of northern England closed down and towns descended on Blackpool en masse.

For Jackie and Victoria, Wakes Week was a veritable cornucopia of spectating delight. Floral shirts, candy floss, and 'kiss-me-quick' hats.

The town became unleashed into technicolour chaos.

'Look at the state of those two over there,' Victoria would comment, and point out of the open car window to draw her daughter's attention.

'Must be making a fashion statement,' Jackie would reply.

'Can't be healthy being so overweight ...'

'Well, as long as they're enjoying themselves, that's all that matters,' ... and Saturday afternoons would drift blissfully on in similar vein for the ladies of number 5 Park Avenue.

The only communal activity for everyone in the family at number 5, with the exception of Joe, was old-time dancing, in the ballroom of Blackpool Tower.

Everyone was dwarfed in the grand and spectacular setting.

Reginald Dixon – 'Mr Blackpool' – rose from beneath the stage, seated on the 'Mighty Wurlitzer', to the strains of 'I do like to be beside the seaside.'

Before taking to the dance floor, Bob and Jackie, and Owen and Victoria viewed the dancers below from the crimson velvet seats in the ornate, gilded balcony at the top of the soaring tiers of seating.

'The modern' was drawing to a conclusion.

Immaculately attired couples were twirling and whizzing

elegantly in a display of pyrotechnic twinkle-toed wizardry, across the inlaid stars of the gleaming parquet ballroom floor.

The Flint family made their way to the side of the ballroom, and waited. The dance floor then emptied to become their domain. The announcement rang out ... 'Ladies and Gentlemen ...Take your partners please for a slow waltz.' The moment had come for the Flints to go on display.

The Eleven-Plus results letter addressed to Joe Flint arrived on a Saturday morning at number 5 Park Avenue.

Joe was lying on the floor in the front room, in his favourite relaxing position.

Although his body at that moment was in Blackpool, his spirit was in St John's Wood Road, London NW8, behind the wicket inside Lord's Cricket Ground. He was opening his packed lunch to the background ripple of polite applause. The Hampshire burr of commentator John Arlott was coming from the radio by his side...And now ... it's Laker ... from the Nursery End ... to bowl round the wicket ... to Sutcliffe ...

Joe jumped to his feet when he heard the letter land on the mat. He ran to the front door ... 'Mum ... it's here ...'

The Bisons

The time-honoured rituals of the Blackpool Lodge of the Bisons required that a pre-initiation visit be carried out at the home of the initiate.

This was one of the duties of the Grand Bison Master, Isaac Ford, who was also to be Frank Lockwood's seconder, with Bob Flint as his proposer.

When the front doorbell of number 3 Park Avenue rang, Sarah gave a cursory glance into each room as she walked down the hallway to the door. She straightened her dress, touched her hair, and composed herself for a second before opening the door.

'Hello. I'm Isaac. You must be Sarah.'

Sarah's first impression of the Grand Master was of a thick set, dark-haired man of medium height, immaculately groomed, and wearing a long olive-green overcoat. She was surprised that anyone could look so sun-tanned and prosperous-looking in England in the middle of November.

It seemed to Sarah that Isaac's soft-sounding voice had a hoarse undertone, but she had been more immediately taken by his deep brown eyes and his disarming smile.

She led him into the hall and offered to hang up his overcoat. 'Frank's in the lounge – I'll take you through.'

'Lucky man,' was Isaac's overriding thought as he followed Sarah, admiring her shapely figure.

He caught the ambrosial aromas wafting through from the kitchen. The smell of percolating coffee and baking bread.

'Looks like someone's been busy,' Isaac commented.

Sarah cast a glance over her right shoulder and Isaac noticed a slight flush had stolen up her cheeks as their eyes met.

'Home-made bread. And cakes. One of my sidelines. When I get the chance, of course.'

Frank rose from his armchair as Sarah and Isaac entered the room.

Isaac let his eyes wander around the room, before settling his gaze on Frank as they met in the centre of the room and shook hands.

Pleasantries were exchanged between the three of them.

Sarah felt that Frank was being excessively effusive in his responses to Isaac's small talk and she attributed this to a certain apprehension he had been feeling in anticipation of meeting Isaac. He was regarding it as an examination to establish if his character made him suitable to be a Bison and was, therefore, too keen on making a good impression, rather than relaxing and being himself.

Frank's anxious manner was transmitting tension to Sarah herself, and causing her to feel a growing irritation with her husband.

'Glad to know you'll be joining us. The Bisons are always delighted to welcome new blood,' Isaac said, reassuringly, flicking his engaging smile between Frank and Sarah.

'I'm looking forward to it,' Frank answered eagerly.

'Would you like a coffee? And to sample my cake-making attempts?' Sarah asked Isaac.

'Or can we offer you something a bit stronger?' Frank cut in.

'Coffee, and cake would be just fine,' Isaac replied, switching a look from Frank to Sarah as she hovered in the doorway, before heading off towards the kitchen.

'I believe your son knows my daughter Molly. She's mentioned him several times. It seems she's a friend of his, and Bob's son, Joe.'

Frank looked surprised. 'I didn't realise Molly was your daughter. Bonny-looking girl. You must be proud of her.'

At this moment Sarah re-appeared with the coffee and cakes.

'I am,' Isaac answered. 'Unfortunately, I can't get to see her as often as I would like.' He made a dismissive kind of gesture with his right hand: 'Business pressures. You know how it is.' Isaac looked at Frank.

Frank didn't know how it was, but politely offered a feigned smile. He then looked down at Isaac's gleaming brown brogues and wondered how much they had cost. And his silk patterned tie. 'Some pressures,' Frank thought to himself. 'Working down the pit, now that's pressure.'

Isaac began to drop sugar cubes into his coffee and to stir. He took a bite from his slice of Sarah's home-made walnut cake. He thought it was about time to get to the point of his visit. 'You probably know, Frank – hope you don't mind me calling you Frank,' Isaac didn't wait for a reply to his presumption, 'but the Bisons require to know a little background detail about an initiate before the day he becomes one of us. Hope you don't mind.' Isaac looked over at Sarah when he said this, so she took the hint, smiled at them both, and elegantly left the room.

Isaac took out a notebook from the inside pocket of his jacket, and flicked back the hard black cover.

'Hope you don't mind if I take a few notes,' he asked Frank as he wound down a small amount of lead into the end of his monogrammed gold propelling pencil.

'I do, actually' thought Frank, but he said nothing, just made a slight movement of his hands from where they had been resting on his knees, a barely distinguishable gesture which Isaac took as agreement.

The pre-initiation questionnaire was completed in fifteen minutes. Isaac had established, to his satisfaction, the calibre of his initiate.

'I'm afraid I really will have to be making tracks, Frank. Look forward to seeing you on the big day. I'm sure that everything will go like clockwork. And, oh, by the way, it will be part of Bob's duties, as your proposer, to rehearse you for the initiation ceremony. I'll ask him to get in touch about it in plenty of time.'

Isaac walked with Sarah to the coat stand, while Frank took the coffee cups into the kitchen, before joining them.

'It's been a pleasure to meet you, Sarah. Hope you don't mind if I call you Sarah? Expect we'll meet again before too long.' Isaac put on his overcoat, and straightened the collar.

Sarah smiled and held open the front door just as Frank joined them.

'I expect so, too,' she answered.

'I hope we'll be seeing you on Initiation Night,' said Isaac, stepping into the street.

'You will,' Sarah answered.

Frank thought at that moment how well the meeting had gone, and that its success must have been due to the good impression he had given Isaac.

Frank Lockwood was initiated as a Bison a month later at the Blackpool Lodge house in the centre of town.

Due ceremony was performed, and Frank passed his initiation with flying colours.

Bob Flint was alongside him during the ceremony, as his proposer, and Isaac, as the Grand Bison Master, presided over the initiation ceremony, seated on his imposing carved wooden throne in the centre of a raised platform.

Isaac's gleaming chain of office dazzled Frank as he stood before him balanced precariously on his right leg, while reciting the Bison eternal oath of allegiance. Word perfect.

At the post-ceremony gathering when the Bisons joined their wives after leaving the Inner Chamber, Isaac was at the bar dispensing largesse in copious quantities with his acolytes at his shoulder, spreading bonhomie to anyone who came into their vicinity.

In recent years Isaac had surrounded himself, at Bisons and most other social gatherings, with a tuxedoed Praetorian guard who radiated inviolable loyalty to the Grand Bison Master.

Isaac glanced down the length of the bar and noticed Sarah ordering a drink. He walked over to her, 'Let me get that.'

'Oh … Isaac. Nice to see you again. Frank's off talking to someone I don't know, so I wandered off to get myself another drink.'

'Glad you did.' The barman put the drinks in front of them. Isaac raised his whisky and soda, and Sarah her gin and tonic.

'Put these on my account,' Isaac said to the barman.

They clinked glasses and exchanged warm smiles. 'I was hoping I'd see you here. I've got something for you. And Frank.' Isaac produced a gold envelope from his inside pocket and offered it to Sarah. She elegantly removed her long black gloves, removed the thick card from the envelope and began to read …

The card had a coat of arms at the top, and, below, in thick bold lettering … CAMFORD CASTLE … FERNLEIGH PEAK …

It was an invitation.

Later in the evening, when Isaac was visiting each table, carrying out his final Grand Master duty of the evening, he came to Frank and Sarah's group.

'Do hope you'll be able to make it,' he said, leaning over close to Sarah.

The rest of the group were intrigued, as Isaac moved on among the cluster of tables. Jackie turned to Sarah. 'That sounds interesting. Do tell.'

'Isaac's invited us to an evening at his castle.' Sarah produced the card from her bag and passed it to Jackie, studying her reaction, not aware of the significance of the invitation. 'I suppose everyone's been invited to his castle at some time or other,' Sarah said.

Jackie ran the forefinger of her right hand delicately along the edge of the card, as though it might snap in two if she were to hold it too long.

'Not to my knowledge,' she replied. 'I don't know anybody who has ever received an invitation.'

The Fifties

On the morning of the Bisons Initiation Evening, Sarah Lockwood was doing her housework. Pushing the vacuum cleaner and polishing the sideboard, while miming to the romantic ballads of her favourite crooners, Bing Crosby and Perry Como on the morning radio request programme, Housewives Choice.

In his bedroom, at that same moment, her son Danny was playing 'Heartbreak Hotel'. After Brylcreeming and combing his hair in Elvis style, he lunged forward, as though to grab an imaginary microphone, curled his top lip, gyrated his pelvis and began to vibrate an outstretched leg in time to the throb of the music.

Although neither Danny nor his mother were aware of it at that moment, their disparate musical tastes were evidence of a revolution that was happening in every household in Britain. And music was the catalyst of this change that was dividing the generations in a way as never before.

For Danny, the Messiah was here. Elvis Presley, the King of Rock and Roll, with his unique blend of blues, gospel and country music. Performed with sensationally charismatic style and dynamism.

A youth icon had arrived who was light years away from the crooners who had gone before.

And Elvis emerged at a time when the shores of a twilight

post-war Britain were being invaded on many fronts from across the Atlantic.

American Fifties prosperity and lifestyle were being marketed to an emerging generation of vibrant post-war baby boomers in a Britain of full employment and growing prosperity.

In essence, the British young were being told they needed all things American and they were in no mood to resist.

A sea-change in style was taking place that encompassed fashion, music, marketing and much more. All being targeted towards the creation of a new culture, a new concept: the teenager.

The young had now been identified as a group, and as a result, they became empowered, and began to change their own world. Forever.

Jukeboxes and pop charts were emblematic of the American infiltration. New popular songs could now compete with each other in a race of public popularity.

In the way that Elvis rose up from obscurity at a propitious moment in history to capture and fashion teenager fantasy in the world of popular music, so also in the cinema of the day, did such an iconic personality emerge, just at the time when the concept of the teenager was being created.

The appeal of James Dean in 'Rebel Without A Cause' lay in his embodiment of the restlessness of the American youth of the 1950s, at a time when the cinema as a medium was still a predominant cultural influence, alongside radio and variety theatre.

Although about to be superseded by television, cinema had been peerless in the way it had appealed to the imaginative part of life from impressionable childhood years onwards, and had imprinted its values in a permanent and easily accessible way, by influencing and shaping thought and behaviour.

As an illustration of cinema's unique capability as a medium with a capacity to make a powerful political statement among a vast audience and thereby provoke controversial debate, the classic western 'High Noon' which Joe Flint had seen with his father, was one of the first psychological mould-breaking westerns.

It was seen, by some, at the time, as a metaphorical attack on those who deserted colleagues during the McCarthy communist witch hunts in Hollywood a few years earlier.

In the way that James Dean in the cinema personified youthful restlessness, so in the British theatre dramatist John Osborne was portraying angst and rebellion in 'Look Back In Anger' and establishing a reputation as the 'angry young man' of the British theatre.

But notwithstanding the cultural impact of music and the cinema during this early post-war era, the most prescient influence was television.

Until the arrival of television, radio, the cinema and the variety theatre were the kings of entertainment and it was thought inconceivable that television could be more popular, particularly than radio.

The advent of ITV in 1955 had a dramatic impact on the lives of everyone in that the British from that moment became a nation of TV addicts. A nation with 200,000 sets grew into 5 million a year later.

It also created a new enduring species of superstars and allowed the public to gaze in on the personal lives of these stars; as the life story of Molly Earle is soon to show.

The quintessence of the mid 1950s is that all these diverse facets of cultural change point to one incontrovertible fact. The young of this time – all of peacetime's children – grew up and, in so doing, they cut the chains of history and broke away.

Elvis Presley flicked on the light switch in a darkened room of young people and they began to party, and it was a party to which their parents upstairs had not been invited.

Seagulls

The paths of peacetime's children were about to diverge. The Alley became deserted, leaving only hollow echoes of laughter and dispute remaining.

The future educations of Joe and Danny had been growing in importance in their respective families and the meetings over the back wall between Jackie and Sarah became more frequent.

'Danny's decided he wants to go to Abbey Grange. It's a public school in Scotland,' was Sarah's unexpected announcement one February morning.

Jackie was aware of both the school and its reputation, but confined her reply to just a pleasant smile.

Sarah, by making her disclosure, had pre-empted Jackie's reason for going over to speak to her that morning. Jackie had also been waiting for the opportunity to announce her own family's important news, but she now held back so that Sarah could tell her more details.

'We just thought that, with the boarding house doing well, we could afford it.'

Jackie was unsure how to respond to the surprise news, but a reply became unnecessary as Sarah continued immediately, 'We've always believed in private education and giving Danny the best possible chance in life, whatever the cost.'

Jackie at that moment was thinking of the reaction to this news when she told her family of dyed-in-the-wool Labour Party supporters at teatime.

'I hope he likes it there. I'm sure he'll do well,' said Jackie, magnanimously, 'How does he feel about going?'

'He wasn't sure at first; leaving his friends and all that, but now he's had time to think about it, he's getting used to the idea, although he doesn't say a lot about it. Frank and I think new challenges are always good for young people. We'll do our part and give him the start, then it's up to him to go and make something of it.'

Jackie took the opportunity of a short silence between them to introduce her news. 'In fact, I've got some news as well. I've been wanting to tell you for a while.

We've decided to move. Not immediately, but after the 11-plus results come out. If Joe passes, and gets a place at Lewis' Grammar School, we're going to buy a house near the school.

We thought it was time for pastures new. We've been looking at the new bungalows at Croft Green. We always did have a fancy for the country life. Don't know how we ended up at the seaside, come to think of it. It's nice and peaceful out there, but still close enough to town if we need the shops.'

'What about your Mum and Dad. Are they staying?'

Jackie pictured in her mind's eye the night all of them had driven the ten miles out to Croft Green to look round the show house.

The salesman had showed them the plans for the plots of land and the diagrams of the two adjoining bungalows. And, when they were back home, everyone became carried away with enthusiasm. 'Be lovely to retire to the country. What we've always wanted,' Victoria had said. 'I'll be able to do some gardening. Grow my own vegetables,' came from Owen. And from Bob, 'All it needs now is for Joe to get into the Grammar.'

While everyone else was engrossed in their own personal visions of the future, Joe was silent. His mind was whirling with all the changes being planned. He had the feeling his life was about to be turned upside down.

Jackie looked back at Sarah and answered her question, 'We've all talked it over. They'll be coming with us. We're going to sell up the business and become homeowners. Adjoining bungalows.'

'I'm going to miss you. Especially our morning natters over the wall,' Sarah replied.

'I'll keep in touch. All the gossip.' Jackie smiled, and a moment of sadness passed between them.

The conversation was interrupted by a call from inside Sarah's house.

'Mum, the oven timer's gone off.' Jackie recognised Danny's voice.

Sarah looked apologetically at Jackie, 'I've been baking bread. Looks like I'll have to go.'

There was so much more both of them wanted to know. 'Wonder what the school fees are costing them?' Jackie was asking herself. 'Wonder what the price of those bungalows is? I've heard Croft Green's expensive,' Sarah was musing.

'I wanted to tell Jackie about the seagulls,' she continued to herself as she went inside the house. She had even taken out the newspaper to show Jackie the article about the old lady at South Shore who had been bitten on the side of her face by a seagull diving at her while she hung out her clothes on the washing line.

Sarah had noticed a few weeks before that seagulls seemed to be flying low and squawking at her when she stepped out of the back door.

Frank and Sarah looked up at the roof and saw two adult seagulls in a nest by the chimney, watching while their young were attempting to fly from the edge of the roof and failing pathetically in the attempt.

Over the weeks they went outside to see what was happening, occasionally being met by one of the protective parent birds diving close to warn them off.

They were amazed by the speed with which the baby seagulls grew to full size, learned to fly and left the nest. Except one.

Then, one day, when Sarah and Frank were standing side by side and looking up towards the chimney, they noticed this last one of the baby birds struggling in its attempts to leave from the roof. It faltered desperately time and again, all under the watchful gaze of the two adult birds. And then, when all had seemed lost, it suddenly rose up in flight and soared away into the sky.

A few nights later, a long, hot spell of summer weather was suddenly broken by a night of thunderstorms and torrential rain.

Sarah was drawing the lounge curtains, and glanced outside.

She saw the same brown baby seagull on the roof of the house opposite, looking bedraggled and forlorn, and, when she looked again before going to bed, noticed it was still there, waiting for rescue, still not having learned the rules of seagull flight out in the vast world, away from the safety of the nest by the chimney pot.

The next morning, Sarah went out in the back with Frank. The storms of the night before had given way to the dawning of a clear, sunny day. The baby bird was not to be seen on the rooftop. Sarah and Frank both glanced round to the roof of their house, and noticed it was deserted. The adult birds had flown. They both noticed the strange quiet. They had grown accustomed to the squawking and to following the blossoming progress of the babies.

For the first time in as long as Sarah could remember, Frank reached out and squeezed her hand, and they turned to smile at each other. They seemed to be reading each other's minds at that moment. They were wondering if the sodden, pathetic baby seagull had got to safety.

At the beginning of September, Jackie Flint was in her front room and noticed a black taxi pulling up next door.

Danny came out, wearing a smart black school blazer with red edging round the collar, a crisp white shirt, and a striped tie.

He got into the front seat of the taxi, beside the driver.

Frank carried a large suitcase down the front steps and handed it to the taxi driver to put inside the boot.

The driver held open the back door of the cab for Sarah and Frank to get in.

Frank, Sarah, and Danny were silent all the way to the railway station. Sarah was surreptitiously taking her handkerchief from her handbag, to dab her eyes. Frank leaned over towards her and put his outstretched left arm around her shoulders and gently pulled her towards him.

Danny hadn't noticed any of this. His attention was busily occupied in waiting for the next click of the meter.

The driver just flicked the occasional glance at the couple when he checked his rear-view mirror, but instinctively felt this should not be one of his idle chit- chat type of fares. So he stayed silent. Anyway, he had three grown-up children of his own, and had known days like the one they were going through.

The silence continued up to the moment the train was about to leave.

Sarah hugged Danny to her, and he thought for an instant that his bones were about to crack by the strength of her embrace. He noticed his mother's cheeks felt warm. He looked into her face, and felt he had never really looked at his mother before, and thought how beautiful she was. If only he could tell her. Instead, he just said, 'I'll miss you, Mum.'

Sarah and Frank, at the same time, looked down at Danny, and both thought how young he looked. How vulnerable.

'And you, too, Dad.'

'It won't be too long before you're back. Half-term. Time will soon go.'

Frank felt these were the right reassuring words at that moment. But they were not the ones his heart wanted him to say.

Sarah gently pushed Danny away from her embrace and proudly inspected him. She adjusted the knot in his tie, and said, 'Take care of yourself, Danny. We love you.'

Danny stepped onto the train. Frank lifted the heavy suitcase and struggled to squeeze it on top of the untidy pile of luggage by the side of the steps.

As the train pulled out of the station, Danny leaned out of the carriage window as far as he could. Sarah blew him a kiss.

Danny continued to wave until his arm was aching, and he was a long way out of sight.

When the train had disappeared from view, and the last wisps of smoke had drifted away, Frank turned to go. Sarah noticed her husband's shoulders shaking and reached out for his hand as they left the platform.

They didn't look at each other.

That morning, on the roof of number 3 Park Avenue, Blackpool, the two adult seagulls had returned to the chimney.

Audition Day

Polish John hired a landau and white horse for the day of Molly's audition for Select A Star.

He had walked to the promenade in the early hours to collect the open topped carriage and drive it to the New Sands.

At John's request, the horse's bridle had been decked with red and white roses – Molly's favourite flower.

John had said to Eva when he'd thought of the idea, 'I want everyone to see how we Old Country people do things in style.'

Molly's face glowed with enchantment when she opened the front door of the New Sands and was met by the sight of the flower-bedecked white horse.

The curtains on the windows of the select Kensington Drive hotels twitched inquisitively as John drove off for the North Pier with Molly in the front seat beside him and Eva in the back.

Molly delighted in being the object of attention on the drive through the town and along the promenade and she bashfully ventured a regal wave to the entranced holidaymakers, in the fashion she had seen the Queen doing on the television.

The carriage presented an exquisitely anachronistic and captivating spectacle as the majestic horse trotted along the bustling promenade of a modern-day seaside town, driven by John in his top hat and tail-coat, and, with erect pose, resembling an Edwardian squire escorting his wife and daughter on a morning tour of his country estate.

John parked the carriage and offered his arm to Molly and then to Eva, to help them as they stepped down.

As he drove off to seek refreshment for himself and the horse, he blew a kiss to Molly and mouthed the words 'Go well, Molly.'

Eva and Molly joined the end of the audition queue on the promenade. A line of hundreds of people snaked back between the north and central piers.

The bright early morning weather had started to become threatening. The wind was beginning to bite as it gusted in from the Irish Sea.

Grey clouds scudded across a glowering sky, and squalls of rain drove in piercingly among the huddled groups of people.

Molly snuggled underneath her grandmother's right arm and pulled her bright red woolly hat tightly over her ears which were now stinging from the icy driving rain.

The long queue slowly started to dwindle as some disillusioned souls headed for the welcoming warmth of the tram shelters.

The buxom woman in the queue behind Eva and Molly, wearing a silk multi-coloured headscarf, and standing with a large, round-faced boy, spoke in a thick Lancashire accent to Eva's back, 'Been 'ere long?'

Eva made a half-turn towards the woman, 'Hour and a half.'

'You from Blackpool?' The woman asked.

'Yes. Near the town centre,' Eva replied. 'You?'

'Preston.'

Then silence.

Pigeons fluttered round their feet, picking frantically among the remains of sandwich wrappings and biscuit packets.

The queue's excited and animated chattering had now drifted into a muffled drone.

'Hope you don't mind me mentioning it, but isn't your little girl a bit small? For the audition I mean? Got nice hair though.' The woman had re-opened her conversation with Eva.

Eva didn't reply, but her mouth formed into a tight hostile line. She told herself she would get her own back. In due course.

'My Richard plays the piano you know.' Richard twitched with nervous embarrassment and looked out to sea.

Eva knew she had to re-establish the equilibrium in this joust of a conversation, so replied pleasantly, 'Things must be quiet in Preston these days. We're full for the season,' hoping the woman would pursue this verbal offering, and thereby take her bait.

'Oh. You've got a boarding house, then?' the woman wriggled her neck and looked towards the sky. Seagulls hovered overhead and squawked demandingly, looking enviously at the feasting groups of pigeons below.

The conversation between the two women had now developed into a verbal duel of thrust and parry.

But Eva had prepared her opening, the trap door had been invitingly opened. And the woman obligingly dropped through.

Eva deftly administered the coup de grace. With a polite smile, 'Hoteliers. New Sands. Best known hotel in central. Always full of show business stars. Business is booming.'

Silence.

'Oh, that's nice.'

Silence.

Smile from woman, fading slowly into fixed grimace.

The queue inched forwards, and the group of four were about to be separated by a lamp-post.

'Good luck, then,' from a triumphant Eva, the point made and honour restored.

'You too.'

The queue moved off the promenade and began to make its way along the pier on its snail-like progress up to the entrance of the wedding cake-shaped theatre.

A conversation taking place among the group in front of them was picked up by Eva, 'Don't hold out much hope. Too many here. The winners will have to be good.'

Eva didn't say anything to Molly, and hoped she hadn't heard.

Eva's resolve had always been formidable, and impervious to attack. 'This is how all the stars have to start,' she whispered to Molly.

Negativity had never been known to throw its insidious shadow across Eva's in-built fortress of optimism.

'What can she do?' Eva and Molly were standing on the darkened stage at last, footlights beneath them.

It was the moment they had both dreamed of from the days Molly had first tap danced in front of the rest of the family on Christmas Eve at the Sands. John had watched her with his inscrutable look, and Eva had sat on the edge of her chair, poised to jump into the air and ecstatically clap her hands above her head, to show everyone else in the room what talent her granddaughter possessed.

Today was the culmination of the long years of dreaming.

'Is she a singer or a dancer. Or both?' The words echoed within the oppressive silence of the deserted theatre.

The disembodied question came from the stygian gloom somewhere in the remoteness of the empty back stalls.

Eva and Molly peered ahead, both trying to stem their rising tension.

The voice was instantly recognisable. It was Roderick Sterne, who, by not personally acknowledging them, was displaying his impartiality. His even-handedness.

Molly at that moment was oblivious to such subtleties of the adjudication process. Her thoughts were totally absorbed in mentally running through her repertoire.

Eva, however, felt a spasm of concern, that, although she would have objected to favouritism of any sort from the impresario, she hoped Molly would not be penalised in any way, to compensate for the fact that he was a family acquaintance, a fact that would come to light if Molly was to be successful, with an inevitable consequence at some stage of accusations of bias being thrown at Roderick Sterne.

An accompanying thought flashed through Eva's mind that he was the type of man likely to have his back well covered against such eventualities, and, if it happened, the only casualty would be Molly.

Roderick Sterne's star was in the ascendant in the show business firmament.

The weekly TV show Select A Star which he hosted was continually top of the audience ratings and sponsors of the programme were clamouring to gain the prized one-minute advertisement slots at the beginning and in the middle of the programme. Demands on the national grid soared when the show ended, with viewers throughout the land rushing to boil kettles for family pots of tea.

The format of the show was the invitation to viewers to vote from six showbusiness hopefuls every week, after a panel of celebrities had vented their vitriolic opinions on the embryonic talent displayed before them. There was only an occasional shaft of encouragement from the panel, but even this was invariably made in a begrudging manner. And then always qualified by compere Roderick Sterne with 'But it's very difficult out there in showbiz land – and only the cream rise to the top.'

Roderick Sterne was mockingly referred to as 'Mr Sincerity' by the television reviewers, due to his slick and urbane manner with the contestants, and his catch phrase 'Tonight – we'll rocket you to the stars,' designed to put them at ease as he placed the microphone in their trembling grasp.

He attributed his public popularity to an ability to portray himself as a 'Mister Nice Guy,' one of the viewers who would have been just as much at ease watching Select A Star at home wearing his carpet slippers and with mug of cocoa in hand, as on the stage in his spangly suit with gleaming white smile and well-smoothed toupee fixed firmly in place.

Now, on the afternoon of Molly's audition for Select A Star, Roderick Sterne's mellifluous television voice had developed a strident edge. To Eva at that moment he sounded brusque and likely to be uncharitable.

'She can do both.' Eva's voice in reply to Roderick Sterne's question was firm and confident as she tightly gripped the quivering fingers of Molly's right hand.

'Whenever you're ready then. Please leave Molly to carry on.' This time the instruction came in the precise, clipped tones of Roderick's female personal assistant.

Eva moved towards the curtains at the left hand side of the stage, looking determinedly ahead as she strode off, and then waited anxiously in the wings.

Molly glanced nervously towards her and Eva gave her a thumbs up and smiled reassuringly.

'O.K. Molly. Off you go. You've got five minutes,' the personal assistant gave the instruction.

Molly gave the performance of her young life. Her legs were tireless, with a pulsating life of their own, and her voice seemed to soar away to the furthest reaches of the theatre. Her five minutes had seemed to vanish in a flash. Then there was silence.

Molly stood centre stage, hands crossed in front of her, waiting for a response.

The judging trio were impressed. Molly was the best so far on the North-West day of their weekly talent trawl. Also the best that week. And the best that year. From all the towns and cities in which the auditions had been held.

'That was good, Molly,' came from the theatre manager of the North Pier, who was the third member of the judging panel with Roderick and his assistant. 'You've obviously worked hard. We'll be in touch. Well done.'

Molly floated off the stage, carried on gusts of euphoria. She had to fight the urge to run into Eva's outstretched arms.

'You were wonderful,' Eva said, tears streaming down her flushed cheeks. 'Let's go.'

They ran helter-skelter back along the pier, hand-in-hand, gulping in lungfulls of cold sea air, Molly's long curly red hair flowing behind her and Eva gasping as she struggled to keep pace.

They stopped to look at a poster advertising the stars of the forthcoming summer season show, who would soon be standing on the very stage where Molly had just enjoyed her greatest moment.

'One day that could be you,' Eva said, pointing upwards for Molly's open-mouthed gaze to follow. 'Anything's possible now you're on your way. All the big stars started like this. Just work hard and be patient.'

But such an entreaty to Molly at that moment was like a command to an astronaut whose lunar module was about to land, being ordered to abort the mission and return to earth so that a later attempt could be made by someone else.

The letter from Select A Star arrived at the New Sands two weeks later. Eva and Molly raced each other to be the first one to pick it up from the doormat.

Eva got there first, opened the letter and read out, 'Dear Molly, We are pleased to let you know that you have been successful in your recent audition for Select A Star and would like to invite you to take part in our televised programme on December 15th.'

John and Eva hugged, and Molly squeaked with delight and jumped up in the air.

Molly went up to her bedroom, took out her paste bottle and brush from the top drawer of her bedside cabinet, along with the brand new, empty scrapbook Eva had bought her. She pasted the letter on the first page.

She studied the name 'Molly Earle', the name her Nan had chosen especially for the audition, at the head of the typewritten letter before she finally closed the scrapbook and gently placed it at the back of the drawer, and placed her clothes on top of it. As she put it away the thought idly crossed her mind as to whether in the future she would be pasting in anything else, such as magazine cuttings, or glossy pictures.

By the end of that month Molly's first scrapbook was full.

That night the celebration in the Goldsmith household was unprecedented.

Polish John's vodka bottle was emptied and a second bottle opened.

He was still sitting by the fireside as the sun came up behind Blackpool Tower.

Eva told him that the night before he had tossed his top hat into the air, and said to Molly, in front of everyone there, 'Everyone here tonight is proud of you Molly. We're all in the presence of a celebrity.'

Molly had then ruffled his hair and gushed with delight at such public praise from her grandfather.

Molly was exhausted at the end of the evening, but she felt, for the first time in her life, a tingling glow of self-satisfaction as she watched the celebrations of her family and neighbours.

She brought her new scrapbook into the lounge and everyone in the room was shown the letter from Select A Star.

Every word was exhaustively pored over, as though the invitation to Molly might be withdrawn if each person there did not scrutinise it.

It was the most eventful day anyone in the family could remember.

The exception was Isaac, who, earlier in the evening, had telephoned his congratulations but also his regret to a tearful Molly that due to business pressures he would be unable to come to the celebration.

After she had put down the telephone, a tearful Molly had run up to her room, and then had to be enticed back into the lounge to meet the people arriving to see her.

The highlight of the evening had been when John had got up on his feet to dance.

Everyone in the room linked arms. Family, neighbours and visitors alike, forming a giant riotous circle.

Molly held John's hand as everyone in the circle kicked up their legs to the strains of the Can Can, the women twirling the hems of their skirts, while the men clapped their hands above their heads in time to the music.

It was a joyous moment and the perfect end to a richly golden day.

Lewis'

Joe Flint's years at Grammar School were largely uneventful. Particularly academically.

The main event may well have been an unwelcome one that happened at the end of his first day.

Just outside the school gates he was approached menacingly by two of the older boys.

Having been brought up to suspect nobody's motives, Joe lowered one foot from his bike, and came to a halt.

The two boys stood gloweringly on either side of him. They snatched his new brown school cap from his head - and sliced the bobble off the top in expert and experienced fashion, in some bizarre sort of initiation ceremony inflicted on new boys. The cap was then abruptly thrown to the ground, to the accompaniment of raucous laughter, as the two boys jumped on it and ground it into the dust of the road.

When Joe arrived home, his mother was not amused and gave full vent that evening to her feeling that this event did not bode well for an auspicious secondary school career for her only offspring.

His father, Bob, puffing away on his pipe in the corner of the room, withheld comment, beyond 'worse things happen at sea,' which, while puzzling Joe as to its relevance, also gave him an odd kind of reassurance and perspective, and helped him to embark on his second day at school the next morning, with the imagery removed from his mind of the same two boys lying in wait by the school gates to inflict even harsher punishment, possibly on his gleaming new blue and white 'Raleigh' bike. The bike which, since the day he had received it as a surprise Christmas present on return home from the midnight family church service, had been lovingly oiled and polished, and had become his most treasured possession.

However, as his school career ground remorselessly on, Joe came to empathise with his mother's expression of foreboding after his first day.

Joe's end of year reports became a growing source of trepidation when presented at home for parental scrutiny and signature, but, much to his relief, were invariably greeted with equanimity by his sanguine parents who were firm believers in the power of hope ultimately triumphing over experience.

The one exception was the momentous year when the Metalwork examination result showed that Joe had come 29th in a class of 28; a disparity caused by Joe having joined the class late in the term, and the records not having been amended to show his inclusion.

Nonetheless, Joe did not feel the mistaken grading was an unjust one, as he knew he had significantly less prowess in metalwork than his class contemporaries. On the one and only occasion all the class were asked to take home a demonstration of their handiwork, his ornate candle holder was greeted with stunned silence when he produced it from behind his back, and placed it in the middle of the dining room table.

Joe took due note of the absence of candle-lit meals at home after that day.

Joe's enthusiasm for football and cricket remained as strong as ever during his school years, but he experienced exclusion from the favoured cliques who established themselves as members of sporting teams during the first year, and managed to continue in the same vein year after year.

These same favoured boys also seemed coincidently to be the same ones who topped the end-of-year academic tables.

At first, Joe with his natural modesty thought that perhaps they were a superior species of being, but he soon realised he was never likely to win in what was an unassailable milieu of academic and sporting elitism, and, in consequence, the answer was to acquire a self-protective shell of insouciance.

Joe, therefore, began to live his life, both at home and at school, in a dreamlike cocoon state that rendered him oblivious to virtually all outside influences except those he occasionally embraced which could not disturb his equanimity.

There was one moment of sporting glory in his school years.

His grandfather, Owen, was now a delivery driver working for a local Wine and Spirits firm.

One Wednesday afternoon Owen was on his way to make a delivery, and had parked his van on the road by the school football pitch.

Joe had mentioned to his grandfather that Wednesday was football day. It was the day for the non-elite. The day when the whole-hearted triers came into their own, and were given use of the football pitch for one afternoon.

Of course, the match was not refereed, and usually developed into a free-for-all. The football kits were uncoordinated, team formations were haphazard, even the goals remained without nets attached to them between Saturdays, when the school teams played against teams from other schools in the area.

But, despite the absence of any kind of refinement, the enthusiasm of the Wednesday afternoon players was always unbounded.

Joe saw the van. That afternoon he played the game of his life, culminating in a moment near the finish when he elbowed his way through a scramble of muddy bodies in the penalty area, and toe-poked the ball past the goalkeeper and over the line for the winning goal.

Joe looked over the road and could have sworn that he saw a smile on his grandfather's face.

Joe always remembered that afternoon, particularly on the day of his grandfather's funeral, over twenty years later, when Donald, as usual relishing the opportunity to relate an anecdote from the past, told him, 'You know that Owen always told people his ambition was to watch you play in a tangerine shirt at Bloomfield Road.'

Joe didn't know, but, from that day forwards, always remained grateful that he had been told.

The Flint family move to rural life in Croft Green was successful and none of them regretted having left the Park Avenue boarding house, from the night Bob Flint had stood in the foundations and lifted Joe and his mother down from ground level to stand next to him, and then over the ensuing months when all the family had watched the two bungalows growing day by day and brick by brick, up to the day the last bricks were slotted into the walls of numbers 1 and 2 Evesham Place, Croft Green, and a new life began for the Flints.

Joe left Lewis' Grammar School with five GCEs and was accepted as a clerical officer in the Ministry of Pensions. He was now a civil servant, and Lewis' Grammar School had completed its obligation of grooming Joe Flint for the world of work.

Joe had been a civil servant for two years when he went on holiday to Spain with a group of workmates. They lazed away hot Spanish afternoons on the beach and he met Lucy, the tall, slim, blonde-haired girl he was soon to marry, after a holiday romance of balmy nights walking together along the sands in the moonlight, and a promise from Joe to phone her when he returned home.

Joe remembered the discontent he felt after his return from that holiday which was fuelled by Jim Fox, a work colleague who was a mountain climber in his holidays, who recounted in graphic detail his climbs in the Swiss Alps. 'Life's passing me by, I want to be up there. In the mountains. Right now. Not just in the holidays. All the time. I'll be off again as soon as I can,' was Jim Fox's continual refrain.

But, one afternoon, Joe was looking out of the window while at work, as Jim Fox was speaking. The sky was blue and cloudless, the late afternoon sun mellow and warm on his face and Joe was able to form pictures in his mind's eye of the mountains Jim Fox was describing.

Jim Fox spoke to Joe. 'Haven't you ever wanted to do something different to this?' As he spoke he looked down contemptuously at the pen in his right hand, 'To do something exciting. To see new places.'

His words, coming at that particular time, took root in receptive soil.

Since the holiday in Spain, Joe had wanted his life to change. And for Lucy to be a part of it. 'And what if Jim Fox is right?' Joe asked himself, 'There has to be more. Excitement. Adventure. And, if Lucy wants the same, then why not do something about it?'

At that moment, the Supervisor wandered along the rows containing the racks of registers, and glanced along to check that all the clerks had resumed work after the coffee break. So Joe pulled down one of the registers, and began to write on a blue slip of paper, with the words of Jim Fox still on his mind.

It was a draft resignation letter.

Joe and Lucy Flint were married in Blackpool in October that same year.

They sailed on the SS Antipodean a month later bound for Perth, Western Australia.

Sailing

AN AUSTRALIAN DIARY

Lucy Flint

December 1970

Perth, Western Australia

Well, we made it!

November 1970

Blackpool
Sadness of the goodbyes before our train left from Blackpool Station.
Frosty morning. Everyone wrapped up in overcoats, scarves and gloves.
Joe and I leaning from the carriage window, waving to the disappearing figures of our families, huddled together in a group on a deserted platform in the early morning sea mist.
Doesn't feel much like a honeymoon – or an adventure – as we sit in a corner of the carriage, in silence, holding hands, with our private thoughts.
Impossible to imagine that this is the first day of a

journey that will end on the other side of the world. That by next month, we will have crossed oceans and be in our new home. Perth, Western Australia.

London
Running across a crowded Waterloo Station, to catch the boat train for Southampton, our rucksack - on Joe's back - splits open. We scramble on hands and knees, in the middle of the rushing feet of a hundred people scurrying around us in all directions, our clothing and possessions on full view to the world, and with the clock ticking relentlessly towards the scheduled departure time of the Southampton boat train.

At Sea
The most unromantic start to a honeymoon it is possible to imagine.
In the Bay of Biscay, the ship begins to pitch and toss. And doesn't stop day or night.
Joe went back to our cabin and stayed there for three days, looking ashen-faced and trying hard to hold off sea-sickness.
A scramble each morning along the sloping deck, grabbing out for a handrail to keep upright against the rocking and rolling motion of the ship.
Once in the half-deserted diningroom, a struggle to finish breakfast, with plates of egg and bacon sliding across sloping table-tops, and coffee spilling out of cups.
Days passed on decks swimming in seawater, and huddled in overcoats against the biting icy winds.

After such a start it was a welcome relief to reach the Canary Islands, and walk ashore into the warmth of a Las Palmas night. The hustle and bustle of the market a contrast to the sedate atmosphere and rigid routine on board ship.

Las Palmas – a turning point on the voyage.

After that, a succession of long, lazy days, each beginning when you leave the gloom of the cabin, with its constant throb of the ship's engine, to step out on deck to absorb the heady intoxication of the sharp morning light, and breathe in the sea-fresh air of the endless ocean all around.
The foaming wake of the Antipodean as it ploughs its furrow through the waters of the Atlantic, and the battalions of flying fish gliding in and out of the waves at the side of the ship.
And all this to the glorious accompaniment of the haunting cries of sea-birds as they skim the surface of the waters and soar up in flight towards the cloudless sky.

Table Mountain made its first appearance as a distant speck on the far horizon and, as we approached, it slowly took shape into a majestic silhouette displaying its grandeur in splendid relief against the backdrop of a setting sun melting into the tranquil waters of the ocean at close of day.

After Cape Town, the long stretch across the Indian Ocean – and the overwhelming excitement of landfall at Fremantle on a dazzlingly beautiful December morning.

Arrival
We ask a fellow passenger to take a snapshot before we disembark.
We look bewildered and forlorn. Like a couple of waifs and strays, huddled together in a lonely corner of the deck, Joe in his suit and tie, the front of his neatly-combed hair being blown about in the morning breeze, and me in a floral dress and plain black cardigan, with handbag over my shoulder leaning with

my head resting under his chin, and his arm round my shoulder.
The man who took our picture reached down to the deck and picked up a wine bottle cork from the last night celebrations. He took out a sixpence from his trouser pocket and slotted it into the cork, and gave it to us – for good luck.
I think he must have felt sorry for us.
How can we now fail?

The Sixties

To celebrate the dawning of a new millennium, Joe Flint, his wife Lucy and their two sons had taken a bottle of champagne to the promenade near to Blackpool's North Pier, the setting for Molly Earle's audition for Select A Star.

Joe opened the champagne on the stroke of midnight and they watched the fireworks from the pier lighting up the night sky over the sea.

When they were back at home an hour later, the Flint family watched the television pictures of celebration in the world's capital cities.

Firework displays over Sydney harbour, Australia. A ticker-tape parade in New York's Time Square. The Queen and Prime Minister Tony Blair joining hands to sing Auld Lang Syne at the opening of London's Millennium Dome.

Joe's son Nick had then put on his compact disc of Beatles 27 No 1 singles and Joe brought out his long playing vinyl record of Sergeant Pepper's Lonely Heart Club Band to show him the inside covers of the long-haired group, all sporting Zapata moustaches, and wearing multi-coloured tasselled uniforms.

Joe smiled in recall of his seventeen year old self with his Beatles haircut and collarless, dark brown, epauletted corduroy jacket.

The talk drifted back from the start of a new century to forty years before. The Sixties.

It was a vivid, extraordinary time, lived to a background of Beatlemania fan hysteria, and the Beatles inimitable blend of black rhythm and blues and Mersey pop.

If the 1950s had brought a tremor throughout post-war Britain, then the 1960s was the ensuing earthquake. A seismic shift from the threadbare drabness of austerity Britain, to a startling new world of dazzling luminosity.

The Britain of the Sixties resembled the outcome of a child with a giant paintbox full of rich, vibrant colours, having been given free rein to splash the paint onto a big blank canvas.

The American invasion of the 1950s ran out of steam, and London assumed pre-eminence as the cultural capital of the world, in a permissive Britain that exuded a new-found self-confidence.

This was heralded in at the beginning of the decade with a ground-breaking 'new wave' in British cinema, depicting the harshness of northern working-class life in a monochrome world of cobbled streets and factory chimneys.

A new generation of star actors was launched upon the British public, speaking with northern regional accents for the first time in the cinema, in films that confronted issues at the heart of ordinary people's lives, and brought cinema into the living room of every working-class person in Britian: Tom Courtenay in The Loneliness of the Long-Distance Runner was a borstal boy at war with the ruling class; Rita Tushingham, a pregnant teenager in A Taste of Honey and, pre-eminently, Albert Finney, a belligerent Sheffield factory worker in Saturday Night and Sunday Morning, portraying youthful rebellion and search for identity in his confining hometown.

The cultural revolution was equally apparent, and even more influential, in the Sixties world of television.

Satire was unleashed from its theatrical origins of Beyond the Fringe, to become That Was The Week That Was (TW3), a Saturday late night event broadcast to a startled nation by the BBC, the mainstay and mouthpiece of the establishment, which launched, every week, a remorseless broadside against the establishment.

Following the politically lampooning TW3 came a new age of

comedy television, of social realism, with programmes such as Steptoe and Son, and Till Death Us Do Part, which were both funny and also had shrewd, controversial comments to make about the society in which we lived.

In the 1960s, television was the medium that provided the compelling evidence that the age of deference was past, and we were now in a new, more provocative world, and the reaction to this challenge to the status quo was incandescent.

The opponents of this new, vibrant and rebellious breed of Britons, who had changed the sound and temper of the times, claim that all that had really changed was that we now had more of what was already going wrong in the world. A growing cult of bored, unwashed youth in a noisier, more disrespectful time of continual revolt.

If Elvis had switched on the light to begin the party of the 1950s, then in the 1960s, the mind-expanding drugs were being passed round among the party-goers.

The changes taking place in Britain in the 60s were mirrored and intensified across the Atlantic.

A watershed era such as the 60s is created from the convergence of monumental events with the appearance of titanic individuals, whose impact on the times becomes so profound that they go on to become symbolic and mythical figures.

It was a world in which a new young American President had proclaimed a 'new frontier' for his country. John F Kennedy, a leader who was confronted by a global challenge, a 'cold war' of polarised enemies, The United States and the Soviet Union, and came on television with a stern-faced announcement that set in motion the Cuban Missile Crisis.

Joe Flint had always remembered the curious feeling of vulnerability he felt at that time.

The television pictures of 1963 showed photographs of the installation of Soviet nuclear rocket bases on Cuba, followed by the warning from Kennedy to Soviet President Khruschev that any missile launched from Cuba would be met by a full-scale nuclear strike on the Soviet Union.

The possibility of instant global annihilation by nuclear

weapons had become a reality to everyone for the first time, and this was to be the paradigm for the new post-war world.

The old world order that Joe's father and grandfather had known was consigned to history on the day Kennedy and Khruschev stared at each other eyeball-to-eyeball to see who would blink first.

But the feelings of the time were also confused and contradictory.

The anxiety and foreboding were paramount, but there was also a backlash towards a new American President who appeared to be offering up a peaceful post-war world as a hostage to fortune to an unpredictable and volatile Russian President. A feeling that the lessons of history had still not been learned.

From the night of Kennedy's utimatum to Khruschev, the world held its breath for six days, waiting for a response.

Then Joe recalled the immense relief when the television pictures came through of the Soviet missile-bearing ships turning back, and Khruschev ordering the Cuban bases to be dismantled.

Kennedy had been vindicated and the world slept easier that night.

But, in Joe Flint's memory, the relief felt at that time had immediately turned to tragedy the moment he had seen a different set of black and white television images, triggered by the announcement of the fatal shooting of President Kennedy in Dallas, which brought, in an instant, the death of a visionary leader of the western world.

Joe remembered the following Monday night at home and the silence between his family as they watched the gun carriage bearing the President's coffin, draped in the US flag. It passed among the crowds, and the overcoated young boy stood to attention and saluted the body of his father as it passed by, to the heart-rending strains of the military band playing 'Eternal father – strong to save.' The President's beautiful widow stood immobile in her silent despair.

The new era of electronic immediacy had united an entire world in grief as it transmitted the poignancy of one family's tragic loss into a multitude of living rooms across continents. Everyone that night was a mourner at the funeral of a President.

This was a new world in which every individual was a part of historic events as they were unfolding.

Joe recalled that night as the first reel of what was to become a running televisual background to his life. Imagery interwoven with daily reality and yet also at a distance from it. The quagmire of Vietnam. The assassination of Martin Luther King, and the conflagration that followed across America in a decade of civil rights landmarks when racial boundaries began to crumble. The emergence of Muhammad Ali as world heavyweight boxing champion, to then go on to become an enduring world icon: a symbol of not only sublime athleticism, but also of racial pride.

And a decade which closed with the world watching man step onto the surface of the moon.

In the 1960s politics became chic in a way that was then lost with the coming of the 1970s, and was heralded by the Watergate scandal of 1972.

It was a time of idealism, before the rot of apathetic disillusionment with political leaders set in as the zeitgeist.

Isaac's Castle

Isaac Ford, although regarded as a 'parvenu' by the worthy inhabitants of Fernleigh Peak, was also admired for his élan, as the majority of them felt that he had been instrumental in putting their village on the map.

Isaac, in turn, felt under a perpetual obligation to demonstrate to them that he was a staunch upholder of tradition and olde-worlde values, in order to gain their esteem.

He now prided himself on being something of a connoisseur of fine wines, an enthusiasm he had recently acquired and which he was keen to demonstrate at the sound of even the merest clinking of two glasses of 1947 Graves Royale.

The inveterate gossips among the members of the Fernleigh Peak Women's Institute had begun to talk of him as the 'bon viveur' in their midst and a man in whose reflection their husbands became exposed as terminally dreary and strait-laced. In fact the older ladies among their number discussed Isaac in such rhapsodic terms that an outsider might have thought that a combination of Errol Flynn and Jay Gatsby had landed in their tiny hamlet.

His repute in the village had risen so highly in fact, that he had now even been forgiven for re-naming their renowned castle in honour of his departed wife and this gesture served to add a romantic lustre to his celebrity.

Invitations to dine at Camford Castle had become highly

prized and carried considerable kudos to one's standing among Fernleigh Peak's social hierarchy.

Reputations were meteorically enhanced upon knowledge becoming known that a gold-embossed invitation card bearing the heraldic emblem of Camford Castle had been received, as this was likely to mean the recipient would be rubbing shoulders with a resident from one of the exclusive clusters of mansions in Fountains Wood.

This was a location that had become so select as to warrant a double-page colour feature in 'Cumberland Corner' monthly magazine, an indispensable publication for the gentry of Lakeland society, but only ever read in doctors' waiting rooms by the rest of Cumberland.

The visit of the magazine's team of photographers and feature writers to Fountains Wood, as well as being a significant event for the residents, also gave them the opportunity to discuss the wealthy entrepreneur who lived in the castle.

It was evident to Isaac that he had been accepted as 'one of us' at Fernleigh Peak, when he read the article about himself in 'Cumberland Corner'.

However, on the departure of the magazine's team, several of the blue-rinsed ladies of the Conservative Club, at the mid-summer sherry evening, could be overheard criticising Isaac's monthly gatherings as being 'infra-dig,' and it was clear that in Fernleigh Peak, there remained pockets of diehard traditionalism that were never likely to succumb to the allure of the new resident within their castle.

Nevertheless, despite such antagonism, no-one in Fernleigh Peak had been known to decline an invitation to dine at Camford Castle.

The approach to Isaac Ford's Lakeland castle meandered through verdant parkland and was lined by rows of soaring trees intermingled with vivid clusters of luxuriant bushes and shrubs.

The castle rose imperiously above a patchwork of fields, inlaid with tiny sparkling lakes.

Isaac had fastidiously selected his guests for the evening and arranged a seating plan for dinner designed to ensure relaxation and conviviality, and an absence of embarrassment. Isaac had arranged the evening to be one of his more informal and intimate gatherings.

He was always anxious when the monthly gatherings comprised an eclectic mix of extremes such as the one that evening.

Isaac was standing on the battlements of the castle, in the falling dusk, impeccably dressed in his double-breasted evening suit, watching his guests arrive in the gleaming black chauffeured Bentleys he had provided.

He was savouring the splendour of the Lakeland setting. The shafts of fading sunlight on the illuminated strands of green and brown in the fields that stretched away to a slowly reddening horizon.

He strolled down to the entrance to greet his guests.

Jennings the butler, the pre-eminent member of Isaac's team of live-in servants, ushered each of the guests along the cream-carpeted entrance hall into the palatial reception lounge, a room decorated in classical creams and golds with heavy curtains and French-style antique furniture.

Introductions were made while drinks were served.

Frank Lockwood positioned himself in a corner of the room and gestured Sarah to stand alongside him. He was always awkward in formal surroundings to the extent of attempting to avoid all polite conversation that contained the possibility of exposing his lack of social sophistication.

'What line are you in?' a jolly man with a rubicund complexion asked Frank, now with Sarah positioned supportingly at his side.

'At the moment, hotels,' replied Sarah.

'Mining management before that,' added Frank.

'I'm in farming, locally,' the red-faced man replied.

Sarah wandered to the other end of the room, to Frank's concern, as it had left him marooned, but much to his relief he was shortly rescued from having to converse with the farmer by the appearance of the local doctor, a tall, greying, distinguished-looking man who joined them just as the conversation was languishing. The doctor's wife, a slim demure woman wearing an elegant midnight blue evening dress was alongside him.

Frank decided to take the conversational initiative by asking the doctor, 'Can you recommend any cures for back pain?'

The doctor who hated talking shop, inwardly winced, but politely suggested, 'One of my weaker areas, I'm afraid, but personally I tend to support alternative remedies when conventional medicine isn't particularly successful. Many of my patients swear by osteopaths.'

As a prelude to dinner, Jennings, at Isaac's instigation, ushered the guests from the lounge and led them up to the battlements.

Isaac stood proprietorially to one side of the group lined up along the wall, his gaze proudly panning his kingdom. He then moved to study the faces of his guests, in the soft, mellow light of early evening as the sun dipped behind the forest.

Sarah was drawing in deep breaths of the clear air, entranced by the exquisite view, and relishing the prospect of the evening ahead. Her eyes sparkled, she felt giddy, and was unable to contain a smile of delight when Isaac came to stand alongside her.

In the tranquillity of the evening, amongst the murmur of animated conversation between the guests, Sarah's imagination began to paint vivid pictures in which this sublime setting was her domain. She felt as though cages in her soul were being opened moment by moment to release gloriously-hued songbirds from their captivity, to fly towards a brilliant blue sky of freedom.

Jennings ushered the guests into the walnut-panelled drawing room.

In contrast to the reception lounge, this room was light and airy and less formal, with a more relaxed lived-in feel. Jennings served vintage champagne in delicate crystal glasses to the guests.

Sarah wandered around the room looking closely at the framed photographs of members of the Ford family. She made a mental note to ask Isaac about them when the opportunity arose.

In one corner of the room, standing in the pale orange shadows cast by the subdued lighting, was the dapper, balding bank manager, who was also a local magistrate, a duty to which he was recently devoting more of his time, in readiness for his imminent retirement from banking. He was gazing intently into the smouldering black eyes of his voluptuous second wife, who was idly fingering the ends of her dark, shoulder-length hair.

She was yet to pass her thirtieth birthday, a fact on which Fernleigh Peak's respected magistrate was more than happy for the rest of the gathering to speculate amongst themselves.

In the centre of the room stood the cheery, red-faced farmer, who was recounting one of his multitude of stories of dubious good taste, and seeming on the verge of imploding with mirth.

Despite appearances to the contrary, he was rumoured to be the wealthiest resident of Fernleigh Peak. With the possible exception of the evening's host.

In contrast to her dishevelled husband, his blonde-haired wife was fashionably dressed and petite, and stood on the edge of their little group, coyly clutching her champagne glass.

The guests took their places in the dining room and Jennings circulated attentively in supervision of his team, as they served a meal of caviar with a soured cream sauce, accompanied with smoked salmon; wild duck with vegetables; and a choice of ice creams to finish.

The serving of the Sauternes with the meal gave Isaac the opportunity to tell the doctor seated next to him about his wine cellar beneath the castle.

The doctor, keen not to be seen by the other guests to wilt in Isaac's conversational afterglow, went on to describe in detail the different fermentation procedures for white, red and rosé wines.

The others within earshot, including Frank and Sarah, nodded in a knowing manner, but were reluctant to venture a view, and were conspicuously relieved when the ensuing hiatus in the conversation was punctuated by farmer Tomkinson's booming laugh resounding across the gentile exchanges between the other diners seated at the long, highly polished mahogany table.

Doctor Bradley was a distinguished hospital consultant who worked in Keswick, specialising in gastro-enterology, and he and Mrs Bradley were regular guests at the castle.

The doctor invariably spent the evening in permanent dread

of being asked to diagnose on fellow guests' embarrassing ailments, such as recommended remedies for haemorrhoids, and he had adopted, for self-protection, the tactic of being the last to arrive, timing their entrance for the tail-end of the pre-dinner civilities, which usually was the time when the occupations of guests was ascertained.

Sarah had scrutinised Isaac's female companion, Barbara Lee, an auburn-haired, statuesque woman in her forties.

The glamorous former fashion model with sparkling pale blue eyes had been an old flame of Isaac's who had remained a close friend and attended occasional social functions as Isaac's escort.

Sarah's initial jealousy upon first sight of Barbara linking Isaac's arm and fearing they were in a serious relationship, dissolved upon overhearing farmer Tomkinson uncharitably refer to her as 'this month's selection from his harem'.

The topics of discussion over the meal ranged between the esoteric, such as the likely effects of an unexpected influx of tourists into north rather than south Lakeland during the coming holiday season, to recommended novels and current West End theatre shows.

Sarah, in contrast to her husband, delighted in every moment of the evening and felt particular pleasure during a literary discussion to be able to venture an opinion on the merits of Proust, when she recalled an analysis of his work she had recently read in the supplement of a broadsheet Sunday newspaper. She had noted, with amusement that Isaac for the first time that night had not offered a view.

Isaac gripped Frank's arm as they entered the smaller of the two smoking rooms, and guided him towards the comfortable deep leather armchairs.

Once settled, Frank accepted Isaac's offer of a Davidoff cigar from his monogrammed cigar box and studied him scrupulously as he prepared and lit it, before he followed suit. They both watched the cigar smoke drift comfortingly upwards towards the glittering chandelier overhead.

The warmth from the glowing log fire slowly melted Frank's apprehension as he swirled around the golden-coloured brandy in his glass.

'What's on your mind, Frank?' Isaac sensed his guest's disquiet and took the initiative, to put him at ease.

'It's Sarah.' Isaac felt a surge of excitement, and immediately assumed an impassive expression to conceal it.

'Everything fine between you? No problems I hope?' Isaac asked.

'No, nothing like that. Things couldn't be better,' replied Frank.

Isaac smiled approvingly, while sensing that this might not be the complete truth, but, to let Frank get to the point, he remained silent.

'Well, it's like this. Sarah and I, we've been discussing plans for the future. Danny's now away at school in Scotland, the guest house is ticking over nicely.' Frank felt he had broken the ice and was getting into his stride.

'And, not to put too fine a point on it, this is Sarah's idea rather than mine, but – she's always had this ambition – to run our own restaurant.'

Isaac still kept his deadpan expression, but felt an increase in his admiration for Frank's wife. 'She's one smart lady. Not like other wives I know,' he mused, 'most of them content to stay at home. Domestic bliss and all that. All personal ambition disappeared.' His thoughts about Sarah ran on ... 'Ambitious and beautiful. What more could any man want? ... lucky old Frank.'

Frank continued, 'Sarah has always had an interest in cookery and catering. She learned about it from her mother. Trouble is, Isaac, we've made enquiries and, with having no previous experience, no track record, no-one will back us, and I know we could make a go of it.'

Isaac sat back in his armchair and drew on his cigar before replying. 'What about the guest house, Frank? Where does this come in your plans?'

Frank had prepared his reply carefully and did not need to hesitate. 'We could pay someone to run it alongside us to start with, until we've got the new business underway. We'll continue to live there and then review things, after say, a year. Then, depending on how well things are going, we could both run the restaurant full-time.

Sarah thinks I could manage the restaurant with her behind the scenes, and she would run the boarding-house, alongside whoever we take on. In time, if the restaurant's successful, we plan to hand it on to Danny. Give him a start in life. If he wants it, that is.

Sarah feels it's time for us to take on a new challenge. To expand. Like the time they made me supervisor at the pit, she says.'

'So, Sarah was behind that as well, was she?' Isaac thought, and an amused smile stole across his face which Frank interpreted as the first inklings of interest in his proposal.

Isaac had never been a believer in easing anyone's path in business negotiations. He liked to test people's mettle.

He was considering everything Frank had said, with the thought of Sarah predominant in his mind, rather than Frank's business proposition.

Isaac's first reaction was that he had no need to give Frank an immediate answer, although as he continued to think about it, he began to realise that he had always supported the credo that fortunes were made on pursuing a dream.

In fact, this philosophy had been the bedrock on which the Fords had built a dynasty, so he could hardly refuse Frank's request. It would be a betrayal of everything he had ever believed in.

Plus, of course, there was Sarah.

Frank's resolve began to ebb away during the silence between them. Isaac tapped the end of his cigar into the ashtray by his side, and looked directly at Frank. 'I'm always in the market for a bright idea.' Frank picked up the slight smile of reassurance projected by Isaac, and relaxed again. 'And yours seems as good as any, and better than most. I'll put it to my people. If they think your idea's got legs, I'll back it. Up to the hilt, don't you worry about that, Frank.'

Isaac stubbed out his cigar, put down his brandy glass and rose to his feet. They shook hands. Isaac, the Grand Bison Master was gratified to note that the recent initiate of the Blackpool Lodge had remembered to use the secret Bison crossover index and middle finger grip before offering his right hand.

Sarah was waiting anxiously among the other guests in the large smoking room. They were talking about the latest proposal from the captain of the Fernleigh Peak Golf Club to allow lady members to play on three weekdays instead of the traditional two. The fact that gentlemen players had played the exclusive course seven days per week from inception fifty years before, did not seem to have surfaced to that point in the heated discussion.

When Isaac spoke to Sarah, he did not feel it appropriate to refer to Frank's business proposition. 'Plenty of time for that later, after we've got to know each other a little better,' he thought to himself.

And so the evening at Camford Castle drifted to its conclusion, with commitments made between the departing guests that they 'must dine together again. Some time in the future'.

The proposal was met with feigned enthusiasm all round. Only Frank stayed noticeably silent. Isaac and his companion, Barbara, stood together inside the ornate castle portal, as the sound of crunching gravel underfoot was followed by the click of closing car doors, and the silken purr of the engines of the Bentleys, as they glided towards the castle entrance and out into the night.

After Frank and Sarah had arrived home from the castle, Sarah was the first to speak,

'How did you get on with Isaac?'

'I think he liked the idea. He's going to put it to the corporation. But he's the man with the clout. What he says goes.'

Sarah didn't reply. She put down her magazine, smiled, and turned to switch out the bedroom light.

As she drifted into sleep, she was picturing herself on the battlements of Camford Castle standing next to Isaac Ford.

Isaac was pensive. The conversation with Frank Lockwood had been an eye-opener. A wake-up call.

'If a man like Frank Lockwood is seeking a new challenge, then what am I doing? Where am I heading? And isn't it time I did the same?' had been his first reaction, even while Frank was speaking to him.

He thought about Cleopatra's. How the hotel and casino were

thriving, more than even he had expected. And this had started from an idea in his head. His imagination had then taken over and the result was Cleopatra's.

At moments such as this, Isaac usually tried to put himself in the position of his father and grandfather, men who had risen to the heights where others had tumbled to earth, and asked himself the question, 'What would they have done in their time?'

The answer came that his grandfather, Big Sam, had brought America to Blackpool when he built Coaster World. 'But that was in an earlier, more innocent age. People expected less,' Isaac mused, 'These days they expect more. A lot more. To be entertained and catered for, twenty-four hours a day, and with variety, choice and originality as prerequisites. Even Frank Lockwood realises that.'

And then the idea for his new project struck him. Big Sam had started he American invasion. He had passed him the ball. Now he was going to run with it. Like the wind ...

The Yankee Experience

The boardroom of the Samuel Arthur Ford Finance Corporation was on the top floor of Manchester's most modern office complex. Isaac Ford, as chairman of the board, regarded it as his exclusive domain.

On a stifling mid-summer afternoon, Isaac strutted along the air-conditioned corridor, and entered the oak-panelled boardroom.

The walls were adorned with oil portraits of each of Isaac's illustrious forebears.

Isaac, as had become his monthly custom as chairman, was the last to arrive and nodded to the sea of faces glancing up at him as he entered.

Among the group of six sitting at the table, Isaac had become the driving force of the flourishing corporation and was regarded by his fellow board members with a mixture of mistrust and grudging respect.

They had all been content to grow rich by hanging onto his coat-tails and, consequently, disregarded any misgivings they felt about his maverick approach to business. Especially as his instincts for progress and innovation were continually being proven correct.

After breezing into the meeting, Isaac rattled through the items on the agenda and came to 'Any Other Business'. He stood up to announce, 'Gentlemen, I would now like to put before you all 'The Yankee Experience' – a S.A.F.F. entertainment complex to be built in Blackpool alongside Coaster World; comprising in one block, a cinema showing the latest American films alongside re-runs of favourite old movies – Bogart, Cagney, Astaire, and, during the day, Walt Disney for the children. A coffee house. A department store specialising in American merchandise – blue jeans, sweatshirts. Specialist music and souvenir shops.

And within the complex I plan to introduce Blackpool to the full range of American fast food.

And the whole enterprise will operate the American way – with an emphasis on speed and convenience; staying open in the holiday season for twenty-four hours a day.'

Isaac's proposal was voted through unanimously, after only token questioning, followed by a chorus of 'Whatever you think best Isaac. We'll leave it in your capable hands.'

Isaac, following his successes, now projected an aura of fireproof confidence. But the other members of the Board perpetually feared that such apparent invincibility could easily tip over into recklessness. None of them, however, believed that now was the right moment to voice such a concern.

'I'll say goodbye, gentlemen. I'll keep you posted. Thank you for your support.' And with this, Isaac left the room in as precipitate a manner as he had entered two hours before, not waiting to partake in the informal small talk that had traditionally closed all meetings of the corporation since time immemorial.

As he walked down the corridor, he glanced back towards the closed boardroom doors with a disdainful thought of how meekly they had acquiesced to his plans.

For Isaac, gaining the agreement of the S.A.F.F. Board was only the first step of his plan for The Yankee Experience.

To get through the next stage required the assiduous application of the influence intrinsic in his role as Grand Master of the Bisons.

For the Bisons was much more than a social hub - it was a hotbed of intrigue and political manoeuvring.

Isaac had often thought the motto of the Lodge should be changed to 'One hand washes the other'.

Within the confines of the Blackpool Lodge meetings, Isaac, under the guise of social conviviality, set his sights on pulling together the disparate economic interest groups within the Lodge, including financiers, hoteliers, building developers and property speculators, and planned to convince them of the benefits that the Yankee Experience would bring both to themselves and to the town.

And, most importantly, from within these groups, those Bisons who were local councillors and were in a position to vote through his plans.

To his advantage was the fact that a significant proportion of Bisons comprising these interest groups depended directly on the holiday trade for their living, and he was able to point to the overwhelming success of Cleopatra's as a blueprint for the Yankee Experience.

Also, the benefits of Isaac's patronage, as chairman of the giant S.A.F.F. Corporation, with his attendant power to determine who would get the contracts for a new enterprise, were immeasurable to a fellow Bison.

For these reasons, Isaac would usually regard what were insurmountable obstacles to other entrepreneurs of his ilk as being, for him, merely convenient stepping stones on the pathway to achieving his grandiose ambitions.

'Frank ... it's Isaac.'

Three months had passed since the night at Camford Castle, and Frank was starting to wonder if his business proposal had been dismissed out of hand, until the morning he got the telephone call from Isaac he had been patiently waiting for. 'Frank, I've got some good news for you.'

Frank desperately searched for a pen and paper in the desk alongside the telephone. He didn't want to risk overlooking anything when he later relayed the details of Isaac's call to Sarah.

'I don't know if this is exactly the sort of thing you had in mind when we spoke at the Castle, but think about it and get back to me if you're interested – I'll give you first refusal.'

Isaac went on to briefly outline his Yankee Experience plans, before getting to the point of his call. 'Where you and Sarah fit in, Frank, is that we're planning an American diner – a theme restaurant – Uncle Sam's; serving American but also British food, with a fast food extension selling hamburgers, fries, donuts, that type of thing. Could Sarah handle that type of cuisine?' Isaac smiled to himself at his ironic question; he had known the answer even while he was thinking of the question.

Isaac rattled off the financial details of his offer, and Frank jotted them down as quickly as he could. 'We'll give you a loan at tiered rates of interest, nominal to start with, but increasing in line with rising profits.

I'll work alongside you, to teach you the ropes, then you'll be manager on your own, and Uncle Sam's will be your full responsibility.

In effect, we're giving you carte blanche – an open cheque – to develop Uncle Sam's as you wish; but don't worry, we'll be in the background for any help and advice you need.

Oh, and one more thing, we'll need the boarding house business as collateral – of course, this means your home as well, as you'll appreciate.

Think it over, Frank, and talk to Sarah.

If you're interested, the three of us can meet up later to hammer out the nuts and bolts. And, we hope to be starting work within the next three months, and will be building the diner first; so I'll need your answer sooner rather than later.'

Sarah phoned Isaac later the same evening, on the pretext of discussing his call to Frank earlier in the day, and to accept his offer.

She mentioned how much she had enjoyed visiting the Castle and that she hoped to see him again at the Bisons New Year's Eve dance at the Tower Ballroom.

New Year's Eve

Just before the moment of midnight, Isaac saw Sarah standing alone, on the opposite side of the crowded Tower Ballroom, and tried to get across to her. They had been furtively exchanging glances throughout the evening.

The moment of the Bison's New Year tradition had arrived.

An expectant hush fell over the ballroom as the lights were dimmed.

A hunched, hooded figure with a long, white beard, clothed in sackcloth and dragging a long scythe shuffled across the deserted dance floor in the semi-darkness.

Gasps rose up from the small children at their first sight of 'Old Father Time' seeing out the old year. He no sooner had appeared than he was gone, and the year had ended.

The lights above the dance floor then went out completely, and all was darkness.

The chimes of midnight sounded, and a young woman swathed in white, cradling a baby, was standing proudly in the brilliant spotlight directed on the centre of the ballroom. To the accompaniment of joyous applause and cheering. The New Year had arrived.

The wonder of that annual moment had remained undiminished throughout the decades. The enraptured faces of the watching children were an enduring testimony to this instant of spine-tingling magic.

'Glad you made it,' Isaac whispered breathlessly to Sarah just as their New Year embrace was unceremoniously shattered by a riotous band of teenagers conga-ing jaggedly across the floor.

'There's been no-one interesting to talk to all night,' he continued when the two of them were eventually re-united. 'I was beginning to think what a dismal New Year it was going to be, but now it looks as though that's all changed – for the better.' As he said it, Isaac thought how trite and juvenile it sounded but at least, he felt, it had the merit of being spontaneous, and sincere.

As Isaac spoke, Sarah was thinking back to the evening at Camford Castle and was concocting an appropriate response that would encapsulate all she had been feeling since that fateful June afternoon; but she was thankfully reprieved by the sudden cascade throughout the ballroom of a multitude of multi-coloured balloons, which dropped out of a giant net on the ceiling, and became trampled under a mass of jigging feet, to the accompanying sound of a host of tiny explosions.

Isaac and Sarah remained undetected in their secluded alcove at the back of the ballroom as they romantically welcomed each other into the New Year.

The symbolism of the moment was not wasted on Sarah. New Year – the time of new beginnings - yet at that moment Frank was far from her thoughts; she was not even wondering where in the ballroom he might be, or whether he was seeing in the New Year with someone else.

After New Year's Eve, the clandestine relationship between Isaac and Sarah began to gather momentum.

The prospect of a temporary dalliance with Isaac had induced in Sarah a tingle of excitement, and a sensation of release from her workaday domestic world. A means to recapture, if only for a short time, the excitement of her youth. To enter again through the door that led to a spangled, carefree world.

When she re-lived the evening at Camford Castle, and then New Year's Eve, she felt coquettish and uninhibited.

The difference between Sarah and Isaac was that, although Sarah knew in her heart of hearts that she was deceiving not only Frank but also herself by nurturing such fanciful desires, Isaac, on the contrary, had never fallen victim to the delicacies of introspection. In his world were only winners and losers, and he had never found himself acquainted with the latter. He had, therefore, no reason to be circumspect in any relationship, business or social. Any casualties in any of his dealings had been, in Isaac's eyes, simply unfortunate.

Isaac was single-minded in all matters of the heart, on occasion to a chilling degree. He had always possessed a facility of disregard, as natural to him as opening his eyes at daybreak.

And so, from the outset of their secret romance, Sarah was at a disadvantage to Isaac, because of her prescience that, if it continued, a day of reckoning would eventually arise which would inflict on her the greater damage.

Already her conscience had told her she had moved beyond the stage where, if detected, ingenuousness could be proferred to Frank as a justification for infidelity. She was now under the influence of more powerful forces which were intent on leading her a long way further down the road signposted catastrophe.

Public School

Danny Lockwood often wondered in his introspective moments if his situation would have turned out differently if he had gone down the same educational path as all his friends.

Perhaps it was genetically preordained that he attend public school as he knew his parents were ambitious, not only for him, but also for themselves.

Despite his frail constitution since birth and the family doctor having remarked on his continual visits to the house that he was never likely to achieve the robustness of other boys of his age, his parents still saw him as the heir apparent to the family business. And to them, that meant education. The best education. At whatever cost.

On his first day at Abbey Grange, sitting on his suitcase, wrapped in a voluminous grey duffle coat, in a cold, lonely room, with an interminable unknown future stretching ahead, to Danny, the cost was already too high.

And then Marcus walked into his life.

Marcus McPhee was big. He lumbered rather than walked. And his clothes looked to be at least one size too small. His trousers were at half-mast, which left his socks permanently on view to the world.

Danny noticed that Marcus' blazer was fastened only by the middle button and that his shirt front was hanging outside his trousers. His unruly curly black hair looked as though it had never come into contact with a comb.

In short, Marcus was a sartorial mélange and, even after he had metamorphosised into an adult, he never experienced an awareness that he had become à la mode during his first rite of passage in life.

Marcus was strong and mean but with the incongruity of having a high-pitched squeaky voice and a refined Scottish accent.

Consequently, he was self-conscious of it and compensated for his vocal unease by displaying an intimidating manner to the world.

However, Marcus was well bred, and in the environs of his leafy Edinburgh prep school, his size and overt pedigree had earned him a respect which he had not used with consideration. For Marcus' over-riding characteristic was that he was an inveterate bully.

He walked into the school bedroom occupied by Danny without knocking and walked over to the single bed by the window. He didn't acknowledge Danny's presence.

'Want a snort?' was his first utterance.

Danny looked blankly at his questioner.

So Marcus dug into his trouser pocket, produced an odd looking badly rolled cigarette and lit it with a match. A strange, sweet, pungent aroma drifted towards Danny.

'Keep a lookout. I don't want to get caught.' Marcus commanded as he blew smoke rings in Danny's direction.

Danny thought at that moment that his stay at Abbey Grange was going to be long and uncomfortable.

He decided not to challenge the sleeping arrangements with the present occupant and jumped onto the bed next to the door. He turned away from Marcus while swiftly unpacking his belongings, all the while being conscious of scrutiny from the overpowering presence on the other bed.

That night Danny read himself to sleep. Conversation had not been resumed and when Danny glanced over to the other bed Marcus was still fully clothed, lying on his back, and with a look of sublime ecstasy on his cherubic red face.

'Where you from then?' The small boy standing next to Danny was asking him the question. They were in a group of boys in a quiet corner of the schoolyard.

'Blackpool.'

The small boy looked up at Marcus expecting him to produce a demonstration of verbal leadership.

'He's sharing my room. Met him last night,' Marcus squeaked, looking at Danny as a scientist would examine a specimen in a jar in his laboratory.

'He looks odd to me,' small boy chimed in. 'His shoes are too shiny.'

'He's a Sassenach,' added Marcus, a word he had heard used by his father to describe the English, and had noticed a disdainful look appear on his face when he said it.

'My mother says Blackpool's common. Says she knows someone who went there once – and never went back.' A third boy added his contribution. 'She said it smelled terribly. Of fish and chips. And there were jellyfish on the sands.' Third boy's voice was plummy and affected, emphasising words intended to sound unpleasant, so as to make his point, and twisting his pointed nose in distaste.

'Where are you from then?' Danny asked third boy.

'Chester. Where the Roman wall is. You been there?'

'No' replied Danny, 'been to *Rib*chester though. They've got Roman ruins there.'

Similar exchanges became a daily event between Danny and the group, and, as much as he longed to be accepted as one of their number, after a month he had resigned himself to the fact that it was never going to happen.

Paradoxically, his isolation proved to be beneficial to Danny in that it forced him to concentrate on his studies, with the result that he was continually among the top three of his class when test results were announced.

This was done at the end of each month by Mr Twiss.

Mr Twiss was the form teacher. He was tall and slim, and always wore his mortar board and gown in the classroom.

He had been a Spitfire pilot in the war.

Mr Twiss refrained from skimming the board duster at

Danny's head as he was prone to do to the badly behaved boys in his class.

His prime target area for this was the back row of the room, in the centre of which Marcus reposed like a beached whale.

Marcus had perfected ducking at the precise moment the wood-backed duster arrived at the spot where his head had been positioned as the bullseye of Mr Twiss' envisioned target.

The relationship between Danny and Marcus as room-mates failed to become any warmer than the awkwardness of their first meeting and Danny sensed a perceptible hostility growing towards him day by day.

He attributed this to an impression that Marcus intended to supplant him as his room-mate, a judgement he had formed after accidentally overhearing a lunchtime conversation between Marcus and his disciples.

This was taking place behind the wooden hut of the Air Training Corps, the domain of Mr Twiss, affectionately known as 'Biggles' by those boys not over-powered by an urge to take to the wide blue yonder.

After the monthly school trips to the local airfield, boys regularly returned with anecdotes of loop-the-loops and other hair-raising stunts, during which they claimed to have taken over the controls from the instructor.

One tale had begun to circulate concerning Marcus' inaugural flight.

Upon entering the aeroplane, he had disregarded the pilot's instruction to step onto the reinforced area indicated, with the consequence that he had put his large foot through the wing.

Also that he had been requested to leave the aeroplane when it was discovered that the passenger seat did not accommodate his ample girth, even though the aircraft was a specially modified training one built for boys of standard build up to seventeen years of age.

One boy had bravely ventured to question Marcus as to the validity of the stories, and was discovered after the close of classes that same day, with four of his fingers jammed inside the ink-well on his desk, but resolutely refusing to divulge the circumstances of his misfortune, despite prolonged questioning by the Headmaster the following morning after assembly.

Danny knew that Marcus was one of the boys behind the hut that day even before he overheard his piggy-like squeak, as a familiar aroma had wafted towards him. He then heard 'Pass it round – quickly – we haven't much longer.' He could not ascertain how many others were engaged with Marcus in the enjoyment of the noxious, forbidden fumes, or who they might be.

'I'm going to get rid of him – for good' were the next words Danny heard, propelling a shudder of terror throughout his body from his head down to his toes. As Frank, Danny's father, had been a Sherlock Holmes enthusiast and used to read to him from his stock of Conan Doyle books, at that instant Danny's mind dredged up from its depths the other occasion when he had heard an identical expression. Moriarty had been referring to the elimination of his arch-enemy Holmes.

'I'm going to need your help.' Marcus was still speaking. To no reply.

At this point, Danny felt he had heard enough and ran at breakneck speed back to the safety of his room.

Danny's existence had turned full circle in a twinkling of an eye, from its erstwhile one of scholarship and docility to a new permanent state of foreboding.

He barely slept at night, and lay awake listening to Marcus' stertorous breathing and the rattling of his snoring, that seemed to loosen the glass in the windows.

Danny struggled to sustain a buoyant tone in his weekly letters home, endeavouring while writing to direct the focus of his thoughts away from galloping dread to the stability needed to write in a firm, legible hand. He usually had to write each page three or four times, continually screwing up the paper in frustration into a ball and throwing it across the room towards his overflowing wicker wastepaper basket.

He withdrew into himself more and more, entire days passing by without uttering a word to a soul and struggling to quell the terrifying bouts of apprehension that assailed him.

And then, after a few weeks, Marcus began to behave in a

friendly manner towards him, tossing out morsels of gang gossip, telling him about his parents, and even making enquiries about Danny's family.

Danny, detecting the possible beginnings of a thaw in the ice between them, decided to invent his own heroic world in an attempt to gain kudos with the Marcus gang. After all, he persuaded himself, no boy at Abbey Grange knew even the slightest snippet about his background, and he had overheard the gang many times bragging amongst themselves of parental exploits and achievements, trying to one-up each another in the way he used to do with his friends Joe and Molly in the far-off days when they played together in the Alley in Blackpool; so this was a sure-fire way of gaining Marcus' stamp of approval.

Marcus was lounging back on his bed, his mind idly wandering. He slowly turned his head to look across at Danny.

'Was your father in the war then?'

It was the chance Danny had been waiting for. To take the first step into the fantastic new world of his creation. 'No turning back now' he told himself, taking his courage in both hands.

'He was a navigator in the RAF – got a load of medals.'

Danny thought he detected a glimmer of admiration in Marcus' eyes but, on reflection, decided it was more likely to be the effect from the roll-up he had just lit beginning to kick into his system. Danny realised he would need to furnish more information.

Illumination from the heavens then struck Danny. He had a brainwave.

Amongst all the teachers at Abbey Grange, Mr Twiss was by far and away the most popular with the boys.

Danny debated with himself, 'They won't dare to question a teacher about his personal life – let alone Mr Twiss .... I know this will work ... it can't fail.'

Danny was aware that desperate measures were called for and he had nothing to lose. Even as he began his explanation to Marcus, his overwrought mind was revisiting that day by the ATC hut and he was starting to feel hot and clammy .... 'Dad was with Mr Twiss in the RAF .... Don't think they actually flew together but when I told him who our form teacher was, he wrote back to me about him.'

Marcus showed interest, 'Let's see the letter then.'

'You idiot,' Danny thought to himself, 'You've done it now. Think … think.'

'Sorry Marcus, Dad wouldn't like anyone to read my letters. I would show you if I could.'

Marcus was feeling in a mellow mood and let it pass, and slowly drifted from silence into soporific sleep, much to Danny's relief.

He knew he had pushed his luck. He was right in believing that his reckless gambit had now rendered him a hostage to fortune. His future safety at Abbey Grange from that moment was in the lap of the gods.

To Danny's considerable surprise and relief, his next few weeks were a period of blessed tranquillity. He felt his spirits begin to rise – and then suddenly soar – when Marcus, on waking one Friday morning, told him, 'We're having a gang meeting – lunchtime today – come along.' Marcus didn't expect a reply from Danny, and, glancing back into the bedroom as he stepped out into the corridor squeaked out, 'Twelve o'clock, by the toilet block. See you there.'

Danny, at that moment, felt akin to a prisoner on Death Row counting the tick of the final minutes to his execution, suddenly learning from the Governor that he had been granted a reprieve.

The morning could not pass quick enough and as noon approached he walked to the toilet block with a brisk and light-hearted step.

Danny thought it strangely quiet when he arrived there, and was just beginning to wonder if he had misheard Marcus, when a sweaty hand shot out from nowhere and clamped itself like a vice round Danny's half-open mouth.

'Keep quiet or you're in trouble,' a sinister voice commanded him. Two more boys appeared, one on each side of Danny, and pushed him through the doors and into the far cubicle.

Danny struggled and kicked but was powerless.

Then Marcus appeared, stepped into the cubicle and locked the door.

The next few minutes were a blur to Danny.

The two boys at his side tipped him upside down, his head poised just above the toilet bowl.

He was dizzy and feeling sick, but still able to distinguish the high-pitched squeal speaking to him in the midst of the scramble and the shouting.

'This is what happens to boys who disobey me. Next time I ask you to give me something, make sure you do it.'

'OK, duck him and pull the chain' ....

Danny struggled to breathe as his head plunged beneath the water .... He fought to remain conscious .... And then they pulled him upright, waited, and did it again .... And again .... Then dropped him face-down, spread-eagled across the cubicle.

Danny, heaving and choking desperately, spat water out over Marcus' feet.

He looked down contemptuously at Danny and rolled him over with his scuffed and grime-encrusted right shoe. 'I want to see the letter ... and ... keep quiet about this.'

He turned to look back at Danny before walking away, 'And make sure you get my shoes cleaned.'

The three of them then left Danny, where he was, crumpled and wretched and forlorn of hope.

A week later the gang held its usual daily meeting by the hut.

Small boy spoke first. 'Has he asked to move out yet? I want to move from my room – it's too cold – I can't sleep and I don't like being on my own.'

Marcus replied, 'He's just gone quiet. But I don't think he's said anything to anybody. He's tougher than he looks.'

'Has he shown you the letter?' a short curly haired blond boy asked.

Marcus knew he couldn't bluff his answer. That they would want to see the evidence. That just saying he'd seen the letter wouldn't satisfy them. 'I'll have to go. See you again tomorrow.'

As Marcus walked off, the look that passed between the other four members of the gang was the signal of the beginning of the end of Marcus' reign as leader.

His attempt to weaken Danny's resistance and force him to ask for another room had been counter-productive.

Danny, after enduring the bleakest night of his life following the incident, awoke the next morning inspired with a fierce resolve to wreak revenge on his room-mate.

'I'll find a way. They won't force me to leave my room and I won't tell him there never was a letter. There must be a way,' he told himself determinedly.

Danny was at a loss to understand why he had such an intense feeling of indomitability.

He rubbed his eyes to wake himself up and clear his thinking.

He remembered going to bed and the pain from his bruised wrists and ankles keeping him awake.

He had curled himself up into a ball and hidden beneath the sheets, and stuffed a fist into his mouth to silence his sobbing, so that his tormentor, in bed a few yards away, would think he was asleep.

He had then whispered a prayer – nothing more than asking someone to help him – and immediately he had drifted into a deep sleep.

And then woken up to a changed world that offered him fresh hope.

'Strange,' Danny thought, now fully awake, and glancing across at the slumbering, snoring Marcus, 'he doesn't bother me any more. Not in the slightest. And I certainly won't be cleaning his shoes. No way.'

Miss Lavender was a curious and unorthodox schoolteacher.

She had taught at Abbey Grange for ten years and no-one had ever spoken to her by any other form of address than 'Miss Lavender'. Even conversations with her closest colleague, Mr Twiss, had been formal exchanges such as, 'The boxing team did rather well this term, Miss Lavender,' and 'They do seem to be showing signs of improvement, Roland.'

She was diminutive to the point of invisibility; the only teacher on whom even most of the first year boys could look down.

She was also charm personified, and had never raised her voice in class throughout her long teaching career.

Yet Miss Lavender was the most feared and respected teacher Abbey Grange had ever known pass through its hallowed gates.

Just a polite cough, immediately followed by a hand to her rosebud lips, as she entered a classroom, was sufficient to bring about silence of a sort that any church in the land would have envied.

Even the fearsome Marcus would hastily remove his chewing gum and stick it under his desk top when the lookout at the classroom door called out 'She's coming', after he had picked up the unmistakeable clicking of Miss Lavender's petite stilettos turning the corner at the top of the narrow corridor that led to notorious classroom 2F.

Miss Lavender for the whole of her ten years at Abbey Grange had been a pottery teacher, on occasions extending this into sculpture for the artistically-minded older pupils. In her private room were miniatures based on the work of Rodin.

Also, in after school hours, she was the school's boxing teacher for senior boys.

Mr Jackson, a senior teacher at Abbey Grange regularly recounted the story to new teachers, of the day Miss Lavender brought into school a scrapbook of her hero, Joe Louis, grinning with pride that she had saved every press cutting about the boxer that had ever appeared in British newspapers throughout his long and distinguished career.

In out of school hours Miss Lavender was a reserve referee at amateur boxing nights in Edinburgh; charity occasions for well-heeled Scottish businessmen to dine lavishly while watching fights.

Miss Lavender heard a knock at her door and opened it to find Danny Lockwood standing before her, 'I need to learn how to box. Can I join your class?' Miss Lavender was thrilled. She had never before been approached for lessons by a junior. But since her days as a student teacher she had understood the need of the underdog to claim his rightful place in the world; so she didn't ask him why he had come. And she had always been a person to take on a challenge; a fight against overwhelming odds.

Over the next three months, under Miss Lavender's tutelage,

Danny's fitness and stature blossomed. He trained three nights a week.

Even Marcus commented to the gang on Danny's frequent absences from the room. And Danny never told Marcus where he had been on his evenings away.

Danny ran laps of the football pitch until his legs ached and his lungs screamed. He skipped. He sprinted. Miss Lavender regaled him with tales of Louis' lightning-fast fists. His subtlety, and knowing when to choose the optimum moment for the killer punch.

'Move and jab ... move and jab' was the mantra Miss Lavender repeated to Danny over and over again as he pummelled the punch bag, each punch landing on an imprint of Marcus' face that Danny had constructed in his mind's eye.

In letters home Danny proudly told his father of his boxing progress.

'Boxing will make a man of him – can't beat the noble art,' Frank had said smiling at Sarah, as he read out Danny's letters.

Sarah could not bring herself to agree with her husband, but sensed a new-found confidence shining through the words of her son's letters so she prudently kept her counsel.

Danny knew that Marcus would not let him forget.

He did not intend to let down his guard as long as Marcus' forbidding presence menaced the corridors of Abbey Grange.

Marcus seemed to have lost interest in supplanting Danny as his room-mate with the gang's small boy. He just could not be bothered with the aggravation of explaining to the housemaster a matter that would only benefit someone else with nothing in it for himself, and, besides, his present room-mate afforded him all the peace and quiet, and discretion, he needed.

But despite the hiatus in the hostilities, Danny continued to worry ceaselessly about the unresolved issue of the letter. Now the gang believed a letter existed, Marcus was obligated to produce it to them sooner or later, and this meant Danny was going to be asked for it again, or suffer similar, or perhaps, worse repercussions than before.

If Marcus didn't come up with the goods then his days as gang leader would be numbered, his credibility shot to pieces. And so

Danny was unwavering in his resolve to be ready for the moment. So he trained on ... secretly ...

It was a cold, frosty December morning. The first snowfall of the winter overnight at Abbey Grange had caught everyone unawares. In the morning, groups of boys were having snowball fights in the playground. Others were skidding down improvised slides. But Marcus' gang, in customary fashion, continued to look on any activity with disdain, and just stood in a circle, hands thrust deeply into coat pockets.

Danny was walking past the gang on his way to his first class of the day when Marcus stuck out a foot and catapulted him headlong onto a frozen patch of snow.

Marcus loomed over Danny's recumbent body as the others gathered round, an eager look of anticipation on each cold, pinched face.

He lowered his opened right palm to the level of Danny's upward-looking face, 'I think you owe me a letter. Hope you hadn't forgotten.'

Danny rose slowly and silently to his feet. His resolution was holding firm.

His moment had to be now.

The scene was a bizarre tableau in the snow. A re-enacted epic Biblical battle, David versus Goliath.

Danny on the ground and Marcus towering menacingly over him. And now becoming slowly encircled by more boys making their way to the corner of the yard to satisfy their curiosity over the noisy scuffling they had heard.

Danny began to chant to himself Miss Lavender's mantra ... 'Move ... move ... move' ... He jumped up off the ground and faced Marcus ... 'Jab ... jab ... jab...' He stabbed Marcus' nose with a quick left fist, and, as he tottered, swung round a clenched right, containing all the power he could muster ... and ploughed it unsparingly into Marcus' flabby midriff.

The boy mountain folded in two, clutching his middle and emitting a high-pitched squeal that rang out in the cold morning air .... 'Get him ... Get him' he cried out to his gang in desperation. But for the first time since the day of their formation, they refused to obey Marcus' orders.

And Marcus in his turn was powerless to stem the mutiny of his crew.

The tableau in the snow crumbled.

Each boy in the schoolyard made his way into the warmth of the school, including Danny, now escorted by the gang.

But minus its stricken leader, who remained, a lone and humiliated Goliath, desolate in the falling snowdrops.

Frank and Sarah Lockwood were in the front row on the day Danny received his prize in front of the pupils of Abbey Grange.

He had gained top grades and was on his way to Sheffield University.

One pupil was not present that day. Marcus had been expelled for extortion of money and valuables from first year boys.

He was discovered when the Headmaster walked in on him unannounced, to search his single room, and observed Marcus reclining on his bed, with more than a passing resemblance to the Emperor Nero, exuding smoke clouds of an exotic aroma towards the approaching Head.

A search of his wardrobe unearthed a pirate's chest of banknotes, small change and assorted schoolboy baubles.

Marcus was led away squeaking pitifully in futile protest of his innocence.

Stardom

Molly Earle's first appearance on Select A Star was a sensation.

The cameras and the occasion seemed to lift her performance into a new dimension from the audition day. She felt the television studio was her spiritual home.

Molly was voted the unanimous winner by the judging panel, with predictions of a glittering future for her. She was also the nation's winner from the TV viewers' vote by a record number of votes.

She had swept all before her.

When Roderick Sterne said before she sang, 'We'll rocket you to the stars, Molly Earle', she giggled infectiously at hearing the announcement of her stage name.

But it was her ingenuous reaction of leaping in the air and then kissing Roderick Sterne at the moment she became the winner that won her a place in the hearts of every person watching that night's show, and prompted a vast number of them to tune in to the programme over succeeding weeks as much to witness Molly repeat her joyful spontaneity as to see her singing performance.

Molly's victory on Select A Star prompted Polish John to secretly arrange his most bizarre celebration; one that Isaac was again unable to attend.

A small group of close family and friends were asked to

assemble at the entrance to Blackpool Tower and told only that the occasion was to be formal.

When the group had gathered at the Tower at lunchtime, John led them inside the building and everyone crowded into the lifts.

The doors opened at the summit of the Tower; Blackpool's giant meccano set, built to compete with the French's world-renowned Eiffel Tower.

Each guest exited the lifts and stepped out to be greeted by a waiter wearing white tie and tails, and offering a glass of champagne from a silver tray.

They all then took up places along the balcony rail that ran around the crow's nest, with Polish John, tall and elegant in his top hat and black tailcoat standing in the centre, with Eva at one side of him and Molly at the other.

It was a day of shining splendour. Clear, brisk and warm. The guests looked down over the balcony rail at the panorama below; the holidaymakers like an army of tiny, scurrying insects on the promenade; the trio of colourful piers edging out into the Irish Sea and the theatrical agency alongside the South Pier.

John had timed his surprise to perfection.

On the stroke of noon, a line of elephants appeared in view and made its stately progress along the stretch of beach directly under view from the Tower summit.

Eva blushed and Molly giggled ...'Oh Grandad, what a surprise ...Thank you ...' and she squeezed his hand.

John, in a ceremonial fashion that befitted a former ringmaster, doffed his top hat and announced to the invited gathering, 'Ladies and Gentlemen, today we are celebrating not only the success of Molly at her audition and then on television, but, also, the day I first met the lady who was to become my wife.'

John then linked hands with Eva and Molly and led them forward to the balcony rail. The three of them smiled as they watched the elephants move away out of view. Not one of the guests, and not even Molly had been told the significance of the elephants to the celebration. John wanted the memory to remain untouched in a small corner of his heart, to be shared by no-one but himself and Eva.

They looked at each other, with shared thoughts in a bygone time, smiled, and moved back among the group of guests.

John the ringmaster straightened his back, puffed out his chest, raised his extended right arm up towards the clear blue sky, and spoke, his words floating away into the wispy white clouds, 'Ladies and Gentlemen. Raise your glasses please. To Molly Earle. To the future. And to show business.'

For Molly, to experience the thrill of an audience's reaction for the first time was enough at her tender and impressionable age to instil a desire for many more such euphoric occasions.

She felt a need for similar experiences was as vital to her as the air she breathed.

As thrilled as Eva had been at her granddaughter's triumph, she now saw her own role as being a stabilising one, as she was only too aware of the pitfalls that lay ahead, and that made it imperative from the outset that Molly's talent be guarded and nurtured.

Although Molly possessed an exciting talent, it was still a raw, fledgling one, and she was an innocent in the ways of the world. Eva knew that Molly was going to need her guiding hand more than ever from now on.

Molly's rise in show business was meteoric.

She won Select A Star for a record twenty weeks, and the tabloid press hailed her as the 'new singing sensation'.

Roderick Sterne became accustomed to meeting Eva at the television studios and a mutually beneficial arrangement was established between them. Eva began to pass on to him for his show the names of any budding stars on her academy books whom she felt were talented enough to recommend, in return for a fee for each.

This agreement came at a time when the Select A Star production team was considering a change in its selection procedure.

The show's popularity ratings had begun to slide, and the producers decided a higher calibre of contestant was essential to revive it .

The Astra Academy, having already carried out a vetting and

training procedure on its own applicants, would obviate the need for Select A Star to continually undertake time-consuming auditions of thousands of people, ninety per cent of whom had no hope of show business stardom beyond the confines of their own imaginations; and only a tiny proportion of the remaining ten per cent had the remotest chance of possessing the talent necessary to progress during the television stage and beyond, as Molly Earle had done.

By agreeing to this arrangement, Eva became, in effect, Roderick Sterne's agent.

She proceeded to cast the academy net wider, employing talent scouts to scour every corner of Britain where any form of show business was taking place, to enrol any potential stars, and at the same time, guarantee them an audition for Select A Star by Roderick Sterne and his panel, with the possibility of progress along the road to stardom to follow.

The Compère

Eva's intention was for her academy to be not only the launching pad for new stars, but also to groom each applicant to look and behave like a star, both while performing to the public, and also in private life.

At this stage in her life, with the worries and responsibilities of running a hotel behind her, and now doing the work she had always wanted, Eva was a fulfilled woman.

After the new selection procedure for Select A Star was underway, a good proportion of the Astra Academy's more polished artistes were now appearing on the programme. As a result, the ratings of the show began to pick up dramatically, and the new improved Select A Star became more popular than ever.

The career of Roderick Sterne was flourishing, as was the profitability of the Astra Academy.

Newspaper reviewers of the hit TV show began to laud Roderick Sterne as the pioneer of viewer participation television, and he gained the reputation of being the man who was personally responsible for making stars out of unknowns.

Roderick had long since stopped reading the reviews, however, since the day one of the more spiteful members of the production team had anonymously left a tabloid newspaper in his office, open at the television page, and he had read, to his dismay, under 'Last Night's Television', 'Select A Star presenter, Roderick Sterne, with the unctuous style and the smile that curdled a thousand stomachs' and '... when Roderick Sterne shakes the winner's hand, and chummily snakes his arm around his shoulders at the end of next week's show, we suggest the fortunate contestant checks immediately to see that he is still in possession of his wallet.'

Eva Goldsmith had known Roderick Sterne from the days when he regularly stayed at the Sands hotel and was a struggling young impresario starting out in the world of entertainment.

In those days he was a judge at North West England regional bathing beauty competitions which were held in Blackpool at the giant Romanesque open air swimming baths.

Eva had always felt lukewarm about him but, at the same time, recently also beholden to him, as by recommending the North Pier auditions, he had been instrumental in Molly getting her foot on the first rung of the showbusiness ladder.

But whenever Eva spoke to him she could never quite eradicate from her mind the image of the day, at 4 a.m., at the Sands, when, climbing the stairs with the poker in her right hand and her hair in rollers, after hearing the loud slamming of a bedroom door, she was confronted by the sight of a curvaceous young blonde who she recalled having seen before, kicking up her shapely legs on the front row of the chorus line in the Winter Gardens 'All Star Revue of 1955'.

The chorus girl was slamming the bedroom door with a ferocity that threatened to wake up every sleeping guest at the hotel, and was mockingly swinging a black hairpiece around her head as she stormed off down the landing.

A youthful Roderick Sterne then sheepishly appeared in the doorway of the bedroom, as bald as a new-born babe, and wearing nothing more than an angry scowl and a pair of long black socks.

Eva knew that he had just returned from his honeymoon the week before.

Although Roderick Sterne hadn't spotted anyone outside in the corridor, he was not prepared to risk the possibility of having been noticed in flagrante delicto, and Eva smiled with amusement when the hotel's night supervisor informed her later that day that room 4 had ordered room service for breakfast, and requested that she kindly leave the tray just inside the bedroom door.

She had also felt obliged to mention to Eva in the same conversation that when she had knocked on the door and stepped inside with the tray, Mr Sterne's room emitted a peculiarly pungent, soporific aroma, as though someone had been smoking a strong, foreign type of cigarette.

After hearing that, Eva always made a point of personally rummaging into every nook and cranny of the furniture in Roderick's room after each stay. She was, however, never able to unearth even one speck of cannabis ash to incriminate her guest as having indulged in nefarious social activities on her premises.

Even in those early days of their relationship, Roderick Sterne was a master at covering his tracks – an accomplished Moriarty to Eva's Sherlock Holmes.

That evening the Sands' young girl receptionist asked Eva who the bald man was who that morning had paid his bill and checked out early from room 4, as she couldn't recall having seen him before.

Eva told her not to ask daft questions and walked off laughing.

Notwithstanding her dubious opinion of him however, Eva had justified to herself her recent business amalgamations with Roderick Sterne as being important not only for the theatrical academy, but also for Molly's future.

In any event, in all her dealings with Roderick Sterne, she smiled amiably at him and kept her thoughts, and early morning hotel recollections, to herself and always adhered rigidly to the maxim, 'If you sup with the devil, make sure you use a long spoon'.

At the Sands Hotel Eva had mitigated her moral qualms about the bewigged lothario, whenever he telephoned to book a room and telling her he was coming to Blackpool to judge a 'Miss Blackpool swimsuit pageant,' by covering the telephone with her hand, summoning over John, and whispering, 'Roderick's coming – put him in room 6 – and move the dancers to share in room 1.' These rooms were situated at the two most extreme points of the hotel and had John and Eva's room situated inbetween. Eva would then add, 'I won't be having any philandering and hanky-panky at this establishment. And, by the way, warn the winner of the pageant to watch out for the judge with the dodgy hairstyle.'

With this, Eva would wink at John. She never could resist ending on a joke.

Whenever Roderick Sterne booked in for a stay at the New Sands, Eva was always the embodiment of proprietorial effusiveness, meeting him at the hotel entrance, with her right hand outstretched in greeting, and wearing her best beamingly radiant smile, and the words, 'How lovely to see you again, Roderick. Do hope your wife's well.'

Winners' Night

A special gala anniversary edition for the winners of Select A Star had been widely publicised, and a record-breaking television audience was predicted.

The producers of the programme were planning a show-stopping finale by Molly and she had been asked for her choice of material.

Molly had remembered 'South Pacific' being the first musical she had been to see at the cinema, with her father Isaac, and recalled wanting to be Mitzi Gaynor ever since that night.

She had made the choice as Isaac had told her he would be coming to the TV studio with Eva and John as members of a specially invited studio audience of family members of the winners who were appearing on the show.

Molly's selection of songs from the show was to be her personal tribute to her father.

Roderick Sterne's backroom staff at Select A Star had baulked at Molly's musical selection, as they wanted something more contemporary. After all, they reasoned, she was the biggest teenage popstar of the day, with her face regularly appearing on the covers of the largest-selling teen magazines.

Molly had now made three records, all of which had gone straight to the top of the hit parade within their first week in the shops.

Eva attempted to question Molly about her decision, but she

had refused to listen, and stormed away, threatening to pull out of the programme if her choice of South Pacific was rejected.

Eva had lately been concerned that Molly's character was beginning to change, and she had a disturbing concern that a malevolent genie had arisen from the bottle labelled 'stardom' which she would be unable to force back in.

Molly was rapidly acquiring a reputation for being waspish with fellow performers, many of whom were often seasoned artists who had served a long, hard apprenticeship in show business, and looked on Molly as a precocious upstart.

Worst of all, it had reached Eva's ears, on the show business grapevine, that Molly was notorious for throwing tantrums while in make-up or with the hairdresser before going on stage.

Eva fretted that the dream could be beginning to go sour when it had barely started.

The New Sands was continually besieged with newspapermen and photographers. The telephone calls to the hotel were incessant ... 'What does Molly like for breakfast? Has she got a steady boyfriend? ...'

After a boom in bookings at the New Sands at the start of her success, most from fans wanting to stay where Molly lived, even though she was usually away performing and living out of a suitcase most of the time, bookings were now beginning to tail off – visitors were becoming peeved at being unable to enter or leave through the front doors of the hotel because of the continual throng blocking the way, day and night.

All the qualities Eva admired in Molly, and that she had been instrumental in developing at the academy were beginning to evaporate. Where once she had been attentive and respectful, now Eva was hearing that she was arrogant and condescending, that no-one liked working with her.

She had always taught her granddaughter the importance of punctuality, but now Eva heard that Molly made a point of never turning up on time, and sometimes not bothering to turn up at all.

To Eva all the evidence pointed to Molly not behaving with professionalism. And, in Eva's eyes, this was a cardinal sin.

If Eva had been in any doubt, the irrefutable evidence was

made glaringly apparent to her during the Select A Star gala night.

Following Molly's intransigence over her choice of South Pacific songs for the finale, the programme content had been passed up to the top floor at Television House for final adjudication by the Executive Entertainment Director.

'TOP PRIORITY' was on the cover of the sealed envelope containing the memorandum for the attention of the director.

Jonathan Maxwell removed his thumbs from behind his stars-and-stripes braces, put down his giant cigar, and lifted the receiver of the red telephone 'hot line' to his senior producer of Select A Star, and barked, 'If any of you value your jobs down there at mission control you'd better do what she says. Pronto. Tout de suite. Get it sorted out.'

He then added, 'Do you know how much our advertisers are paying for the two minute slot before Molly comes on? My daughter loves this girl. Her bedroom at home is plastered with her pictures. Don't you realise who we're dealing with here?'

Molly's chosen songs that night proved to be inspired. From the first bars of 'Honeybun' all the way through to the final bars of 'I'm gonna wash that man right outta my hair,' the audience exploded into wild cheering and applause.

Molly was reluctant to leave the stage, and noticed that the cameras were still trained on her, waiting for the credits of the show to roll on TV screens across the land, showing a picture of Molly accepting a bouquet of flowers from the host Roderick Sterne, and the words running across the screen in front of them while the studio orchestra slowly faded.

Roderick Sterne put one foot onto the stage, ready to present the flowers, when Molly signalled him to move away.

His usual aura of unflappability disappeared like a fading mist, into the arclights, and he hovered on one leg, glancing anxiously from side to side, listening to the frantic instructions being relayed into his concealed earpiece from the control room '...Give her the flowers ... Now ... Switch to camera two ... Start the closing credits...'

Still Molly refused to move. So everybody else remained frozen.

And then she strolled nonchalantly over to the conductor, and leaned over to whisper in his ear... 'Do you know 'Let's dance the night away'?' ... He shook his head, indicating his unfamiliarity with Molly's current number one hit record ... 'Just follow me' ... Molly said to him and walked back to centre stage and grabbed the microphone with the authority of Ella Fitzgerald. She felt an exhilarating sense of freedom and, at that moment, was being borne along on a wave of adrenalin and euphoria.

The cameras continued to roll, and focused on her in centre stage under the spotlight ... 'Stop the credits' ... rang out from the producer .... Molly started to sing the first few bars of 'Let's dance the night away,' without musical accompaniment, the audience clapped in time to the familiar lyrics to help her get underway, and the bemused conductor picked up the tempo, waved his baton to the orchestra, and the backing began ... Molly even did a reprise of her song, then, as it closed, she moved away to the side of the stage, twisting and moving in time to the throb of the music. Like a gyrating marionette.

Eva in the front row of the audience was on her feet, mimicking her granddaughter in her movements.

All the other performers - all previous winners – were circling the stage, clapping and dancing.

When Molly had left the stage, the studio was buzzing with an electric excitement.

Watching on his screen in his office from on high, Jonathan Maxwell leaned back in his swivel chair, put his thumbs behind his braces and gave them a resounding twang of delight. He extended his legs and kicked off his brown brogues. He took out a cigar from his top pocket and set it aglow, blowing big circles of smoke towards the pale yellow shadow on the office wall thrown from the standard lamp in the corner of his office. He picked up the hot line to his senior producer, 'What chutzpah the kid's got ... what nerve ... what a gal ... get me the ratings first thing in the morning ... and ... well done ...'

At the after-show champagne party in the studio's hospitality suite – the blue room – Eva and John came over to congratulate Molly who was engulfed in a sea of well-wishers ....'Where's

Dad?' was Molly's immediate question which she mouthed to them through a gap in the throng, as she saw them approach. 'I'm sorry, Molly,' John said when he reached her, kissing her on the cheek. 'He asked me to send his apologies. He wasn't able to make it. It was a last minute thing. He gave me this to give to you.' Molly took it off Eva and glanced at it. It was a good luck card.

Drifting

By the end of the 1960s Molly had been a big star for over ten years, with a string of hit records.

The Astra Academy had grown to become the largest theatrical agency outside London.

Even Polish John's undertaking business was experiencing a boom.

However, the publicity machine that Eva had set in motion, as Molly's manager, had grown into a juggernaut careering downhill out of control with Eva as the driver being unable to prevent it jack-knifing and crashing into pieces.

The scale of Molly's success had outgrown Eva's capacity to control it, let alone develop it.

Molly was beginning to feel she was treading water, and could see the sands of time rapidly running out for her ambition to top the bill at the London Palladium before she was thirty. Also her dream of taking the U.S.A. by storm, perhaps even Hollywood, was beginning to vanish.

Molly feared she had gone out of fashion with the young.

The Beatles had conquered Britain and then America. It was now the age of rock groups on both sides of the Atlantic.

Sales of her singles and albums had slumped.

Select A Star and subsequent audience participation 'trial by jury' shows for aspiring performers had all passed their sell-by dates and departed from Britain's TV screens.

Gnawing doubts about Eva's part in her decline from the

pinnacle of public acclaim had begun to intensify as the close of the decade came into view. 'Perhaps Eva's drifting, reacting too late to changing trends rather than attempting to chart a new path for my career; maybe her finger is no longer on the show business pulse', Molly would muse.

Molly had been living a reclusive private life for many years, in a mansion on the Thames, close to the London nightclub scene in which she had recently been working as a cabaret singer, specialising in medleys of her hit songs, which she sang while moving seductively between the tables of the diners. A present-day style that was a world removed from the unbridled dynamism of her glory days.

She then returned in the early hours to her lonely mansion by the river.

There had been relationships in her life, but even the most serious of these had not succeeded in diverting her from her single-minded devotion to showbusiness.

Roderick Sterne in the latter part of the Sixties had been compelled to re-invent his public persona in the wake of the demise of his ground-breaking Select A Star.

When the show hit the rocks, he had immediately concentrated all his efforts into expanding his impresario business, using the contacts the show had given him as its host. He was, by the close of the decade, the number one showbusiness agent in the south of England, based in London, and Eva Goldsmith had cemented her position as the unrivalled agent in the north.

Roderick Sterne had metamorphosised during the 1960s to such a degree that he was one of the first celebrities to go over to America to lend himself to experimentation in the hair laboratories of San Francisco which, towards the end of the decade, had announced a breakthrough in the battle against premature male hair loss by means of the revolutionary new treatment of follicle transplantation. He had crossed the Atlantic unannounced and incognito.

He returned after six months with a luxurious mane of dark

curly black hair, a droopy black 'zapata' moustache, and attired in black leather trousers, floral shirt and matching tie.

If he had visited his doctor at this time he would have been diagnosed as being a classic example of premature male mid-life crisis.

Upon his return to England Roderick Sterne immediately launched a television and newspaper nationwide publicity campaign advertising the first hair transplant studios in Britain, which he initially set up as a 'loss leader' arm of his showbusiness empire, at vast financial outlay, and with a selection of willing celebrities who, for lucrative reward, allowed their pictures to appear in newspapers and on hoardings showing their hair at different stages of its decline.

As a guest on a late-night television chat show – the successful new TV genre – the Irish compère of the show had impertinently asked Roderick if there was any particular motivation behind his missionary zeal to broaden out into the battle against baldness in such a innovative and unusual direction. Roderick replied in all seriousness, 'There were certain traumatic occasions in my younger days when self-consciousness over my gradual hair loss had caused me anxiety. I seem to recall it began about the time I was starting my career in Blackpool.'

Eva happened to be watching this programme at the New Sands. She turned to John and said, 'I can back him up on that any time he likes.'

The chat show compère followed up this question with another one, 'And what did you decide to do about it? As a young man that is?'

Roderick fastened his grave expression on to his face before he replied, 'Well, I knew I could never wear a hairpiece – under any circumstances.'

Eva and John just looked at each other with expressions of pure disbelief. They turned off the TV set and went to bed.

They found difficulty dropping off to sleep that night. This was not due to business concerns and anxieties.

It was just that hysterical laughter tends to have that effect at bedtime.

Of the many young performers who had come to the attention of Roderick Sterne in his life at the top of the entertainment tree, only one had succeeded in gaining a serious foothold on the mountain slope of his affections. Molly Earle.

Roderick was in one of his rare reflective moods at home.

His drifting mind had been toying with ideas.

He had recently been thinking that his life had arrived at a crossroads.

His marriage had ended five years earlier in acrimonious divorce, with a punitive financial settlement in favour of his wife.

'My life's crowning irony' Roderick thought. 'In a life pervaded with recklessness, I paid the heaviest price of all – the collapse of my marriage - as a result of an accusation of which I was completely innocent. It's all too preposterous and tragic for words.'

The Diver

The Mercury, Britain's leading Sunday tabloid newspaper, had published a front page scoop.

A woman living in a squat in London's Notting Hill had claimed that one of Britain's foremost show business impresarios was the father of her two-year old child.

It did not help Roderick's plea of innocence to his wife that the photograph of the mother and child on page one showed a thin, hollow-eyed woman with unkempt long black hair holding a cherubic blond baby boy who bore an uncanny resemblance to Roderick.

Fortunately for Roderick he had picked up the newspaper before his wife had seen it that morning, and so had been able to drop it behind the sofa cushion as he walked into the lounge after breakfast.

Sonia Sterne had been too busy with her housework that morning to stop and read the newspaper, but she was looking forward to getting round to it after tea, when she could finally relax for the day in a steaming hot bath.

Sonia was so busy, she had not even thought it strange when Roderick had offered to take her into the city for the day, for a walk in Hyde Park.

While setting up the ironing board alongside the pile of clothes in a corner of the lounge, Sonia had declined the offer because she still had more jobs to do, so Roderick had slumped back into his seat on the sofa, his thoughts in overdrive as the happy chubby face of a two-year old child continued to flash accusingly in the front of his brain.

And then the telephone rang.

Roderick was on his feet faster than a hundred metre sprinter hearing the starting pistol in an Olympic final.

But Sonia had a standing start and was able to get to the telephone before him.

Roderick walked out into the hall and stood alongside her. He watched the expression on his wife's face change, as she held the receiver against her right ear, from neutral, through puzzlement, and finally settling into fury.

Sonia put down the receiver and glared at him. 'Did we get a newspaper today?'

Roderick walked back into the lounge, lifted up the cushion, picked up the Mercury and handed it to her, in the manner of a small boy caught by his mother with his hand in the cookie jar.

At that moment the years tumbled away, and Roderick's mind took him back forty years; he remembered the selfsame feeling one particular day in his kitchen at home.

Roderick had been playing at his friend Freddie's house next door, and had gone with him to the bathroom, where Freddie had locked the door, put in the plug, and run the water to the brim.

Freddie had then tip-toed back to his bedroom so as not to be heard by his mother downstairs and returned to the bathroom, locked the door again, and produced a toy diver from behind his back.

'What do you think of this?' Freddie asked Roderick.

To Roderick, whose finest present up to that time had been an admired and still uneaten selection box of chocolates designed in the shapes of different animals, the diver was a revelation. He looked at with covetous eyes as it dangled from between Freddie's right thumb and forefinger.

The diver was perfect to the minutest detail.

Freddie inserted a small lead weight into a tiny hole in the base of the tiny rubber diver and placed him on the surface of the bathwater, where he slowly sank to the bottom of the bath.

Roderick remembered Freddie had said, 'Look – he's now on the ocean bed – among the sharks.' Roderick expected a miniature shark to appear from behind Freddie's back, but instead his friend began to pump air into the long rubber tube that he held in his hand and which was attached to the diver's back.

Roderick was open-mouthed in wonder as the diver first fell forward as the air billowed into his costume and appeared as though about to swim, and then magically rose up to the surface of the bath, bubbles appearing from behind the grill of his helmet, as though coming out of his mouth. Roderick could have sworn the diver actually opened his right eye and winked at him.

A call then came from Freddie's mother, 'Freddie ... come down here ... where've you been all this time?'

'I'd better go,' Freddie said, 'she sounds mad. Wait here.'

Roderick had never wanted anything as much in his life.

He didn't stop to think of consequences, as he lovingly lifted the diver from the water, dried it on a towel, and put it in his coat pocket.

He slipped out of the bathroom, crept downstairs, hesitating for a second in the hall as he wondered whether to shout goodbye to Freddie and his Mum – decided against it – and stepped out into the street.

That night Freddie appeared in the kitchen of Roderick's house, holding his mother's hand. His face looked as though it had been crying. Roderick could still recall the looks on the faces of the two mothers.

'Don't worry – I'll make sure it doesn't happen again,' his mother had said. 'It's been so difficult for us since his father left. Roderick's been such a handful.'

Roderick remembered the silence in the kitchen just before he went up to his room, took the diver from the top shelf in the corner of his wardrobe, his special secret place, and handed it back to Freddie downstairs.

Freddie examined the diver with forensic efficiency, and then looked at Roderick with a expression that combined bewilderment and abhorrence in equal measure ... 'My diver's broken ... Look Mum.'

Freddie's Mum looked at the diver and handed it to Roderick's Mum without comment.

The diver had been sliced open from below his chin to his stomach.

Roderick could never remember playing with Freddie after that day.

Nor the two mothers speaking to each other again.

He did however remember sitting in the lounge with his mother and her boyfriend while they ate every single one from his chocolate selection box without offering him any, and then screwed up the box and passed it to him without saying a word.

He also remembered his bath-time that same night and the contorted face of his mother as she leaned over him in the bath and scrubbed his back until it felt raw.

'I'll give you divers. You've brought shame on this family. How will I be able to look her in the face again? You've to stay in for a month. Do you hear me? And what about the neighbours? When they find out? You know how Freddie's mother gossips. What on earth were you thinking of? How will I be able to hold my head up in this street ever again?'

If Roderick had been old enough to assess character he would at that moment have been able to discern in his mother's personality an overly-developed sense of the dramatic that, on occasions of extreme stress, veered unpredictably towards the explosively theatrical.

When older he looked back on scenes such as these as ones in which a mother genetically programmed for performance, even in front of her own children, was being watched by a son with similarly inherited genes but, in his case, programmed for observation.

As an adult, Roderick Sterne dined extensively from the menu of human frailties. He became a flawed man, a solipsist devoid of scruples, who showed an open disdain for life's moral boundaries; someone who lived by his own rules and was unable to comprehend that every action has a consequence.

He remained a man forever wandering and lost in that vast hinterland that exists between the poles of good and evil.

But one thing Roderick Sterne never did as an adult was inflict malicious damage on someone else's property.

That Sunday morning, in the hallway of his home, the face of his wife mutated to become that of his mother of forty years earlier.

Within six months Roderick and Sonia Sterne were living separate lives.

The decree absolute had been a formality.

The only consolation to a desolate Roderick was that there had been no children of the marriage, to be damaged by the bitterness of the private recriminations, and the fearsome vitriol unleashed against him by a merciless media publicity machine.

And then, at the start of the New Year, Roderick's nemesis – his woman accuser – was discredited in the same Sunday tabloid that had published the original story, when it blazoned across page one a lead story that one of the men from her Notting Hill squat had claimed the original story had been concocted by the two of them, and that he was, in fact, the child's real father.

Their relationship had soured since publication of the original story and the woman had subsequently refused to share the considerable financial proceeds from the story with him, and had spent the money on herself and not on the child, which had been the original intention of both of them.

Roderick felt that his philandering chickens had come home to roost, in that Sonia had not even given him the opportunity of insisting to the newspaper that the woman take a blood test to verify paternity.

Over the years she had listened to too many of his claims of innocence and, on the same Sunday the original story broke, she packed a suitcase and walked out.

A poignant rider to the entire debacle was that Roderick had a peculiar feeling that the woman in the story was a past acquaintance.

He seemed to recall a chorus girl in Blackpool who looked just like her.

In the days when he used to stay at Eva Goldsmith's place ...The Sands hotel,... 'a crazy hippy sort of kid who had run off screaming and shouting when she found out I wore a wig ...

Hazards of fame, I suppose' ... he smiled ruefully to himself, 'always at the mercy of some screwball ... even so ... a heavy price to pay for a harmless bit of slap and tickle.'

The Proposal

'It's strange how my mind drifts so often to thoughts of Molly. After all, she was only one of hundreds I either auditioned or managed. Admittedly, the one who became the most famous,' Roderick mused to himself, sitting at the fireside of his country house in rural Surrey.

His golden Labrador at his side looked up into his master's face as Roderick tickled the inside of the dog's right ear, as though the dog was in tune with Roderick's changing mood and was offering him spiritual comfort as well as physical companionship.

Roderick's lonely contemplation ran on ... about Molly '...Particularly strange that she should be the one who overruns my mind, when she was the only person in my entire career to have humiliated me ... that gala night ... left me floundering ... not knowing what to do ... still ... that's a star for you ... and I should know ... I've discovered plenty in my time ... but Molly ... she had class ... and with me to manage her ... well, who knows ...'

He poured himself another double scotch and added a short dash of soda. His Labrador had rolled over onto his back, legs outstretched, and face in an ecstatic smile ... an invitation for a tickle ... Roderick obliged ... 'You and me, boy, eh? And this big house. Just to ourselves. Perhaps it's time we had a woman's touch about the place again ... eh boy?'

The dog yawned and rolled over on to his side to let Roderick step round him. Roderick walked into the hall and picked up the telephone.

He dialled the number of Jake Sullivan, his gopher, who could always arrange anything. At any time. 'Jake, get hold of Molly.' Roderick had no need to say any more than that. Jake knew who he meant. Molly Earle might be a fading star, but she was still that famous. A single name star. Just like the ones peacetime's children had idolised in the far off Alley days.

It had been a bad night for Molly at the Blue Grotto nightclub.

Admittedly, the dank evening had not helped the attendance for her late night cabaret.

But the applause from the audience as she finished her act had not merited even the description of being a smattering.

And, for the first time in her celebrated career she had been heckled by a drunk lurching around at the back of the room.

Molly stormed offstage and made straight for the sanctuary of the dressing room.

She slammed the door behind her, and drained her half-full bottle of vodka before the compère of the cabaret had finished the introduction of the next act.

Molly pulled up her stool to the dressing table and examined her face in the mirror as she carefully removed her make-up with a tissue.

She did not like what she saw any more.

Lines were appearing at the corners of her eyes and mouth, and faint frown lines across the centre of her forehead.

The flaming red hair that had been her trademark was now limp and lifeless.

The eyes that had flashed and sparkled in the dazzle of a thousand spotlights now wore only a remote and haunted look.

Her face told the story that she was now well and truly on the skids.

Molly was so preoccupied in her self-scrutiny that she gave an involuntary jump from her stool when the telephone rang. She picked up the receiver ... 'Yes?'

'Molly, you don't know me, but ...'

'If you're press, go away ...' Molly had almost slammed down the phone when the persuasive lilt of the suave Irish voice on the other end jumped back in... 'Molly. I'm not press.'

'If you're a fan then, wait at the stage door, I'll give you an autographed picture.'

'Molly, will you please listen? I'm not press, and I'm not a fan.' Jake realised what he had said and gave a snicker that did the trick in breaking the ice between them '... rather, I am a fan, but that's not why I'm calling you. I work for Roderick Sterne.'

Molly did not ask for further elaboration. Jake now had her attention.

'If you'll just give me five minutes of your time.'

'You've got five minutes. Not one second more.' Molly took off her diamond-encrusted wristwatch and placed it on the dressing table in front of her.

Roderick's subordinates were of the highest calibre, and Jake's pitch to Molly was a cameo display of slick salesmanship, especially when he hadn't been told why he was calling such a famous star. And he finished with two minutes to spare.

Molly had agreed to visit Roderick at his country house the following Sunday at 11 a.m. For pre-lunch drinks.

'It's been a long time, Molly.'

Roderick and Molly were sitting opposite each other, both feeling ill at ease and sitting stiffly in the upright armchairs, Molly with a glass of vodka and tonic, and Roderick with his customary scotch on the rocks.

Roderick's sitting room was bright and expansive, and the two of them could look out through the large patio doors onto a vast expanse of immaculately-cut lawn bordered on each side by rows of perfectly trimmed and shaped conifers.

Molly noticed a gardener and his assistant trimming a hedge in the distance. She tried to distinguish the shape of the animal they were creating.

From the moment of her arrival at eleven, Molly had been making a running assessment of Roderick's financial worth, and been thinking, 'How can a glorified agent be higher up the greasy pole of show business than Britain's number one entertainer ... well, perhaps not quite number one at the moment.'

Molly had enjoyed a lavish lunch at the end of which both of them knew the ice had still to be melted between them. She was growing impatient as to when Roderick would cut to the chase, but held her counsel, reasoning to herself, 'If someone of his clout is prepared to go to this amount of time and trouble – after all, he must be a very busy man – then I'll go along for the ride.'

When the occasion demanded, Molly could effortlessly conjure up the allure that she possessed even when she was a young girl from the New Sands hotel, playing in the Alley, whose attributes Eva had honed at the theatrical academy ... 'One day you'll be a sophisticated woman, who will be at home in any company, Eva used to tell her.'

Molly was feeling that this was such a day and that the over-indulged enfant terrible of show business that she was when Roderick had last seen her had matured into a radiant, captivating woman and she intended to make him aware of that.

It was now mid-afternoon, and the bright early morning sun was fading away. The mellow shades of orange and green in the garden were becoming slowly etched into deeper focus.

'I can't believe that the beautiful, elegant woman with me now was the same little red-haired girl who ran around playing at the New Sands. Eva must be very proud of you,' Roderick said to Molly.

Molly was unsure how to respond, as she always had been exasperated by references to those earlier times when she was a young girl, or a 'child star,' as the newspapers continually titled her. She wanted to move on in the public perception.

'Well, we all change, I suppose,' was Molly's bland response to Roderick's compliment.

'Not all to the extent you have, Molly.' Roderick continued.

'I suppose we do go back a long way,' Molly tried to switch the conversation away from herself.

'Lot of water under the bridge, Molly ... lot of water ... for both of us.'

Molly was aware of the notorious story of Roderick's fight to preserve his integrity in the face of vilification at the hands of the unscrupulous woman who had claimed to be the mother of his child. And the woman's subsequent humiliation – all at the cost to Roderick of his marriage.

As someone who herself had lived the greater part of her life trying to preserve some vestiges of privacy away from the white hot glare of the media spotlight, Molly looked at him at that moment with a sympathetic and understanding smile, and, just for a split second, the two of them seemed to connect in some strange, almost mystical fashion. At a level above the façade of the self-constructed personas that both of them had honed to such a degree over the years that they had come to forget that they had ever been normal people.

They understood each other, as the people they used to be. Two people now lost forever in the swirling, fading mists of a more innocent time.

Talk of the past had presented Roderick with the opportunity to manoeuvre the conversation into a different area, 'Eva's done well for you. How is she?'

'We don't see a lot of each other lately. The academy has taken off in a big way.'

Molly detected a flicker of irritation crossing Roderick's face, and back-tracked in an attempt to cover up her faux pas. The thought also struck her 'Why should I be so considerate of this man's feelings ... I'm not usually like that ... I speak my mind and if anyone doesn't like it, then it's their look-out – not mine.' Still, she was determined to try and eradicate her clumsiness '...Well, I know you're in the same line as Eva, and, I should imagine you've done just as well.'

As she said this, Molly raised her gaze towards the patio doors and the garden, and noticed that Roderick's glance had followed hers.

'Much too big a place for only one person, I'm afraid,' Roderick replied. 'Still – the price of fame, I suppose,' he added, with a wry smile.

Now it was Roderick's turn to realise he may just have committed a verbal gaffe, as he knew that Molly also lived alone in her mansion. He hoped she had not drawn any personal inferences from what had been merely a throw-away inconsequential remark. He hastily moved on. He did not want to risk either of them straying into any territory replete with verbal landmines, so he decided to get straight to the reason for his invitation.

'Molly, I know your grandmother is a rival of mine. But she's always been a close and valued friend. And that's why what I'm about to say is not going to be easy for me, so I hope you'll hear me out.'

Molly looked at Roderick and wondered to herself how true in fact his statement was, as she conjured up in her mind a picture of Eva and John laughing between them when she had once wandered unnoticed into the room, and had overheard Roderick's name being discussed at length. When she had asked them who they were talking about, she had been summarily silenced with 'Nobody you know, Molly. Just one of the visitors.'

At the time the incident had just served to add an extra layer to Molly's already confused view on the peculiarity and duplicity of the adult world and to her firmly established conviction that it was a world to which she would prefer to postpone her entrance for as long as possible.

Molly fixed a penetrating gaze onto Roderick, and asked herself why he was such an object of mirth to Eva and John. 'I think he's rather buttoned-up and serious. Certainly not a song-and-dance man. The type of man most people would tend to feel sympathy for rather than laugh at. Not a bit like the television man he projects himself to be. Perhaps it's only that he needs to loosen up more. To be himself and not some distorted self-manufactured image of himself. Pity is ... he probably doesn't know which is the real Roderick ... that's what this crazy business can do to you ...'

Roderick cut into Molly's musings, 'Molly, I've been thinking for quite a while of branching out into new areas. The band scene ... is beginning to grow stale. Apart from a few, right at the very top of the tree. The market's saturated. Every kid fresh from school now thinks that, with the right suit and haircut and with three of his mates, he only needs to buy some guitars and a drum kit ... and ... hey presto ... overnight stardom ...

I've always tried to anticipate the public mood. That's where fortunes are made. Walking down the lesser walked path. Never doing the obvious, the predictable. You were an original, Molly. The people could see it. You can never fool the people, Molly. Never fool them, but you can lead them. Lead them and they'll follow. And that's just what I intend to do. With your help.'

Molly was intrigued. And impressed. By this man's intensity. His utter conviction and self-belief.

'What do you mean – my help?' Molly asked the question and experienced a twist in her stomach. A twist mingled with excitement.

'I've been making contacts in the States. The people I've been speaking to are movers and shakers in the music business. High rollers who control the music business in the big cities ... New York ... Los Angeles ... San Francisco ... across the whole continent. They're always looking for the next trend. They think, like I do, that this one's about to play itself out.'

'Where do I come in?' Molly was forced to gulp back a breath before the question was completed. Her throat was beginning to tighten.

'This is how I see it, Molly. I'm going to have to talk straight to you. But I'm speaking with over twenty years' experience at the top – so you can draw your own conclusions.'

Molly was beginning to see how Roderick had got to where he was in the business. It had not been by accident, that's for sure.

'I see your career running out of steam. And a star who has been as big as you can fade as quickly as they arrived. I've seen it happen too many times. The public are fickle – just look at the news – one day the world's about to come to an end and the next they're dancing in a street carnival. It's the same with the music business. Adapt or die. Survival of the fittest ... and the smartest ... that's the key, Molly ... that's what we have to be, Molly, ... the fittest and the smartest.'

Molly was going to interrupt, but let Roderick continue. He was on an inspired roll ...

'I see your career changing gear. I see you as a new type of singer. Glamorous. Dynamic. Dramatic. A combination of actress and singer. Singing operatic pop. A pop music diva. It's a revolution, Molly. With you carrying the flag – alongside me.'

Roderick sat back in his armchair. He had given Molly his best sales pitch.

Molly was impressed. In her mind's eye she wound back to the night she had taken Jake Sullivan's telephone call ... the humiliation of the heckler ... trembling in her dressing room ... a world away from the picture Roderick was painting for her, before her eyes. Perhaps it was meant to be. That telephone call had been destiny reaching out for her hand and leading her towards Roderick's vision of her bright new world. She had nothing to lose. Only a future of a slow, remorseless slide into obscurity. A has-been on the show business scrapheap.

Molly looked directly at Roderick, 'Why America, and not here? And why me? There are others ...'

'Not like you, Molly. I spotted it at the first audition. You were the best who ever appeared before me. You caught the public's imagination. I've seen artists who are liked ... artists who are revered ... you were loved. And you fulfilled everything I expected. And more. But you were a kid. You've grown up. And while you've been growing up you've outgrown your public. In time, that same public will come to pity you.

And America, Molly, because in this country the public have formed a particular image of you. A stereotype. Of you as a singer of pop songs. For the young. Nothing beyond that. That's why you're finding things so difficult now. But in America, you can make a fresh start. As a new type of performer. A more sophisticated singer for a new market. Make a breakthrough over there and you can come back to Britain as an established American star. The old Molly will be history in the public mind. You will have re-invented yourself. Leave the youngsters to their pop groups, Molly, and grasp a new challenge. Before it's too late.'

Molly felt a surge of nausea, but knew the question had to be asked, 'What about Eva?'

'Molly, you're not going to like what I'm about to say.' Roderick leaned forward in his armchair, his arms resting on his knees and his hands clasped together. He continued with the initiative as he could see Molly's face had blanched.

'Molly, Eva can no longer do for your career what I can. At the moment she's running just to stand still. She's done amazingly well to achieve all she has, but now she's hit a brick wall.'

Molly felt a distaste at hearing Roderick's words, but this was combined with an awareness that his words had the bitter taste of truth. Like the man summoned to see his doctor must feel, she thought oddly, being told he has a terminal illness, and hoping against hope, but also having to accept the inevitable.

Also, she had always respected candour in her dealings with people. Liked to know where she stood. As each minute passed, she was coming to realise there was more to Roderick Sterne than met the eye. And then again, the odd image of Eva and John laughing at him shot into her head, as if to test her changing perception ... 'Perhaps that's the difference,' she thought, 'they were laughing at him because they had only seen the surface of the man, and had never had the opportunity to touch his considerable hidden depths. And someone with such depths is the kind of person I need right now. Someone who can see the big picture for my life ... perhaps even ...' She smiled ruefully as the accompanying thought came to her, and Roderick looked at her, wondering what on earth she was thinking about at that moment '... can see the big picture before I can ... yes ... that's it.' The word her mind had been reaching for popped in unbidden, from out of the ether '... perhaps this man ...the man they laugh at ... is going to be my Svengali.'

Molly delayed breaking the news to Eva that she was taking on a new manager, and who that manager was.

She managed to stall Roderick by telling him she wanted to see out the contract she had signed with Eva, which took her up to the end of the year. So she continued to work the tables at the nightclubs, singing her past hits, but now throwing in an occasional blockbusting ballad just to test the waters of audience reaction, in preparation for her new career.

Even amongst the world-weary clientele of the Blue Grotto

the response was enthusiastic, and Molly felt a new surge of life running through her veins, on seeing again an audience rising to its feet in appreciation of her work, instead of shuffling away sheepishly to the bar during her act, something she noticed had been happening more often recently.

This reaction had given Molly a growing conviction that her decision had been the right one. But having to break the news to Eva was a different matter.

Since the day at Roderick's she had been in continual debate with her conscience. 'Nan has been with me even before the audition day at the North Pier – the day that started it all. Been there for me every step of the way, through triumph and despair. That day we celebrated at the top of the Tower had been meant to cement my singing future with Eva and the academy. My family life and my performing life have always been inseparably entwined, and were never intended to be unravelled. And the success of the academy has been on the back of my own success. Eva has used me as a trailblazer that has led to her becoming the North's number one show business agent. Now to change all that, to pull the rug away, who knows what might happen ... And yet, Roderick won't keep his offer open for ever – he'll find another singer from his books. To mould. To fashion into his pop diva, and the chance will be gone for good ... And then where will my career be...my future? In dingy cabaret clubs continually singing songs that are fifteen years out of date. Ridiculed by drunken hecklers, and left with nothing but looking at the reflection of a lost stardom through the bottom of an empty vodka bottle.'

And yet Molly still continued to prevaricate. To justify to herself having to do nothing.

Molly knew she was living in a fool's paradise. That Roderick would not allow her the luxury of honouring her contract being allowed to stand in the way of fulfilling the vision he had mapped out for her.

And then a telephone call, summoning her again to Roderick's country house, brought reality abruptly back into focus.

'Molly, believe me, I appreciate the difficult position you're in. But you must also try to appreciate my situation.'

They were sitting in the same armchairs as on Molly's last visit, but this time there were no gardeners on the lawn, and no mellow, soothing shadows being cast on the deep green carpet.

Molly considered his remark before replying, 'I do, Roderick, I know what I need to do, I really do, believe me. But can't you give me just a little longer? And, like I told you, there's still my contract to consider.'

Roderick barely let Molly finish her explanation, 'The contract's not worth the paper it's written on, Molly. You know that. If it was in front of me right now I'd rip it up into little pieces and no lawyer in the land could do the slightest thing about it. And that's another reason for coming over to me – I've got the best lawyers working for me. Better than Eva's. Legal men who can tie up the best deals for you. Watertight. To safeguard your interests – even against me.'

Roderick smiled sardonically at his last remark. But Molly felt unable to appreciate his humour at that moment, and the corners of her mouth curled up in distaste at his callousness.

She felt that Roderick had changed since their last meeting. His hard edge was now lacerating both her self-regard and her love for her grandmother. But, despite this, she still knew that she had no alternative but to go with him, such was the vice-like grip in which she had always been held by her pitiless talent.

Roderick then spoke more sympathetically, 'I've just heard about a vacancy on a cruise ship, the 'S.S.Antipodean', sailing from Southampton to Perth. For a cabaret singer. Top of the bill. The singer's fallen ill at the last minute. Gallstones. Needs an operation – then rest. It's a golden opportunity to try out our plan. No old hits. A completely new repertoire. Big ballads, new costumes - the works. I can arrange a tour in the big cities – Sydney, Melbourne, Brisbane ... and then a cruise ship back home – through the Panama Canal. Stopping at Acapulco, Barbados ... a chance to see the world ... and then, next year ... the States ... as we planned. I hear it's a cruise taken by a lot of newly-weds ... honeymooners ... so I've booked the tickets ... in my name ... and yours ... also in my name ... '

Molly thought she was hearing things. She thought Roderick's nerve was astonishing, and that any rational response from her would be impossible.

That his presumption was beyond her outrage.

Roderick was impervious to Molly's failure to respond to his veiled marriage proposal, so he ploughed ahead, 'Molly, we'll be good for each other. Both now living in big, empty houses. We need each other.'

Molly had no intention of clearing away any rocks from the path he was building, and her continued silence, and deadpan expression she had deliberately locked onto her face gave him no clue as to whether his prepared proposal speech had borne fruit.

Roderick felt that Molly was leaving him no alternative but to now set foot into unknown territory, to improvise and speak from the heart.

'Molly, I'm tired of being lonely. I need someone to share things with – the good and the bad. I need to laugh again. You can make me laugh again ...'

Molly looked deeply into Roderick's pleading eyes.

Roderick reached into his blazer pocket and produced a small black box. He opened the lid, which sprang back and displayed the most magnificent diamond ring Molly had ever set eyes on.

'I would like you to be my wife. Will you marry me, Molly?'

Roderick took the ring from the box and placed it on Molly's finger.

Molly was still silent. Her face expressionless.

They could both pick up the rustling of the conifer trees in the swirling breeze.

Molly moved her gaze from Roderick's face and looked towards the patio. She spotted a leaf gently fluttering from the tree and delicately touching the ground. It prompted her memory to return to a summer's day. She was in a field with her father Isaac. She had no other memory more sublime than that day. The only picnic she had shared with her father. Just the two of them. An entire afternoon as endless as a lifetime stretched ahead. There was a tartan rug spread underneath them. An open picnic hamper. She recalled that her father had plucked something from the air as it drifted past them in the cooling afternoon breeze. He held it in front of Molly '...Blow, Molly ... gently ... blow ...' It was the most delicate, the most exquisite thing Molly had seen in her life. A thistledown ... a present from her father just for her. She wanted to keep it. To take it home. To look at on those long, lonely days in her room at the hotel. But she blew and it floated away into the breeze. And she was left with a stem in her grasp. A stem stripped of its beauty, its wonder.

'My life's been like the thistledown,' Molly thought to herself, as she looked at the conifers, 'ephemeral. At the mercy of every passing breeze.'

After the eternity of the few seconds of silence between them, Molly looked back to Roderick ...'I'll leave it on. Seems a shame to take it off, when it's such a perfect fit.'

With a star you never quite know what they're likely to do. From one minute to the next. And Molly was not the granddaughter of Eva and Polish John for nothing. And she never had appreciated being outdazzled when an impact was to be made.

Roderick sauntered across the room to an ornate oak cabinet that was tucked away in an alcove. Molly glanced over and noticed him pull out a tiny gleaming key from the small top pocket of his waistcoat and use it to open a drawer hidden beneath the lowered desk top.

He didn't look at Molly as he spoke. His tone was hushed, even conspiratorial, 'We must celebrate this special moment in style – our special moment. I dare say you're familiar with this.' Roderick began to pour a trickle of fine white powder with practised delicacy from the opened corner of a white envelope across the surface of a piece of glass contained within the palm of his left hand. He then placed this on the desk top and took out a banknote from his wallet and rolled it into a tube. He turned to face Molly and proceeded to give an expert demonstration in snorting cocaine. 'This is top quality – the buzz you get is incredible. These days it's essential for top stars to achieve peak performance – to bring out the best that's within – at the moment it's needed. That's what separates the true stars from the also-rans. In fact, I could give you a few names you wouldn't believe, who use it regularly at some of the house parties I've been to.'

Molly gave him a wry smile. In fact, she had never in her life taken a drug stronger than alcohol, and not even a great deal of that until recently, when she had felt a growing need for an emotional crutch – something to help her relax and wind down after a show.

Molly had not so much as smoked a cigarette.

But, at that moment, she wasn't prepared to let Roderick know any of this; she was unwilling to exhibit an aspect of her personality – her will-power – that he might regard as a flaw in her make-up; in his eyes a character weakness which she had always regarded as a strength. Molly wanted to show Roderick that she had it in her to be his diva; a sophisticate versed in the avant-garde mores of celebrity society, and no longer just a naïve wunderkind. And if this meant being complicit in Roderick's freemasonry of silence that turned a blind eye to social drug-taking, then so be it. And, above all, she reasoned, a unique event in her life had just occurred that very afternoon, one that merited celebration – she had consented to become Mrs Sterne, Roderick's wife – and accepting his offer of the white powder was no more than a sealing of the moment – a toast - and would be an action she need never repeat from that day on.

So Molly took the glass from Roderick and placed it on her lap. She opened a nostril with the index finger of her left hand and picked up and twirled the rolled-up banknote with her right .... The tentacles of the cocaine slowly opened out and stretched themselves seductively towards the extremities of her senses.

There was now no turning back.

Molly had supped from Roderick Sterne's poisoned well.

Molly and Roderick said goodnight at the entrance to the mansion and Molly walked away to her car.

Roderick turned to go back into his mansion. He closed the door behind him as firmly as if he was closing the door on his old life.

Polish John, Eva and Molly were sitting together in the spacious lounge of the New Sands.

Isaac was expected to arrive within the hour.

The meeting had been arranged by Molly. It was the first visit she had made to her home town in over two years.

Roderick had wanted to come with Molly but she had told him it would be better if she broke the news to them on her own.

One reason for her reluctance was the image that came into her head of, not only her grandparents, but also Isaac, abruptly ceasing their mocking laughter when Molly, with her husband-to-be alongside, appeared on the front doorstep of the New Sands, and the thought that her father had perhaps now been let in on their peculiar little secret while she and Roderick had been travelling from London to Blackpool.

In visualising this, Molly failed to reason that her father was usually too preoccupied with business matters to concern himself with any inconsequential tittle-tattle.

On the journey to Blackpool, Molly rehearsed different ways of breaking the news to her father and her grandparents, and when she arrived she had still not resolved how she was going to do it.

John and Eva had been speculating on the importance of a meeting having been arranged between the whole family, and various ideas flew around between them, ranging from the realistic to the wildly fantastic.

Molly had asked Eva if she could telephone Isaac and ask him to come as she had been having difficulty contacting him …

'Isaac. It's Eva. How are you?'

'Fine, Eva. Yourself? John?'

'Molly's been in touch. Says she's coming up here, and wants to see us all – together.'

Silence on the other end of the line, and a rustling of papers.

'Going to be difficult, Eva. Did she say what it was about?'

'No. She didn't. Only that it was important we were all here.'

Eva could sense the irritation in his voice, a tone she had

recognised before whenever his daughter's name arose in conversation.

'She needs to realise I'm a busy man, Eva, and can't just drop everything on one of her whims.'

Eva reminded herself that this was not going to be different to any of their other conversations, with both of them always selecting words and phrases as though walking on eggshells.

'I don't think this is a whim, Isaac. But, if you can't make it, you can't. I'll have to explain. As usual.'

Eva knew that she shouldn't have added the last two words, and wanted to take them back into her mouth the moment they had entered the mouthpiece of the telephone.

'I don't expect you to understand, Eva. I'm sure you'll get a great satisfaction from putting me in a bad light with my daughter. As usual.'

Isaac did not feel the same compunction as Eva had to withdraw the same last two words.

In fact, he felt a buzz of satisfaction at being able to say to Eva what he really felt, rather than indulging in their perennial verbal shadow-boxing, sheltering behind platitudes.

'Isaac, could we just put our opinions of each other to one side on this occasion, and consider your daughter.' Eva was attempting to take the rising heat from the conversation.

She did not succeed.

Isaac's combustibility when roused was legendary, and the developing situation was akin to two warships approaching each other on the high seas, with the cannonballs having been loaded into the barrels and the gunpowder about to be ignited.

'I don't need you – or anyone else – to tell me what's best for my daughter.'

Eva, too, had wanted for a long while to get things off her chest, and was now determined that this was not going to be yet another to add to the interminable list of occasions on which she had to kow-tow to her son-in-law so as to keep the family peace.

'As a matter of fact, Isaac, that's precisely what you do need. And have needed since the day Molly was born.'

The pent-up words of condemnation poured forth from Eva in a bitter flood, and she readied herself for an onslaught in return.

'How dare you? Who the hell do you think you're speaking to? Tell Molly I'll be there at three.'

The slamming of Isaac's receiver reverberated in Eva's ear.

She noticed her hands shaking violently.

Eva had managed to get Isaac to come to see his daughter by pricking his conscience about her.

'I only hope that what Molly has to tell us is worth what I've just been through,' Eva told herself, as the noise of an army of skeletons continued to rattle around in the cupboards of her throbbing brain.

Molly's intention to get her news off her chest in one fell swoop was foiled immediately upon arrival at the New Sands and being told by her grandfather of her father's delay. This threw her into confusion, and, not wanting to hold off completely until his arrival, she decided to speak to Eva on her own first of all.

John made himself scarce in another part of the hotel while Molly began to speak to her grandmother.

'Nan, you know I've always been grateful for everything you've done to get me where I am in show business.' Molly was feeling hesitant and apprehensive. She decided to proceed step by step.

Eva, in her professional capacities of manager of the theatrical academy, and as Pandora the fortune teller, had become conditioned to taking the initiative in dialogues with others, and responding, especially to her granddaughter, was going to be an unfamiliar reversal of the role she had become used to adopting.

'What's bothering you, Molly?' Eva was attempting to tune herself in to her granddaughter's vibes, but the messages coming to her she found to be mixed and confusing, especially as Molly looked to be her old self again; radiant, lively, and talkative. When they last met she had appeared remote and uncommunicative, to the point of being monosyllabic.

'The grapevine tells me the clubs are going well. I'm now trying to line up a summer season for you. There's a good chance I can arrange a booking here in Blackpool. Top of the bill. You can see the headlines now...'Local girl Molly Earle returns home in triumph.' We could pack the house every night with you back here, Molly.'

'Yes, Nan, everything's been fine. Don't worry.' Molly was feeling that Eva was not going to make things easy for her. Quite the reverse in fact.

'The fact is, Nan, I've been offered the chance to work abroad. Australia first, on a cruise liner. It's going to be a chance for me to see the world...and then – what I've always wanted – what you always wanted for me, too – America.'

Eva wanted to smile back at Molly but her features were unable to respond.

'Who's arranged this? Must be someone with clout in the business.'

Eva had a sickening feeling that she knew the answer to her question even while she was asking it.

'Roderick – Roderick Sterne. We've been seeing a lot of each other recently.'

'I see,' said Eva, 'I'm thrilled for you, Molly. Truly, I am,' Eva reached over and clasped Molly's hands within hers.

'Nan. The clubs. It's not what's meant for me. I need this new challenge. If I don't take it someone else will. And then my career will just die.'

Neither of them had realised how long they had been talking, and the appearance of Isaac and John in the doorway brought the conversation to an abrupt halt.

Molly walked over to her father and embraced him.

Isaac and Eva did not greet each other.

The awkwardness in the room between the four members of the same family was intense to the point of volcanic eruption.

'I've been telling Nan some of my news,' Molly continued, glancing between Isaac and John, 'But the main reason I needed to see you all – together – was something else – something more personal.'

Eva was already partly prepared for the bombshell about to explode, as she had correctly interpreted Molly's 'seeing a lot of him lately' with the romantic connotation that Molly had intended.

Eva took over '... Molly's been telling me she's been given an opportunity – America – that will mean she'll be leaving us – and the academy.'

John and Isaac rose to their feet. Eva put up her hand ... 'No. Sit down. I agree with her, It's what she needs at this stage of her career. And I've given her my blessing. It's now just a matter of settling contracts, which shouldn't present any problems.'

Eva was at ease again. The reins of the family meeting were now firmly in her hands. She intuitively realised it had to be her responsibility to steer the family through the impending seismic impact of Molly's disclosures.

'Carry on, Molly,' Eva smiled at her. The two men sat down.

'Well, I also came back to tell you all that I'm going to be married.'

Eva jumped in again, to soften the impact of the news, 'She's going to marry Roderick Sterne.'

'Over my dead body.' Isaac was on his feet again, and made for the door.

'He's old enough to be your father, Molly,' John came in, realised what he had said, having just passed Isaac standing in the doorway, and immediately went silent.

'Molly's old enough to know what's best for her own life, John,' and, looking at Molly, 'We're both delighted for you, Molly. We hope you have a happy life together.' Eva looked towards Isaac, 'I'm sure we all hope that for you.'

The future of the family as a group of four people hung on Isaac's response.

Molly looked into her father's eyes, with an expectant half-smile on her face, 'You must have known about the man you've agreed to spend the rest of your life with, Molly. You could choose anyone you wanted. A lawyer. A doctor. A businessman. Instead, you've chosen a sad, pathetic womaniser, with delusions of grandeur. Didn't you know about his reputation? He'll ruin your life. You do know that, don't you?'

'You're talking about the man I've agreed to marry, Dad. The man I love. Please be happy for me.' Molly looked at all three of them ... 'All of you. Please.'

'I want no part of it.' Isaac left the room, and slammed the door.

They all heard the powerful roar of his Mercedes erupting into angry life.

John made for the door, leaving Eva to comfort a sobbing, hysterical Molly.

He felt an odd sort of nausea rising in his throat, struggling for breath.

John never managed to turn the door handle, as, at that moment, a pain with the force of a thunderclap from hell, hit the centre of his chest.

He didn't even have time to lift his hand from the doorknob to protect his own body.

Polish John was dead.

Polish John's funeral took place at the height of a sizzling Blackpool summer. Molly stayed over at the New Sands for the week.

Isaac pleaded unavoidable pressure of business for his absence.

Eva shed no tears. She immediately got on with arrangements for a funeral that was to resound in the annals of Blackpool history as marking the passing of one of the grand old town's magnificent eccentrics.

One of the mourners that day, walking in the procession alongside someone he knew as the plate-spinner from the Tower circus, casually remarked to him, 'Today marks the passing of our Blackpool – the real Blackpool.'

That night, inside Blackpool Tower, the majestic lion in the cage didn't bother to rise to his feet and pace by the bars when the mocking crowd approached. He just lay. Head resting on his giant paws. Resigned to his fate.

On his walk past the cage that night many years before, John had struggled to understand. Perhaps at that moment he now knew ...

Eva could not remember ever visiting a doctor since the days when she was a child, and her mother had lain awake with her for nights on end, as she fought the ravages of whooping cough, and 'survived only by the grace of God,' as her mother had continually reminded her well into adulthood.

Since Molly's marriage to Roderick, and their voyage to Australia and a new life, there were many times when Eva thought her loneliness would overwhelm her.

Working more hours than ever at the academy failed to assuage her plight.

Such was Eva's desperation at the onset of the dark winter nights, that she visited the doctor for a tonic, even though she mistrusted the efficacy of any kind of medical intervention, either professional or bogus.

The doctor had prescribed a pick-me-up, and also taken a routine range of tests.

Eva returned to him to tell him in terms that brooked no contradiction that his tonic had not worked.

When she sat down in the consulting room, the doctor noticed the slight tremor in her right hand, as she placed the bottle of tonic between them on the desk.

'I've got your test results back.' The doctor was formal and precise in his manner. There was a neat pile of prescription pads in front of him, and a stethoscope hanging from his neck. Eva looked at his immaculately manicured nails.

'How long have you suffered from hand tremor?' he asked coldly.

'Not long. A few months probably. At most.'

'I'm afraid your condition could indicate the onset of Parkinson's disease.'

Eva did not bat an eyelid. Did not ask a single question.

She just said, 'Thank you, doctor. I'll leave the bottle of tonic with you.'

She stood up, pushed her chair back under the desk, and left the surgery.

The doctor stared at the closed door after Eva had left.

He shrugged his shoulders.

He was thinking that never in his long medical career had he seen a patient so untouched by such devastating news.

Eva had known friends who had been diagnosed with the disease.

She had witnessed their deterioration.

She also knew it was often brought on as a result of shock. Never confirmed as such by the doctors of course. 'Too imprecise. Not scientific enough,' Eva told herself, as she walked home along the promenade, past the shadow of Blackpool Tower.

But shock it is. But, for Molly's happiness, a small price to pay.

Eva threw back her head and looked upwards. Towards the very top of Blackpool Tower, and began to laugh '...Isn't it, John?'

Backstage

And so, two of peacetime's children, Molly and Joe, began the new decade of the 1970s as married people. At the beginning of new chapters in their lives.

And, by a strange quirk of fate, they found their paths crossing, when they least expected it.

On the voyage to Australia.

Joe was walking along B deck of the S.S. Antipodean with his new wife, Lucy, and noticed the poster advertising that night's cabaret.

'The S.S. ANTIPODEAN PRESENTS AN ALL-STAR CABARET'

'FEATURING THE SINGING SENSATION ... MOLLY EARLE'

The glossy photographs of the glamorous singer stopped Joe in his tracks. The flaming red hair ... The vivid blue eyes ... He had to meet her ...

Joe and Lucy arrived early for the cabaret, and sat on the front row.

Molly was brilliant. Superb.

Joe was scarcely able to believe the woman he was watching was the same person as the girl from the Alley.

The urge to speak to her again was overwhelming.

The moment Molly's act had finished, Joe made his way backstage.

He felt apprehensive. 'I don't know where to begin ... my life's been so ordinary ... school ... a job ... and now on a search for adventure ... And she's been a big star during the same years.' He was having second thoughts and was on the point of turning round to head back into the cabaret room when something told him to wait. The three of them – Joe, Molly and Danny – had talked of their hopes. Their dreams. Children's fantasy talk. Pipe dreams. But for Molly they all seemed to have come true. And Joe was fascinated to know one thing from her; had it all been worth it? Was she happy? Fulfilled? If she said she was, it would in some way justify his own sacrifice, his yearning for adventure. Molly had proved that any achievement was possible. By anybody. Even three kids from an Alley in Blackpool.

And then Molly appeared.

At the far end of the passageway that led from the stage to the star's dressing room door.

Joe began to make his way down the passageway, when a thin, smartly-dressed man blocked his path. Joe noticed his odd hairstyle. Also that his face seemed familiar, but he couldn't quite place where he had seen it before. Although when he spoke, Joe recognised his voice. Select A Star. That was it.

'I'd like to have a word with Molly. I'm an old friend.'

'If it's an autograph you want, leave your name and cabin number and I'll make sure you get one. A signed photograph.'

'Just tell her Joe Flint was asking about her. Joe from the Alley. She'll understand.'

They both turned round and went their separate ways down the passageway.

Roderick Sterne never gave the message to his wife.

As far as he was concerned, from the day of their marriage Molly had severed all ties with her past.

During the rest of the long voyage to Perth, Joe looked for Molly as he walked along the decks. Looked to see if she was sitting in a deckchair by the rail. Reading or looking out to sea.

But, in the last few days before landfall at Perth, he finally gave up his search.

She's like an exotic flower, Joe thought, that can only blossom in the dark.

A tinge of sadness passed through him. A sudden awareness that, in those days in the Alley, their lives had been so simple.

Uncomplicated. No need then for Molly to be protected. Joe knew what she had lost in the years in-between, despite her wealth and fame she had lost the very thing he still had. Freedom.

In fact, in thinking this, Joe Flint's perception was far more accurate than he could possibly have imagined, for shortly after he had caught sight of the back of Molly Earle as she hurried down the passageway, she was unconscious in her dressing room; the result of an inflammable combination of cocaine and alcohol taken to contain her exploding nerve-endings following a violent row with Roderick after he had criticised her performance.

The honeymoon cruise of Mr and Mrs Sterne had become notorious for wild, after-show parties, attended by members of the crew and selected star-struck passengers, but without the knowledge of the ship's Captain.

The boisterous gatherings took place in the Sterne's luxurious suite and ran through from the moment the stage curtain was lowered until the serving of breakfast to the first sitting the following morning.

Roderick, as host, always ensured that conviviality was maintained undiminished throughout by lavishing on his guests copious quantities of succulent food and strong alcohol.

The surreptitious introduction of cannabis and cocaine was made during lulls in the proceedings, and offered only to those guests who appeared to be the most discreet.

Molly's objections to her husband's excesses were invariably met with a hostility which escalated into ferocious argument.

However, Molly's collapse that night proved to be a cathartic event, both for Molly and the marriage.

Her recovery, after medical attention, brought home the extent to which she had fallen in such a short time, both psychologically and emotionally, and she resolved to free herself from the drug and alcohol dependency that had dragged her down so far.

Roderick, for his part, after experiencing the fear that came from nearly losing his wife that night, began, for the first time since the day of their marriage, to give Molly the emotional support she had been craving and for need of which she had propelled herself headlong to the precipice of self-destruction.

Engagement Night

Danny intended to ask Faye to marry him on a moonlit night in Greece, after a romantic meal for two at a quiet secluded taverna.

He had bought the ring and booked their flights to Rhodes.

Danny had known she was the one from the night when the small, dark-haired girl with the soft brown eyes had accepted his offer to buy her a drink and had then come over to join him and his group of University friends at the table in the corner of the country pub.

Faye hadn't said a word that night amid the disconcerting hubbub made by his friends, but to Danny her diffidence only served to make him even more smitten with her.

He noticed the way she analysed his friends in a shy yet composed way that intrigued him, and increased his determination to make sure there would be only the two of them when they next met.

Over the three months after this first meeting, Danny had continued to remain unsure as to whether Faye shared his intensity of feeling.

On a moonlit night in Rhodes he would know for certain.

The misery of Danny's years at Abbey Grange had long ago faded into distant memory, and he now often thought that this period of his life had happened to someone else; particularly as his years at Sheffield University had been so carefree and fulfilling.

And he had met Faye.

He had graduated from University with an English degree and plans to begin a career as a journalist.

He had not had the heart to tell his parents he would never be fulfilling their plans and dreams for him to join them in the family business, and one day take it over. He had decided to postpone that task until the day it became unavoidable.

The holiday in Rhodes with Faye was idyllic.

On a first night of shimmering heat they strolled along the walled approach into Rhodes town, looking in the windows of tiny shops that lined the steep descending path leading to the ancient square.

They wiled away the long and languorous Greek night, drinking wine on a taverna terrace overlooking the square, watching the bustle and flurry of Greek nightlife.

The next day was a boat trip to Lindos, with a walk through the narrow, meandering white-walled streets, down to the bay, and then a donkey ride up the stony hillside path to the ruins on the summit.

It was a week of flawless enchantment. Sailing to a deserted monastery in the cool of the morning and then waiting for the crowds to disperse and leave them alone together on the island, to sit by rows of empty fishing boats on the deserted beach and watch together as the fine grains of sand filtered through their entwined fingers; a scene set against the magical backdrop of the sun setting below the distant islands.

The last day of the holiday had arrived too soon.

Danny hired a car for the day, at their hotel in Rhodes.

At dusk they pulled up outside a small, deserted taverna.

Neither Danny nor Faye had felt the need for conversation during the meal and the bottles of red wine. They were both re-running mental images of a glorious, carefree week.

Tomorrow they would be back home, and for Danny that meant decisions to be taken. How to tell his parents he was not going to be involved in the business; that instead he had decided to be a writer, a journalist, and had already been offered his first job; working as a reporter with a Sheffield evening newspaper.

But he also planned to tell them at the same time that he would be starting his new career as a married man; that Faye had consented to be his bride, and that they would shortly have a daughter-in-law in the family.

And, for them the best of all – there would be the prospect in the not-too-distant future that they would achieve their ambition – one that they had often teased him about; they would become grandparents.

Everything in Danny's life was now falling into place – in perfect synchronisation.

Both Danny and Faye were beginning to feel drowsy from the effects of the meal and the wine.

They decided to stretch out in the mouth of a cave at the far side of the beach.

They drifted off to sleep and awoke an hour later in a cave now in pitch-darkness. The only discernible lights were scattered dots from within the houses skirting the bay.

Danny had the disquieting feeling that the moment he had been planning and anticipating for so long was about to vanish, if he hesitated any longer.

Danny and Faye walked hand-in-hand from the gloom of the cave onto the beach. 'Faye, will you marry me? As soon as we get home, let's not wait. Please say yes.'

Faye looked tenderly into Danny's eyes, 'Yes, Danny. Of course. Yes.'

Danny took out the ring from his trouser pocket and placed it gently on Faye's finger. She let go of his hand and started to run towards the sea, lost in the ecstatic thrill of the moment, and wanting to capture it before it flew from her grasp forever.

Danny chased after her and they raced one another pell-mell towards the edge of the beach, Danny overtaking and shouting out a challenge for Faye to beat him in a swim to the first rock out to sea.

They plunged, fully-clothed, into the icy waters.

They started neck-and-neck, both swimming smoothly and rhythmically.

Then Danny pulled away with long, fast strokes.

The crescent-shaped moon was casting a thin beam of pale light ahead of them in the water. Danny slowed and pointed up to the stars in the night sky as Faye approached. She waved her left hand into the air to show him the new engagement ring. They burst into joyous laughter, as Faye then took the lead, teasing Danny to catch her.

Danny shouted a warning not to swim much farther out to sea, but his words drifted away into the eerie silence of the Greek night air.

The current of the water changed as Faye neared the rock, and the waves began to rise and swirl.

Danny saw Faye's right arm shoot upwards towards the sky and her body jerk upright.

She began to twitch and writhe, her thin frame shuddering violently, as though shot through with a charge of electricity.

He shouted to her to hold on. To stay calm.

But his words were lost.

He gained on her.

His chest throbbed, his arms and shoulders ached, with the extra effort needed to increase his speed against the rising current.

He feared to look ahead but knew he had to.

Only Faye's long brown hair was now visible above the waves.

But he reached her before her head was submerged beneath the water.

He spoke to her. Shouted her name. Over and over again as he began to drag her body along through the churning waters towards the shore.

They staggered from the sea and fell together on to the sands in a twisted, exhausted knot.

Danny retched as he rolled Faye over and tried to resuscitate her.

But he had known as he was pulling her through the waters that she was already dead.

Danny began to run.

He was consumed by a terrible anguish.

'If only I could have reached her a few seconds earlier.

If only I could get to that light at the bottom of the hill, someone might still be able to save her.

Might still be able to save us both.'

Frank and Sarah left Danny alone after his return home from Rhodes.

After the funeral.

They felt this was what he wanted from them. Needed from them.

Danny tried to occupy his every waking minute by activity. Any activity, no matter how futile.

He isolated himself and sought to subdue his crazed thoughts and divert them from the fateful moonlit night among the Greek hills.

The night he lost a wife. And a future.

As the months passed, Danny began to socialise again at night.

His friends became concerned at the extent of his drinking, and the increasing signs of erratic, unpredictable behaviour. However, they rationalised this as being a necessary part of the grieving process; a move away from his self-imposed seclusion, and could, therefore, be looked on, in one way, as his first steps on the road to recovery.

So they all left Danny to his own devices, and refrained from attempts at admonishment; and they especially encouraged him not to be alone on the night of the anniversary of his engagement to Faye.

The Cherry-Red Sports Car

As Danny opened the door of the George and Dragon he thought to himself that he had got through this night he had been dreading for so long. The anniversary of his engagement.

The heady mixture of the cold night air, the soothing influence of alcohol and the boisterous company of his friend Gordon Francis had dulled his painful thoughts, and, eventually, towards the end of the evening, taken them away. 'Perhaps, from tonight, even the nightmares will begin to fade, and I can start to dwell on just the happy times we shared,' Danny told himself consolingly as he strolled across the car park with Gordon.

'Don't you think you'd better let me drive?' Gordon said to Danny, attempting to reach for the car keys of Danny's beloved cherry red Spitfire two-seater, as he twirled them round the fingers of his right hand.

'You're not insured – and I'm fine.' Danny closed his fist around the keys. 'Don't worry about me. Tonight's the start of my new future.'

And, with that final assurance to his friend, they reached the car and stepped in.

Danny turned on the ignition and the car burst into life.

He over-revved the engine, crunched through the gears, and skidded through the entrance of the deserted car park with a screech of tyre rubber, out into the main road.

Gordon didn't seek to reprove Danny, as he knew from

experience the regard in which Danny held his own driving skills and his sensitivity to any hint of criticism.

In any event, he had always been too mild-mannered to confront anyone, especially Danny in a mood of repressed fury.

He merely gave Danny a cursory sidelong glance as he sped off at breakneck speed down the main road.

But a knot like a fist was forming in his stomach.

In that momentary glance Gordon had detected a look on Danny's face that told him the evening had far from exorcised his demons, and that they were now beginning to re-assert their grip on his tormented psyche.

Danny's driving became more reckless, and oncoming car headlights flashed angrily as the blast of screaming car horns rent the night air.

Gordon sensed that Danny was about to lose control completely, and he fought desperately, but unsuccessfully, from the passenger seat, to pull on the steering wheel to get the car out of the path of an oncoming car.

Danny was now on the wrong side of the road.

Gordon covered his face with the palms of his hands, as they careered through a red light ...

Danny's memories of Faye were now returning vividly and harrowingly.

Lacerating his mind. Tears were streaming down his cheeks.

He heard in the distance a whirring, insistent siren, and, glancing into the rear-view mirror, saw a flashing blue light ...

Danny accelerated through another red light, racking his throbbing brain to form a clear map of the area so he could escape his pursuer. But the siren gained on him. Came nearer ... and nearer ... until he could make out the outline of the following car in his mirror.

Danny made a last, despairing attempt to swerve off the main road into a side street, to lose the police car.

He veered sharply to the left and drove up on the kerb ...

His misted and confused mind could not distinguish in time the brick wall that loomed ahead ... He swerved and skidded ...

The moment of impact was horrific in its intensity.

The last thing Danny remembered was letting go of the

steering wheel and throwing his head downwards towards his knees. The movement saved his life but meant that the passenger side of the car crumbled into the face of the wall.

Gordon screamed pitifully before ... Silence ... His head lolled to one side.

Like a torn rag doll.

The steam from the radiator beneath the concertinaed car bonnet formed circles as it drifted upwards towards the frosty night sky.

The night echoed in its menace, as the engine of the police car cut to silence, and an eternity seemed to pass while the two policemen approached Danny's slumped, desolate figure lying across the steering wheel.

The first officer to reach the wreckage peered through the side window and began to tap insistently to rouse Danny, and, when he eventually raised his head, motioned to him to wind down the window.

Danny slumped back down in response, so the two officers opened the driver's door, and reached inside to help him out of the car.

Danny's crumpled form dropped in an eternity of agonizing slowness out on to the road.

They led Danny away to the police car. To the background static of the police radio, and the accompanying urgent, precise exchanges.

When questioned by the officers, Danny's mouth opened wordlessly in his doomed, contorted face.

Simultaneously, frenetic activity surrounded his crumpled shell of a once-adored cherry-red sports car.

It was five hours later when Gordon's twisted, lifeless body was winched through the cut-out hole in the roof of the tangled wreckage.

From behind the bars of a police cell, Danny's haunting scream cut chillingly into the stillness of the night.

Danny felt strangely serene as he stretched out his aching body along the narrow mattress of the police cell.

First had been the indignities of the body search.

Followed by the probing questions. And the clanging thunk of the keys in the lock of the bolted cell door.

He was now numb.

He had surrendered himself to whatever else fate may have in store for him.

Even the cold and the hunger had now ceased to pierce the suit of armour his brain had mercifully enclosed around his anguished thoughts.

Danny's mind was now seemingly locked, vice-like, in the grip of an irredeemable past. The unbounded future he had planned with Faye had been cruelly washed ashore on a desolate Greek beach.

His anaesthetised brain was now protecting him from any awareness of pain, but, at the same time, also not allowing him to single out those consoling recollections of Faye he was desperately seeking in order to comfort him in the extremities of his distress.

The lonely hours ticked by, minute by agonising minute, until, to the sound of birdsong drifting in through the bars of the cell to welcome in the dawning of a fresh new day, Danny was finally granted the merciful benediction of sleep.

The next morning Danny tried to force himself to think clearly.

The effects of alcohol had worn off, and the morning brought with it shafts of remorse for his own weakness that had resulted in the wanton manslaughter of a close friend.

He felt an urgent need to tell his father. Before the news leaked out. Before the local newspaper discovered the awful details.

As he thought this, Danny had to fight off an increasing feeling of panic.

He tried to focus his thoughts in some kind of positive, constructive way. To dig a clear new channel through the quagmire of his brain, so that fresh, clean water could begin to trickle along it.

Frank Lockwood was already in the police station. His first sight of his son told him Danny was beyond his help.

He began to ask himself unanswerable questions:

'Why has this happened? I gave my son the best start possible in life; he had the best of education while I was laying the foundations of a thriving business so he could step into my shoes when he had finished.

His life was mapped out for him. A seamless transition. He should have been unstoppable on the way to success. But now this, leaving me helpless. Impotent.

To come back from Greece and tell us he didn't want any part of the business, that he was going to work as a writer on a newspaper; and then turning down the job at the last minute – just to lie around at home, grieving for the girl, never wanting to let go of her. And this is the result...

What did we do wrong? We only ever wanted the best for our son.'

While engaged in this tortuous self-scrutiny, Frank's mind was simultaneously picturing the fall-out from the crash. The potential impact on Sarah, the business, and, potentially worst of all, on his own marriage ... Action was needed ... 'I can try to hush it up,' he said desperately to Danny, 'We have no alternative.'

'Leave it, Dad,' Danny said in reply, grabbing his father's arm as he walked off to ask to use the telephone. There was a frenzy in his appeal that stopped Frank dead in his tracks.

'It will only make things worse. Listen to me, please.'

'But I know people who can keep it quiet. People with friends in the right places, to sort out things like this. Leave it to me.'

But despite his attempt to give comforting words of hope, Frank ached for his son's pain.

He felt that the cruel tide of fate was sweeping Danny out to sea as remorselessly as it had carried away Faye.

'It has always been this way – from as far back as I can remember,' Danny said to himself, 'Even right back to primary school; my failure then, and being sent to private school to cover it up. Everything always made right. My world always being conveniently slotted away into the right compartment of the

Lockwood family box. Never allowed just to be me. My own person. An individual.'

Frank looked into his son's pained face, and knew this time he had to respect his wishes. For the moment. 'I can't use the old boy network to get him off the hook. At least not while I'm here with him.

I'll have to sort it out myself when I see Isaac again. And tell Danny afterwards,' Frank reasoned to himself. 'He'll be relieved. Grateful even. And then things will soon return to normal, and, before long, all this will be a distant memory; one which we'll never need to think about again.'

'We'll leave it for now,' Frank said to his son, stilling the fraught atmosphere that had sprung up between them, and feeling the tension begin to dissipate.

'Perhaps that was the moment when the breakdown started,' Danny told himself many times in the future after that morning. 'The final turn on the ratchet of my sanity and my buried sorrow. Another vicious throw of fate's dice.'

And so, Joe Flint and Molly Earle had arrived in the 1970s having driven on clear, hazard-free roads. They took wrong turnings along the way there, but always recovered their course and carried on straight ahead towards futures burnished with gleaming promise in Australia.

Danny Lockwood's road to the 70s was also straight and open at the start, but became strewn with potholes of broken dreams and roadblocks of shattered hopes.

And now ahead loomed a cul-de-sac.

Scoop

From the day Molly Earle set foot on Australian soil at the end of the cruise from England, to launch her transformation from teenage singing idol to sophisticated diva, the next ten years became the high-water mark of her career.

In this decade Molly developed into not only an accomplished performer but also became the epitome of celebrity chic in the public esteem and renowned worldwide for her outlandish displays of ostentatious self-promotion, behind which it was not difficult to detect the machiavellian hand of her husband.

Roderick Sterne had spent a lifetime searching for a raw, natural talent such as Molly's, that he could mould and then launch into the entertainment stratosphere and he now intended to capitalise on his opportunity to the utmost.

As she blazoned her unstoppable path across the footlights of arenas around the world, Molly grew to believe that Roderick possessed the Midas touch and that both her marriage and her career were unassailable.

Molly achieved her ambition of topping the bill at the London Palladium before she was thirty, with her grandmother Eva in the centre of the front row on her great night.

Roderick played the key role of masterminding Molly's career from behind the scenes, shielding himself from the glare of the public spotlight, whilst carrying out his role as negotiator of deals and signer of contracts.

And yet although Molly had now realised her aspirations – twice – as two distinct types of performer, nonetheless at times she felt strangely unfulfilled.

There were times when she yearned for the life she used to know and which had now vanished forever.

Molly felt there was now an aching void in her life in the place once occupied by Eva and John, which Roderick had been unable to fill.

The wide-eyed, red haired ingénue who had so bewitched Roderick on first sight at her audition, was still intrinsically the same entertainer who was now enrapturing audiences on both sides of the Atlantic, but with an added veneer of sophistication which Roderick's tutelage had given her.

But, as she now approached her fortieth year, the same gods who had singled out Molly for super-stardom, decided in their capricious wisdom that the time had arrived to exact retribution for the lavish gifts they had bestowed.

It began with a telephone call to Roderick from a police station in a seedy area of London surburbia, to tell him that his wife had been arrested for shoplifting. She had been accused of the theft of two bottles of vodka.

The fact that the Sterne's solicitor, 'the lawyer to the stars', as the tabloid press referred to Roddy Barber, subsequently managed to arrange for the charge to be quashed, important as this was to Molly and Roderick at the time, did not disguise the fact that the incident became significant in that it caused the first crack in their marriage and one which became too deep to be papered over.

Molly explained to Roderick the circumstances surrounding her arrest, and her innocence of the accusation. 'While in the aisle of the supermarket, I experienced a blinding headache, followed by an urge to panic and get out of the store.

At the check-out I must have left some items in the trolley when I pushed it through and not noticed them in my rush to load everything onto the conveyor belt, pack and pay as quickly as possible so I could get outside into the fresh air.'

Roderick had not asked why the vodka, so Molly was spared

for the time being from having to confess to her recent heavy drinking.

While she was explaining, her thoughts were flickering back to one particular night ... the horrific night her voice failed completely on stage.

Molly had stood rooted beneath the spotlight in abject terror while the conductor improvised an ending in order that she could run off the stage as the curtain came down to muted applause from the puzzled audience.

Molly looked back on this night as the one when her infatuation with performing turned into alarm and a need to have recourse again to the consolation of her vodka bottle. Before, as well as after performances.

Molly feared the bad old days were returning with a vengeance, but even at the height of this present anxiety, she refused to resort again to cocaine. And yet her dilemma was that she knew she still needed the support of an emotional crutch – something outside herself that could both give an edge to her performance and also re-establish her equilibrium following the high of performing. And she saw reflected in her vodka bottle the answer to her dilemma and one she believed, on its own, did not contain the inherent capacity for catastrophe that she encountered on the cruise to Australia. But her deepest fear lay in the knowledge that the demons within had not been exorcised and were determined to return.

Molly chose to put off telling Roderick of her new terrors – her voice worries, the stage fright, the return to drinking and just when she felt that the shoplifting incident had now provided her with the opportunity to unburden herself completely now that he knew about the headaches and the absent-mindedness in the supermarket, the telephone rang and the chance was lost.

Roderick walked over to answer it. He heard the gruff croaky voice of Des McIntosh, the editor of the Sunday Enquirer on the other end of the line. He told Roderick that one of his freelance paparazzi and a reporter from his paper had tailed Molly that morning and later called in at his office with incriminating photographs showing her being apprehended outside a supermarket and that the story was to be published in the next edition of the Enquirer.

The impact on Molly of seeing her private life splashed over the front page of one of Britain's biggest selling Sunday newspapers was shattering.

Amazingly, Molly's army of fans actually swelled in number after she appeared the following week on the nation's favourite Saturday night chat show, and broke down sobbing in response to questions about the shoplifting affair, which she announced had been a misunderstanding for which the supermarket had apologised. She began to catalogue in graphic terms the plethora of problems that had assailed her since the day she had stepped into the limelight and become a public figure, and fair game for a media determined to hound her day and night by inspecting and dissecting her every move, however trivial, and offering it up for public titillation.

To the astonishment of the dumbfounded interviewer, Molly held back nothing. Having been denied the opportunity to explain everything to Roderick by the interruption of the fateful telephone call, she now opened up her soul to an incredulous television audience of millions. An audience who for decades had been spoon-fed threadbare banalities under the guise of showbiz revelation.

The switchboard at the television studios was jammed for several hours following the programme, with each caller expressing total support for Molly and her treatment at the hands of a callous tabloid press.

The next morning Molly was front and back page news on all the Sunday tabloids, including the Enquirer which printed an ingratiating public apology for the misguided actions of its reporter and photographer in trailing Molly Earle and impinging on her private life without justification.

When buttonholed by Roderick at breakfast-time, in answer to his demand to know why the whole nation knew more about his wife than he did, Molly regarded him with one of her faraway gazes; a practised look induced by several furtive, early morning vodka martinis, tossed back her hair and walked out of the kitchen.

Molly's chat show performance did for Bob Brewer, the Sunday Enquirer photographer, and Jimmy Evans, his sidekick reporter on the Molly Earle story.

Evans' career was torpedoed below the waterline by the extent of the vilification launched on the Enquirer in its readers' letters pages, and the plummeting sales of the newspaper over the ensuing weeks of the Molly Earle exclusive.

Bob Brewer was forced to return to the local paper on which he had started his photographic career ten years earlier.

In the circumstances of the public furore he had started and the opprobrium he had caused to his ex-employer, he felt relieved to find gainful employment of any description and made a particular point at his interview with the Reading Herald of asking the Editor to respect his wish for anonymity when publishing any of his photographs.

And never ever send him to a scoop.

Cruelly and paradoxically for Molly, as her drinking began to spiral out of control, the stirring dramatics which were an indispensable part of her stage performance, began to lose their impact to the stage when it needed only a slight nudge to tip her completely over the edge.

The downfall occurred on the first night of a one-month booking at the West End's chic Flying Flamingo cabaret club.

The plush nightspot was a popular haunt of well-heeled Londoners and was regularly frequented by such luminaries as the Chancellor of the Exchequer, the England football captain and minor publicity-conscious members of the Royal family.

Molly had rarely performed at her best in milieux such as the Flying Flamingo; her preference had always been for large theatres in which she could ignite a vast audience with a Rolls Royce combination of power and subtlety that had become the hallmark of a Molly Earle performance. And, afterwards, delight in the hero worship of her travelling legions of fans with whom she could reminisce over past glories, while she obliged every request for a personally signed autograph or posed photograph.

When Molly topped the bill at a small intimate venue, even one of world renown such as the Flying Flamingo, she always felt the need to draw upon inner reserves to overcome an unnatural inhibition that seemed to invade her.

Molly had been feeling such a customary tension in the build up to her opening night.

Rehearsals had been a struggle, and she had needed to take long periods of rest in the afternoons and evenings. This was always facilitated by slugs of vodka martinis to wash down the sleeping pills she felt were essential to unwind the tightness and ease herself into sleep.

Relations with Roderick had been strained since the time of the Enquirer episode.

Molly's behaviour had been growing more extreme and they were now sleeping apart, because of her continual thrashing about and moaning, which had led to her attempts at sleep becoming a nightly return to an existence in a personal purgatory.

Roderick had begun to go missing from the theatre for long periods in the afternoons and, on his return, always refused point blank to discuss his whereabouts. In any event, Molly was usually in no fit state to enter into confrontations with a husband who she was becoming increasingly convinced no longer cared for her.

The moment she opened her eyes on the day of her first appearance at the Flying Flamingo, Molly crushed her headache pills into a large tumbler of vodka and stirred with her finger, and continued in this vein until an hour before she was due on stage.

Roderick was absent during the day on his usual covert activities and returned only moments before the opening of the doors to an audience of specially invited celebrities.

Roderick came backstage and entered Molly's dressing room to discover her staggering round and colliding with the furniture, her make-up smeared across her face.

He walked over, gripped her by the shoulders, and shook her violently, 'Molly, do you hear me? Sober up. You're on stage in half an hour.'

'I'm fine. Have you been enjoying yourself?' Molly tottered towards Roderick, glass in hand, struggling to keep him in focus.

He dragged her by the right arm towards the shower, turned

on the powerful blast of cold water, and pushed her fully-clothed into its full blast.

Roderick shouted at her through the noise of rushing water, 'Did you rehearse today?'

'No. I needed to rest. Don't worry. I'll be fine,' replied Molly, propping her throbbing head against the tiled wall of the shower and letting the steaming warmth of the water ooze luxuriatingly down her back.

The following burst of icy water cleared her head and she briskly towelled down, feeling reinvigorated.

Molly sat down at the dressing table and began to prepare herself. When she had finished, not even the most vitriolic of the newspaper critics among the first night audience would have been able to describe her appearance as other than breathtaking, in his following morning's reviews.

Molly's performance on stage that night was scintillating.

Until the middle of the big number that closed the first half of the show. Then, inexplicably, she froze.

The first night orchestra was not able to extemporise in time to cover up Molly's plight, so she began to invent lyrics, just to break the silence, and the song then became rambling and tuneless.

And then she tripped over the lead of her microphone.

She shrieked with loud, cackling laughter as she lurched unsteadily back to her feet.

The flabbergasted audience shuffled and coughed in embarrassment.

Roderick was standing in the wings, transfixed with horror at the sight of his wife – his superstar protégé - disintegrating in front of his eyes.

'Bring down the curtain. Now,' he screeched at the stage hands.

Roderick ran on stage and led a stumbling Molly to her dressing room, where she collapsed face down and unconscious across the chaise longue in the centre of the room.

He walked over to the telephone and dialled the number of a nearby West End theatre where a young understudy singer in the current London hit musical was standing backstage, watching the first half performance.

The seductive Rita Gonzalez had recently received a string of rave reviews when she had been forced to take over the lead role in the show from the star who had been summoned home to Los Angeles to see her critically ill father who was in a coma following a road crash.

'Rita – you're needed – right away – at the Flying Flamingo. I've ordered a cab.' The instruction came from the theatre manager, who had just put down the telephone after speaking to Roderick.

He had been seeing a lot of Roderick lately, and had been wondering why he was taking such an interest in his theatre's production when he should have been fully occupied at the Flying Flamingo.

Rita arrived at the club and was directed to the star's dressing room.

Roderick was standing in the open doorway waiting for her arrival.

She ran into his welcoming embrace.

'You're closing the second half – tonight – and for the rest of the month,' Roderick whispered into her ear breathlessly. 'Change into your costume.' He pointed to the wardrobe by the far wall.

Rita stood with a stunned look on her face.

'They might not fit me,' the pencil-slim Rita spoke excitedly, as she drew apart the wardrobe doors, and gazed spellbound at the dazzling assemblage of glamorous garments displayed on the rack in front of her.

Parkers

Roderick dropped Molly off at the door of Parkers with her two large suitcases and left her standing there. In the rain. He had leaned across and opened the door of his dark blue Daimler from the inside and gestured to her to step out on to the gravel driveway.

Roderick did not want to risk being spotted by the paparazzi who had been known to lurk behind the giant conifers that lined the sweeping driveway of the exclusive London clinic, in the expectation of snapping a celebrity.

But, also, he had reasoned, apart from an understandable desire for anonymity, he did not feel it necessary to feel guilty about not accompanying his wife inside the premises, as he had already made prior arrangements over the telephone with the manager for Molly to stay at Parkers for an indefinite duration, to be concluded only at their discretion. So there was nothing further to be gained by his staying longer than necessary. She was now out of his hands.

Molly shambled up the steep stone steps, a suitcase in each hand.

She didn't turn to look at the Daimler as it drove away.

She laid the suitcases at her feet and struggled to turn the big brass doorknob.

A nurse in a crisp white uniform opened the heavy door from the inside and stood aside to allow Molly to pass, welcoming her affably as Molly walked on towards the reception desk, not turning to respond as the nurse closed the door and came alongside her.

'Hello, you must be Molly. I'm Jane. Let me take those.' Jane lifted up the two suitcases, and carried them over to the reception desk.

Molly still did not answer.

Nurse Jane, who considered herself unshockable fought back an overwhelming urge to retch, and managed to sustain her fixed, professional, welcoming smile.

Molly was a glitzy, glamorous star no more.

She now had the unmistakeable appearance and odour of a down-and-out.

Jane was the first point of call in Parkers processing system.

Her manner was jovial and no-nonsense, and contrasted sharply with the dreary shabbiness of the décor in reception, with its peeling wallpaper and stain-encrusted chair. She tried to recall a previous occasion when a patient had arrived unaccompanied but was unable to think of a single one.

The manager had left details of the morning admissions before his staff came on shift, and Jane thought, on first sight of Molly that she must have misread the admissions form. The details page had shown 'entertainer' in the occupation space and Jane was anticipating the usual rich, pampered celebrity type who returned to Parkers at predictably regular intervals, in order to boost a flagging career, with a few weeks stay at the renowned clinic providing the publicity impetus of a page one exclusive in the tabloids, and a place back in the forefront of public awareness.

Parkers, over the years, had become uniquely qualified to validate the time-worn adage that 'all publicity is good publicity.'

Such recidivist personalities would invariably indulge themselves in a personally tailored programme of meditation and massage, interspersed with speeches at group support meetings, followed by autograph-signing sessions for fellow patients in the exotic garden courtyard. And all this at the same cost to the celebrity as a stay at a luxury hotel, but with an attendant media hype of incalculable dimensions.

Also, as Parkers' clientele of famous personages increased, so also did its reputation burgeon, and it became 'the place to go', and then announce as widely as possible that you had been, not only for the stars, but also for those well-heeled members of the general public who were feeling either addicted, or burnt-out from any one or more item on an extensive menu of over-work, over-eating, over-drinking, over-drugging, over-worrying, over-relating with people other than a spouse, and a correspondingly countless variety of 'under'-related problems.

The entire à la carte ensuing, in fact, from nothing worse than the condition of being alive, along with everyone else.

But on that morning, as she looked into Molly's dark-rimmed, haunted eyes, and Molly looked back with a lost and distant smile, Nurse Jane's preconceptions were swept away.

Just for a fleeting instant, Jane saw just a human being who had lost her way, pleading in desperation to another human being to lead her out of the blackness of the pit into which her tortured mind had tragically stumbled.

Molly reached behind her head and untied the knot of her headscarf. Her unwashed hair tumbled over her gaunt cheekbones. The hair with the famed resplendent red glow that had once been her emblem was now long, straight and dank. Shapeless. Faded into a nondescript mousiness.

Jane sat Molly down in the chair by the reception desk. Molly put her tiny black handbag on her knee, flicked open the gold clasp, and began rummaging absent-mindedly among the contents '...This was a present from Eva ... my Nan ... lives in Blackpool,' Molly said, to no-one in particular, and carried on rummaging. Jane smiled, 'That's nice ... won't be long now, Molly.'

Nurse Jane took her blue biro out of the top pocket of her uniform, and began ticking the boxes on the pink admissions form. She was categorizing Molly. She dashed boxes A and B, the ones she normally ticked immediately an 'entertainer' breezed through the double doors.

Box A allocated the patient for an initial examination and assessment by the duty doctor, to be followed the next morning by Box B – prescribed treatment, and recommended duration of stay by the appropriate consultant.

Jane had assessed Molly differently.

Her pen moved immediately and swiftly down the form to Box C – immediate admission to Special Care Ward.

This was a large, modern room bathed in bright fluorescent light, situated on he ground floor. Away from stairs and windows.

New intakes were accommodated in a separate purpose-built corner room of the ward for the first week, and then, if progress was satisfactory, moved into the shared main ward.

Nurse Jane had a particular reason for her decision to categorize Molly as a C. When Molly had passed her the two suitcases she had noticed deep cuts on her right arm, close to the wrist, and a large round burn mark on the left arm.

Jane's nursing colleagues at Parkers had always admired her for the meticulous approach she brought to her duties. The more acerbic ones had commented that it bordered on obsessiveness.

In any event they were all agreed on one thing. Nurse Jane was the ideal person to run the reception desk.

Nurse Brenda arrived and led Molly by the arm the short distance along the corridor to the small room of the special care ward.

Molly sat down on the narrow single bed.

She opened her handbag again, and took out an old dog-eared photograph. Her head was feeling too fuzzy to question why the door had been left open. Or why a nurse was sitting guard by it.

Molly held the photograph up close in front of her eyes. It was of a little girl with her father. She was holding a thistledown stem. Molly pressed the photograph against her face, and tears slowly began to trickle down her cheeks. The nurse on guard craned her neck around the door and saw the new intake making a silent blowing motion with her pursed lips pressed against the photograph. The nurse wasn't in the least surprised.

After all, she told herself, you can expect all sorts on 'suicide ward'.

After Molly had eaten her tea, alone in the room, she was given the routine medication for a new intake to the Special Care Ward.

She then drifted into a deep sleep.

In her dream she was sitting on the front row of an audience in a vast theatre, with Eva, John, her grandfather, and her father Isaac.

She was watching herself on the stage. She was wearing her most glamorous, spangled, figure-hugging costume. She sang a medley of her hit songs. The audience rose to its feet in a rapturous explosion of cheering and applause.

Molly looked beyond the spotlight, and the faces in the middle of the front row mutated into herself and her friends, Joe, and Danny, playing in the Alley in Blackpool on a summer's afternoon, long ago.

Just as she was thinking how carefree the three young faces looked, each of them changed ... one by one ... each smile became a demonic, taunting sneer. Molly peered into the blackness of the front row, attempting to substantiate who the monsters were ... they had become Roderick ... with his arm around a young slim, blonde-haired woman ... and ... herself ... standing apart from the two of them ... and the cabaret room had become her dressing room.

Molly's whole body was soaked with perspiration, as she flung herself from side to side, slinging the sodden bedclothes on to the floor. Her brain told her to wake up, to sever the insidious horror out of her seething head before it embedded its unyielding roots of treachery. But another part of her brain was demanding that she see the nightmare through to its end.

Then this three-person tableau in the forefront of her mind began to slowly move ... to change position ... hideous apparitions beckoning her to join them in the realm of the damned. Molly could see herself rising from the sofa in the dressing room, her head had cleared from its drunken stupor and Roderick and Rita were standing before her ... Molly noticed that Rita was wearing Molly's favourite black, spangly, sequined costume. Roderick was speaking ... not to her ... to Rita ... the same words he always said to Molly before she went on stage ...

'Go out there and knock 'em dead, kid…' Roderick walked over and closed the door behind Rita as she ran off down the corridor to captivate the waiting audience … Molly was now alone with Roderick … he turned to face her, and she recoiled at his twisted, malevolent expression of disdain. 'As for us – we're finished…' and he walked out, slamming the door … Molly was left alone … frightened … and then Eva walked in … and held Molly in her arms, and began stroking her hair … 'Oh, Molly, our little Molly … how could he do this to you?' Molly saw herself looking up into her grandmother's face. 'Take me home, Nan … please take me home.'

Molly woke from her nightmare, and lay motionless on the bed. Afraid to move. Waiting for the fiends to retreat from her frenzied brain. And then the realisation hit her. She was alone. No Eva. No happy ending. The grotesque torment was not a figment of her pitiable, psychotic mind. It was her reality. Real life. Now.

Molly felt the upsurge of a sudden glacial conviction.

She reached down to the side of the bed and lifted up her handbag. She reached into the corner of the bag and moved her fingers to distinguish the shape of the metal object she had painstakingly secreted. She spoke to herself in the pitch blackness of the tomb in which she imagined she was encased '…I knew that nurse wouldn't find them … the same way Roderick never found my hidden vodka bottles.'

Molly sprang from the bed and gripped the nail scissors tightly in the fingers of her right hand … she exposed the veins of her left wrist … she drew back her right hand … blood spurted upwards and Molly screamed … an appalling wail that rose up from the depths of her being.

The nurse ran in, and pulled Molly's arms behind her back. The scissors dropped to the floor. Molly collapsed … and then dropped into blissful blackness as she looked up at the shadowy figure in the long white coat looming over her head. She felt the stab of the needle easing its merciful way into her right arm … the screeching in her head slowly drifted down into the fathomless reaches of her mind.

Over the next few weeks Molly's treatment at Parkers began to be successful.

The night-time deliria began to diminish, and, eventually to evaporate, into the safe enclaves of her mind.

After two weeks in the isolation ward, she was moved into the main ward. Molly didn't speak to the four other women in the ward for three weeks. Just ate her meals. Looked lovingly at her photograph, and between times drifted soporifically into a comforting land suffused with nostalgia.

Molly never had a visitor. Roderick had told no-one of his wife's deterioration that had resulted in her admission to Parkers.

Molly would look longingly, with a tender knowing smile at the other women in the ward after their visitors had left and peep over her blankets to try and see the presents they had unwrapped and placed on their wooden bedside cabinet.

She wondered why Eva hadn't been to see her.

What a triumph she would have if the others could only see her grandmother. Her own personal visitor.

After a month on the shared ward, the doctors and nursing staff, at their weekly meeting decided it was time for Molly's detoxification programme to be intensified, and, at the same time, for her to take the first steps in joining the larger world at Parkers.

Over the next few months Molly became the chief talking point at most of the staff meetings.

None of the staff had witnessed a recovery to compare with Molly's.

She led the women's daily group support meetings, and became in increasing demand to give motivational talks to new intakes.

She drew on her past life to tell them about arriving in Australia as a new bride ... and then how her heart had soared when she first caught sight of the Statue of Liberty as she sailed into New York ... and then her two lifelong dreams coming true on he same night - her grandmother watching her at the London Palladium ... how she had given the performance of her life that night ... had held the audience in the palm of her hand ... spellbound ... on the stage of the most famous theatre in the world ... and the moment her Nan had run up to the footlights at the end and reached up to hand her a bouquet ... tears were streaming down her cheeks.

Molly always took most of the morning to prepare herself for her talks. She wanted to ensure that she set an immaculate example in appearance and presentation to her audience.

Many of the watching patients assumed Molly was under treatment for extreme delusional fantasies, and was probably in need of increased medication, but, nonetheless, they listened in rapt fascination, as each of them could recognise a star performer when they saw one.

Molly still possessed the panache to beguile an audience.

God had protected her magic.

Four months had passed since the day Molly had walked through the doors of Parkers.

The October agenda of the staff meeting showed that Molly was item number one for group discussion.

Discharge was recommended. As priority. Unanimously.

Molly was singing to herself as she walked through the double entrance doors.

She tossed her headscarf into the waste paper basket by the reception desk and ran her fingers through her glowing, red, bouncing hair.

Molly put up her hand to shield her eyes as she stepped out into the dazzling sunshine of a majestic autumnal day.

On that morning even the sun itself was at risk of being outdazzled.

Point Walter

AN AUSTRALIAN DIARY
December 1970

The cab driver drove Joe and I out to Point Walter – beyond the Perth city area.
Everything passed in a blur of contrasting images. A host of new sensations that assailed the senses each passing second.

Point Walter Hostel

Instant Impression
The shock of arriving at an open, treeless, dusty wasteland.
Row upon row of corrugated-roofed huts, all surrounded by a perimeter fence of barbed wire. A forbidding aspect everywhere you looked.
To come to this after three weeks being cosseted and indulged in the tranquillity of an ocean liner. Joe says 'What do you expect for ten quid assisted passage?' followed by 'I expect to get some change after seeing this little lot.'

Meal Times

Meals in a self-service cafeteria the size of an aircraft carrier.

Sitting on hard wooden benches at long wooden tables, amid a chaotic, cacophonous intermingling of nationalities all around us: English, Greek, Italian – Joe says we'll be fine as long as we don't come across any Scots; evidently a joke to do with after the World Cup when they sat on the crossbar at Wembley and then dug up the pitch. I just smiled at him without comment. Daft sod.

I can't seem to get him to appreciate the seriousness of our predicament. In fact, I'm beginning to think he might actually like it here, and prefers it to the ship, when he seemed to be miserable most of the time. Peculiar man.

Takes all sorts, I suppose.

Living Quarters

Ours are in a large wooden hut set apart from the main grouping of small huts, and at some distance from the aircraft hangar.

Rows of single and double beds along each wall, separated by a canvas curtain down the centre of the room, and from each other by a wooden partition.

Only furniture is a small wooden cabinet by each bed.

Luggage stored underneath and alongside the bed.

The Perth Hilton this isn't.

Washing and Toilet Facilities

A long walk away, along a well-worn dusty path, to an isolated building by the far perimeter fence. Rows of cubicles, washbasins and showers, and a handful of baths.

Our first purchases in Australian dollars have been a portable radio and a map of Australia.

Whenever we switch on the radio it seems to be

playing one of the same two songs: either Neil Diamond's Cracklin' Rosie, or Montego Bay, don't know who by.
The music from the radio merges seamlessly into the daily hubbub of multinational jibber-jabber.
If the main purpose of this place is to motivate people to move out and begin their new lives as a matter of urgency, by not providing home comforts, then it could not have been designed better, and no doubt Point Walter achieves its objective with flying colours, and is the flagship of the Australian Department of Immigration.

Joe has been keeping his feelings to himself recently, but I think he is concerned that I am homesick, although I try not to let him see when I am feeling unhappy, which lately has been most of the time.
We need to get away a.s.a.p.
Joe said yesterday that he is rounding up a group of Brits to form an escape committee.
Some official from the Department of Immigration called yesterday to give a talk on 'Your new life in Australia after Point Walter – all you need to know and do' – One look around the audience would have told him his words were falling on receptive ears.

Tonight we decided to use our savings of four hundred dollars to buy a second-hand Volkswagen Combi van.
We spread out our Australia map across the bed and Joe traced his finger along the journey we plan to take – from Perth, across the Nullarbor Plain; then the ferry from Melbourne across the Bass Strait to Tasmania.
We are going to be apple pickers.
Point Walter will soon be a distant memory.

The Nullarbor

THE NULLARBOR

January 1971

Today we left Point Walter.
Our pale green battered old Combi is our life support from today on.
A thin floral curtain divides the driver's seat from the back of the van, with its small sink and concealed cupboards.
There is enough room to stretch out in the back; so we will be able to take turns to have a sleep.
We have a jerry can filled with our reserve supply of petrol, and have it propped up in the back, between our suitcases and rucksack.
We have a portable ice box, and have bought enough supplies to live frugally for a week; we can cook meals on our hot plate.
Our new life will be basic and bohemian.
But we have never felt happier.
We now realise why we have come all this way.

We soon left behind the civilisation of Perth and its skyscrapers fringing the sparkling blue Swan River.

The smooth, fast surface of the Great Eastern Highway led us out of the city.
As daylight faded we passed through isolated country towns, with wide streets, a handful of stores, a few shuttered, red-roofed bungalows, and a single-pump petrol station.
We parked off the road at night. Indescribable sunsets of changing shades; from deepest red to palest pink; before total blackness and silence.
Woke each day to a vast majestic emptiness of biblical dimensions. Overhead: huge, clear, encircling skies of brilliant blue. Underfoot: an endless expanse of red soil, broken by outcrops of scrub and saltbush, twisted gum trees, stunted and skeletal eucalyptus.
A timeless landscape sucked dry of life by a remorseless sun.
One morning, a baby wallaby hopped up to the van. I kneeled to feed him a few scraps of food.
After the famed gold town of Kalgoorlie, the desert plain began.
The road became a rutted and pot-holed track.
It was like driving across an enormous corrugated iron roof, rattling and jarring the van's suspension.
As the hours pass and the sun rises overhead, there is now not even the occasional country town, only the odd forlorn roadhouse to break up the wilderness.
Groups of kangaroos appear from nowhere and bound along by the side of the van.
We share the driving – through days of unrelenting heat.
The single dirt track disappears ahead of us into a shimmering pinpoint in the far distance – a point we never reach along the interminable gun-barrel straight highway.
An occasional dust-encrusted truck passes within a hairs-breadth of us, a driver's hand pressed up against the windscreen in greeting – and instantaneously vanishes in a billowing shower of red dust.

At the end of eight days of this, and eking out our meagre rations, we are feeling as desiccated as the forbidding, baking landscape around us.
We are consumed with a terminal lethargy.
And then – we see a speck of blue in the distance, which beckons us on as it grows larger and larger as we approach.
The end of the journey is in sight.
We have reached the sea. The Great Australian Bight.
The track soon becomes a road again – the Flinders Highway into South Australia … through Streaky Bay … Anxious Bay … Coffin Bay … to Port Lincoln on the Spencer Gulf.
Now there is water everywhere in view. We can't take our eyes off it.
We have crossed the Nullarbor.
That night we stepped from the van and looked out to sea, letting the sight of the waves wash away the heat and the dust from our thoughts.
We can now head on to Adelaide – and then Melbourne, and the ferry to the apple orchards of Tasmania.

The Woolly Fleece

A TASMANIAN DIARY

January 1971

How refreshingly different Tasmania seems to the Nullarbor and mainland Australia.
A green and lush island with blue ranges of hills and distant mountain peaks never seemingly out of sight.
We have driven down the island and are now in the south-east corner, near Hobart. Close to apple-picking country.
I am writing today's diary from the front seat of the Combi.
Joe is fast asleep in the back.
We are at the foot of Mount Wellington; we walked to the top today.
After so much interminable flat, arid scrubland only a week ago, it was strange to be climbing towards the top of a snow-capped mountain, along steep tracks which meandered among dense green pine forests, and alongside tiny streams glistening in the soft morning sunlight.

I am writing this two days later.
In the kitchen of the Woolly Fleece hotel in Swan Vale, a tiny town in the Heron Valley.
Yes! We have left the confines of the Combi for the first time since Point Walter.
The intoxicating aroma of steak and eggs, and percolating coffee is wafting towards me at this very moment as I write.
We are about to have a traditional Woolly Fleece breakfast before setting off to find work as apple pickers.
The Woolly Fleece is not a conventional hotel in any sense whatsoever, as will shortly become apparent.
We are in the heart of rural Tasmania, and I must record the events of the past 24 hours while they are still fresh in my mind, to show how different life here is to anything we know at home.
To set the scene:
Swan Vale is a small country town with a population of 500, in the Heron Valley – the most famous apple-growing district in Australia.
The area is spectacularly pretty.
On the drive here, all around were meadows and rolling hills, in every lush shade of green, with herds of cows grazing on the tall grasses; and tiny hamlets scattered along the way.
Swan Vale is so sleepy and old-fashioned, and seems to be permanently bathed in the sweetest bright sunlight.
We were given the last room in the only hotel in Swan Vale when we arrived late yesterday afternoon.
The Woolly Fleece was the first building we came to on Swan Vale's main street – an imposing black and white cross-beamed building that would not have been out of place alongside the River Avon.
From the dazzling heat of the afternoon, the interior of the hotel was welcomingly cool and shady.
The locals, attired in stained white singlets and

battered bush hats, were drinking ice-cold schooners of beer, lined up along the bar; with swirling clouds of cigarette smoke drifting upwards towards the clanking fan cooler in the centre of the ceiling.

We encountered our landlady, Maria, at dinner-time, when, in the middle of our meal, she barrelled through the door, and came crashing and careering among the tightly-packed tables, in breathless pursuit across the dining-room, of a gaggle of squawking and flapping geese, just escaped from the hotel yard.

The landlord, Rupert, Maria's husband, made his appearance in no less dramatic fashion, just before bedtime, when he was summoned to the upstairs bathroom by a distraught elderly female guest, wearing dressing gown and with hair in curlers, pointing in wide-eyed, open-mouthed horror, towards the toilet - at a spider emerging threateningly from below the rim.

'No worries, mate – she's a redback,' said Rupert insouciantly, 'Get them regularly this time of year. Leave her to me. You get yourself off to your room.'

Rupert then told us, with worryingly excessive glee, how 'over a dozen people had died in Australia in the past year from redback spider bites,' and that, 'the Woolly Fleece is long overdue a funnel-web spider – the world's most poisonous insect, mate – makes the redback look tame, with its single bite causing seizure, turning blue, and death – all in the blinking of an eye. And its Aussie, too. One of our very own. Fair dinkum.'

Not surprisingly, Joe and I did not get to sleep easily after that, especially as we then came to bed and did not get to see the fate of the redback at Rupert's hands. And, this morning, I was particularly reluctant to use the toilet, as I had told myself during the night that at least Joe was able to stand up, and then, if need be, make a run for it, if it turned out that Rupert had decided to leave the redback where it was as a talking point with future guests.

When we were in Hobart we bought a small, battery tape recorder, to record messages to send home; so this will be my last diary entry for some time, as, after today, we intend the complete record of our travels to be a combination of my diaries to date, plus tapes. We may even write a book someday, who knows?
I'll take the diary up to the start of our new jobs. If we get them.
That seems as good a place as any to take a break.

Bye for now
Lucy
P.S. Wish us luck today.

In the Orchard

Joe Flint drove the Combi to the Billy Forrest orchards in the secluded southern corner of the Heron Valley.

After an hour meandering along the tree-lined lanes with the heady aroma of apple-scented air from the surrounding orchards drifting on the afternoon breeze through the open windows, he brought the van to a halt at a line of tractors and pick-up trucks parked against a hedgerow.

Joe and Lucy left the parked van and walked through a gap in the hedge, to find themselves in a vast orchard with apple trees, large and small, stretching as far as the eye could see, into the sweeping dip of a broad vale of deep green grazing land in the far distance.

Giant ladders were positioned amongst the groves of apple trees.

The Flints walked over to the nearest tree, and, peering upwards, at the soles of a battered old pair of hiking boots, resting on the top rung of a rusty metal ladder, Joe called up, 'We're looking for Billy Forrest.'

The hiking boots descended the ladder, and a wiry man of Joe's height jumped down from the bottom rung, and squinted at Joe from a wrinkled, walnut-like face, which was topped by an old khaki-coloured bushman's hat.

He was immediately assailed by a swarm of flies that appeared from the lower reaches of the tree. He shook his head violently from side to side, blew out from his mouth and nose, and began slapping his sallow cheeks.

'Looks like you've found him, mate,' he answered in a slow, laconic Australian drawl.

'And who might I be talking to?'

'I'm Joe Flint. And this is my wife, Lucy.'

Billy Forrest and Lucy nodded and smiled at each other.

Lucy was unsure what protocol she should adopt: whether shaking hands was appropriate in such a setting. So she decided against it.

Billy Forrest certainly didn't intend to; he dropped his dark brown, canvas apple-picking sack, full to the brim with shiny green Granny Smiths, on to the grass by his feet, and plunged his hands into the pockets of his black corduroy pants.

The rest of the picking gang had stopped working. The sight of any female, let alone one of Lucy's undoubted allure, setting foot into the hallowed south orchard was an event of such fascination as to preclude any further activity.

Joe was the first to speak, after what had seemed like an eternity of communal microscopic examination, 'They told us in Hobart you were looking for apple pickers.'

'Can you start now?' Billy Forrest asked the question, and immediately spoke to the man alongside him, without waiting for an answer, 'Lew, give 'em two sacks.' He turned back to Joe and Lucy, 'Ten dollars a person a day. That do yer? Eight till six. Plus packing at night in the shed if you want it. Seven-thirty to nine-thirty. Time and a half.'

Joe and Lucy agreed. They picked up the canvas sacks, clipped them round their shoulders, and went to work; under Lew's supervision.

At six o'clock they leaned wearily against a tree in a now-deserted orchard.

Billy Forrest approached, 'Where are you two staying?'

'We sleep in the Combi. But last night we stayed in Swan Vale. At the Woolly Fleece,' Lucy answered.

'Bloody good gaff, the Woolly Fleece. Finest in 'Stralia.

Biggest spiders you'll find in a month of Sundays – live on left-over steak and eggs.' A trace of a wry smile stole across Billy Forrest's sun-weathered face, and he gave a slow wink at Lucy.

'I've got a pickers' cottage up on the hill. Empty at the moment. Goes with the job.' Billy lifted his bush-hat and wiped beads of sweat from his forehead. He pointed into the distance, 'Yours if you want it. Just say the word.'

Joe and Lucy glanced at each other with a look which signalled to Billy that they were keen to accept his offer.

'I'll drive you up there. You can pick up your van later.'

The cottage was isolated on a hilltop at the end of a steep, stony path, with a panoramic vista that encompassed in one glorious expanse the sweep of the valley below, with the orchards a tapestry of contrasting greens that blended exquisitely into the glittering blue waters of the river Heron.

They were entranced and speechless.

Billy stood by the front door, 'Make yourselves at home. The door's not locked. We don't need keys in this part of the world. See you both tomorrow morning. Eight sharp. At the west orchard.'

Billy Forrest drove off in his dusty pick-up truck, bouncing down the track, and glancing back at them, his black spotted cocker spaniel, Spike, standing up in the back, his large ears pointing up and his tail wagging excitedly at the prospect of tea.

Joe and Lucy's first season working in the Heron Valley orchards was a period in their marriage that they subsequently looked back on as a blissful idyll.

There was the camaraderie of working with the fellow apple pickers: local Tasmanians, Americans and Canadians, and, at the end of each day, feeling tired, hot and dusty, walking along the winding lane to the shore of the Heron river. They would swim for an hour in the still, refreshing water, before returning to work for two hours in the packing shed; sorting and packing apples into their different varieties, for collection by lorries and transportation to the deepwater port at Heronville; there to be loaded on to the fruit ships for shipment overseas, to the markets of Britain and Europe.

In September, with the close of the season in the Heron Valley orchards, the Flints returned to the mainland and travelled up the east coast, with stays in Sydney and Brisbane, and sailing out to the Great Barrier Reef from Cairns.

In January of the following year they wrote to Billy Forrest, asking if they could be taken on for the approaching apple season. Billy replied immediately, letting them know that the cottage would be kept available until their arrival.

As their second season in the Heron valley neared its close, Billy Forrest invited Joe and Lucy, much to their surprise, for a night out in Hobart.

Billy drove them in his red Falcon estate to the gleamingly sleek and modern Tasman Sporting Club in the centre of Hobart.

Billy was shown to his usual table near the centre of the room, and a complementary jug of beer was placed on the table between the three of them.

Billy was in a jovial mood, and enjoyed being the focus of attention as people came up to his table and he introduced them to Joe and Lucy.

He even paid them a compliment, 'You've done a good job, these past two years. Most Poms we get over here can't stick at it past the first few weeks, before they want to be off somewhere else.'

But as the evening wore on, and more foaming jugs of beer appeared at the table after each signal Billy waved in the direction of the crowded bar, he retreated into the taciturn persona they knew from working with him in the orchards, and the silences between them became protracted and awkward, as they gradually exhausted topics of conversation.

A cabaret singer opened the floorshow, much to the relief of all three of them, and she slinked over provocatively to Billy's table, to the accompaniment of ribald cheering and clapping from Billy's friends at the bar.

She leaned forward and embraced a self-conscious and flustered Billy, and placed the microphone in his hand. He reluctantly accompanied her in a few bars of her mournful country and western song of lost love, and then, after she had left the stage, Billy murmured soulfully, 'Jeez, I still miss Grace.'

'... my wife,' Billy added, looking ruefully at Joe and Lucy.

'Sorry,' they replied in unison, both knowing this was a hopelessly inadequate response, but at a loss as to what to say.

'We've got two boys. The legacy of our marriage. Of our love for each other. Nathan lives on the mainland. Melbourne. I see him now 'n' again. Big man in finance. Done well for himself. Married. Two kids – my grandkids.'

No further details were forthcoming from Billy. His explanation died as quickly as it had begun, and his sorrowful voice trailed away into his next swig of beer.

The Flints interpreted this as a sign to move on.

'You remind me of us two when we were first married. Except you're Poms. Grace would have liked you. Fair dinkum.' With this, Billy returned to his morose mood, and remained in his own private reverie until the close of the floorshow.

The three of them walked out into the cold Tasmanian night air.

The drive back to the Heron Valley in pitch darkness was precarious as Billy swung his car around the hairpin bends of the winding country road.

He was now in a mellow mood, singing an upbeat Sinatra song as he drove up the path to the cottage.

'You know, for Poms you two can certainly take your grog,' were Billy's parting words.

He drove off, waving and doffing his bush-hat out of the car window as he swerved down the path, with a screech of tyres as they skidded along the gravel on the sharp left turn into the road.

The next day Billy Forrest was dead.

No-one in the orchard that day admitted to having caught the ladder in the hectic rush of pickers to unload their apple sacks into the collecting truck. But they all heard the cry. Followed by the dull thud of a body hitting the ground. Then the spine-chilling moan. Then silence.

'His ladder was too near the tree, mate. Not balanced properly. That's why he caught his head on the tree when he hit the ground,' said one of the pickers, picking up Billy's bush-hat and dusting it down respectfully, as Billy's body was taken away in the Swan Vale ambulance.

The dusk of a Tasmanian afternoon began to close in on a scene of Spike, Billy's cocker spaniel, running after the ambulance and emitting a pitiful yelping sound; the heart-rending noise mingling eerily with the comforting familiar drone of a tractor in a nearby field.

Joe and Lucy were picking apples from the tree next to Billy when he fell. The brutal speed with which it had all happened had left them stunned.

This was not how either of them envisaged a life should end.

They were thinking that it shouldn't be as mundane as this; that Billy would now have been strolling back to his house on the hill, bush-hat tilted jauntily on the side of his head, chewing gum, and delighting in the thought of a day's work well done as he wandered along, idly chatting to Lew his foreman, arm round his shoulders.

No. Not like this. Taken from his beloved orchards. Never to return.

Joe and Lucy walked down to the river that night, but only to stand in the moonlight and look at the mountains across the water, and think of Billy.

Two days later there was a gentle tapping on the cottage door.

Standing outside was Lew the foreman.

'Can you both be at the big house at two? ' Lew asked, propping himself up against the open door.

Inheritance

When Joe and Lucy got to Billy's house, a row of cars lined the driveway.

They entered the lounge and were met by the sight of a man they presumed was Billy Forrest's lawyer, standing on one side of a long, mahogany table, and faced from the other side by a seated group of people, with two empty chairs positioned at the end of the row, which Joe and Lucy walked over to occupy, exchanging nods of acknowledgement with the lawyer as they sat down.

After everyone in the room had settled to his satisfaction, Mr Pettigrew, the lawyer, introduced himself, and, to the accompaniment of the sound of restless shuffling of feet and the clearing of throats, began to speak, 'Today is a particularly sad occasion for me.

I have been Billy Forrest's lawyer for many years, and, as I have never believed in beating about the bush, let me get right to the point.

I have been authorised by the coroner's office in Hobart to let you know that, because of the particular circumstances that have taken place, of which everyone here today is sadly aware, there is to be a post mortem, followed by a coroner's investigation, which is a protracted procedure likely to take a considerable time.

Because of this, I have come here today to disclose the provisions of the last will and testament of Billy Forrest.'

There followed a stream of legalistic jargon from Mr Pettigrew which sounded absurdly formal and inappropriate removed from the confines of a lawyer's office.

Mr Pettigrew then, in less stilted manner, proceeded, 'We all know the regard in which Billy held his family, and, in particular, his love for Grace. And, recently, he had developed a strong affection for an English couple working for him, Joe and Lucy Flint.'

Everyone in the room looked perplexed at the latter reference and its possible significance, and several glances were cast in the direction of Joe and Lucy, who were beginning to feel uneasy at being the focus of attention in the overcrowded room, which now started to become stiflingly hot and stuffy.

The tension was now palpable, with stirrings of hostility in the air.

Mr Pettigrew continued, 'Although Billy felt that he was not always perceived as such by members of his family,' he made a conscious effort not to glance in the direction of Billy's son, Nathan, 'and that unfortunate ...' Mr Pettigrew struggled for an appropriate euphemism, '... disagreements ... had occurred over the years, he was a deeply sentimental man, and he wished you all to know of his fondness, his love, for each one of you right up until ...' again the search for a moderating phrase, '... his sad demise.'

Mr Pettigrew hesitated for a second and glanced at his papers before carrying on, 'However, although Billy wanted me to make this clear, he also wanted me to tell you all that he had continued to love Grace as strongly, following her untimely death, as he did on the day they first met.'

The puzzled frowns among the rapt audience on hearing a lawyer departing from a prepared legal script and entering the realms of his client's private feelings towards his family prompted Mr Pettigrew to clear his throat and take a sip of water. He was beginning to feel as ill at ease as his audience evidently were, despite the fact that, in his capacity as senior partner of Pettigrew, Miller and McDonald, he had carried out similar duties on innumerable occasions.

However, none of these had presented Mr Pettigrew with the

requirement to deliver a qualifying clause in a will such as the one he was now obliged to announce, and his unease in such a circumstance was therefore understandable; for Mr Pettigrew regarded the moment about to come as being a unique one in his esteemed thirty-year legal career.

He began to steel his resolve in anticipation of the expected reaction. In his wide experience, disinherited offspring tended to exhibit few, if any, charitable reactions towards the messenger of their misfortune. Mr Pettigrew thought to himself that this was especially likely to be the response on this occasion, for Billy Forrest had been a wealthy man.

'I think Billy would have liked you all to know his exact words at this point, so I will read the following clause verbatim, in order to avoid any possible later misunderstandings as to his intentions.'

Another, longer, sip at his water. Another, deeper, throat clearing, but this time, also the need to brush away a fly that had been persistently hovering around his perspiring forehead, 'Over the past two years I have come to know an English couple ... Joe and Lucy Flint. My marriage to Grace ...'

'Where on earth is this leading?' the faces before him were asking, 'What has Grace to do with THEM?'

'... was the happiest time of my life. We had planned a long and exciting future. And then to grow old together.'

The colour was beginning to drain from the face of Nathan Forrest.

Mr Pettigrew was now warming to his task, his apprehension starting to dissolve, as a picture took shape in his mind of the day in his office, only a week earlier, when Billy Forrest had sat before him, and relayed his wishes, in his inimitable, matter-of-fact way, but this time in a tone suffused with embarrassment at his need to expose the innermost workings of his heart.

Mr Pettigrew had emotionally connected with Billy that afternoon, as a man he instinctively felt was cut from the same piece of cloth as himself. A man who measured his words as circumspectly as he measured his feelings.

'Make sure they understand my wishes...' Billy had said that day ...

Mr Pettigrew snapped himself out of his reverie, which had been imperceptible to the gathering. He adjusted his rimless eyeglasses and adopted his formal tone of voice, fixing his gaze again on the immaculately squared off stack of typed foolscap pages in front of him, from which he had been reading and continually forming into a neat adjacent pile sheet by sheet as he methodically proceeded.

'... But Grace and I were tragically denied the opportunity to grow old together.

I respect the need for independence felt by members of my family, and my heart will always be with them in all their future endeavours. I deeply regret past conflicts that have taken place within my family. I also fully understand any reluctance members of my family have felt to succeed me ...'

The suspense in the room had now become unbearable. A hush of such intensity that the drone of the air-conditioning fan in the middle of the ceiling sounded deafening and intrusive.

'My fondness for Joe and Lucy has revived memories of the early years of my marriage to Grace, when we, too, had plans to see the world together. A need for adventure. Dreams we were not able to realise due to the demands of business. And then the passing of Grace.

I have seen in Joe and Lucy a relationship similar to ours, and would like them to have the opportunity to fulfil a future for themselves in which their dreams can be realized. A future that would only be fully possible without a continual struggle for financial survival.

I feel that by bequeathing my apple business to them, its continued success will be ensured and the orchards will be in safe hands. Alternatively, if they should decide to sell at any future date, I want them to know they have my full blessing to do so.

My dairy farm, I bequeath to the present manager, Stan O'Neill.

I stipulate that Lew Burke remains in his capacity as foreman of the orchards for the duration of his working life, if he so wishes, with full responsibility for the running of the orchards.'

And, finally, my house I leave in trust equally to my

grandchildren, Oliver and Christina Forrest, for them to assume ownership in their own right upon attaining the age of majority. If he so wishes, Lew Burke can assume immediate occupancy of the property, subject to payment of a monthly rental payment to the trustee of my estate, Mr Arthur Pettigrew, who will decide the appropriate amount. This provision is contingent upon Lew Burke remaining as orchard manager.

Mr Pettigrew will also ensure the provisions of this will are notified to all parties concerned, and complied with in full by such parties.'

There were gasps of astonishment throughout the room.

Nathan Forrest was ashen-faced. Drained of all emotion.

Isolated groups began to form, standing in separate corners of the room.

Lew approached Joe and Lucy and offered his hand, 'Fair go, you two. Billy liked you both. He always had a soft spot for the larrikin spirit. Never could abide wowsers. He could sink his grog in his younger days. Drink us all under the table. Grace going did for Billy though. Never the same again after that. Poor old bastard.'

A masterly antipodean synopsis of a man's existence. Concise and affectionate.

People in the room were shuffling around. Dumbfounded.

Talking in whispers. Absorbing the impact of Billy's bombshell.

Mr Pettigrew boxed his papers into one complete tower, straightened his tie, folded his eyeglasses and placed them precisely in their shiny maroon case. He was feeling a warm glow of satisfaction at his consummate performance. Never in his experience had a shock so profound been delivered.

Joe and Lucy decided not to remain any longer. They both felt unable to meet the eyes of Nathan Forrest, who brushed brusquely past them on his way to the cool of the terrace.

Back at the cottage, Joe and Lucy were silent for what seemed like an eternity. Frozen in amazement.

They were both feeling at that moment that in the previous few hours their world had been turned on its head and nothing would be the same again.

'We'll need Lew to help us and it means we can't now return to England. We'll need meetings. Quickly - with lawyers and accountants.' Joe began to spell out what he felt they had both been thinking. Thoughts that had been crowding in by the multitude.

As the first shadows of evening began to appear, Joe and Lucy walked down to the river, deep in conversation.

At the same moment, Nathan Forrest could be found on the terrace of the Big House, engaged in heated conversation with Mr Pettigrew - 'I don't accept this. It's an outrage. I'll fight it all the way. What was he thinking of – Ma wouldn't have wanted this. Why would he have just changed his will – he was still fit and healthy. Never had a day's illness in his life.'

Mr Pettigrew peered at him, squinting against the glare of the late afternoon sun in his eyes. He shaded them by putting his right hand across his forehead. 'Perhaps he intended to tell you. Would you care to sit in the porch for a moment?' Mr Pettigrew asked Nathan, 'There's something you need to know...'

Billy Forrest had received a telephone call from his doctor, asking if he could call in to see him as soon as possible.

When Billy entered the surgery, he noticed the grave expression on Doctor O'Malley's face and the absence of the customary genial greeting.

'Take a seat, Billy, thanks for coming over so quickly.'

Billy didn't reply. He was composing himself. Attempting to relax, to put his racing mind into a neutral passive gear.

Doctor O'Malley went straight into it. In his long experience he had always found it was the most compassionate approach. That small-talk only added to anxiety, making bad news all the more devastating.

'Your recent test results have come back from Hobart General. They aren't as good as the earlier ones, I'm afraid. There looks to have been a significant deterioration.'

He was secretly hoping that Billy would not want too technical an explanation. 'Leave the lab boys to do their jobs and leave me to do mine. I've got the worst part as it is – having to give news like this,' he was saying to himself. 'Anyway, I know

Billy – he won't want to know more than he needs to. I know I won't when my time comes.'

'Doc, tell me straight. Simple language. No frills,' Billy said.

'I thought so, I was right about his reaction,' Doctor O'Malley thought.

'It's not good, Billy. I'm afraid you've got a brain tumour.'

Billy felt a strange beatific sort of calm. Not at all what he would have expected, being told such news.

'How long have I got?'

'Difficult to say. Could be six months. Could be longer. Everyone's different.'

Back on the porch at the big house Mr Pettigrew looked at Nathan and spoke quietly. 'Your father had been told he had a terminal illness and wanted to put his affairs in order without delay.'

Nathan was still reeling from the earlier reading of his father's will, but now felt the added shock and confusion from the impact of Mr Pettigrew's new disclosure.

He stormed off. 'You'll be hearing from me ...'

Mr Pettigrew had expected no less, and was, in fact, to be seen wearing an ironic smile on his face. He was at that moment recalling a comparable occasion five years earlier. A widow had also just been witness to her anticipated fortune filter away through cupped palms like sand picked up from a beach, to a twenty-five year old Melbourne beauty queen with whom her deceased husband had recently begun a secret passionate liaison. She chose the moments immediately succeeding the reading of the will to launch a violent attack on her glamorous rival that resulted in the curtailment of her budding cinematic career.

Mr Pettigrew had never before witnessed a head-butt. Let alone one delivered by one woman to another. 'But with this job you just never can be sure how people will take the news,' was Mr Pettigrew's closing thought on the Forrest family as, with an audible sigh of relief, he got into his car and made his way back to the enticing tranquillity of his Hobart office.

The Billy Forrest Story

It is difficult to pinpoint the precise moment when the Flints, albeit unwittingly, became involved in the affairs of the Forrest family, but the day of Nathan's visit to see his father during Joe and Lucy's first season apple picking, would seem to be he most apposite, as being the beginning of the compelling story of Billy Forrest.

It was lunchtime in the south orchard.

The pickers had formed into their customary nationalist clusters: Americans with Americans. Australians with Australians. And the English Flints.

All eating from packed lunches, in their usual areas of the orchard.

Joe and Lucy had chosen a secluded part of the valley where they could unwind for an hour in the shade of a giant oak tree, after a morning working in blistering heat.

Billy Forrest had wandered off on one of his tours of inspection of the orchard. He never liked to take breaks from work, and the pickers always sensed his impatience as the lunch hour moved along closer to one o'clock and picking had to be resumed for the afternoon.

The voice the Flints heard first was broad Australian. But not one of the pickers; it had a deep soft tone. They were unable to see anything, due to the size of the oak tree they were resting against, and distances in the silence of the orchard could be deceptive.

'How are you, Dad?'

'Fine. Yourself? The kids?' The voice that replied belonged to Billy.

Before that afternoon in the orchard, it had been over a year since Nathan had spoken to his father.

Billy had been invited to spend Christmas with Nathan and his family in Melbourne.

Nathan and his wife Evelyn had been reluctant to invite Billy to their new bungalow in the exclusive suburb of Kookaburra Heights, situated in Melbourne's stockbroker belt, a recently gentrified area popular among the city's business community.

Nathan's career as an investment banker had been flourishing since his move from management of a Hobart finance company five years earlier.

The reluctance to offer the Christmas invitation to Billy had been on Evelyn's part rather than Nathan's. She felt their annual Christmas Day sherry morning with the rarefied company who always attended at the Oaks was too important to Nathan's progress at his city bank to risk being jeopardised by a careless remark from his father or any other embarrassing manifestations of rustic gaucheness.

In fact, when he had arrived on Christmas Eve, the warmth of the welcome Billy received from his grandchildren, Oliver and Christina, had served to prick Evelyn's conscience that perhaps she needed to adopt a more charitable approach towards her father-in-law.

Billy delighted in sitting round the tree on Christmas morning, opening the presents with his grandchildren.

And the sherry morning, later on, far from being the hazardous social ordeal that had been feared, on the contrary proved to be a resounding success, with Nathan's banking colleagues relishing the opportunity to talk to someone from outside their tight-knit financial community, and finding that Billy brought a breath of fresh air to the annual gathering.

Nathan and Evelyn had firmly resolved before Billy's arrival to try and avoid the usual delicate family topics which in the past had provided a minefield which someone in the family invariably walked into.

Following the departure of the guests to their own homes for Christmas lunch, after the sherry morning, more presents were opened in the lounge, and Billy played with his grandchildren while Nathan helped Evelyn prepare Christmas dinner.

Billy was seated at the table between Oliver and Christina and pulled crackers with them before the meal; everyone was now wearing a coloured paper hat, and turns were being taken to read out the jokes on the slips of paper from inside the crackers.

After the plum pudding doused with brandy and aglow with a swirling blue flame had been brought in from the kitchen by Nathan, Billy raised his glass and proposed a toast to 'a bumper apple crop next year'.

Evelyn followed her muted response to Billy's toast by proposing one of her own, 'The future – for all of us.' She deliberately chose an optimistic yet innocuous toast, aware of the raw sensitivities around the family table that Christmas – the open emotional wounds that were still a long way from having healed over.

'Delicious lunch, Evelyn,' Billy said to his daughter-in-law, as she began removing the dishes from the table.

'Let me help you with those,' Billy offered.

'Let's sit and watch television for a while. The dishes can wait until later,' Nathan suggested to the two of them.

So Billy, Nathan and Evelyn settled round the television set in the lounge, while Oliver and Christina, for the first time that day showing signs of exhaustion, after the excitement of the morning, stretched out on the carpet and drifted off to sleep.

'At this joyous time of Christmas, we, as Australians ...,' the words came from the television; Dan Archer, the Australian Prime Minister, an urbane fifty year old man with grey hair, was speaking from the study of his home, with a background of a book-lined wall, and with his hands resting on his desk, on which stood strategically-positioned photographs of his wife and their three young children.

Dan Archer was wearing a facial expression of concerned

gravitas with its 'You can trust me, I'm your friend,' look which had been an instrumental factor in his achievement of a landslide victory for the Progressive Democratic Party at the previous year's General Election.

'... are all looking to the future,' he continued, 'but with an awareness of, and therefore a respect for the past.'

As he spoke the opening words of his annual television address Dan Archer felt a surge of gratitude for the skill of his speechwriters who had meticulously crafted the phrases that were to follow, phrases that he was hoping would succeed in uniting the hearts and minds of his fellow countrymen.

'We do this for ourselves, but most of all, for our children and our grandchildren.'

The television screen at that moment showed scenes of families swimming in the surf at Sydney's Bondi beach, cutting instantaneously to a modern Melbourne of skyscrapers, parks, and bustling crowds. All these emotive images taking place beneath brilliant blue Australian skies.

'We have all lived through difficult times in the past year ...' the Prime Minister continued. 'Brave young Australians, as in other periods during our troubled twentieth century, have been called upon to uphold the values of the free world. To ensure that the values we all cherish can be preserved. Values which mean that today, on this special family day, we are all free to celebrate together.'

The pictures on the screen then switched, in rapid succession, to grainy monochrome freeze frames of troops entering a transport plane ... a small group of American soldiers surrounded by laughing Vietnamese children ... an Anzac Day parade in Sydney, with decorated war veterans marching past and saluting the Australian flag ... then a cut back to a reprise of Bondi beach and Melbourne ...

It was slick audience manipulation designed to show time's unremitting lineal rush across the generations, but artfully containing the message of the necessity of war in order to ensure the prosperity of peace. Cynical viewers would have referred to the broadcast as blatant government propaganda.

As the images faded from the screen, the silence in the room began to intensify, the children began to stir.

Nathan and Evelyn glanced across at Billy. Tears were streaming down his cheeks. 'My boy. Then my wife.' Billy tried to choke back words of grief. 'Both Australia's finest.'

The television pictures had probed into the recesses of his memory. 'He was always headstrong. Never told us he'd joined up; we only knew the day the letter arrived. But that was Michael. Impulsive. Patriotic. I told him not to go. That it wasn't Australia's fight over there - Grace told him as well. But he wouldn't listen. He always knew his own mind - even as a little boy.'

'Do you want to give us a hand with the dishes, Billy?' Evelyn said, making a move towards the kitchen, 'Can you see if Oliver and Christina want to play out in the garden?' Evelyn addressed her question to Nathan.

'It's too hot, Mum, and we're tired,' the children complained.

'Do as you're told – plenty of time to play inside again later on.' Evelyn answered irritably.

Billy showed no sign of diverting his attention from the television screen. He was still lost in his thoughts, 'I think I'll go back tonight,' he spoke to nobody in particular.

His spirit had been crushed by the broadcast.

'You're welcome to stay longer, Dad. You know that.' Nathan walked over and put his arm round his father's stooped shoulders.

Billy wanted to give voice to the myriad thoughts flooding his mind, but knew any words he spoke would only lead to resentment; their respective pain was deeply buried and each believed they would never now be able to open up to the other. So they each donned a civilised mask of pretension while preserving a private grief which had become a warm, comforting blanket for an anguished soul.

Billy had always felt at an emotional distance from his older son, but in the past year this had deepened to become an unbridgeable chasm – since the death of Grace. She had been the cornerstone of the Forrest family, the cohesive force that had ensured the maintenance of harmony across years of turbulence, so that the family ship continued to sail sublimely on over the storm-tossed seas of life.

Grace had been tireless in soothing brotherly squabbles and jealousies, and as a mediator between a father and his two growing sons. Often to her own emotional cost, and, she often felt but never openly admitted, at a cost to her marriage to Billy.

But, of course, there were also the good times, when they all felt they were the archetypical Australian family. Strong, healthy, and free, with an unbreakable bond. A family in the true sense of the word and all it was intended to mean – a unit that was the acme of solidarity and mutual support. That was until the drizzly Tasmanian morning when the official-looking letter was delivered to the Forrest house. And a shadow of gloom descended which enveloped them all in its darkness.

The letter was for Michael Forrest. To summon him for induction training in the Australian army.

There was silence as the letter was opened, and Michael was forced to admit to his family the reason for his visits to Hobart several months earlier, when he had put his signature on the series of forms, and answered the host of questions that were the pre-requisite for admission into the military.

Over the succeeding months Michael had intended to tell them all at home what he had done, but, on those occasions when he felt the moment was right, a powerful opposing voice within had told him that his family would not understand his motives and the result would be a torrent of condemnation, and the unleashing of needless distress on the people he loved.

So Michael remained mute as the months passed.

Until the day the letter arrived, and he was called upon to account for his impetuosity.

'You know what you've done, don't you?' Grace spoke the first words after the letter had been opened and passed to her by Michael.

'What this might mean?' As the question left her lips, Grace felt herself clinging to the word 'might', in the manner of a drowning man seizing a piece of driftwood as it floated by.

She passed the letter on to Billy.

'Yes, Ma, I know,' Michael answered softly.

It was left to his older brother Nathan to say the dreaded word Vietnam and, in so doing, to give the signal for the floodgates to open.

'It was on the news last week. Another moratorium against the war. In the centre of Sydney. Thousands protesting,' Nathan added.

Grace had been hushed by her older son's intervention, which spelled out starkly the implications for Michael and which, before he had spoken, had already begun to exert a vice-like squeeze on her consciousness.

'In America, they're burning draft cards in droves. And protests. And marching. Every day of the week,' Nathan continued relentlessly.

Then Billy felt the need to add his weight to the verbal blitzkrieg.

'It's true, Michael. The war's going to end. The writing's on the wall. There's too much opposition from the people.'

Michael leaned against the refrigerator, listening attentively. But he had been counting the days to the letter's arrival. The prospect of adventure, even danger, had stirred his blood, and stiffened his resolve against even the most vehement persuasion to alter his chosen course.

Also, some of his friends had gone to war and he didn't want to lose face.

In any event his life had become dull. Without any challenge. A future in the orchards, mapped out for him by his father, while his brother was carving his own independent niche in life, in the world of business – going his own way, free of parental influence.

'We can tell them you're needed. On the land. The orchards. Essential industry classification. I've heard of families doing it every day of the week,' Billy suggested, with desperation at the apparent impenetrability of his boy to reason.

'We could tell them you've had second thoughts. That you acted hastily. Then, while they're re-considering, the war might come to an end.' Grace's voice came in, softly, feebly.

'But I want to go, Ma, I don't care about any of that. My

mind's made up. I need this.' Michael's eyes were unblinking and remote in a face showing a look of fierce conviction.

Grace had seen the television pictures, and read the front pages of the newspapers. Body bags being carried out of cargo planes in America. In the streets coffins draped with the stars and stripes. Distraught mothers everywhere. 'No, not my son, our future,' she thought, as she met Michael's unswerving gaze, her eyes piercing his. 'I always said half jokingly I could tell what he was thinking before he thought it himself – that I would always know him that well,' she thought.

Perhaps now – even now – Grace hoped that this instinct, almost primaeval in its intensity, that mothers had felt for their children since the mists of unrecorded time – could transmit itself to her son and he would viscerally respond, and that a corresponding instinct within him would rise up and lock onto hers, as it had when he was a baby in her arms.

But it was not to be.

Grace knew at that moment her son had become a man.

And she had lost him.

The family discussion ended. An ominous silence descended on the kitchen.

Michael left the aborted discussion hanging in the air. He folded the letter carefully and placed it in his back pocket. He walked from the kitchen into the lounge.

The next time official correspondence arrived at the Forrest house, Nathan opened it. He was on a visit home to tell Billy and Grace about his recent promotion at work and the plans he had been making with Evelyn to move to a larger house.

Billy and Grace had both said how pleased they were for him, but, to Nathan, as always, they were merely paying lip service with their lukewarm enthusiasm. Nathan felt his success was regarded by them as really just a matter of course, and he was even prompted, over breakfast, to irritably snap 'If Michael had told you news like this, you'd put out the red carpet for him.'

'Michael is fighting for his country,' Billy replied angrily, tossing his knife on top of his unfinished piece of toast. 'You can't speak of pen-pushing in the same breath.'

'But you know we're just as proud of you too,' Grace sprang to her son's defence. 'It goes without saying. We always have been. Since you were both small boys.' Grace felt her usual proviso was required to her older son in order to avoid having to give him unqualified praise.

The clinking sound of the letterbox interrupted the simmering breakfast-time quarrel.

Arguments in the Forrest family had always developed from similar beginnings to this, and Nathan was relieved to bring it summarily to an end by leaving the kitchen to get the letter.

He picked up the letter from the mat at the foot of the front door and brought it back to the kitchen, without giving it a glance.

He passed it to Billy.

He hadn't even noticed it was not a letter, it was a telegram.

'When Michael returns, they'll be killing the fatted calf,' Nathan thought ruefully to himself, his thoughts still locked into the breakfast discussion of a few moments before. 'But I'll never get any more than grudging praise from them. No matter what I achieve. It's never been any different. And never will be. Yellow ribbons round the trees for the war hero when he returns. Nothing surer.'

Billy opened the telegram untidily, running his right forefinger underneath the flap of the envelope, a terrible dread gripping the pit of his stomach. He began to read.

And so the Christmas of Billy's visit to the Oaks on Kookaburra Heights was ended by the hand of an unwitting Prime Minister, who by the medium of television had reached into the body of the Forrest family and sliced open an unhealed gaping wound.

Having taken a detour in the Billy Forrest story, we can now return to where we left Joe and Lucy Flint. Eavesdropping on the conversation between Billy Forrest and his son Nathan, over a year after his Christmas visit to his son at Kookaburra Heights.

'I'll get some of it off my chest now, and the rest later,' Billy said, standing with his son, behind the giant oak; Joe and Lucy reclining on the grass on the other side, resting from their morning's work.

'I need to talk over the business with you,' Billy said to Nathan, and, as he spoke thought that perhaps inside the house and over dinner would have been a more appropriate place and time than out in the middle of south orchard, but reasoned that, by later in the day, the usual awkwardness between them would have re-asserted itself and the chance for resolution of matters would have gone.

'I want to know what you think I should do with the businesses – the orchards and the farm.'

Nathan was still puzzled at the reason for the urgency of his father's summons to come over to speak to him, but left this point in abeyance.

'Dad, you know that Ma had grown bored with the businesses – both of them, especially the orchards. She wanted to sell up.' Nathan thrust his hands deeper into his trouser pockets as he spoke, the early afternoon sun was making him feel hot and uncomfortable, and he wanted to remove his suit jacket.

'Did she tell you this?' Billy sensed his son's discomfort as he barked out the question.

'Well, no. But we all seemed to know. Except you.' Nathan removed his jacket and swung it over his left shoulder. He tried hard not to meet his father's eye.

Billy appeared not to have heard his son's answer, as he immediately turned away as though about to end the conversation by heading off down the valley. But Nathan knew he had to continue – that his father had to hear everything he had to say.

Nathan's immediate concern was that Evelyn would interrogate him when he returned home. He could picture her now, at home, in the kitchen, hands threateningly on hips, 'Well. Did you tell him? Everything?'

'If only for my peace of mind,' Nathan thought to himself. 'It needs to be said now. It could have been said that Christmas at the Oaks, but another year's gone since then. Time's passing so quickly - burying things deeper and deeper.'

'Don't go, Dad. Let's sit down.'

Billy obeyed his son, and, at that moment, a wave of weariness drifted across his consciousness and he felt one of his migraines forming behind his temples, ready to launch an onslaught as he began to speak.

'But the businesses were meant to be for ...' Billy only just stopped himself in time from saying 'Michael' and, instead, hastily substituted 'you and Michael.'

'Dad, you know that's not true. Michael was always your favourite.'

'We always treated you equally – even from the time you were nippers.'

Nathan let it pass. He was being side-tracked from his mission.

'Dad, Evelyn and I have talked it over. We think you've only one option.'

'And what might that be?' Billy pulled the brim of his bush-hat down across his eyes as though this could in some way help to ward off the intense throbbing behind his eyes.

'You have to sell the orchards.' Nathan smoothed his jacket that was now lying beside him on the grass, and pulled up his legs to rest underneath his chin. Billy looked at his son from underneath the cover of his hat and thought he looked again like the seven-year old boy who always sat in that huddled position when the two of them used to sit together fishing by the side of Freeman's Creek all those lost summers ago.

'Grace and I – we built up these orchards – from nothing. A bit of land, and a few scrawny trees. Look now,' Billy took off his hat and gestured it in a wide sweeping motion of his right arm.

Nathan had continued looking squarely at him. 'Not the look now of a seven-year old boy,' Billy thought to himself, 'Now a cold, emotionless businessman, who looks on this land, Forrest land, as nothing more than a line of figures on a bank statement.'

'The farm as well. Always been in the family,' Billy continued, 'You don't understand. Never have. Michael, he understood.'

Nathan suppressed his rising anger at the mention of his younger brother's name, even though he had been expecting it sooner or later.

'Dad, I'm a businessman, dealing every day of the week with accounts of businesses like yours.' Billy noticed the use of the word 'yours' and not 'ours', coming out from a Forrest mouth.

'Times are changing. The big corporations are taking over. Family businesses are dying. The apple business is no more immune to change than any other industry. It has to play by the same rules. Also, Tasmania is isolated in expanding markets; higher trading costs cutting into profits - greater overheads all round. Anyway, Ma wouldn't have wanted you to continue, Dad. You should retire now. While you're still fit and well.'

Billy listened, and would have told him about the visits to Doctor O'Malley. But not now, 'He can go to hell,' he thought to himself. 'Back to his balance sheets. His cosy office. His bossy wife.'

Instead, Billy stopped his son in full flow, placing an upraised right palm an inch from his face, 'Don't you ever tell me what Grace did or didn't want for me, for us. I was her husband. She was your mother. Don't you ever, do you hear me – ever - forget that.'

Billy stabbed his pointed right forefinger into Nathan's chest.

Nathan took a step backwards.

Billy's head began to pound like a road drill. Full blast. A thick blue vein was protruding across his forehead. All the warning signs to one of his blackouts.

'Now I've got work to do ...'

'O.K. Dad. Fine. You know best.' Nathan straightened his jacket lapels and lined up the knot in his tie.

Joe and Lucy knew the time to resume work had now passed by half an hour ago but they remained on the other side of the oak tree until they heard Billy storm away, the crackle and snap of breaking twigs under his heavy boots - away into the depths of south orchard and Nathan's lighter step moments later, in the opposite direction, back to the house.

Later that same day, in the cool of the evening, Billy and his son were sitting by the log fire in the lounge of the big house, a half-consumed bottle from Billy's stock of Barossa Valley wines positioned on the coffee table between them.

Tempers had cooled and Nathan had firmed his resolve to tell his father the rest of what he needed to know. A resolution thrust upon him by his wife Evelyn from the moment they had received Billy's invitation to go over to see him.

Evelyn had insisted to Nathan that everything had to be said. She had given him a now or never ultimatum, adding 'In the long run it will be kinder for him to know,' and finished off with 'After all it's his right to know, I would want to if I were in the same situation.'

Nathan had thought at the time she said it that she made it sound as though they were a pair of social workers on a visit to soothe a recalcitrant client, but, then again, he had reasoned, she always had been a persuasive person, so he didn't argue.

Nathan made his move. He placed his wine glass on the table and was unaware that his right hand immediately formed itself into a rigid fist of tension as he spoke. 'Dad, this afternoon - the businesses and all that.'

Billy was feeling warm and mellow by the fire. The throbbing taut band of pain behind his eyes had now softened into the stillness of a millpond 'Let's just leave it, son.'

'O.K. Dad. Fine.' Nathan began to picture Evelyn wagging a formidable finger in front of his nose. 'But there's something else we've thought for a while that you should have known.'

Billy was intrigued and sensed immediately Evelyn's hand on the tiller, steering Nathan's boat to heaven knew where. He smiled to himself, but let his son continue.

'Dad, it wasn't only the businesses we needed to talk about. Like I say, we did mean to have a talk to you about it a while ago, and thought that last Christmas we might have. The time has never seemed to be right - you know how these things are - what with Michael and then Ma's ...' Nathan was not able to bring himself to say the word, and so it stayed lodged somewhere in the recesses of his brain. He had not been able to say it since the word happened, and now he felt he probably never would.

'It's about Ma.'

'No going back now,' Nathan told himself.

'What about Grace?'

'Well. There was one time. Evelyn and I were shopping in Melbourne, and we saw her. She didn't see us, and, at first, we didn't think it was Ma - just someone who looked like her. But it was.'

'What are you trying to tell me, Nathan?'

Billy recalled Grace had gone away for a week and asked him if he could manage on his own. He remembered the ensuing argument - 'Leaving me at peak picking time,' he had told her. In reply, she had told him she had 'received a letter from an old school friend who lived just outside Melbourne. Class reunion. Week-long celebrations. Chance of a lifetime. She wanted to go, and hope he didn't mind too much.'

'That's the thing Dad, she was with somebody else that day. A man. Hand-in-hand. I'm sorry, Dad.'

'No. It's not true. There has to be an explanation.'

'That's what we thought,' said Nathan, 'I wanted to forget all about it. Forget we had seen anything, but Evelyn thought you must be told. She thought what if Oliver and Christina find out, by accident, and, you know children – always say what's on their minds.'

'Oh, so that's it,' Billy thought to himself. 'But for the grandkids they'd have kept me in the dark forever.'

'That's the reason that nothing's been said – for so long – we couldn't agree between us what to do for the best,' Nathan continued. 'You remember the children's school holidays, when we brought them over to see you. Well, we confronted Ma about it then. Well, in fact, Evelyn did.

You were working in the orchards on that blazing hot summer afternoon.

Oliver and Christina were climbing a tree at the far end of the back garden.

The three of us were sitting in the porch. The two women were discussing the children's schools. How Oliver was good with his hands, always trying to fix things when they were broken. And Christina never seemed to be interested in playing, and preferred reading her books. The quiet one; and Oliver the lively one, always up to mischief, getting his younger sister into trouble.

Evelyn had been thinking of a way to manoeuvre the conversation away from the children. I went inside to pour the cold drinks, and she used the opportunity to find out some answers from Ma ...'

'You wouldn't recognise Melbourne these days. New buildings springing up all the time. Nathan and I don't go into the city unless we have to. Last time, we took the children to the Botanical Gardens, and then went for a walk by the Yarra.'

'We find Hobart a bit quiet,' Grace replied. 'Small for a city. I love to go to the big stores in Melbourne, clothes shopping; so much more choice. The country life's fine but there are times when you feel like you need to have a change. More life. To be among crowds. The noise. Go to a show.'

Before they could move onto another topic and the chance lost, Evelyn took her opportunity, 'In fact, when we were last in Melbourne we thought we saw you, but Nathan said, No. She'd pop in to see us if she'd come over to the mainland. Must have been someone who looked like you.'

Grace shuddered and gave Evelyn a quizzical look. She disputed with herself, 'Should I play mind games with my daughter-in-law, or take her into my confidence? It's impossible to know what to do for the best, but if I try to brazen it out and she actually knows it was me, I'll forever be covering up, with things never again quite right between us. But, on the other hand, if I explain the situation, woman to woman, perhaps she'll understand. But then there's Nathan. She'll obviously have to tell him. Let alone what to do about Billy.'

Her racing mind attempted to process the tangled complexity of possibilities that were strewn along the moral minefield into which she had strayed, and their potential implications. 'But, if I decide to own up, it has to be right now, or else my relationship with Evelyn, and also my son, will forever be one of mistrust. His mother a cheat. Our whole lifetime together under question.'

So Grace told Evelyn.

'Evelyn. Can I tell you something? In confidence.'

Evelyn nodded but stayed silent.

They were poker players playing against each other for high stakes. They had examined their hands of cards and the moves could not be signalled in advance. But the initial advantage was with Evelyn. Grace had made the first move and laid her opening card on the table. Evelyn had no option but to counter with the cheapest card she held. To stonewall until the hands they were both holding became more apparent to each other. However, both players knew when the cards were dealt and Grace had asked the question that Evelyn held a full house in her hand and it was a simple matter of the cards being laid down. One by one.

Nathan had left the tray of drinks on the table, and, sensing the tension between his wife and his mother, had silently moved away, without comment.

'It was me you saw – in Melbourne,' Grace confided. 'The man I was with ...' Evelyn's expression did not alter. Not even the hint of a raised eyebrow. Grace took this as confirmation she had indeed been rumbled that day in Melbourne, and that her decision to reveal all had been justified.

'... was someone I'd met by accident a few months before, in Hobart.

He'd been my first boyfriend. So that day in Hobart we had a coffee together. To catch up on old times. His wife had died, In fact I felt sorry for him. That's not strictly true. I have to admit some of the old feelings were still there. It surprised me really. Come to think of it, I don't think they ever fully went away.

We parted that day in Hobart agreeing we should meet up again some time, but neither of us really expecting any more to come of it.

I'd told him about Billy. And the boys.

He had children as well - three. Grown up and living away.

We walked to the ferry terminal together, and he gave me his business card as he got on the boat to go back to Melbourne, where he lives.

Evelyn, you won't tell Billy, will you? I expect you'll have to tell Nathan - I'd rather you told him than me – it's not the sort of thing a mother should have to tell her son.'

Evelyn looked sympathetically at Grace and replied, 'I won't tell Billy if you don't want me to – but don't you think perhaps he should know?'

Grace ignored the question. She felt a powerful need to complete the story while her nerve was still strong. With what she had told already she was feeling lighter.

'Anyway, I know I shouldn't have done, but one day, when I was feeling more bored than usual - life in the country can sometimes get to you like that - I picked up the phone and rang him. Just a silly impulse really - nothing behind it, he just made me laugh - like when we were kids. Suppose he made me feel young again.'

Evelyn noticed that Grace had not used his Christian name, and attributed this to embarrassment and her need to downplay the relationship. An intention which would be assisted by the anonymity of not naming him.

'Anyway, after that phone call there was no going back. It got out of hand. Beyond our control. Of course, I feel guilty – we both thought we could finish it any time we wanted to. Funnily enough, on that day you saw us – that must have been the day we ended it, before anyone found out, and any damage was done; I suppose we both realised that you can't ever turn back the clock, and that we'd had our fun. That's all it ever was, Evelyn – fun, a harmless fling.'

Evelyn looked at her closely, and was convinced this was a long way from being Grace's true feeling about her anonymous man, but both their hands of cards had now been played, and to Evelyn it appeared as if Grace was the losing player of the two, and had just thrown in her last card – the best one in her hand – but in the knowledge that all the cards she had held were overpowered by her opponent's from the moment they were dealt.

Nathan tried to bring himself back to the reality of the present-day, and the conversation with his father in the front room of the big house. After all, he told himself, the events between Evelyn and Grace in his reverie now seemed to have happened so long ago. It seemed like a lifetime.

All the agonizing he had been through with Evelyn caused by that afternoon. And all the time the turmoil was going on Billy knew nothing. He was in blissful ignorance.

And then the deaths … not one … but two …

Billy's anger shook the dust from his brain, and he was forced to continue to confront the present. The now.

'You're trying to poison my memory of your mother. How dare you?'

Billy was more out of control than Nathan had ever seen him. But the damage had been done, and all that was left was to try to limit his father's pain.

'Listen, Dad, it's not like you think. Ma said he was just an old friend. She didn't even use his name when she was telling Evelyn. Told her she had ended it anyway. That she loved you. That it was only an unavoidable fling that she regretted.

She always talked most to us about the early years of your marriage as being her happiest, when you built up the orchards together.

But nothing stays the same forever, Dad. Things change. And people change.

Try not to judge Ma too harshly, please.'

Nathan studied the desolate look on his father's face. 'Because it was over, she asked us not to tell you. She didn't want to hurt you.

Then - we lost her.

No-one will ever know why she did what she did at the end, Dad.

Only Ma knew.

Everyone assumed it must have been caused by Michael – and the telegram that tipped her over the edge.

But it could have been guilt from the relationship as well - and not having told you about it. The combination of both causing her a terrible mental overload that nobody could be expected to bear.'

Billy was just listening. Eerily composed. Externally. Not wanting to assess the options about his wife that his son was presenting matter-of-factly to him. 'I'd let Grace go. In peace. Now this,' Billy thought, his mind now in dreadful confusion.

'Why tell me now?' Billy asked his son, a contorted look of anguish now on his lined, weather beaten face.

'We thought it important that you know what she really thought about you.'

'You mean in case I ever happened to find out. About the affair. By accident. During a family argument say,' Billy came back at his son in ironic anger.

Of course, to Nathan, family concern, including altruism

towards his father, was not a paramount motivating force, as, since the moment of picking up the telegram from the doormat, and handing it to his father, in his own mind he had wanted it to be the affair that had tipped his mother over the mental edge of reason, and not that of his brother's death in Vietnam. Michael, who, even up until the moment of his mother's suicide, may still have been the most important person in her life – even to the extent of being the cause of her passing.

In fact Nathan feared that Michael may have been the final thought in his mother's mind as she slipped despairingly into eternity.

'You and that wife of yours. Ever since you met her,' Billy ranted at his son.

'Don't blame Evelyn, Dad.'

'Get out. Now,' Billy blazed, his hands shaking.

He pulled open the front door and gestured to his son to leave the house.

'About the businesses, Dad...'

'Out ... Now ...'

'Get in touch, Dad. If you want to talk it over.'

Billy slammed the front door. He went inside the house and slumped at the table, resting his aching head in his upturned palms. Images raced through his mind ... Grace ... everything his son had just told him ... it couldn't be true ... she was always faithful ...

Billy's felt dizzy. His head throbbed with a ferocity which verged on the edge of derangement.

The coroner's investigation was completed. Witnesses had been questioned. The result was unequivocal: Accidental Death. How could the coroner have concluded otherwise when he learned of Billy's recent medical history. For anyone suffering dizziness and blackouts, a fall from a ladder was inevitable.

The final farewells were said to Billy Forrest. Everyone who knew Billy from miles around came to the funeral in Swan Vale.

Nathan and Evelyn and the two children came over from Melbourne, pointedly spoke to no-one and then returned. Never to set foot in Tasmania again.

Lew asked the apple picking team to continue for two more weeks, until the end of the season, and everyone agreed.

Joe and Lucy had wanted to seek advice following the announcement of their inheritance, but had held off approaching anyone, as it seemed insensitive; there still hung over the orchards an air of unreality, as though no-one wanted to acknowledge the tragedy that had taken place in their midst.

In the week following Billy's funeral, the Flints were taking their lunch break in the south orchard, under the giant oak, when Lew came over to join them. Their relationship with him had been amicable enough over the two years they had been apple picking, but had never stepped over the boundary into friendliness.

Lew gave the impression that he had joined them to discuss confidential matters, although he was such an enigmatic character, it was difficult to be categorical about anything connected with him.

Lew Burke was a shy and solitary man. The salt of the earth. Hard as teak, and the type of man who, if ever the call came in war to leave the trench and charge at the marauding enemy with fixed bayonet, then he was the one you would want at your shoulder.

The studied politeness of his 'Do you mind if I join you?' took them both aback, as this was, with the exception of his approach following the reading of Billy's will, the longest continuous sentence he had spoken to them.

Lew stretched out his legs, opened the top button of his red gingham work shirt, and leant back against the oak tree. He opened the greaseproof paper containing his salmon paste and cucumber sandwiches.

In a scene rife with incongruities, Joe and Lucy noticed how his sandwiches had been prepared. Cut in triangles – not halves – the crusts surgically removed from the slices of white bread.

Only Billy ever knew, among the workers in the orchards, precisely what Lew's domestic circumstances were, and Lucy speculated on this while she studied how immaculately Lew's lunch had been prepared.

A delicate-looking sandwich appeared to disappear into

Lew's massive, large-veined brown fist as he took it from the plastic box before raising it slowly to his mouth, all the while keeping them in suspense as to the reason he had joined them. However, they concluded that, to Lew, such a leisurely speed of action was probably habitual, and that he would need to progress at his own leisurely pace through still more stages of his lunchtime routine before the reason began to be divulged.

They were now beginning to wonder, in fact, if several one-hour lunchtimes would still be insufficient time for a conversation with Lew to be completed.

Lew, for his part, felt that he had come to trust the English couple. It usually took him much longer than two years' acquaintance for him to embark upon any discourse of any substance with anyone.

Lew had known Billy and Grace from the day they met, and had been Billy's closest confidant. After his lunch was finished, he spoke. No small talk. Straight to the point ... 'Billy was a sick man. Very sick. Brain tumour.

The job hadn't got any easier for him. And he had big responsibilities – family worries. Especially after his wife died.'

Since the day of the reading of the will, the Flints had been hoping that someone would unravel the mystery of Billy's cryptic statements that had resulted in their inheritance, but had remained uncertain what action they should take after hearing the news. They felt as though they had been on the front row in a theatre watching a Shakespearean tragedy, and had been thrust violently onto centre stage to play the lead roles.

'What happened?' Lucy asked, sensing that Lew wanted to tell them a lot more.

'Suicide ... Michael, Billy's youngest boy, went to serve in Vietnam. Never returned. Missing in action. Fine boy. Fearless. Brave as a lion. I remember him at school; loved to play Aussie Rules. One match, he jumped high to collect a pass and fell badly. Broke a collarbone. Trainer never found out until the final hooter went. He'd played on through to the end. Even kicked two goals.'

Lew was visibly relaxing, letting his words flow, as though he had returned from a mountain climb and was removing a heavy pack from his back, placing it on the ground, and starting to remove the contents.

'The Anzac club, in Hobart,' Lew continued. 'After we got the news- about Vietnam – the place was packed to the rafters – everyone there that night was an old soldier. I drove Billy to Hobart that night. He was guest of honour. Grace stayed at home.'

Lew was beginning to feel he had gone too far. That he had stepped into unfamiliar territory in opening his heart, particularly to people he didn't really know. That Billy wouldn't have approved.

But even while that particular feeling was developing within him another equally powerful one arose that these were the people who had inherited the land on which the three of them were now sitting. The same land he had walked across with his dog before he was tall enough to pluck his first apple from the branch of a tree.

His land. Not theirs. Tasmanian land.

Lew, as he was speaking, felt sensations growing within him that he could not remember having felt before. Feelings he didn't welcome, and with which he was uneasy, and which, because they were not part of his nature, felt as though they had appeared supernaturally, and, if made light of, would evaporate.

But these new feelings were controlling, crushing ones.

He began to realise that the rancour he was feeling was not directed towards the English couple as much as to Billy. His boss. The man who had rewarded his thirty years of back-breaking toil with the weekly pittance of a meagre wage envelope, and then disdainfully handed over his birthright to a pair of foreigners.

And so Lew knew inside that this was the reason he was going to tell them the rest of the Forrest story.

Because Billy had forfeited all rights to his respect.

He wanted them to know that if integrity had been a Forrest attribute, then it had been laid to rest with the youngest son in a field of a far-off foreign land.

Lew knew his conscience was clear, and he would continue the story.

He had never told anyone about the night at the Anzac club,

and, as he began to talk about Michael Forrest, he felt his heart begin to swell with pride.

'The Aussie flag was hanging over the doorway of the Club. A roomful of war survivors from Galipoli ... and the Second World War.

And at the end of the evening we put our arms round one another's shoulders and all sang 'Waltzing Matilda'.

Billy and Grace used to hum it to Michael when he was a baby in his cot, to send him to sleep.

Then a bugler played the 'Last Post' – everyone in the room stood to attention and saluted the flag ... never known a moment to match it ... before or since.'

Lew's pride in the boy was now shining in his eyes. His unwanted invasive bitterness had been washed away by an innate tenderness within his spirit that reminiscence had engendered.

The orchard was hushed as Lew's words in commemoration of Michael Forrest drifted away to become one with the timelessness of the apple groves of his homeland.

'That night Billy shook hands with each and every man in that room.

Then, when Billy got home, to the big house, Grace was gone. The car was missing. Billy was frantic. No note. Not a word. We went searching.

Down to O'Rourke's glen. There she was. In the front of the car. Down the embankment. They found a photo of the boy in her hand.

Billy had lost his son – and then his wife.

Time I did some work.'

And with that Lew was gone.

He hadn't told the Flints the part in the Forrest story about the day he had deliberately given Billy's ladder a nudge with his boot as he walked past, among the pickers who were busy unloading their bags into the cart.

Nor about the sleepless nights he had been having for months before deciding to do it. Worrying how to find the money the bookies were asking him for – Billy had been warning him for years that backing the horses would one day get him into strife.

Mind you Billy had always promised to see him right. He had a favourite saying that they used to laugh at together, 'If I drop off the twig, Lewwy, you'll be well taken care of – no worries.'

And when Billy had told him about his blackouts, doctors, hospital tests and that he hadn't told anyone else ... well.

But time went on. Bookies were still putting pressure on.

'People with money just don't understand how desperate things can get when you haven't got any,' Lew had told himself. 'And, well, people who are ill ... you just don't know for sure - some can go on for years.

Then again, who was to know that Billy would have gone and changed his will like that.'

Amazing the hidden depths that can be discovered lying just below the surface of even the most upstanding and mild-mannered people.

Uncle Sam's

The launch of Blackpool's Yankee Experience and, within it, the Lockwood's Uncle Sam's American diner was a masterstroke of timing by Isaac Ford.

It caught the wave of 1950s Americana that was sweeping the post-war nation.

And it was built in Britain's premier holiday resort, alongside the well-established and phenomenally successful Coaster World.

To Isaac, Frank and Sarah's venture was insignificant; a minor cog in a gigantic corporate wheel that he had agreed to, not least as a means to occupy Frank so that he could continue his affair with Sarah.

Only when Isaac was satisfied that the restaurant had been professionally established and was up and running in a way that satisfied his exacting standards, with Frank fully equipped with the necessary management skills and Sarah's background support, did he then take a permanent long-distance supervisory role.

Within three months of opening, Uncle Sam's became the 'hot spot' in town – the place to go to and to be seen at.

Sarah continually teased Frank that Uncle Sam's had become his obsession, to the exclusion of everything else in his life, including herself.

Isaac, on those few occasions he was also present when this marital banter was taking place, would smile benignly and refrain from comment; and Sarah was, in fact, not as concerned as her remark to her husband implied, as she, at the same time, was pre-occupied with an infatuation of her own; that between herself and Isaac.

Frank had failed to notice how his wife had changed. How she was now happier. More carefree.

Danny, however, on his visits home, had noticed that his mother seemed different in some way, even to him, a son who was accustomed to his mother's habitually mercurial approach to domesticity.

However he was happy to admit that he liked the new Sarah.

It is not too much of an exaggeration to say that Frank, due to working in close proximity to Isaac, came to revere him, both for his urbanity, and also his business acumen and accomplishments.

Nevertheless, such esteem would never have stretched to the extent of sacrificing his wife to his newly-acquired idol.

Isaac, for his part, assumed that everyone regarded him in a similarly reverential way, and had always taken for granted his ordained place at the summit of the order of things, and that the material evidence of this, in terms of his castle and his other lavish accoutrements, had been no more than his just desserts and his birthright.

From the days of his youth, Isaac's single-minded commitment to whatever endeavour he undertook had singled him out as a man apart from his peers, and his relentless pursuit of success over the years had provoked their grudging admiration towards him rather than their affection.

Even Frank felt no more warmth for his mentor than he would have looking at a basilisk.

It was destined to be Sarah Lockwood who became the seismic force that cracked the implacably iron surface of Isaac's emotional defences, and who then burrowed beneath to reach the vulnerable core.

Initially Isaac desired Sarah as a trophy; no more than one of his expected rewards in life. But as their relationship deepened and she became the first woman since his wife Camille to prise open the locked door to his hidden sensitivities, he came to place her in a separate, altogether more protected compartment of his life, and, with this change, an exquisite irony of role reversal took place, and Isaac came to envy Frank.

At first, clandestine meetings were easy to arrange between them, as Frank was so preoccupied with his burgeoning Uncle Sam's.

Isaac had even told Frank that it was good experience for him to operate more on his own, so that the day could be brought nearer when the complete handover of the restaurant could be made without any further involvement from himself.

And, even while he was saying this to Frank, Isaac would be visualising his next meeting with his wife.

Both Isaac and Sarah wanted to believe it would always be just a harmless dalliance between them, with no casualties involved, and a relationship on which they could call quits at any time.

But the more serious their feelings grew, the more difficult became the pretence.

Because both of them were in denial that a serious romantic entanglement was developing between them, they were able to agree readily on several occasions over the years to separate, each time ostensibly being a final split, but somehow a malign force always conspired to intervene and arrange for a crossing of their paths, usually in the least expected situations and circumstances. And then the hidden emotions would be re-ignited and all the good intentions they had made to return to their old and trusted lives and forget one another, would be swept away on a tide of renewed fervour which then re-united them even stronger than before.

Amazingly, the affair continued in this way for over fifteen years, spanning a decade of success for Isaac's Yankee Experience, and Frank's Uncle Sam's, which retained its position during that time as Blackpool's most popular restaurant.

As the 1960s drew to a close, Frank's plans as he had outlined them on the night he had spoken to Isaac at the castle, had been realised, and he had started to envisage Uncle Sam's with his son Danny learning the business, in partnership with him, and then eventually taking over.

But, in the early years of the 1970s, storm clouds of recession began to gather over the renowned seaside town before sweeping away the clear blue skies of the prosperity years.

British holidaymakers, in ever-increasing numbers, began to forsake traditional week-long seaside holidays at home, in favour of the continent and beyond, with the result that Blackpool, the nonpareil of the British tourist trade since the dawning of the railway era, was compelled to look towards ways of regeneration if it hoped to compete with the Spanish costas, and avoid the onset of a long and painful terminal decline.

Sixties Blackpool was beginning to resemble a dinosaur which had lived unchallenged in its prehistoric world and was now to be seen lumbering blindly towards the edge of a precipitous cliff.

Blackpool needed to adapt or die. The choice was that stark.

And it had to do it quickly.

The town's luminaries, however - the movers and the shakers – possessed the requisite attributes to weather the approaching storm.

They had traditionally been visionaries and innovators. And gamblers. And they had always ferociously guarded their reputation for pre-eminence against all-comers, both at home and abroad.

They were not going to go down without a fight.

Isaac Ford had pioneered the way to the future and had ensured that Blackpool reigned supreme throughout Europe in the previous two decades with his monumental Cleopatra's, followed by the Yankee Experience.

He now began to resist the continental threat by plans to overcome the long-standing drawback to a holiday at home compared to across the Channel – poor British weather.

He planned a giant indoor sun centre, supplying all the essentials of a typical British holiday, but under the cover of a moveable roof.

The focal point was a huge swimming pool fringed by synthetic palm trees and heated to a constant Mediterranean temperature.

As well as the pool, every other modern holiday amenity was

to be found in Isaac Ford's 'Sea City' – from entertainment to shopping – and all were to take place in artificial sunshine – Isaac's pièce de resistance.

The project was an inimitable fusion of foresight, ingenuity and inspiration, and because of the timing of his brainchild, Isaac's S.A.F.F. Corporation suffered no more than a sideswipe when the British holiday migration began to gather momentum.

For Frank Lockwood, however, and the rest of the town beyond the confines of Sea City, the situation could not have been more different.

The restaurant trade, in particular, felt the full impact of the chill wind of change.

Frank, with the aid of periodic S.A.F.F. loans over the years of growth, had financed more and more improvements to Uncle Sam's, which placed him in an especially vulnerable position when the recession began to bite.

Isaac, as Frank and Sarah's principal creditor, in his capacity as S.A.F.F. chairman, began to scrutinise the financial situation of Uncle Sam's, along with the other holiday enterprises in which S.A.F.F. had substantial investment, one consideration in so doing being his intention to divert loan funds from continuing to be invested in the more precariously-placed businesses, to go instead into the embryonic Sea City, which was being projected as requiring unprecedented capital investment.

As a starting point, Isaac proposed to the S.A.F.F. board that existing businesses be subject to a freeze on new loan capital for projected expansion plans, with regular reviews to take place for the foreseeable future.

By this time, the financial arm of the S.A.F.F. empire had grown to such an extent that it had become impossible to ascertain any personal involvement on Isaac's part in any particular business from the myriad of S.A.F.F.-backed enterprises.

He was, therefore, able to claim corporate necessity for loan freezes and requests for early repayment, in his dealings with the Lockwoods and other proprietors, and that he was merely a figurehead doing his master's bidding, even though this was far from being the unvarnished truth, as the master in question was, in fact, his father in the United States, Samuel Arthur Ford Junior, who had always given his son full autonomy to run the British offshoot of the U.S. Corporation in any way he thought fit, subject to fellow directors' approval.

In fact Isaac planned to use Frank's current financial impasse at Uncle Sam's to attempt to lure Sarah away from him for good, leaving her to confront the heart-rending decision of having to choose between the two men in her life, which was also, for her, a choice between her past and her future.

Trevi's

It was hard to believe that the two people facing each other across the corner candlelit table at the Trevi, Manchester's exclusive new Italian restaurant, were the same Isaac Ford and Sarah Lockwood who first met over twenty years earlier on the doorstep of number 3 Park Avenue.

Isaac's hair had receded from his forehead, and was now grey at the sides of his lightly-tanned face, and he was broader at the midriff.

In his appearance, he was the archetypal cultured middle-aged businessman who continued to personify wealth and power as ostensibly as he had on the day they had met.

Sarah, on her part, had acquired a serene elegance over the years, and a taste for the sophisticated trappings that were de rigueur for the wife of a successful businessman, a status which Frank had now indisputably acquired.

The meal was over, and Isaac and Sarah clinked their champagne glasses together for a closing toast to their next meeting, before retiring for coffee and liqueurs in Trevi's sumptuously-furnished lounge.

They had always tried to arrange an annual celebration of the day of their meeting, and they shared a mutual conviction that Frank had never, over all this time, suspected for one moment that he was being cuckolded.

To compound her twinges of guilt over the years, Sarah knew

that Frank had never strayed from the marital path, nor ever would.

Her husband radiated integrity, and dependability, as conspicuously as the garishly-coloured patterned ties he had taken to wearing with his dark blue pin-striped suits as his sole concession to the necessity for a touch of flamboyance in a successful restaurant manager who was on view to his customers.

Isaac, by contrast, having always lived his life in the empyrean realm, had never experienced a Frank Lockwood-type of congenital self-consciousness, so had not the slightest compunction to display to the world even in a token way his status as a proud peacock with a need to preen and display its fine feathers.

And Sarah loved them equally, albeit differently, in the same way that she loved Danny differently to Frank.

She saw the calibrations of love as infinite and intriguing, and defying the cold, forensic approach of a rationalist.

Love was not meant to be analysed or categorised. It had always been at the heart of everything, just as it was the essence of the heart itself.

And, Sarah told herself, as she had been fortunate in being the recipient of several of love's innumerable varieties – chosen in an unknowable way by some kind of perverse invisible romantic force – then why shouldn't it be a delight, a joy to be savoured, and without this wonderful gift of love needing continually to war against equally powerful countervailing ethereal forces, such as guilt and loyalty, thereby enforcing choices that engendered not only inevitable confusion, but also sadness, leading to eventual loss.

Such, therefore, was the force of Sarah Lockwood's conscience - the scales of her emotions and her thoughts – perpetually weighing these eternal forces in the balance of her life.

Isaac Ford, on the other hand, no longer experienced such complex entanglements of the thoughts and feelings.

His veins had received the injection of an anaesthetic when his wife died, which had spread remorselessly over the years through his being, until reaching his heart, and rendering him emotionally sclerotic.

But Sarah coming into his life, however, had slowly massaged his ailing heart into life and caused it to beat with excitement once again, as his feelings for her had deepened into an abiding love that tormented him because it was unable to be fulfilled.

For Sarah was married to Frank, and already committed for life; and Isaac's life partner was now only a memory, a treasured one, but, nonetheless, a love of the past.

And he had grown tired of being a lonely man.

He needed a woman to share his life with again.

And, at Trevi's restaurant that night, he intended to make Sarah that woman.

The question of a permanent future together had never been openly addressed between the two of them, and Isaac that night was waiting with intense agitation for the right moment to begin his impassioned entreaty.

He had felt ill at ease all evening at the prospect of having to pour forth his emotions.

Isaac's milieu of expression had always been the blunt world of the boardroom, with its own sort of inimitable challenges, but on this evening with Sarah he felt he was encountering a far greater test than he had ever faced in his enclosed business world.

From being a young man he had habitually had to deal in the currency of hard, cold fact, and had rarely needed to articulate from the concealed and delicate realm of the emotions.

The difficulty he now found himself facing was that each word to Sarah needed to convey the afflictions of the heart and not the contents of a balance sheet.

At that moment Isaac was sailing into uncharted waters.

His cultured veneer had been stripped bare, to reveal the essence of who he really was.

A part of the emotion he was feeling was a terror that this essence of himself might never have been a heart, but always no more than a gaping void, and the words he was about to speak would be damning testimony as to which of the two it was.

He leaned forward and spoke.

'Please come with me, Sarah. Leave Frank. You know you want to. That you need to.'

Isaac reached out and held Sarah's hands between his, underneath the table. He sought a change of expression in her bright, pale blue eyes, 'Your future's with me. Look at all I can give you. We should be together. For keeps.'

Isaac felt Sarah's small, thin hands trembling.

Her gaze left his and she glanced away, realising the significance of what she was about to say.

'You know I want to. But I still love Frank, too. He needs me. Always has. Always will. He's not a survivor like you. And what about Danny – where does he come in all this? You're asking so much from me. It's unfair, and cruel on others. Others who are blameless. Innocent.'

'It's not a question of blame, Sarah. Or guilt. Never has been. And never will be. We only have one life, and deserve our chance at happiness. Together. You and me. Please say yes.'

Isaac wanted Sarah to hesitate, to weigh his words – to picture the two of them together in her thoughts right now, as he was doing. Not thoughts of herself with Frank.

'Where is my famed power of persuasion now? Where's the point in feeling such anguish if Sarah can't feel the same way. Or won't feel the same way – yes, that must be it – it's loyalty that's stopping her, and she's just as torn right now as I am,' Isaac frantically debated with himself.

But Sarah did not hesitate. Not for one second.

In her heart of hearts she supposed she had always known what her answer to Isaac was going to be when the fateful moment arrived that she had always dreaded.

She raised her head and looked directly at him, and knew she was about to say the most painful words she would ever utter in her life.

'Not at other people's expense, Isaac. I don't know if I could live with myself. As much as I love you, the answer has to be no. Please try to understand. I'm so sorry. So terribly sorry. Please forgive me.'

Sarah's face looked pale and agonised, and she rose to her feet to leave, but Isaac reached forward and grasped her hand.

He could not conceive that he had lost her. Forever. And to someone like Frank.

But he refused to surrender the initiative in the conversation.

No-one ever walked out on him. Not even her. Especially not her.

He thought she was saying these things because her anxiety had taken a grip on her imagination, and, if given just a little time, she would see that he was right. But he could not let her walk away now. Out of his life forever.

'Sarah. Just listen to me. Please. Everything I have. I've ever worked for. It can all be yours. Just say you'll leave him and come with me. What more can he possibly offer you than I can?'

The image of her standing alongside Isaac on the battlements of his Lakeland castle on that sublime summer evening flashed into her mind. 'Be careful what you wish for, as you might one day get it,' had been her mother's favourite aphorism, and Sarah pictured her saying those prophetic words, but then immediately felt a shaft of shame – a little girl's guilt – peeling away the years between childhood and maturity in an instant, when she realised how much her mother would have disapproved of her affair with Isaac.

'I can't bear to be torn like this,' Sarah wanted to scream up to the heavens, for everyone within earshot and beyond to share a part of her intolerable burden, even though she knew that all the people there in that room had problems of their own, many worse than hers. Problems of life and death. Problems beyond emotional entanglements, however deep.

But the picture of that magical evening at the castle would not leave her mind. 'That night was beyond my wildest dreams,' she heard herself thinking, 'And mother's adage has come true. It's now all within my grasp.'

And yet she knew the die was cast.

'Frank has been my whole life. The father of my precious Danny. We have built everything together. And it has taken what's happened tonight to make me really appreciate what I already have – probably for the very first time. I've taken it all for granted. My life's been too easy, too comfortable, too happy. If that's possible. And now I'm thinking of throwing it all away.'

Sarah's internal dialogue was becoming feverish and out of control.

She thought she was hallucinating with the speed at which these conflicting thoughts were flashing through her head, and, just as quickly, being replaced by equally extreme thoughts cancelling out the preceding ones. She began to think she might be suffering from some form of emotional insanity. All taking place in the blinking of an eye, while the conversation with Isaac continued. She wished she had walked out when she had the chance, and put an end to the madness of her thinking.

A brooding silence fell between them, and Isaac took this as a signal to end his persuasion.

He realised that his attempt to win Sarah had failed, and resolved there and then to put a reserve plan into operation the following morning.

Isaac formulated an outline of the plan in his mind as he walked with Sarah towards the cloakroom by the entrance of Trevi's.

They had both accepted that any possibility of a romantic end to the evening with coffee and liqueurs in the lounge would be an absurdity now that a sheet of glacial ice had formed between them.

On the drive to Sarah's home, not a word was spoken.

Sarah gave Isaac's cheek a summary peck as he stared straight ahead through the car windscreen.

She stepped out and closed the passenger door with studied accusatory slowness, and prepared to tiptoe up to her bedroom so as not to awaken her slumbering husband.

As he watched her walk away, Isaac mentally finalised his scheme for Frank's destruction with venomous intent in his heart.

The obstacle in his path to Sarah lay sleeping blissfully just beyond the front doorway in which he was watching her turn the key to enter and go to lie by his side.

Isaac felt an intense yearning that it should be himself, not Frank, whom Sarah was joining that night, and every night in the future.

He vowed there and then that he would not give her up.

No-one had ever inflicted a defeat on Isaac Ford in his life, and, as he stared at the closed front door of the Lockwood house, his poisonous thoughts began to crystallise.

'She's chosen him. A man like Frank. The type of man I despise. Weak. Not worthy to breathe the same air as a woman like her. And yet he's got her. She's chosen him rather than me.

But I'm going to win her back. At all costs. Starting tomorrow. And, if everything fails, and I can't have her, then neither will Frank.

Because, rather than lose her to him, I'll destroy him. In my own way. Destroy him in his wife's eyes, so she'll see him for the man he really is, and realise what she's given up tonight.

From tomorrow Frank Lockwood's finished.'

Early the next morning Isaac contacted his corporation's financial heads, ostensibly to discuss possible expansion plans for Sea City, but instigating, during the conversations, an immediate profitability review of the corporation's restaurant enterprises in the North-West, as a first step to financing these plans.

Staff redundancies and dismissals where appropriate were mentioned as a priority in the current depressed business climate, and, where applicable, an overhaul of management structures.

The accounting department was set to work by Isaac, and the upshot was a summons to Frank Lockwood, proprietor of Uncle Sam's diner, the one-time flagship of the S.A.F.F. Corporation North-West restaurant outlets, to attend corporate headquarters at the end of the week.

Frank left the building late that afternoon in a state of shock, and with his head reeling.

He had been given an ultimatum that could lead to the loss of his business and his home.

When he had received the call to go for an interview, he had tried to get through to Isaac, but without success. He had wondered what was so important as to warrant a visit to headquarters at such short notice that could not have come from Isaac himself.

Frank had known there were cash flow problems with the

restaurant, but he felt he knew the financial aspects of the business better than anyone at the corporation and there was nothing to justify a call from the powers on high.

After all, it had been his business. His and Sarah's. His dream made flesh. With Isaac's backing and support.

But he had always regarded himself as considerably more than a mere front man for some faceless bureaucracy. And the cost of failure would be borne by him. It had always been his head on the block. It was his debt and his home that had been on the line – right from the day he proposed the idea to Isaac at Camford Castle.

Frank had been concerned about the increasing amount of his financial commitment to the expanding restaurant, and the spiralling costs and debts that went hand-in-hand with ambitious expansion plans. And, recently, customer numbers had begun to show a tailing-off.

But Isaac had always reassured him in the past whenever he had voiced any concern, and had emphasised the necessity to continually keep moving forward instead of looking to consolidate; a suggestion more compatible with Isaac's temperament, not Frank's.

And Frank would tell himself at such times, that Sarah had never been happier than during the years the business had been growing and, if Sarah was happy then so was he, and that was more important to him than any restaurant business, as much as he thought of it.

So Frank had always stilled his concerns by following Isaac's advice and tried not to anticipate problems.

But the last thing he had expected, even in his moments of deepest concern, was personal annihilation.

Frank had left Sarah sleeping fitfully on the morning he had driven to Manchester.

He looked at his wife as he gently closed the bedroom door and wondered for a second if her unsettled sleep meant that she had something on her mind, and perhaps he should try to find more time to talk to her and find out what was worrying her.

Five hours later, outside the offices of S.A.F.F. , Frank was a shattered man.

The financial team who had faced him across the oak table had refused to extend his overdraft facilities beyond six months, unless economies to the business had been shown to have been effective within that period, by means of staff redundancies and dismissals. Accompanied by increasing profit flow as an essential requirement alongside these cost-cutting measures.

And, after that time, foreclosure on Uncle Sam's and his boarding house would be undertaken.

An exact date for Frank's execution had been set.

But he had not realised that the executioner was Isaac Ford.

In fact, within an hour of receiving his ultimatum he had telephoned Isaac for advice on any recourse open to him, looking for a glimmer of hope.

This time Isaac was available. He told Frank 'Not to worry,' to 'Leave it to him to see what influence he could bring to bear,' and 'Hadn't he always been there for him?'

This was sufficient to assuage Frank's incipient panic, and, when he was back home, Sarah also consoled him, despite her own sickening foreboding in the pit of her stomach which was instigated by a conviction that she knew only too well the hand that had wielded the dagger that had just been plunged into her husband's back, and that she had been the unwitting cause by what she had said at Trevi's.

Frank, after that fateful day, began to be squeezed in Isaac's iron palm, as though he was an orange and the juice spouting forth was his life-blood.

He undertook his duties at the restaurant as though nothing had changed, but at night he began to crave sleep, to give him temporary relief from a situation in which he was certain there was no way out.

Sackings and redundancies began to take place at Uncle Sam's and Frank, with a heavy heart, was the one to carry out the unpalatable task.

Customer numbers continued to decline, bills remained unpaid, and threatening letters from suppliers began to escalate.

Sarah fought the corporation onslaught side by side with her husband, to save both businesses and the home, everything they had built together to be passed on to their son.

As the end of the six months ultimatum period came closer, Frank and Sarah scoured the books of the business together, night after night, in an attempt to find any chink of light that might be the entrance to a tunnel leading them to safety.

But Frank knew the searches were futile, and had been secretly preparing for several weeks to play one more card before they resigned themselves to their fate and went under.

But his heartfelt hope was that a miracle would still happen at the last moment to prevent him playing it.

The Seventies to the Millennium I

From the Mersey-led British rock group dominance in the sixties, popular music gravitated between polar extremities during the 1970s.

A decade that was heralded in by the dazzling flamboyance of the Swedish group Abba and glam rock, to the politically embittered late 1970s which brought forth both the anarchic Sex Pistols and punk rock, and a culturally symbolic feminist anthem, Gloria Gaynor's 'I Will Survive', a record destined to be one of the most enduring hits of all time.

The rapid progress of technology, evidenced particularly in the development of computers during the 80s and 90s, influenced the sounds with which musicians were able to experiment, and the result was techno pop, which reflected the musical tastes of a society with an ever-changing ethnic composition.

One year in particular showed the momentous impact possible when popular music was harnessed to humanitarian concern in an era of modern global communications.

The Live Aid concert in July 1985 was a follow-up to 'Do They Know It's Christmas?' – a record by forty pop stars gathered together at the persuasion of Bob Geldof, which raised proceeds of £8 million for famine relief.

The concert was a sixteen-hour spectacular of pop music performers which took place simultaneously in England and America, and was broadcast to every country in the world.

By the end of the evening an estimated 1.5 billion people had watched the unique event and fifty million dollars was raised to aid the Ethiopian people.

Throughout the 1970s, and for much of the 1980s, British television came to be regarded as the best in the world, noteworthy for a series of landmarks: Civilisation and the Ascent of Man; epic documentary series such as The World At War, and the historical literary dramas Brideshead Revisited and The Jewel In The Crown.

A pre-eminent figure in British television from the early years of the decade was David Attenborough, Controller of BBC2 in the 1960s, and pioneer of world-renowned natural history productions.

The era was also notable for the plays of Dennis Potter, and the innovative comedy of Monty Python's Flying Circus.

The period was one in which British television advanced to become one of the most dynamic and significant creative cultural influences ever known in popular entertainment.

In the British political arena, 1979 saw the election of Margaret Thatcher as the first female Prime Minister, who, during her first term in office, sent British troops to recapture the Falkland Islands from Argentina.

The first decade in power of her Conservative government witnessed head-to-head confrontations with trade unions, and thousands of British workers were faced with redundancy.

The most controversial was the Miners Strike of 1984-85, which ended in the miner's defeat, and a shift in power away from the unions.

On the world stage, Ronald Reagan's inauguration as the 40th U.S. President coincided with the start of the Thatcher government, while in South Africa, in 1991, a worldwide television audience saw the African National Congress leader, Nelson Mandela, walk to freedom and to the Presidency of a multi-cultural nation, after twenty-seven years in prison.

Disclosure

Sarah Lockwood's distress at the Trevi restaurant had not been caused purely by Isaac asking her to leave Frank. The affair with Isaac had not been the only secret she had been keeping from her husband.

A year earlier Sarah had felt so overwhelmed with having to carry the knowledge of her new secret that she had telephoned Jackie Flint to ask if she could go over to talk to her.

Jackie and Bob Flint had moved from Croft Green after the deaths of Owen and Victoria within nine months of one another in 1978.

Bob Flint had taken early retirement and, with Jackie, had bought a converted farmhouse in Silverdale, a village in the Ribble Valley.

Jackie and Sarah had kept in touch by telephone and letter since the days when they had been neighbours in Park Avenue, and their two boys had played together in the Alley, and they had continued to meet once a year in Blackpool at the Bisons Ladies Evenings.

Sarah expressed admiration for the embellishments she assumed were Jackie's skilful touches to the renovated farmhouse, as she looked into each room with Jackie at her side: colourful floral arrangements in the bedrooms; glass-fronted display cabinets of miniature thimbles and tiny silver clocks highlighted by secluded lighting in the hall, and oil paintings of soothing pastoral scenes in the downstairs rooms.

As they looked round the house, Jackie updated Sarah on the recent developments to the news of Joe and Lucy having become owners of an apple business in Tasmania that she had described in detail when she had last telephoned after receiving Joe's twenty-page air mail letter.

Sarah talked chirpily about the guesthouse, and the success that had come from the expansion of Uncle Sam's.

Jackie studied Sarah while she was talking, and thought how light-hearted she seemed, but, within only half-an-hour from sitting down together for coffee in the living room, she realised what a false impression this had been, and how much Sarah had been keeping a tight rein on her emotions.

Sarah and Jackie moved into the open plan living room and sat side by side on the green velvet two-seater settee, with cups of coffee next to them on small, glass-topped, patterned tables.

In the rush to tell each other everything that had happened in their lives since they last spoke, both of them had exhausted the primary topics that had always been at the forefront of their conversations.

Except one.

A subject too delicate even for close friends of many years standing such as Sarah and Jackie to broach without concern for the possible consequences that could ensue.

It had now lain dormant for so long it had become almost taboo, even between them.

But as it was the cause of Sarah's visit to see Jackie that day, the subject needed to be introduced into the conversation in some way.

However painful it was going to be.

Sarah put down her coffee cup and fixed her gaze on the hypnotic candle flame in the alcove at the side of the brickwork fireplace.

She was looking at it as though she was conjuring up someone's face in the flame.

'I've seen Danny.'

Sarah didn't want Jackie to respond.

She hoped she would just allow her to talk uninterrupted for as long as she was able to do so coherently.

Jackie understood and stayed silent.

The telephone rang, and Jackie cursed the day the instrument had been invented.

She let it ring.

'I had a phone call. Out of the blue. A month ago. It was Danny. Asking me to meet him. At a house in London ... Lewisham.'

Sarah choked back her tears and took a few seconds to collect her thoughts before continuing,

'You can't imagine how I felt, hearing his voice for the first time in thirteen years.

And then driving down there to see him. All he gave me over the phone were directions. No news.

You musn't tell anyone, Jackie.

Not even Frank knows.'

Jackie was shocked by the disclosure, but attempted to hold an impassive countenance as Sarah glanced towards her. She felt at that moment it was important for Sarah to hold her equanimity so she could continue, and not break down.

'You don't know how much it means to be able to speak to someone about it. At last.'

Jackie was thinking how she and Sarah had shared the joys and sorrows of their respective families over the years, but this .... her feelings were a disorientating mixture of disbelief at the revelation, compassion for her friend, and indebtedness that Sarah had chosen her to share such a confidence. The thought crossed her mind that if their situations were ever reversed in the future, she would feel secure in choosing Sarah to entrust with her innermost hopes and fears.

The memories came flooding back to Sarah as she resumed.

'You know that the last we heard of Danny was when he had broken police bail after the crash and gone into hiding.

How I told you I went up to his room that day and found that his suitcase and clothes were gone and that he hadn't even left a note.

You can understand why Frank and I stayed silent at the time of the accident, and for all these years since.

Even though the police, in the early days, were continuously questioning us about Danny's whereabouts – not believing us – thinking we had something to hide – that we knew where he was.

So did everyone else.

But, in fact, we've known nothing all along.

Until last month.

And, even if he had contacted us in all that time, we couldn't have said anything, because of the consequences for Danny.

I know that's the reason he's kept away all these years – he didn't want to incriminate us.

And, do you know, Jackie, we still miss him as much after all this time as the day he left. The hurt never goes away. It's been worse than if he'd died – at least then you can grieve – and move on.

Jackie, where did we go wrong?'

'Sarah, listen to me. You didn't do anything wrong. You did the best you could. We all do for our children.

But things happen.

The days at Park Avenue can't be brought back. Ever.

We just have to cope the best we can, and move on.'

Jackie, at that moment, felt Sarah's pain as though it were her own. 'There but for the grace of God,' she thought; not only towards Sarah as a mother, but also as a wife, as she had heard the rumours about Sarah and Isaac, which were spoken in whispered tones between the Bison ladies at the yearly get-togethers.

Sarah clasped her hands together, feeling the need to wipe off the perspiration that had seeped into them.

'I was horrified when he met me at the door.

The house is no more than a hovel.

He's living in one room on his own.

He's gone so thin ... You wouldn't recognise him ... My Danny who was always so particular about his appearance ... Always combing his hair ... He's been living rough all these years ... Surviving God knows how ... '

Sarah felt a lump forming in her throat.

Jackie kept quiet.

The silence between them became oppressive. The poignancy of the story had become almost unbearable.

Sarah took a sip from a glass of water Jackie had brought in from the kitchen, and began again.

'Danny asked me not to tell anyone that I'd seen him. Not even his father. 'The fewer people who know I'm still alive, the better', is what he said, 'In case the police find out.'

A few weeks before I saw him he had collapsed ... in London. Close to the Palladium ... Exhaustion. And hunger.

He told me a strange tale.

That the last thing he remembered before he lost consciousness was having walked up to the entrance to the Palladium to look at the photographs outside the theatre – showing the stars who had topped the bill there. You know who one of them was, don't you, Jackie?... Molly ... Molly Earle ... little Molly from the Alley.'

Jackie smiled tenderly, but didn't want to take Sarah down a detour into the past which would recall the young Danny. So she stayed quiet.

'Danny told me a crowd gathered round him and he blacked out.

And the next thing he remembered was waking up in a hospital bed.'

Sarah's words trailed away, and she fell back into the backrest of the settee.

Jackie put her arm round Sarah's hunched shoulders. Her head was buried in her hands, and she began to sob.

Jackie held the glass while Sarah took more sips of water.

'You don't have to tell me any more if you don't want to, Sarah, you know that.'

Sarah took out a tissue from her side pocket of her brown suede jacket and blew her nose. While doing it, she seemed to Jackie to draw upon some reserve of strength as an act of pure tenacious will.

'He said he'd phoned me as he wanted me to know he was still alive, after the scare of the collapse, in case ... you know ... next time he wasn't so lucky. I just think he'd come to the end of his tether.

He said he would pay me back every penny of the bail money we'd lost, but I know he never will – and we don't want it anyway – we just want him home again with us.

He hasn't got anything. He didn't even have change to feed the meter for the gas fire.

He sat huddled up on the floor in a corner in his overcoat, wearing his balaclava and mittens, and blowing on his hands to keep warm.

It was freezing in there
It broke my heart
He didn't say what he planned to do
I asked him to give himself up
Told him that it wasn't too late
That Frank and I could help him straighten everything out
But he said things had gone too far
I think deep down he just wanted to let us know we were still in his thoughts
He knows if he comes out of hiding he'll go to prison and he wouldn't survive
Not like he is now
He didn't say as much
But I saw it in his face
I am his mother after all
I put fifty pounds in his hand
It was all I had on me
He tried to give it back
But I went quickly before he was able to
I knew I'd never see him again
I didn't want my last memory to be my own son repaying me
He owes me nothing
I didn't want to leave him
He's just a little boy again
Frightened of the dark
He always asked us to leave his bedroom door open
So he could hear our voices downstairs
In those days we could make his life right again
Just by sitting next to him
On his bed

Stroking his head
And holding his tiny hand
But now...'

'I know. I know.' Jackie Flint took Sarah Lockwood's tired, anguished face between her hands and looked into her eyes.

Mother to Mother.

And at that moment Sarah knew she had chosen the right person to tell.

Inferno

Frank Lockwood lay awake in the dark, waiting for Sarah to drop into a deep sleep.

He listened closely to her breathing before he moved.

He dressed hurriedly and, after quietly closing and locking the front door of the house, started the car and backed it out of the driveway.

He glanced at his watch. It was 1 a.m.

The drive to the diner was along deserted roads.

He parked the car a mile away, down a deathly quiet unlit alleyway.

He moved swiftly to the rear of the building and crouched behind a low brick wall.

Earlier that day he had made sure he was the last to leave.

When everyone had gone home, he had opened out some cardboard boxes and placed them on a table underneath the open back window.

He then spread a small pile of newspapers haphazardly on top of the opened boxes.

He wanted it to look as though one of the staff had been reading the newspapers and smoking, during a late-night break, and the window above the table then left partly open as an oversight at the close of business when the premises were locked up.

Frank waited ... and waited ...

A man with his Alsatian dog walked by, almost within touching distance, the dog sniffing at the foot of the wall.

Frank held his breath and tried to still every muscle in his body.

The man tugged the dog's lead and walked away.

Frank's cramped legs were beginning to lose their feeling, and, after a seeming eternity of suspense had passed, which was, in fact, only half an hour, the planned moment finally arrived.

Frank's heart was racing.

He focused his mind completely on the task at hand, and ran the short distance from his hiding place to underneath the window.

Now he had to act quickly to avoid detection.

Frank tried to strike a match. A sudden waft of breeze blew it out.

He tried again, holding the match downwards after it was alight, to keep it burning while he removed the crumpled and folded page of a newspaper from the inside pocket of his black leather jacket.

He held the burning match against the end of the newspaper and waited until it flared into a glowing taper.

Frank stood up from his crouching position, extended his right arm through the gap of the window, and dropped the taper onto the newspapers below.

He reached into the side pocket of his coat and removed a small pile of used cigarette butts, which he then scattered through the open window.

A light appeared from a nearby bedroom window and a dog barked.

His heart began to pound as though about to burst through his chest.

Frank ran.

He reached his car and fumbled in his trouser pockets for the keys.

He started the ignition and eased the car away, hearing above the muffled drone of the engine the urgent screeching in the distance of a smoke alarm.

The shaking of his hands as they dug into the steering wheel was beginning to ease, 'I've done it,' he said to himself, with a maniacal gleam in his eyes, 'our problems are over.'

A few moments passed and his frenetic thoughts began to slow down and be replaced by plans emanating from the cold, calculating part of his brain ... 'When I arrive at the diner in the morning, I'll act as shocked as everyone else there. No-one will suspect it's been anything else but a careless accident ... and then the insurance company will take over. Our debts will be wiped out.'

The destruction by fire damage of Uncle Sam's meant that Frank avoided his six-month appointment at the corporation headquarters.

The corporation was too preoccupied with police and insurance ramifications following the inferno that had gutted the restaurant.

The findings of the investigations concluded the cause to be accidental, although lack of essential safety measures were highlighted in the report: inadequate provision for smokers on the premises; carelessness in the storage of packaging materials, and failure to replace an outdated sprinkler system that had failed to activate, were all cited in the report as significant points of criticism.

But no suggestion of criminal intent arose throughout the enquiry period.

Frank, who had always been as conscientious in paying the yearly premiums on the insurance policy as he had been with all his other business obligations, even during the recent times of financial troubles, was paid the full sum insured by the insurance company, a figure substantial enough to enable him to repay his debts and thereby keep the boarding house.

But the planned future of the Lockwood family had been wiped out by the restaurant fire, and Frank and Sarah had been returned to the position they were in on the day they moved to Blackpool from Mansfield.

Although their dream of passing on Uncle Sam's to Danny had died in the flames of the fire, Frank and Sarah had found each other once more and they committed their future to becoming a family again.

This meant Sarah admitting to Frank that she had visited their son in London, finding him again, persuading him to take his punishment, however harsh, and then come back to them.

From the aftermath of the fire had come the belated realisation that a home was not a building of bricks and mortar – that was a house; a home was people.

The Lockwoods sold their boarding house and moved to a flat in a large terraced house in Lewisham, to begin a new life. And to search for Danny.

While making enquiries as to his possible whereabouts over the following months they heard many rumours as to what might have happened to him in the years since that day Sarah had seen him, and they diligently followed up each one.

But they were all false trails, leading down blind alleys.

So the Lockwoods began their new life with a son who had become a ghost, lost to them forever, but who was also an apparition they seemed to see in the face of every man of Danny's age they passed by on the crowded streets of London.

Both Frank and Sarah would cast sidelong glances and their hearts would begin to soar in expectation that their long search was at an end, but, just as quickly, hopes were dashed, with the realisation he was not their Danny.

Until the next person they saw like Danny.

But there always remained hope.

Isaac and his corporation weathered the economic ferocity of the recession.

Cleopatra's, the Yankee Experience, and Sea City all flourished, going from strength to strength.

But Isaac never recovered from his loss of Sarah, and, without her, he became a shell of a man.

Sarah neither saw nor heard from Isaac after the fateful night at Trevi's, and her pain eased with the passage of time between them.

But she never forgot him, and never grew to hate him, despite all he had done to attempt to destroy her husband and her family's future.

If there was a winner then it was Frank, and Isaac was the one who was destroyed, as he was faced with living the rest of his life without the woman he loved, who would haunt his every waking moment for the rest of his days.

Frank never spoke of his part in the burning down of Uncle Sam's, but Sarah knew where he had been in those hours when he had left their bed at midnight, not least because of the nightmares he had in the early hours that morning after he had returned, and had every night for weeks afterwards.

It remained unspoken between them, in the same way that Frank's knowledge of his wife's long-standing affair with Isaac had remained unspoken by him over the years.

Financial recompense had not been Frank's only motive for leaving the marital bed on the night of the fire.

Frank salved his conscience over the ensuing years by the rationalisation that if Sarah wasn't going to come clean to him about her secret relationship with Isaac, then, he, on his part, had been justified in burning down his own restaurant in an action that had not only saved his family financially and emotionally, but had also slaked his thirst for revenge against a man intent on taking his wife away from him.

Frank had never believed that Sarah had any real feelings for Isaac, but had been swept along by a man who fulfilled her longings for ostentation and the finer trappings of life.

After all, Frank was a realist. He knew the person he was, and the person Sarah was, and had known back in the days in Brackley.

He knew he had only got to where he had in life because of Sarah, a woman who had always been a unique fusion of wife and go-getter.

Sarah, for her part, held her silence, about both her affair with Isaac, and her conviction that her husband had been responsible for the fire, because she did not want to risk losing the only man who now remained in her life, now that two had been lost to her – her son by tragedy, and her lover by agonizing choice.

No-one in Blackpool who had been a part of their old lives saw or heard from Frank and Sarah ever again.

Of all their old friends, Jackie Flint was the one who missed Sarah most of all, and spent many afternoons after they had gone, wistfully longing for a chance once again for the two of them to shoot the breeze together like they did in the old days. But the postman didn't deliver a letter from her, and the telephone remained silent.

Frank and Sarah talked about their son round the open fire at home on winter nights. That maybe he was happy somewhere living alone, or that he had found somebody and built a shared life and didn't need them anymore, and, on such nights, their pain melted mercifully into nostalgia, and Danny was a little boy once again in their thoughts, carefree in the Alley of Park Avenue.

And, through such consolation, he was, in a way, with them forever, and the Lockwood family had become united again.

Such scant consolation, meagre as it was to the Lockwoods, was great riches when set against Isaac Ford, who was, with Sarah's departure, a man of no more tangibility than the tragic ghost of Hamlet's dead father at Elsinore, walking the battlements of his own castle domain in the evening mists of a Lakeland summer's evening.

The villagers of Fernleigh Peak, walking in the empty fields on their evening stroll, could be seen shading their eyes from the glare of the setting sun behind Camford Castle, as they looked upwards to discern his solitary figure.

They all knew Isaac by repute, and, in some cases, acquaintance, but not one amongst their number in those days envied him, and most of them pitied him, for the devastation loneliness had visited upon him, amidst a setting of such magnificent grandeur.

Paradise Lost

On the cold winter mornings when he was driving his van to the fruit and vegetable market, having left Lucy to her last two hours of sleep in the flat above 'Flints', their greengrocer's shop in Lytham St Annes, Joe Flint's thoughts were often inadvertently drawn back to Tasmania, and he would be compelled to mentally re-live that period of time when Billy Forrest's legacy of a pot of gold turned into a poisoned chalice.

That episode in his life still seemed unreal to Joe, and, whenever the recollection came to him, he would consciously switch his reminiscence to a particular image during the unspoiled part of those years; walking with Lucy from the cottage in Swan Vale, down the lane to the orchard, on a glorious misty morning, with the dew twinkling like jewels on the grass beneath their feet, and without a care in the world.

Only six years before in time, yet another lost lifetime away from his present-day reality of unremitting worries, such as Lucy faced in two hours' time when Jack Grime, the landlord of the shop, was due to make an early morning visit before Lucy opened up for the day, demanding to know when he was going to get his quarterly rent, already a month overdue, and issuing thinly-veiled threats of the serious implications if he did not receive payment. All disguised behind a smiling, urbane facial expression of feigned chumminess.

Joe also preferred to dwell upon the happy times in Tasmania rather than the events of just over a month before, which still haunted him, and which had been instrumental in provoking Jack Grime's visit.

Events that were all of Joe's doing, and which for every waking moment since meant that he had been riddled with guilt for the anguish his reckless actions had caused his wife and himself.

Flints, over recent months, had been making barely enough money to put regular meals on the table for Joe and Lucy and their two young children, and an unsympathetic bank manager had warned them that overdraft facilities would not be extended beyond the following summer unless he started to see the beginnings of an upward trend in the accounts of the business.

But if Joe had not gambled with his own family's future then at least there would still have been capital in the bank to tide them over the quiet autumn and winter months, until the spring and summer, when holidaymakers and passing customers would have boosted the shop's takings to ease the financial pressure.

Joe attributed the current difficulties they were experiencing to Billy Forrest's legacy.

Although he was not trying to exempt himself from blame by doing this, he refused to waver in his belief that misfortune was set in motion the day they became the owners of the Forrest orchards.

Joe's belief, misguided as it might have been, was founded on his conviction that, before that fateful day, his and Lucy's lives had been happy and uncomplicated, and they had been masters of their own destinies.

In fact, this had remained the case for the Flints for five years following the inheritance, as their lives had continued in more or less the same vein, only without the daily necessity of having to pick and pack apples to earn a living, and with the acquired status of apple business owners.

Everything in the Swan Vale orchards was left by the Flints to run as before, only with Lew Burke in charge of operating the business, which he had been doing in effect anyway while Billy Forrest was still alive, as Billy had occupied himself, especially in his later years, purely with a low-key supervisory role in both the orchards and the packing shed.

Billy's accountants in Hobart continued to handle all financial matters, providing the Flints, as new owners, with monthly statements in the same way they had to Billy Forrest.

The Flints moved to a Hobart tower block apartment overlooking the Derwent river, and paid monthly visits to Lew, for a run-down on everything they needed to know since the previous visit; a routine monthly meeting similar to the ones Billy used to have with Lew after he had received his accountant's statement.

In effect, nothing at all changed in the Heron valley with Billy Forrest's death.

Stan O'Neill, the new owner of the dairy farm under the provisions of Billy's will, changed to a new accountant, as he wanted, as he put it at the time, 'To give a spring clean to the books of a business I now own instead of managing on someone else's behalf.'

The Flints' new lives were centred round the upbringing of their twin boys who had been born during their first Christmas in Hobart.

They saw no reason for this idyllic new life not to continue, and did not question the beneficent hand of fate that had showered them with such undreamed-of good fortune.

And it did continue for five years.

Until the Great Tasmanian Bush Fire of 1978 destroyed the apple industry.

The monthly reports from Hobart following the Great Bush Fire brought to light the unpalatable fact that Billy Forrest's orchards had been uneconomic for many years, and had been supported by the thriving dairy farm.

Billy Forrest, blinded by his sentimental attachment to the orchards, had chosen to disregard any harsh economic reality, and had been blithely unaware of the financial state of his businesses, including the fact that for many years the orchards had been a financial drain on the farm.

He had left it all in the hands of the accountants, who, after the years of prosperity in the Tasmanian apple industry, had neglected to draw attention to the imbalance, caused by several years of recession, that had slowly crept into the accounts of the

Forrest joint businesses which had always been under one financial umbrella.

And so the monthly reports, which Billy Forrest never read anyway, and which, following Billy's death, Joe Flint merely rifled through, assuming all was in order as they had been prepared by highly-paid financial professionals who knew the businesses better than he was ever likely to, or cared to, had become, over the years, misleading at best and duplicitous at worst.

The Great Bush Fire had changed everything.

A succession of the driest Tasmanian summers on record had produced orchards that were tinder dry, and at the mercy of a devastating bush fire which denuded the Heron valley countryside, leaving Billy Forrest's beloved orchards barren and echoing with an eerie silence.

Disastrously, the Flints had chosen to disregard two opportunities to sell their inheritance.

They had seriously considered this option just after the inheritance when they recalled eavesdropping on Nathan Forrest's warning to his father, and also later when Stan O'Neill, the new owner of the farm, pointed them towards reality after his newly-appointed accountant had carried out his first scrutiny of the Forrest farm accounts.

But they had decided to hang on through one more season, their fifth as owners, at the end of which they had agreed to sell up and return to England.

And then the bush fire hit.

Stan O'Neill decided to sell the dairy farm after he came to realise, after four years, that he was not cut out for ownership. He 'went bush' and was last seen entering the Alice Springs racetrack with pockets stuffed with dollars and a sizeable personal account having been opened at his Hobart bank before he took off.

Lew Burke was left stranded by The Great Bush Fire.

He managed to find employment as a barman at the Woolly Fleece hotel in Swan Vale but remained an insecure sitting tenant at the Big House, purely because Mr Pettigrew, after extensive study of legal precedent, had been unable to find a case to provide a parallel to Lew Burke's predicament.

Billy Forrest's will still continued to intrigue the Hobart lawyer in its uniqueness.

The Tea Party

The Flints sold their Hobart apartment and flew home to England, eight years almost to the day on which they left. They returned to their home town with enough capital salvaged from the Tasmanian debacle to set themselves up in a leasehold greengrocery shop with living accommodation above, in nearby Lytham St Annes, and £20,000 in savings, inherited by Lucy on her grandmother's death and intended strictly as a safety net for their future security.

Everything the shop earned in profit in the early years was ploughed back in just to keep it afloat.

A competitor greengrocer opened up a few doors away, and the small profits Joe and Lucy had been making were hit immediately.

And then Jack Grime raised the rents of both the business and the flat.

Arguments in the flat above the shop became a nightly occurrence, and the common thought the Flints shared at these times was that the Australian dream – the adventure – had gone sour and their present plight was the result.

But, despite their predicament, they refused to renege on their agreement that the shop had to be self-supporting, and the £20,000 remained untouched.

Joe's musings as he loaded up the van at the market returned to the day five weeks before when he had decided to take matters into his own hands ...

The morning was still vivid in his mind's eye.

Several of the shop customers had recently been talking to him about how the way to make money was to invest in the stock market.

Joe had paid little attention at first, and then his instinctive love of a gamble, which had remained dormant since the return from Tasmania, began to establish a foothold in his imagination, having been fired by the notion that his customers may have been the unwitting providers of the means by which he could resolve the Flints' financial plight.

Joe began to read the financial pages of the newspapers, to learn as much as he could about stock market investment, waiting for the day when he would be able to put his knowledge to profitable use.

And the more he learned, the more excited he became.

He enjoyed the buzz that came from selecting companies and following their progress on the 'Sharecheck' text pages on the television, especially as there was no money at risk. It was just an exciting game with no losers.

As Joe pored avidly over the business sections of the papers, there always seemed to him to be a story of someone making their fortune on the market, purely by buying and selling shares at the optimum moment.

He began to feel he was about to join an elite gaming club from which he had previously been excluded. And that he had a large enough pot of money to not only gain admission, but also buy enough chips to place on the roulette table and just wait for the wheel to spin and the little silver ball drop onto his chosen number.

Whenever he thought about the stock market, Joe felt he knew how Alice felt when she gazed open-mouthed in wonder when chancing upon the Mad Hatters' tea party.

Joe kept all this to himself as a sort of private hobby, but felt his motive was an honourable one and justified him in going ahead with his plans when the opportune moment arrived.

In his mock selections, Joe came to favour, firstly, the pharmaceutical companies, and then the utilities sector, the latter including companies who were in the vanguard of the current Thatcher government plans towards privatisation.

A revolution was taking place in the enticement of the British public towards becoming a share-owning democracy, with television and newspaper advertisements incorporating a fictional iconic British working man named 'Sid' and entreaties between people in the street telling each other to 'tell Sid' about the opportunities to buy shares in leading British industries now being offered for share ownership for the first time. The ultimate objective of the Conservative government being to entice the 'Sids' of Great Britain out of their pigeon lofts and into the golf clubs wearing a new attire of pin-stripe suit and red braces to replace the traditional cloth cap and anorak.

A similar transformation was taking place throughout great swathes of British society as part of a process known as 'gentrification', by which areas such as derelict docklands were being revamped into ultra-modern luxury flat complexes for up-and-coming young city-types.

Lucy Flint, for her part, was more than content to leave her husband each morning with his pink financial newspaper, and his set of multi-coloured marker pens, and at night to retire first to bed, happy in the knowledge that anything had to be welcomed that could produce such a change in him from the disillusioned, morose man he had seemed in danger of permanently becoming; in fact, recently, she had even heard him whistling while taking his shower at six o'clock in the morning.

Of course, in the midst of his unbridled enthusiasm for his new interest, Joe disregarded the continual warning he was reading that 'the value of shares can go down as well as up.'

Joe Flint was a contradiction.

Despite his recently gained fixation with the world of high finance as typified by the stock market, he and Lucy still remained bohemians at heart.

On their return from Tasmania, they decided a fresh start back in England should also mean a return to an uncomplicated lifestyle; consequently, they decided not to own either a car or a telephone. They acquired a van from the previous shop owners, but used this solely for the collection of shop supplies from the market, and they travelled everywhere either on foot or by bicycle.

The Flints were determined to return to the days of simplicity and freedom they knew before the later Tasmanian days, and, even though, as shop owners they now belonged to a class of people totemic on the prevailing government template of a society of materialistic go-getters, they only planned to make enough to live within their own self-imposed boundaries, and never again to step beyond them. An aim that looked not much beyond living a comfortable, fulfilling family life with the two children.

They were looking to get back to their starting point, when they had everything that was important already within their grasp but had not realised it.

Perversely, this awakening had turned out to be the real legacy left to the Flints by Billy Forrest, and was one that would not have displeased him.

But fate had decreed that a fresh start for the Flints could only be bought at a punitive price.

Joe recalled the Monday morning five weeks before, and that the previous day's financial supplements of the newspapers had included an advertisement by Jackman Jones, a Cardiff stockbroker, offering concessionary rates of introductory commission for new investors.

Beneath the advertisement was an article by a city analyst about oil companies with potential for success.

Joe had cut out both from the newspaper and clipped them on to the folder he had been compiling of cuttings taken from investment articles, and his own scribbled pages of indecipherable company names.

Alongside each name was a line of figures in red and black, each with an accompaniment of either a plus or a minus sign.

Joe had been assiduously monitoring company performance, ready for the day when he felt able to proceed.

He decided on that Sunday that the following morning he would become a client of Jackman Jones.

And that he was going to invest in oil.

But first he had to secure Lucy's agreement.

Joe and Lucy were having breakfast in the kitchen later that morning when Joe decided to sound out Lucy about his intentions the next day.

He chose his moment while the twins were still asleep in bed, before the hurly-burly of a typical Flint Sunday exploded in full force.

The pile of Sunday newspapers was spread out untidily over the salt and pepper pots and the empty coffee cups.

Joe pulled out the financial supplement, kept his head lowered, and casually addressed his preoccupied wife.

'I've been thinking about our savings. That we need to do something. With interest rates falling I mean. I know we both agreed never to touch the savings, no matter how tough things got, but sometimes opportunities come up which are too good to miss.'

Joe jabbed his right index finger several times at the headline on the front page that he felt confirmed his assertion.

Lucy frowned impatiently, put on her spectacles and leaned across the table.

Joe continued before she could comment, 'I've been thinking about the stock market. Customers have been talking about it lately. Seems it's the 'in' thing these days. I've been keeping some cuttings.' Joe walked over to the desk in the lounge and came back with his buff-coloured folder which he placed in front of Lucy.

'There's a firm offering discounts for new clients. Cardiff stockbrokers.' Jackman Jones' advertisement was paper-clipped on the top of the folder. Lucy gave it a cursory glance and continued crunching her toast.

Joe wasn't sure what she was thinking. What mood she was in. But he ploughed on, fearing an outburst of negativity, always possible at that hour of the day, and which would blow his plans out of the water.

Joe opened the folder and placed the city analyst's article on top of the Jackman Jones cutting.

'And oil's big at the moment. Manaco has made an oil field find off the coast of Chile, and this article forecasts the price to soar within weeks. So we need to be in right at the start. It's a gold mine.'

Joe was oblivious to his Goldwynism, and Lucy smiled at him enigmatically, but was loathe to point it out as she didn't want to interrupt his enthusiastic flow and risk bursting a hot air balloon she could see floating above the clouds heading for the stratosphere and carrying them along in its basket beneath.

'But then that's my Joe,' she thought, 'Always trying to find the end of the rainbow. Never content with what he's got.'

'If you think it's a good idea, Joe, then we could find out more details.' Lucy looked up at Joe and smiled.

This wasn't what Joe wanted to hear.

He wanted Lucy up there in the basket with him. Not standing on the ground looking up.

He wanted her to dive in with him at the deep end of the pool from the high board. Not dip a toe in the water.

'What if I phone this Cardiff firm – this Jackman Jones – in the morning – first thing say – and find out more about the discounts, and, if everything seems straightforward, we could buy a few shares – say in an oil company – this Manaco maybe. Just so we can say we've given the stock market a try. And then see how we get on.'

Lucy rose to her feet and began to put the breakfast dishes on a tray, and moved it towards the serving hatch.

She heard one of the twins shouting from the bedroom.

'O.K. Go ahead. I'll open up the shop. But don't do anything silly. Those savings are all we've got. And not likely to have much more the way things are going.'

Lucy walked over to Joe and gently kissed the top of his head, 'After all, it won't be the first crazy thing we've ever done.'

With that, Lucy walked out of the kitchen and climbed the stairs to attend to the impatient demands of the twins who at that moment were laying into each other with the full force of their flying pillows.

It was still dark when Joe woke up the next morning.

Even though he had slept fitfully he felt alert and tense.

Joe had always liked this hour of the day.

He felt the silence enfold him like a cloak. It seemed to set the ideas racing sharp and clear through his brain.

It was his high-octane time of the day.

He looked over at Lucy, still soundly asleep, while he hurriedly put on the same clothes he had casually discarded over the chair by his side of the bed the night before.

In the kitchen Joe poured himself a mug of strong black coffee and buttered two slices of toast, and then wandered through to the lounge for his share folder which he kept in the drawer of the desk in the corner of the room.

He settled himself in his big red armchair and began to read through his newspaper cuttings.

Joe had become infected by the city analyst's enthusiasm for the riches to be made from investment in oil, and, in his eagerness to believe every word of the analyst's speculations he decided it was time to adjust his portfolio of sector preferences and promote oil at the expense of his erstwhile favourites, pharmaceuticals and utilities.

He was in no mood to heed the words of caution about oil that equally-eminent financial writers were continually citing in their articles aimed at new stock market investors.

Joe had never been a man to deal in half measures.

He had no intention of spreading the risk - something the city page writers emphasised, without exception, as being priority for all new investors.

In Joe Flint's investment dreams, in order to get big returns then big gambles had to be taken.

He always had been an 'all or nothing' man.

However, even Joe, with all his meticulous and painstaking stock research and preparation, was helpless when confronted by the vagaries of the economic relationships between nations – particularly the oil-exporting ones and Great Britain; or boardroom power struggles within the giant conglomerates.

Such lack of discernment on Joe's part was about to deal him a severe blow.

By the time Joe had finished reading his notes it was daylight.

Joe looked at his watch. It was 8.15 a.m.

He put his small green tin full of £1 and 50p coins in his coat pocket, his folder under his arm, and walked to the garage for his black mountain bike.

Joe cycled to the call box that was over the nearby main road and outside the post office.

It was a dull, overcast morning and a fine drizzle had just started to fall.

Joe propped up his bicycle against the wall of the post office and, in the call box, settled his folders and money tin on the narrow ledge. He dialled the number of Jackman Jones.

Joe's first transaction as a stock market investor and the newest client of Jackman Jones was easier than he had anticipated.

When Joe was through to the dealing room of Jackman Jones, after completing the registration formalities, he felt his chest swell when the broker on the other end of the line opened the negotiation.

'Are you are a client of Jackman Jones, Sir?'

'Yes, I am.'

Joe gave his newly-acquired client details to confirm his authenticity.

'Do you wish to buy or sell, Sir?'

This was the moment Joe had been waiting for, over all the months of preparation. 'Buy, please.'

'Company name and amount of investment, please.'

Joe glanced at the lined sheet of foolscap paper he had placed on top of his folder, although he had no need, as he had rehearsed the reply many times earlier that morning.

'Manaco Oil.' Joe hesitated a moment. He felt his gambler's instinct come to the fore and surrendered in the face of it. He knew all caution was about to be lost, and was powerless to resist it.

'Twenty thousand pounds.'

'Just to confirm, Sir. That's Manaco Oil. Twenty thousand.'

The voice was monotone and matter-of-fact. Coolly professional.

'Yes, that's right.' Joe felt a tingle of excitement.

'One moment.'

Joe gulped, and began to feel the blood rushing to his cheeks, and his palms becoming clammy.

He had done it. No turning back now.

He fed a second £1 coin into the slot, and the urgent metallic ticking registered the money. He heard the faint sound of voices chattering urgently in the background and the soft continuous ringing of telephones.

The sounds of deals being done. Buying and selling. The start of just another normal working day's business at Jackman Jones of Cardiff.

And then the dealer's voice came back in the foreground on the line.

'That's your purchase completed, Sir. Manaco Oil at £4.50 per share. Investment £20,000. Investment completed 8.45 a.m. Thank you, Sir.'

'Thank you.'

Joe replaced the receiver and felt relieved.

He placed the foolscap sheet back into the folder, tucked in the flap neatly and then wiped his hands on the sides of his trousers. He picked up his money tin and placed it, along with his pen, into the inside pocket of his jacket.

Joe returned to the shop and switched on the text pages on his television screen, to check the latest quarter-hour price update.

Manaco... £4.60 ...

He called out to Lucy in the front of the shop.

'Lucy. Come and have a look. What did I tell you?'

That same Monday evening, the teatime television news announced the resignation of the Chief Executive of Manaco Oil over misleading newspaper publicity at the weekend concerning an oilfield find off Chile; a story had been leaked to the press by a former Manaco director who was seeking revenge on the company for his sacking a year earlier for his alleged part in accounting irregularities at Manaco.

The credibility of this perfidious director had not been verified by the newspaper's chief financial reporter.

The closing price of Manaco Oil at 4.30 p.m. on Monday was £2.10.

Joe stayed silent all that night.

He did not even play with the children after tea.

Lucy always went out with her friends to the local pub on a Monday evening, so Joe felt relieved to be spared any questioning.

His mind was in a turmoil.

The wait until the opening prices at 8.30 the next morning was going to be interminable. He was unable to settle, and paced the floor for hour after hour, feverish thoughts thrashing around inside his head seeking the best way to put right his foolish impetuosity.

He wanted with all his heart to turn the clock back twenty-four hours, but, instead, was forced to face harsh reality and consider rationally and coldly the various permutations now open to him, and to hope that the news story had been some sort of crazy mistake which, by the morning, would have righted itself with profuse apologies from the guilty parties.

'... I can sell immediately in the morning and take the losses in the expectation that prices might fall even further when the full impact of the news announcement sinks in,' was Joe's first thought.

'... I can monitor the price on the text screen, quarter-hour by quarter-hour and try and guess where it's heading – if there looks to be a trend – upwards, downwards or stabilising – in the hope that the fall had bottomed-out and recovery was on its way ... But doing this means holding my nerve for maybe hour after hour ... like hoping for something substantial to suddenly materialise from out of the depths of a black hole in space ... and even then still needing to make an inspired guess as to the moment to sell ... maybe when three or four upward figures have come up, indicating a recovery trend.' Joe began to feel easier, that perhaps he had found the answer, but, almost immediately his mind catapulted him back into the midst of its whirling vortex of anxiety.

'...But, then again,' Joe told himself frantically, 'If I opt for this approach, I might then decide not to sell at all, as these upward figures could mean the crisis was over and a long-term recovery was taking place, making a decision to stay or sell even more difficult.

Also, tomorrow, there might be an announcement from Manaco, reassuring investors, which could lead to the share price picking up immediately ...'

Joe's head was starting to throb from the effects of this lunatic game of mental tennis, and, no sooner had he started to soothe his anxieties with the balm that this last possible eventuality brought than the sharp needles of destructive negativity speared through the layer of protection that had only just begun to form.

'But even this outcome would mean a waiting game that would certainly involve having to endure another night of uncertainty at least – with our life savings at risk of being completely swept away, if the markets confidence in Manaco then proves to have been permanently undermined by the bad publicity, and this sudden rise was only due to over-optimism brought on by a desperate need to regain investor confidence quickly.'

Joe felt his temperature oscillating crazily.

He seemed to be boiling over.

That night was anguished and sleepless for Joe.

The next morning he left Lucy to sleep on a while longer, and, with trembling hands, gathered together his money tin, folder and pen.

He poured himself a glass of water and took a large gulp, to loosen the tightness at the back of his throat.

He quietly closed the front door and hurried to the garage for his bicycle.

Joe had to get through to Jackman Jones at 8.30. At the start of trading for the day.

The traffic was heavy on the main road, and Joe, to his relief, saw that the call box was empty.

He had only to cross the road when the first gap in the line of traffic opened up. Joe glanced at his watch. 8.25.

Joe made to move into the traffic in the hope that someone would give way, and then he heard his name being called ...

'Joe ...'

Joe glanced to his left. It was his next door neighbour, Jim Johnson, on his way home after taking his golden retriever for his morning walk to the nearby field.

Joe made an effort to compose his thoughts and to form a neighbourly smile across rapidly clenching teeth.

The dog lurched forward towards Joe, stretching his lead to the limit. Joe jumped back sharply.

'Get down, Goldie. Sorry about that, Joe. Looks like we're in for a drop of rain soon.' Jim Johnson said, glancing up to beyond the tops of the trees in the distance. 'Must be due for some soon, though, after this dry spell. Must say, the lawns need it. Full of bare patches these days. Mine's never been as bad.'

Joe, knowing that Jim fortunately wouldn't expect a response to his pleasantries, glanced over anxiously at the call box, while Jim patted Goldie and then tugged him abruptly to one side to let a tiny paperboy, weighed down on one side by a bulging grey canvas bag full of newspapers across his shoulders, shoot along the pavement in the gap between the pair of them, raising the front wheel of his bike as he went by.

'Damn nuisance,' said Jim, casting a scornful look in the direction of the rapidly disappearing bike.

'Betty alright? Not seen her for a while,' Joe asked, and at that moment he noticed a woman pushing a pram making a beeline for the call box.

'Must go, Jim.' Joe nodded his head in the direction of the call box. 'Have to make a call. See you soon.'

Joe pushed his bike ahead of him, out into the traffic, and was met with an angry blast of car horns.

It was touch and go as to who made it to the call box first.

The uncharitable thought crossed Joe's mind that she looked to be the type of woman who would happily take root in the call box for the rest of the morning.

Joe dropped his bike on the ground and stepped inside first.

He placed his folder and money tin on the ledge.

The woman with the pram glared at him through the glass side of the call box, tossed her head to one side, and hurried on in disgust.

Joe tried to settle his nerves and concentrate as he dialled the number of Jackman Jones.

He got through first time and breathed an audible sigh of relief.

The woman's voice on the other end of the line sounded formal but friendly. Joe tried to picture her, sitting upright and briskly businesslike behind her desk, as she led him through the unavoidable routine ...

'Name?

Account number? How can we help you, Mr Flint?'

Joe crossed his fingers, something he had always believed was a ridiculous demonstration of nonsensical superstition, in the same way he remembered as a small boy his mother pouring salt on her left hand before tossing it over her shoulder for good luck. But, after he became an adult, he always felt guilty when he recalled his childish irritation at his mother's occasional harmless self-indulgence in frivolities. He found that his thoughts of his mother would gravitate towards a myriad of moments such as tossing the salt, which now all blended together in his memory to become a radiant mosaic of her uniqueness.

'Can you give me the present price of Manaco?'

Joe's nerves had got the better of him – he had forgotten the procedure.

'One second, please, I'll just put you through to the dealing room.'

'Dealing room, can I help you?'

'Can you give me the present price of Manaco?'

'One second. £2.50.'

It was 8.45 a.m.

Joe fed more coins into the slot. The last thing I need now is to be cut off, he thought anxiously.

The silence seemed endless as the dealer waited for Joe's response.

A queue of four people had formed outside the call box.

Joe sensed their impatience seeping through the glass side. He turned his back on them in an attempt to isolate himself into a cocoon of ice-cold concentration.

Bizarrely at that moment a picture formed in his mind of Arthur Ashe the American tennis player, in the Wimbledon final against fellow American Jimmy Connors. A famous image. Ashe sitting on his chair by the side of the umpire between sets. Back erect and head motionless. Eyes locked tight. A man totally in control of his world. A monument to stillness in the eye of the storm. A man consciously willing indomitability into his soul, to lead himself on to victory and sporting immortality.

Joe experienced a surge of relief.

A safety valve had been opened to release a gushing forth of the pent-up anxiety that had insidiously built up during the night and occupied his entire being since it first expressed itself as a tight block of tension across his forehead.

'What was the opening price at 8.30?' Joe looked at his watch as he asked. It was 8.50.

'£3.00.'

Joe felt a spasm of tension rising again.

The price is going haywire.

£2.50 wasn't a recovery price from last night's close of £2.10 after all.

His mind was now frantically searching for some kind of pattern to help him make a decision. Whether to sell now or to hold.

'Think straight ... think straight,' Joe implored himself.

The rapid cut off bleepings of the phone began to sound into his receiver.

Joe looked inside his money tin. Empty.

He ransacked his coat pockets. His trouser pockets.

Nothing.

The line went dead.

His folder symbolically fell to the floor and his pen dropped off the ledge and rolled out underneath the door.

A dark-haired, weary-faced woman opened the door of the call box and handed Joe his pen. She scowled out words that sounded like a threat, but barely managed to penetrate the outermost layer of Joe's sludge-like, spinning consciousness.

'Will you be much longer, love? I've got an urgent call to make.'

She thrust out the pen at Joe, who replaced the receiver and stepped out into the street.

The woman brusquely elbowed him aside and squeezed her angry bulk through the gap between Joe and the wall of the booth.

When Joe had arrived back home he avoided Lucy, who was serving in the shop, and hurried to the lounge to switch to Manaco on the Sharecheck text page.

There had been no price changes.

He waited until 9.15.

The figures flashed and skittered in a mass of reds and blues across the page, against the lists of company names ... MANACO was on the march – a lovely blue plus figure of +1.90 against its name, being the price change since Monday's close of trading, and, next to it, 4.00 – the current price – only 50p short of the price Joe had paid yesterday.

Joe sank back in his armchair, kicked off his shoes, and tossed his folder across the room.

He returned to check the prices as often as he could throughout the day, when he was able to get away from serving in the shop.

The price remained steady. Although he was still down on the price he had paid a day earlier, Joe felt that the pressure was now off and he could breathe easier again. For the time being.

Much to his relief, Lucy had too much on her mind, with problems the twins had taken to her after school, to raise the issue of shares with him, and the rest of the week passed quietly, and Joe slept the sleep of a new-born babe.

... Until Friday morning, when the newsreader on the 10 a.m. radio news bulletin announced that OPEC was raising the price per barrel of crude oil by 20 per cent, with further price reviews to follow, in response to possible hostilities breaking out in the Middle East.

Joe and Lucy were working together, serving a shop full of customers at the time, and Joe did not catch the full announcement, or its potential significance.

The share prices of all the major oil companies plummeted in dramatic and unprecedented fashion, in response to the OPEC announcement and the anticipated global economic instability that would result from it.

When Joe heard the full details on the 10.30 news, he knew that, this time, his decision had been made for him. He now had to come out at any price. And quickly.

Joe resigned himself to his fate, and realised that all the previous week had merely been a succession of false dawns.

However, even in his new mood of despondent realism, Joe was unprepared for the reply of the dealer at Jackman Jones when he finally got through, after several abortive attempts, due to a continually engaged line ... 'Manaco, to sell, Sir ... 85 pence.'

Joe was stunned into a temporary silence. He didn't even bother to calculate on his piece of paper what this meant the £20,000 was now worth; after taking off buying and selling charges he knew they had been virtually wiped out.

He uttered a faint and strangulated reply, which echoed back to him from the recesses of his brain as he spoke ... 'Sell.'

He left the call box and pushed his bike home, in a befuddled daze.

He didn't even notice the strange tight feeling across his chest as he stumbled along.

Joe dreaded the moment when he had to break the news to Lucy, and began to prepare himself.

In fact, Lucy's reaction was silence.

A silence absolute and condemning in its intensity.

She stood up and walked out of the room without a glance in his direction, closing the door as slowly and as pointedly as a jailer closes his prisoner's cell door just before he turns the key in the lock, to condemn him to another long night's isolation, with only the haunting thoughts of his wrongdoing to fill the silent eternity of night.

Joe Flint still vividly recalled the moment it happened.

He had returned from the market anxious to hear the outcome of Lucy's meeting with Jack Grime.

It had been as bad as they had been expecting.

Lucy had pleaded their case. To be given more time. Told him that their problems were only temporary. If he could just bear with them a while longer he would have his rent.

Joe still recalled every sentence of Lucy's re-telling of the meeting ...

'He was in no mood to listen to anything I had to say, Joe.

His mind was made up before I even let him in.'

Joe remembered looking at Lucy, and thinking how calm she was, how composed, and how Jack Grime must have had a heart of stone not to even give her a hearing.

'I sympathise with your problems, Lucy, but please try and understand my position too. If all my tenants couldn't pay their rent, where would that leave me? You must try and understand. I've been more than generous so far, but I have to set a time limit. I've given you longer than I usually allow anyone else.'

'Then he just sat there, Joe, none of his usual smarm. A face like thunder. I thought he looked like one of those Easter Island statues, and with about as much feeling inside him.'

Joe recalled the smile that spread across Lucy's face as she said it, and his laugh in response.

But Joe felt he knew the Jack Grimes of this world better than Lucy ever would. She always saw the best in everyone. Never would suspect that people had hidden agendas. He had known for a long while before Jack Grime's visit that he would be in no mood to listen to any entreaties for a stay of execution, even from people he had always claimed were friends rather than tenants.

Joe had known from the moment they had first shaken hands to seal the tenancy how blunt and uncompromising Jack Grime would turn out to be beneath his smooth veneer of bonhomie, if the going got tough.

'Then he seemed to soften a bit, Joe,' Lucy carried on, I'll tell you what I'll do, Lucy,' he said. 'If you can find two quarters' rent payments – the one you owe and the next one – I'll accept payment of them together on the next due date. That should give you time to get the money together.'

'He musn't have seen anything in my reaction, Joe, to lead him to expect his offer was going to help us, because he followed this up with a threat.'

'If you can't come up with the rents on that date I'll have to put the matter in the hands of my solicitors.'

'And with that, Joe, he just got up and walked out, slamming the door.'

Joe remembered that no sooner had Lucy finished telling him

than the strange feeling he had first noticed in his chest the day he sold the shares came back. And then moved into his neck and jaw, and he began to feel woozy and clammy.

He had walked out into the hall to look in the mirror and was startled at the deathly pale grey pallor of his skin.

He began to struggle to catch his breath.

The pain suddenly shot down his left arm.

This was the last thing he remembered with any clarity.

Lucy had told him later that he had collapsed on the shop floor and was then carried out into the ambulance.

He vaguely recalled listening to the dramatic strident urgency of the noise from the ambulance that seemed to be all-encompassing, as he sank into a blissful sleep.

Joe knew Lucy was beside him in the ambulance, and was holding his hand ... He remembered thinking, 'Perhaps she's now forgiven me,' as this was the first time they'd touched since the day he'd sold the shares, and, with them, had also sold their future.

A Walk in the Park

The ivy-clad cottage on the banks of the sleepy, willow-shrouded stream in the idyllic Cotswold village of Oxbury, possessed such unique prepossessing charm as to stop visitors in their tracks as they sauntered out of the Farmers Arms to be greeted as they turned the corner into Primrose Lane by a thatched-roof dwelling of glorious Cotswold golden-hued stone, shimmering in the afternoon summer sunshine, that could have been taken straight from the pages of George Eliot's Middlemarch.

Such transfixed onlookers would have been blithely unaware that Lark Cottage was the home of Britain's leading television star of the late twentieth century; a woman of middle age and striking vivacious red-haired appearance, and instantly recognisable, as claimed by a recent newspaper survey, by seven out of ten of the entire British population.

This staggering statistic resulted from this celebrity's appearance each week in the nation's living rooms as the star of 'A Family in War and Peace,' the number one drama in which she had become immortalised as Jenny, the family matriarch.

Molly Earle, OBE, had occupied this exalted position in the national psyche for ten years, to such an extent that she often felt that her earlier incarnation as a singer was not herself, but someone who was a long-lost acquaintance with whom she had once been inseparable, but who she now regarded with a certain degree of disdain for the flippancy of her approach, both to life in general, and to her inborn talent in particular.

Molly basked in the rays of acclaim that streamed down upon her from her role as Jenny; a part that had opened the door to her personal renaissance, and her apogee from that momentous autumn morning when she breezed out of the front door of Parkers into the dawn of a new life.

After that morning, Roderick Sterne's path through life was equally dramatic, but in a diametrically opposite way to his wife and protégé, for, while Molly scaled the heights of public recognition and renown, he plumbed the depths of notoriety.

Parkers was a watershed in both of their lives, and the story of how this came about became the stuff of show business legend.

Molly Earle's first port of call after leaving Parker's was the New Sands to see her grandmother Eva.

It was a moot point as to which of the two of them was the more surprised at the other's appearance, for Molly noticed that Eva had lost her vivacity.

The mischievous sparkle in her eyes had vanished, and she looked jaded and careworn.

By contrast, Eva, who had expected her granddaughter to be diminished by her harrowing experiences, in fact found her radiant and reinvigorated.

'You look well, Nan,' Molly said, holding Eva at arm's length, and using a loving smile to mask her searching gaze into Eva's tired blue eyes, as though she could draw out the cares from her soul and share them with her.

'It's lovely to have you back here again, Mol,' Eva said, in a vaguely subdued sort of way, using the same phrase she always had when Molly returned to the New Sands, only this time it was lacking her usual tone of suppressed excitement.

Over the next few days, they were both reluctant to divulge the difficulties they had been through since they last met.

Such disinclination towards mutual soul-searching was totally consistent with the type of character with which they had both been endowed, one which viewed the world as a realm of promise and opportunity rather than a place suffused with gloomy despondency.

Light over shade. Day over night. Perversities of fate were to be brushed away as being of no more consequence than an autumn leaf is to a tree when it falls from the branch and is gently swept away across the grass by a passing breeze.

To both of them, indomitability of spirit was all, and would always triumph over adversity, no matter how cruel.

Eva had become reconciled for a considerable time to the progressive physical deterioration caused by her Parkinson's disease, and had chosen to disregard any of its distressing manifestations such as her hand tremors.

But Molly had noticed immediately how much more stooped Eva was than the last time she saw her, and her slow, shuffling gait as she moved about the hotel.

Eva was simultaneously both aware and yet dismissive of the likelihood that concern over Molly had been a factor in the acceleration of her recent physical and mental decline, and, in particular, sadness over the collapse of her career, which Eva now regarded as having been like a shooting star which had lit up the night sky for all to see, only to disappear from view forever after only a few brief, glorious seconds.

Molly had been back at the New Sands for over a week.

Eva and Molly had settled down in the lounge after lunch on a quiet Wednesday afternoon, and Eva decided the time had come to tell her granddaughter what had been on her mind since the week before she arrived; knowledge which had blighted her every waking moment and rendered her nights sleepless and tormented, because she knew the devastating impact the news was going to have on Molly's life.

'I've had a visitor.'

Eva decided on a circumspect beginning as she was uncertain of Molly's likely initial reaction.

Molly thought this was nothing more than the introduction to one of her grandmother's gossipy chit-chats, and was only half-listening.

She reached for a magazine from among the untidy pile of old newspapers on the coffee table between them.

'It was Roderick.'

Molly closed the magazine and placed it back on top of the pile.

'What did he want?'

Molly felt her cheeks go red as mention of his name provoked a picture to form in her mind of the last time she had seen him – disappearing into the distance down the driveway out of Parkers, and abandoning her to walk alone through the doors that opened on to her own private hell.

'I don't know how I'm going to tell you this.'

Eva shuffled uneasily in her armchair as she spoke,

'He said he wanted to make plans for the future - plans that couldn't wait.

It seems the clinic had told him when you were expected to leave, but he'd told them he was going abroad for a while.

He said that, as you were bound to come here first, he thought if he told me what you needed to know, I could pass it on, and he could then get on with what he wanted to do.'

Molly felt a potent mixture of anxiety and intrigue beginning to seep through her veins as she braced herself for the bombshell that was about to explode.

This was immediately supplanted by a blast of visceral anger towards her husband, that he should be so craven as to unburden himself, and the intimacies of their marriage, onto a sick old woman.

Molly smiled comfortingly at Eva, and let her continue without interruption, knowing how difficult she was finding it, having to make such personal disclosures to her own granddaughter.

'He's sold your house, and moved out.

He says he saw you in the clinic, and you signed some papers, stating your joint agreement to a legal separation, because marriage problems had resulted in your admission into Parkers.

He also said that he had decided to make a fresh start, that he has met someone he wants to marry, and wants a divorce.

I was shocked, Molly, and wanted to throw him out, there and then, but I felt you would need to know it all. All he wanted to tell me. That I should let him get it all out in the open. Once and for all.

You're better off without that man, Molly.

I never trusted him. I thought he was wrong for you; but you seemed so happy at the start, and were with someone who could open all those doors into show business for you, to help you achieve everything we always dreamed of together when you were little.

How could any of us know it would all turn out like this?'

Molly felt shell-shocked.

Her mind was racing in an attempt to make some kind of sense from all Eva had just told her. She felt she needed time to absorb it all, and the implications involved.

A dim recollection began to gather shape in her anguished thoughts.

It was of a man standing by her bedside at the clinic, talking softly to her. She had thought at the time, in her confusion, that it was her father, Isaac, and that she was a little girl again, and he had come to take her walking in the meadow on a summer afternoon; and she recalled being puzzled as to why her father should be giving her a pen, and asking her to write her name on a sheet of paper he was placing in her hand.

'Now it all makes sense', she explained to herself. 'It was Roderick. Asking me to sign his forms; pieces of paper that would end my marriage – and my career.

Trying to crush the remnants of me. Making sure there was going to be no future for me when I was well again.'

'I'm sorry, Molly. But I was so confused and upset by it all. It all took me by surprise. I'm not able to cope with things like I used to. I'm so sorry, but what else could I do?'

'Nothing, Nan. You couldn't do any more than you did. Try not to worry, I'm sure there's a way out, I just need some time to think. Where is he now? I'll need to speak to him.'

Molly was trying to stay calm and rational.

'He told me to tell you not to try to get in touch with him; that there was nothing you could do; that his legal people already had arrangements underway.

But he did say you'd be well provided for.

He left me this card, with the name of someone you can speak to; I think it's his lawyer, who, he said, will tell you all you need to know.'

That's it, Molly, I don't know any more.

Sorry, Mol.'

Eva rose unsteadily to her feet, and passed over the card to Molly with a shaking hand.

Molly got up and put her arms around Eva, and they stood, locked together in a huddle of misery, in the centre of the room, the muffled sound of sobbing resounding in the emptiness, broken only by the metallic clanging of the grandfather clock as it registered the passing of a crisp, autumn afternoon, and the encroaching dusk of early evening.

From that afternoon onwards, Molly and Eva bolstered one another in a mutual resolve to create a new future for themselves; but, in later years, Molly traced the beginning of the rapid decline in her grandmother's health back to the trauma of that afternoon at the New Sands, and its aftermath, when the full extent of Roderick's treachery, born out of his innate weakness, was unmasked to shattering effect.

Molly's discussions with Roderick's lawyers merely added the confirmation she anticipated: that all the i' s had been dotted, and all the t's crossed, to ensure that not a single legal loophole was left open to her.

Her husband had employed the cream of legal expertise, no expense spared, and she would have expected no less from a man of Roderick's fastidiousness.

He had indeed cut her off at the knees, with no means of redress, legal or moral.

Roderick tossed Molly a consolatory morsel, in the guise of sufficient remaining cash to buy a small home for herself, plus a few thousand pounds to open a bank account, to help her with a fresh start.

But Molly had known that her career was on the rocks from

the time she had entered Parkers, and that Roderick, as her agent, held the keys to any revival by having taken with him his extensive portfolio of contacts in the entertainment business, thereby removing her means of earning a living.

Roderick had severed the lifeline to Molly's future, and left her in desperate straits.

But she refused to wallow in thoughts of reprisal and pointless self-pity.

Instead, she firmly closed this door in her life, and set out determinedly again along the corridor that was her future, intent on searching for any door that might be ajar, waiting to be pushed open.

The door of her life marked 'Nan' concerned her.

She had decided she wanted Eva with her, and, with a feeling of considerable trepidation, raised the issue a month after her final meeting with Roderick's lawyers, who, on that day, closed their file on Roderick and Molly Sterne.

Molly, at this meeting, finally decided against seeking redress against her husband, as her psychological state during the period prior to her admission to Parkers had been regularly referred to by the lawyers at the meeting, in several of the documents quoted to her, and she had no wish to re-open a chapter of her life she wanted expunged from the marrow of her being.

Also, there was the potentially serious effect on Eva that may ensue from pursuing such a perilous course.

Molly, therefore, gave her agreement for the lawyers to proceed with the divorce Roderick wanted so much, and turned her thoughts to Eva's future, and the small amount of time she might have left to share with her.

From somewhere deep within, Molly always felt that Parkers was not the finish for her, but was merely a staging-post in her life and her career and so, after the initial shock of Eva's news about Roderick, and the ensuing legal formalities for her divorce, had been absorbed, she felt at times she could see tiny diamonds of hope glimmering in the debris of her life. And she chose one of such moments to have her talk with Eva.

The time Molly chose was a frosty October morning, and the setting was the park.

The two of them walked along, arm-in-arm, Molly easing her stride to keep pace with her Nan as she shuffled her feet among the crisp and crackling red and brown leaves, as they walked on the grass, among the trees by the lake.

The park was deserted, save for three fishermen, separated by some distance from each other, seated on small canvas chairs, along the banks of the lake. Their shoulders were hunched, and their heads bowed in concentration over the gently rippling water, fishing rods near their feet, with lines taut and extended beneath the water, in anticipation of a bite.

Molly thought how fragile her Nan was now looking, her face so pinched and sallow in the chill morning air.

She studied Eva's moving shadow on the grass as they walked, and noticed the way the sharp, glowing sunlight, framing them in their movement between the trees, magically elongated her frail body, huddled in a thick, grey overcoat, into a long, thin shadow, and the strange thought struck her that the Eva of old would have dwarfed her own shadow, not the way it was now, when the shadow seemed to Molly sinister and portentous.

The thought disturbed her, and she gently led Eva away from beneath the trees, and they sat together on a rickety wooden bench.

'It's been nice being home again, Nan, especially after all that's happened to me. I'd forgotten how it used to be; the days out in the park, like today.'

'I know, Molly – for me, too,' Eva reached for Molly's hand and placed it on her knee, tenderly squeezing her fingers.

The gesture was evocative to Molly as being one she used to do herself to Eva when she was a little girl, and a momentary shiver of sadness skipped across her memory.

It seemed to Molly that perhaps such awareness of the turning of life's wheel in small, tangible ways such as this, may have been the intended gift from an empathetic higher power, as a form of transitory consolation during the cruel, inevitable passages of life, typified by old age, and that such tiny, exquisite moments must always be held delicately, and lovingly, for the fleeting seconds they appear, and then placed gently in whatever corner of the mind this same higher power fashioned for us at birth for the single purpose of storing those jewels that magically appear along life's path.

'Nan, I've been thinking lately that it might be time for a change, for both of us, and wondered what you thought.'

Eva didn't answer, but continued to look straight ahead, in the direction of the lake.

So Molly continued, 'It might be good, for both of us, if we left Blackpool. Made a fresh start. If you sold the academy, and, with the money I've got as well, we could buy a new place together.'

Molly thought she may as well finish the speech she had rehearsed that morning. 'Somewhere in the country, Nan, like the Cotswolds, where we used to go on holiday. What do you think?'

Molly had anticipated fervent opposition to her proposal, but Eva let her finish, and was silent for a moment, watching the swans as they glided along the surface of the lake, finally settling in a pool of sunlight that sparkled on the still water.

She was thinking how peaceful it all was in the park that morning, as peaceful as the Cotswolds had remained in her memory, and she pictured a cottage of golden stone, and herself, standing in the open doorway, and Molly as a little girl in pigtails, running down the path, holding out to her a yellow rose she had picked from the garden.

That was her favourite holiday … so long ago …

'Yes, the Cotswolds, Mol, why ever not? We'll do it. There's no future here for me now. All I do is sit at home, living in the past. I've not even been involved in the academy for donkey's years.

Yes, Mol, we'll do it.'

Eva turned to Molly and they joyously threw their arms around each other, and Eva let out a girlish giggle, as the two of them walked out through the park gates into their new future together.

Molly helped Eva arrange for the sale of the academy, and, by the end of the year, they had found their idyll – Lark Cottage in the Cotswolds.

Eva painstakingly worked her way through the books of the theatrical academy, telling everyone of the imminent start of her new life, and it was while she was about to close the books for the last time that Dame Fortune played her hand, to launch the new career of Molly Earle.

A face flashed into Eva's mind as she closed the last book.

The image was of a friend she had last seen ten years before; a fellow theatrical agent – Maxie Walker.

Eva knew of no earthly reason why she should have thought of Maxie at that particular moment, but she felt an eerie premonition that she needed to let him know that she was about to leave Blackpool.

In later years, Eva used to tell everyone who would listen that this had been Gypsy Pandora's parting gift to her for all the years of fun they had enjoyed together in the booth on the promenade.

Eva remembered Maxie had told her when she last saw him that he had just moved into the world of television drama.

She leafed through her box files of papers, to find anything that might show his number, and eventually she found an old, dog-eared calling card.

She dialled the number on the card, and a youthful sounding female voice answered.

'May I speak to Maxwell Walker, please?' Eva asked, strangely convinced as she spoke that Maxie would still be at the same address.

'Hang on a second. Who shall I say is calling?'

'Can you tell him it's Eva; just say Eva from Blackpool.'

Eva heard the clinking of cutlery and the rattle of teacups in the background.

'Hello, Eva, well, well, well, what a surprise. How are you?'

Eva thought Maxie's voice sounded exactly the same, whereas she felt sure she must sound a lot older to him.

'I'm fine, Maxie, just fine. Listen, Maxie, the reason I'm calling is that, well, to be honest, I don't really know why I'm calling.' Eva began to feel weepy; hearing Maxie's voice, the thought had struck her that this might be her last contact with a friend from a past that was about to vanish forever.

'I just wanted to talk to an old friend, and you just sort of popped into my mind.'

Maxie sensed the upset in Eva's voice, and changed his tone from its customary crisp, businesslike, rat-a-tat-tat, to soft reassurance.

They talked for over an hour, and told one another about the ups and downs, the joys and sorrows, that life had brought them, and neither of them wanted to end the call.

Eva decided it was her obligation to make the first move, as it was she who had contacted Maxie.

'Well, Maxie, it's been lovely to speak to you again, after all this time. We must keep in touch. I'll give you my new number, after we've moved.'

Maxie, whose mind never strayed from business for too long, even in the most sentimental of situations, decided, before he said farewell to his old friend, to sound her out on a dilemma he was currently trying to resolve, 'Oh, by the way, Eva, has your girl Molly any plans these days? Just thought I'd mention it, as I might be able to put something her way. A new venture. A T.V. drama series. I'm looking for a face that's well known to the public. Someone famous they can identify with, to get the programme good ratings from the start.'

'I don't think so, Maxie, Molly's never been a serious actress. She's always been a singer, an entertainer.'

'She could always learn, Eva, and grow into it. She'd have the lead role.

It's a wartime story of a family; husband and wife, and two sons. It's the story of all their lives, during and after the war. The main part is the mother.

'A Family in War and Peace'. It's a long-term project, and it's going to be big. You just mark my words.'

'I'll mention it to her, Maxie, but I don't think she'll go for it. In fact, I'm not really sure what she plans to do.' Eva paused for a few seconds before continuing. 'Although, now you come to mention it, she did have some acting training at my academy in

Blackpool, and, I seem to remember, showed promise too. I'll mention it to her, Maxie, leave it with me.'

'Get back to me, Eva, if she's interested, I'll put it on hold for as long as I can.'

Maxie then remembered the original reason for the conversation, and wished Eva all the best for the future, and said his goodbyes.

He didn't expect to hear from her again about his offer.

To Maxwell Walker's surprise, he received a call from Molly a week later, to say that she would be delighted to audition for the role of Jenny, the mother in A Family in War and Peace.

Molly Earle, teenage singing sensation, diva, was about to embark on what was destined to become the most famous performance of her life, one that would carve out for her a special niche in the celebrity consciousness of the British people, and make her a 'national treasure'.

The Water Mill

Molly Earle had played the role of Jenny for two years, and A Family in War and Peace was continually the nation's number one television programme during that time.

Molly had become indistinguishable to her adoring public from the fictitious character she had brought to life and made her own.

Her recently-acquired iconic status was officially acknowledged from within the country's political corridors of power when she received a letter from 10 Downing Street, informing her that her name was to be submitted to the Queen, recommending Her Majesty's approval to appoint Molly Earle to the Order of the British Empire, in the forthcoming New Year Honours List.

On the morning it was delivered, Molly opened the imposing-looking letter, and passed it, without comment, across the breakfast table, to Eva. The old lady promptly let out an ear-piercing squeal of delight, and grandmother and granddaughter danced a jig of unrestrained glee in the centre of their Cotswold country kitchen.

It was said in Oxbury, and not without excessive exaggeration, that from the day this letter was received at Lark Cottage, Eva never again bought her own afternoon pot of tea and tray of assorted cakes at the Water Mill and the number of village residents who had not had recounted to them the precise details of the day of Molly and Eva's visit to meet Her Majesty could be counted on the fingers of one hand.

The typical scenario took place at the corner table of Oxbury's quaint Water Mill tearooms, eponymously named because of its picturesque riverside setting, alongside Oxbury's famed tourist landmark.

It usually ran along these lines ...

'This might take a while, I don't like to skimp over any details, and might need a little refreshment to remember everything properly.'

Eva would then hesitate long enough for her specially invited afternoon companion to offer to buy tea and cakes for two, and Eva, after taking a decorous sip of tea from her patterned china cup, accompanied by a bite from her favourite cherry slice, would lean forward, in a companionable manner, as though her guest was the first one ever to have been told about the special day, and begin her narration in a faltering voice which barely rose above a whisper throughout its entirety.

'We both spent a fortune on our outfits for the day. Bought them in London. Molly looked gorgeous. My husband John would have been so proud of her. Her father's an important businessman and was too busy to be there. I suppose he must have known about it, it had been all over the papers; all the names of the celebrities who were being honoured. It would have meant so much to Molly to have seen him there.'

Eva would pause at this point, as though lost in the past, before continuing. 'We wore the fanciest hats you've ever laid eyes on. And the sun was cracking the paving stones.

Anyway, we all gathered in the quadrangle of Buckingham Palace, early in the morning.

The presentations were being held in the Ballroom, and this is where I went, while Molly and all the other OBEs went off to the Picture Gallery, the room next to us. Molly said that the OBEs were lined up along one side of the wall, and the MBEs on the other.'

At this point, Eva would tilt her head back slightly, and raise her eyes to the ceiling, to add a touch of theatrical elaboration to her story.

'Someone up above must have known that my Molly was at the Palace that day, because, in the Musicians' Gallery overlooking the Ballroom where we all were, the guards began to play excerpts from South Pacific, the musical that made Molly a star on television, all those years ago. Molly said she was watching on a T.V. screen in the Picture Gallery. It sent a shiver down my spine – as though it was all meant to be.

Molly told me about all the different sorts of people waiting with her, to meet the Queen. Hundreds of them. And people were coming up to speak to her, and say how much they enjoyed A Family in War and Peace, and never missed an episode.'

Eva would then take several sips of her second cup of tea, and finish off her first cherry slice, before continuing. 'The ceremony was wonderful. I was so nervous, waiting for the Queen to arrive. Heaven only knows how Molly must have been feeling.

It all began when the Yeomen of the Guard came in, and took their places by two thrones in the centre of the room. After this, the Queen came in, with her escorts, and you could have tasted the silence.

The band played the National Anthem. The Queen asked us all to be seated ...

First came the Knights and Dames.

Poor old Mol, waiting all that time for her big moment.

Mol's grandfather, my John, would have been smiling, looking down on her from up there,' Eva would then cast a look at the ceiling again. 'He was always one for a big build up, and a lot of kerfuffle. He was a circus ringmaster, you know.

Anyway, at last the OBEs went in, in groups of ten.

The Queen spoke to Molly for longer than anyone else, and Molly looked so happy.

How proud I felt.

I nudged the lady next to me, and told her who I was, I hope she didn't mind. She said she'd always liked my Mol, from right back when she first started, in Select A Star. That was the T.V. audition show, to find new stars, the first one ever. Don't know if you remember it, or not; it was very big at the time. Molly won for more weeks than anyone else. It was her big break into showbusiness.'

Eva's guests rarely interrupted, even during the occasional discursive reminiscences, partly out of respect for Eva as a delightful, and enthusiastic old lady, but also because they were genuinely engrossed by her colourfully descriptive narration, which had the effect of transporting them to Buckingham Palace on the auspicious day.

It made them feel they had been there, amongst the onlookers, so vividly had Eva honed her exposition, with only the minutest of changes to each telling, so that it gained each time in grandiosity, and had even been timed to conclude at the same moment as she drained the last drop from her pot of tea, and wiped away the cake crumbs from the corners of her mouth with her table napkin.

Eva's favourite waitress at the Water Mill, Ella, at this juncture in the story, would be hovering, poised just out of view, in the back room, and knew precisely when the story ended, as she could then add her own inimitable dramatic conclusion, by appearing at Eva's corner table, at the exact concluding moment, and solicitously place the itemised bill in the centre spot of the table, between Eva and her companion.

Complicity between Eva and Ella in the performance was never openly acknowledged by either of them, although Eva came to look on the timing of Ella's entrance as indispensable, in that it provided the ideal histrionic concluding flourish that a dyed-in-the-wool theatrical trouper such as Eva regarded as essential.

Ella, for her part, came to relish the chance to play support to so consummate a performer as the grand old lady of Oxbury.

After Ella had gone, Eva would always say, before she rose from the table, 'When we met up, we both had a good cry, but had to compose ourselves, because, outside the Palace gates, we were crowded round by reporters and photographers, and Molly was holding up her medal, and linking my arm.

They wanted a quote from me, for the next day's papers, and, do you know, I could only think of one thing to describe how I felt, 'Wonderful, Simply Wonderful'.'

The end of Eva's life was a blissful fading away.

She often told Molly in her last days that, 'After seeing my lovely Mol talking to the Queen, my life was complete.'

Eva felt that her life had been a perfectly composed and directed theatrical production, with her as the lead, and each act complete in itself, with tragedy and ecstasy in equal measure, the essence of all good dramas.

Shafts of shadow and sunlight amid the grey, dreary longueurs.

And all leading to a perfect third act. A glorious finale.

She had played her part to perfection and could now leave the stage.

Only quietly.

Without fuss, fanfare, or kerfuffle.

That was for her Mol.

She had always been the real star.

Eva died peacefully in her sleep.

Molly found her when she took her early morning cup of tea up to her room.

Molly touched her cheek, lightly and lovingly.

Eva's face wore a beatific smile, with traces of mischievousness at the corners of her mouth, as though her final act on this earth had been to rifle through her lifetime's collection of Donald McGill saucy seaside postcards, of buxom women bullying henpecked, skinny husbands, and pick out her favourite one to accompany her into eternity, so that she would never be short of a good laugh if her new home turned out to be a bit on the grim side.

Lying by her side was a recent copy of the Australian newspaper. The Brisbane Record, and Molly removed it, and then placed Eva's lifeless arms across her chest, and gently closed her eyelids.

The night before, Molly had sat at her grandmother's bedside.

Eva had called to Molly to come and sit with her, saying that she had something important to tell her.

Eva then said she had heard from Michael, her nephew living in Brisbane.

Molly knew Eva and Michael had been sending Christmas cards to each other for as long as she could remember, and probably since Michael was a little boy. He was as gossipy as Eva, and, in the long letters they enclosed with the Christmas cards, both of them had always taken great delight in trying to one-up each other, as to whose titbit of scandal had been the juiciest over the past year.

Eva was on the verge of reading to Molly from the Brisbane Record, she had received from Michael in the late morning post. She was intrigued why he would have sent her an Australian newspaper, something he had never previously done during all the years they had corresponded.

Eva looked up at Molly, and passed the newspaper to her, with an impish twinkle in her eyes.

At no time during her recent weeks of painful struggle had Molly seen her Nan's face brighter than the way it was at that moment.

Eva whispered to Molly that she had been sleeping all afternoon and dreaming. Her expression changed to one of sublime serenity as she spoke. 'My dreams are all mixed up, Mol, as though I'm living in the past again, back in Blackpool, with John, when we were young.'

Eva struggled to find sufficient breath to form each word, 'I read the headline in this newspaper, the one young Michael sent me, and I saw the photograph inside, page four ... read me the article, Mol.'

Eva touched the copy of the Brisbane Record, lying open on top of her bedside cabinet, underneath her reading glasses.

'You must rest now, Nan.' Molly patted her hand, and plumped up the pillows, before placing her hands underneath Eva's tiny head, and smoothing down the strands of wispy white hair, before easing her head down onto the pillows.

Eva struggled to continue, 'But my dream, Mol, I must tell you. I was in a theatre, it was packed with people.' Eva's voice was now deep and rasping, and Molly became concerned. 'Everyone was there, everyone we've ever known. I was in the front row, next to John ... you were on stage, Mol ... rapturous applause ... for you, Mol, rapturous applause.'

At this, Eva smiled tenderly, and fell into a blissful slumber, from which she never awoke.

'Rapturous applause, Mol,' was the favourite phrase Eva and Molly had always shared, ever since the time Eva had read it to Molly from a newspaper review of Molly's performance on the all-winners' Select A Star.

Eva's funeral was quiet and restrained, and took place on a still June morning, in Oxbury's tiny, timeless, parish church.

The mist that had been hanging over the valley since dawn had just begun to evaporate, and be replaced by the beginnings of a heat haze, which brought with it the promise of an idyllic Cotswold summer day.

Eva was laid to rest in the shade of an ancient oak tree, whose branches cast their protective shadows seemingly to all points of the churchyard, and, in the process of so doing, formed an exquisite pattern of twisting, tranquil beauty, upon the deep, soothing green of the ancient lawn.

Molly had been preparing herself for the day of Eva's death with persistent dread, but, now it had happened, her feelings were the opposite to those she had been fearfully anticipating.

Molly felt no sadness, only an all-suffusing ethereal reassurance, and a radiant happiness, that seemed to emanate from somewhere way beyond her physical self, yet, at the same time, occupied every fibre of her being.

This feeling remained with Molly, and she waited, with foreboding, for the day to arrive when her pent-up emotion for the loss of Eva would manifest itself in an uncontrollable outpouring of grief.

But that day never arrived, and Molly felt her spirit was now able to pass through an invisible curtain that had separated her past from her future, on to the next stage of her life.

The corner table in the Water Mill tearooms remained unoccupied for a week after the funeral, as a mark of respect to Eva.

Ella, the waitress, had reluctantly handed in her resignation.

As she told a friend, 'My heart's no longer in the job. Not now the old lady's gone. She was such a lovely old girl. She used to brighten up my day. The job's boring now.

And what a card she was. Do you know, when she invited someone for afternoon tea, me and her used to play this little game between us ...'

A Wedding in Las Vegas

During the week following the funeral, Molly, in an idle moment, picked up the copy of the Brisbane Record, and opened the newspaper at the page she presumed Eva had folded down at the corner.

The headline she read made her involuntarily catch her breath sharply in shock:

SHAMED TYCOON JAILED FOR FIFTEEN YEARS

Underneath the stark, bold, dramatic sentence, was a grainy, black-and-white photograph of a man with head bowed, beneath an overcoat, held in place, on either side, by two policemen, and about to be lifted through the open back doors of a police van.

Molly read on rapidly, in astonishment, picking out the salient points of the article:

'Show business baron Roderick Sterne left court in Brisbane yesterday morning, on his way to serve a fifteen year prison sentence ... renowned throughout the entertainment business as being the ex-husband and agent of former singing superstar Molly Earle ... now an actress in both Britain's and Australia's number one television drama series, and recently honoured with an OBE in the British New Year Honours List.

Mr Sterne was convicted of bigamously marrying fifteen year

old Julie Hegarty, in July last year, in a civil ceremony at a Las Vegas wedding chapel.

Mr Sterne and Miss Hegarty have been living in Brisbane since the wedding.

The Brisbane police department had been tipped off to investigate Mr Sterne, following information passed on to them by Miss Hegarty's father.

Mr Sterne's entertainment business empire has also been investigated and found to be built on sand ... convicted of embezzlement ... also attempting to pervert the course of justice, by attempting to bribe Mr Hegarty.

Mr Sterne's wife, Rita, from whom he had been living apart ... had married Mr Sterne following his divorce from Molly Earle ... Rita used to be an understudy to Miss Earle ... discovery by Miss Earle of their affair led to her much-publicised breakdown, and resultant drink and drugs dependency.

Rita Sterne broke down in court ... when interviewed later by reporters, said Mr Sterne has left my life in tatters.'

As Molly continued to read the full-page article, her initial feelings of amazement, followed by contempt, gradually began to become tinged with pity for a man who, after all, had once been her husband, and was now being vilified, and his reputation torn to shreds.

Molly read on further ... 'Mr Hegarty said that his daughter, unbeknown to himself, had replied to an advertisement by one of Mr Sterne's theatrical production companies, seeking an audition for a part in the chorus of one of Mr Sterne's Australian stage shows. Mr Hegarty said that his daughter had been stage-struck from being a very young girl.

Our enquiries have disclosed that Mr Sterne has shown a predilection for the company of chorus girls since his early days in Blackpool, England, when he was starting out on his climb up the showbusiness entrepreneurial ladder.

Miss Hegarty was subsequently reported missing by her father, who had identified her from a magazine photograph of her alongside Mr Sterne, which had been taken secretly as the couple left the Las Vegas wedding chapel, and which was then published in a well-known glossy weekend magazine, renowned for its disclosures of the activities of the rich and famous.

Mr Sterne made unsuccessful attempts to offer substantial financial inducements to Mr Hegarty to remain silent, and has maintained his innocence of knowledge of Miss Hegarty's true age from the day he met her.

Miss Hegarty, when interviewed by reporters outside the court, yesterday, said, 'Obviously, I was unaware that Mr Sterne was a married man when we met. Neither of us had ever considered age to be a relevant factor – on either side. The only thing that has ever concerned me since I was little was getting into showbiz, and Mr Sterne was able to make this possible for me, and, by marrying him, I knew that my career would take off.'

When asked whether she would stand by Mr Sterne, Miss Hegarty snapped curtly, 'What has he got to do with me, now? He already has a wife, let her have him. My future's now in showbiz, and I'd like to thank him for helping me onto the first rung of the ladder.'

Rita Sterne refused to speak to reporters after the trial, and is presently receiving hospital treatment, following her collapse outside the courtroom.

The unravelling of Mr Sterne's ruined financial empire, by the Brisbane fraud squad, is expected to take several years. Estimates of the extent of Mr Sterne's embezzlement run into many millions of dollars.

Mr Sterne will become a pariah in the entertainment world, and it is anticipated that the careers of many showbusiness household names will be terminally undermined during the investigations.

Mr Sterne was unrepentant on entering court, and announced to the waiting crowd that, 'Whatever the outcome of today's trial, I have done nothing I am ashamed of. Everyone will soon hear of the name of Roderick Sterne again.'

Molly's first thought was, 'If only I had read the article to Nan, like she asked me to. Her reaction would have been something to behold.' This was followed by, 'Poor Roderick. Another chapter of my life has just closed for ever.'

In the same way that her grandmother, Eva, had felt complete at the time of her death, so, with this news of Roderick's ignominious downfall, Molly also felt that her life had now turned full circle.

The same edition of the Brisbane Record newspaper proved to be an unlikely instrument that linked the lives of two of peacetime's children across time and generations, in a peculiarly bizarre and coincidental manner, and neither of them, ironically, had the slightest inkling that this had occurred.

The story, occupying three columns of the middle page held not the slightest interest to Molly, but would have been of intense interest to her childhood friend of bygone Blackpool days, Joe Flint.

The story concerned an elderly man, living in Brisbane, who had made a dramatic deathbed confession, in his own words, 'To put the record straight in this life before I move on into the next one.'

The man in the story had been the foreman of a Tasmanian apple orchard, who had harboured a lifetime's grievance about the treatment he had received from his employer and whose death from falling off a ladder which was leaning against a tall tree in an apple orchard, he had carried out by kicking the ladder away, while his employer was picking apples from the tree.

The foreman subsequently took over residence in the employer's house, under the terms of his controversial will, which he said on his deathbed, was 'The least he could have done for me, for having exploited me over a hard lifetime's service lining his pockets. And even then I was only keeping the house warm for his grandchildren.'

In his choice of dying words, he became perversely linked to Roderick Sterne, similarly quoted on his way to prison earlier in the same edition of the newspaper, by also refusing to show even the slightest morsel of contrition in saying, 'I feel I have done no wrong. My conscience is clear. I am now ready to meet my maker.'

Molly Earle took the news of Roderick, following, as it did, the trauma of her grandmother's death, as her cue to withdraw from the limelight of public life, and began to lead an increasingly reclusive existence, particularly for a celebrity who had been so feted.

Molly's life came to revolve around her part in A Family in War and Peace, at the Birmingham television studios, and her private life in Oxbury, where she assiduously attended charity functions, when asked, but this apart, she was rarely seen outside the village boundaries.

She became most proud of the voluntary work she undertook, a few years later, when, after providing a major share of the financial backing for the opening of a centre in Oxbury to provide help for people with alcohol and drug problems, she undertook duties there as a senior counsellor, in her spare time away from the television studios.

The only public appearance away from Oxbury that Molly felt compelled to undertake was to visit Kensington Palace in the week following the death of Diana, Princess of Wales, and, on that day, she endeavoured to remain as inconspicuous as possible, wearing a long navy blue raincoat, and a black headscarf.

The compulsion to show her respects for a woman she had not known, except through the medium of her television screen, arose from a feeling that they had shared not only glamour and celebrity, but also a mutual vulnerability, a need to be loved and wanted, and to express the same in return, that Molly had chosen to satisfy by her driving desire to be an entertainer, and the Princess had still been seeking to express and fulfil, by means of her various admirable initiatives, when she was lost.

Molly became swept along on the tide of national mass hysteria of the time, and, upon arriving in London, bought flowers at the railway station, and placed them, with her written message, among the enormous mound of tributes outside the Kensington Palace gates.

Molly joined the queues snaking around the side of the palace, to sign the books of condolence, and, as dusk slowly fell around the palace lake, she moved quietly among the hushed small groups of people sitting cross-legged, with heads bowed, over the glow of candle flames.

The sweet fragrance of a hundred candle flames drifted intoxicatingly on the gentle breeze of a darkening London summer evening, the reverential silence interrupted only by the drone of traffic moving along the road outside the palace gates, into the heart of London.

The Seventies to the Millennium II

End of Empires

Two moments towards its close epitomised the century in which peacetime's children had lived.

Both were significant events which revealed the global role being played by television at the turn of the century, and the extent of its advance since the afternoon, almost fifty years earlier, when the New Sands threw open its doors to a communal gathering who watched spellbound as a flickering black and white screen showed the Coronation of Queen Elizabeth II.

Unlike that momentous day, we were all able to be present on the day an Empire ended, to witness the closing of the curtain on 500 years of history.

At just the push of a button on the remote control of a colour television set you could be transported to Hong Kong on the last day of June 1997.

We had already seen, a decade earlier, the tearing down of the Berlin Wall – the symbol of a post-war world divided between east and west – and the collapse of the communist bloc; but on this day in Hong Kong it was our own Empire coming to an end. The British Empire.

Great Britain, at the forefront of the Industrial Revolution, and the building of the modern world; whose flag had flown for hundreds of years over vast territories of diverse populations across the face of the globe.

And now, on a chilly, rain-swept afternoon, in Victoria Harbour, the British were giving back Hong Kong, their last overseas colony, to China.

We were all part of a moment in history, marked by a host of elegiac images: the lowering of the Union Jack and the coloured flag of Hong Kong; the vision of a lone piper playing Auld Lang Syne; the Royal Yacht Britannia, on her last voyage, heading out in the harbour while the Royal Marine band played Rule Brittania.

In the summer of the previous year, 3 billion of us across the world had shared a moment which had stirred the emotions of everyone privileged to witness it.

The setting was the opening ceremony of the Olympic Games on a summer night in Atlanta.

In a darkened and hushed stadium, to audible astonishment, a spotlight picked out a lone spectator.

Muhammad Ali stood with the Olympic torch extended before him to open the Games.

Now long into retirement, and shaking from Parkinson's disease, he carried off the moment with the majesty of a man who at the peak of his epic career had been known as the most famous person on the planet.

We were all there when a moment of sublime drama had moistened the driest eye and softened the hardest heart.

Revival

On the 1st of January 2001, the middle-aged Joe Flint looked at the family photograph standing just behind the black and white one of his boyhood self, with Molly and Danny; it provoked a recollection of twenty years earlier.

'How pale and thin I looked back then,' Joe mused, 'I remember it particularly because it was the first picture taken after my recovery from the heart attack.

Lucy had linked my arm, to help me keep my balance on my shaky legs, as we strolled along the promenade at St Annes.

I still remember the heady intoxication of walking in the open air again; sensing life pulsating sublimely in everything around, with an awareness that I was part of it all again.

That day, the twins had just come back to walk alongside us after having run off on to the beach, chasing the dog in a race to be the first to the ice cream van.

We all sat on a bench overlooking the sea, and Lucy asked a passer-by to take our photograph.'

Joe Flint's road to recovery had been long and difficult.

He had been told by the young white-coated consultant on his mid-day ward rounds in the cardiac care unit that he had suffered a 'myocardial infarction' on the day of his admission to Blackpool Central hospital, and that a further attack had taken place in the early hours of the next morning, which had needed the implant of an electrical pacemaker to regulate his heartbeat.

The consultant concluded that Joe was 'A fortunate young man to be still with us, was now hopefully through the critical phase, although needed to rest and be carefully monitored over the next few days.'

Joe's recovery to fitness was throughout most of the following year, which meant that Lucy, as well as looking after the twins, was required to carry out both their roles in running Flints, until Joe was fully recovered.

Joe and Lucy had been determined from the day of their marriage that they would stand on their own feet, and, if misfortunes happened, as they were bound to do, they would attempt to resolve them without asking for family help.

But, during Joe's convalescence, their parents had offered not only to help with the twins, but to pay the overdue rent on Flints.

Lucy kept this from Joe, but accepted the offer, on condition that they accept repayment as soon as the shop was up and running again.

Lucy struggled along single-handed, including opening up late on the days she drove to the market for supplies.

But fortune smiled on Flints one particular day, when Lucy's mother left her daughter a homemade fruit loaf on the shop counter during a visit.

A customer walked into the shop at the same moment, asked the price of the loaf, and was given it without charge by Lucy.

Such a seemingly insignificant incident led to the transformation in the fortunes of Flints.

After that day, Lucy and her mother spent all their time making the loaves and other types of cake, and displaying them in Flints shop window.

All the loaves and cakes were sold every morning before lunchtime, and, on Saturdays, within an hour of opening the shop.

Building on this unanticipated success, Lucy then began to make sandwiches for sale, and Flints developed into more of a take-away food shop than a greengrocery.

It appeared that the corner had been turned at last, and the rise in profits gathered momentum when the competitor greengrocer sold up and moved on. He had been experiencing a sharp downturn in trade due to his customers deserting him for Flints, to buy cakes, and then, while in the shop, also buying their fruit and veg.

After this, Flints went from strength to strength, and their dramatic reversal of fortune was aided still further by Joe's return.

Joe and Lucy knew their problems were in the past once and for all on the day a grinning Jack Grime left the shop with his quarterly rent cheque in his hand, calling out from the doorway, 'I always knew you two would do well with this place,' and then closing the door quietly with a cheery wave and 'Keep up the good work.'

Joe and Lucy just laughed.

Joe Flint was never lured into playing the stock market again.

The debt to their families was repaid.

The Flints were on their way to achieving all they had hoped for on the day they left for Australia.

peacetime's children

The story of peacetime's children has now been told.

We were three children, my two friends and I, who grew up in an era free from world war.

Unlike our parents.

And our grandparents.

We lived through a turbulent, exhilarating post-war age that was an epic journey along a path that led to the end of the century; and we now look around with a wistful longing at this path which has now faded from view, because we feel we took for granted what history could come to view as a golden age.

So now we had arrived at the beginning of a new millennium.

And, as a day to make resolutions, the first one of a new century – and a new millennium – takes some beating.

In fact, it was the day I had the idea to tell the story of peacetime's children.

On a good day to be alive
I had decided to clear away the dead wood from the past
And start afresh
Whatever the cost
And what better day than a sublime January morning
At the start of the year
To take your wife and daughter on a visit
A wife and daughter my parents had never met
It had taken me a long time to find them
Even though it was only a short journey
Across London back to Lewisham
But it was one that had taken my whole lifetime
My mother opened the front door
She looked at Sarah standing by my side
Her granddaughter
Her namesake
If only you had been there to see her face

The story continues...

To follow shortly...

'DÉNOUEMENT'

The sequel to peacetime's children.

Printed in the United Kingdom
by Lightning Source UK Ltd.
9754400001B/1-24